# Chapter One

SHE WAS GOING to die today.

He'd all but promised that. Now it was time, and he was coming for her, moving quickly above. His heavy footsteps headed for the cellar door, the solid footfalls confident, but uneven.

He'd developed a limp. Funny. She hadn't noticed that until now.

Death, just over the horizon, sharpened her senses, she supposed.

Or was it the dark, the complete pitch black of the windowless space? Her mind was shrouded in pain and despair, her senses hyper-alert, the smells and sounds crisp and vivid. The musty scent of the basement. An old oil furnace in the corner emitting a metallic smell. His footsteps in the distance, growing closer as he headed for the cellar door.

For her.

Painful desperation swallowed everything around her.

*Please, please, please don't let him do this.*

She heard each groan of the house. Each creak of the floor. Heard him reach the cellar door.

Her heart kicked hard, sounding a loud echo in her chest.

A key slipped into the deadbolt at the top of the stairs with a firm *snick*. She could picture the shiny new lock he'd dragged her past the first night. Remembered her hands clutching at anything to stay aboveground, her nails breaking as they scratched to take purchase. Raw and ragged now.

Then the descent. Down the rickety wooden steps. Kicking. Fighting. The fist to her jaw. Seeing stars before her vision cleared. The light burning bright, revealing metal castings stacked on old rotting shelves. The shackles she now bore around her wrists lying limp on the scarred linoleum floor, waiting for her.

The jars. *No, stop.* She didn't want to think about them.

She'd thought of little else since she escaped from this madman who, in the late nineties, had pretended online to be Adam Smith, a man in his early twenties who'd developed a crush on her though she was only fifteen. She should have known better than to believe him, even when he'd given her a photo that showed how handsome he was. But as a foster kid, she'd craved love desperately, and he seemed to want to give it.

So she'd gone to meet him, but it turned out the picture he'd sent her had been retouched. His face was grotesquely scarred, and he soon had her handcuffed. Her foster sister, Lauren, had figured he was bad news so she'd followed, and he'd abducted the two of them. But they'd both eventually escaped.

The rusty hinges on the door groaned open like those on an old coffin. Only a stairway separated them.

Bile rose up her parched throat, gagging her. She swallowed hard and strained against the coarse rope digging into the oozing sores circling her wrists. Days of struggling had left them open. Maybe festering. But that didn't matter. What mattered was the door groaning open. The air around her stirring, dragging a putrid current into the vortex. She retched at the smell of her own body. The stench of her own fear nearly overpowered everything. She hadn't showered in four days or had access to a bathroom for as long.

She was disgusting.

She'd die like this. Be found like this. Would her family have to see her this way? Identify her?

*God, please, no*, she begged. *Spare them.*

A shadow of light filtered through the open doorway. His foot hit the top tread with a thud. Then the next, each step an earthshaking roll of thunder in her ears. His flashlight bobbed on the stairs. Quick circles of light moved down like a slinky before jerking back up. She saw his foot now in an arc of light. A big work boot. Size twelve or larger. Heavy lug soles, worn and scarred. His jeaned leg came next. Then a flannel work shirt. Red, she thought, but the light suddenly danced ahead.

He reached the bottom. His boot struck the linoleum with a solid thump. Not a word came from his mouth, but his flashlight spoke for him. Sliding across the space. Searching.

She recoiled. Dug her heels into the floor. Scooted back and tried to cover her nakedness by drawing her knees into her chest.

*Nowhere to go.*

She needn't worry about her family seeing her. No one would find her here. He'd chosen the perfect location, an abandoned metal fabrication plant with rows and rows of buildings. Some were in use. Others had fallen into decay like this one.

He snapped the dangling string overhead. Light from a bare bulb flooded the area.

"Hello, Molly," he said, as if they were meeting at a social event. But this wasn't social—he was coming to kill her.

Her eyes ached from the sudden brightness. She blinked. Thought to keep her eyes closed and avoid seeing her killer's face one more time.

Hadn't she seen him enough in her dreams since she'd escaped his capture two decades ago? In nightmares replaying the torture of long ago. Now she was his captive once again, facing him for the last four days, his torment a blur of pain.

Yet, she couldn't look away. She didn't have the nerve to ignore her own death. She had to see him. To see the end of her life in his eyes.

She blinked hard until she could focus. His face was a mirror of the one in her dreams, except the passing years had etched wrinkles like a road map across his skin. The dark, dead eyes hadn't changed. Hadn't dulled. His chin was angular and covered in graying whiskers. Scars puckered his cheeks, and his nose was nothing more than a red knob, as if an afterthought.

Memories of their first meeting sixteen years ago came flooding back. The same revulsion curdled her stomach. It wasn't the scars, the stub of a nose. She could handle the deformities from severe burns. It was the sneer of his lips and vile hatred in his gaze. The steady stare that never wavered.

Like now. His gaze sought her out, a hunter looking for prey. He smiled. Wide, toothy, a hint of contempt keeping his lips tight. "I hope you've had enough time to think and give me what I want."

She couldn't abide his stare, and dragged her gaze away. It landed on the shelf. Nine mason jars were lined up, a set of human ears in all but two of them, preserved in clear liquid. The jars were labeled with the numbers one through nine. Detectives had dubbed this madman Van Gogh for his penchant for removing his victims' ears. There had been only five jars the last time he'd captured her. Now there were four more. The jars marked four and five were empty. Waiting. She wasn't surprised to see those jars. Not when she and Lauren had both escaped. She'd figured he'd come after them again, even though they'd both done their best to disappear.

"Well, Molly. Where is Lauren?" he asked, his tone insistent and threatening.

*Lauren.* Shortly after Molly had overpowered him to escape, she'd seen a news report indicating that Lauren had died in a car crash. But Molly didn't buy the story. At first, it seemed real, but the police slipped up on one little detail that only Molly would know, proving the detectives had faked Lauren's death and given her a new identity.

*Rebecca Lange.* The regal name fit the current-day Lauren, a woman who had become a defender of foster children and a top-notch FBI agent. It was the name she'd always dreamt of having.

"Where's Lauren?" Van Gogh asked again, this time removing Molly's gag.

She gathered what little moisture she had in her mouth and spit at him.

He lurched back, anger darkening eyes she didn't think could get any blacker. He looked up at the ceiling. Took a few breaths. "Don't worry,

Mother. I know she's gone off the deep end. She will be cleansed today. Her funeral will draw Lauren out. I can cleanse both of them, and my collection will finally be complete."

He often talked to his mother who was never present, so this wasn't new. But Molly had never been successful in getting him to explain the cleansing ritual.

"Mother says it's time to get you dressed." He opened a box sitting on the shelf and lifted out a virginal white nightgown. "You remember this, don't you, my pet? You will be cleansed and free. Too bad you won't help me find Lauren so she can know the joy of cleansing sooner."

He leaned close, an ugly smile parting his lips. The whisper of his breath, the acrid smell of his unwashed body, made her stomach roil. She couldn't speak. And she wouldn't, even if she did know where Lauren lived. She'd never betray the trust of her foster sister.

Never.

If she did, he'd go after Lauren and kill her. Molly wouldn't let that happen.

"Let's get you cleaned up." He went to the corner and ran a bucket of water, then put it on a table near the sink. He shoved a knife with sharp teeth lining the edge into a sheath on his belt. The knife that had once carved into her body, leaving the number four. Into Lauren, who bore the number five.

Humming, he crossed the room to stare at Molly while snapping on a pair of latex gloves. "You really are a mess, aren't you?"

She thought to try to cover herself, to maintain her dignity. But after the last few days, what dignity did she have left?

He unlocked the shackles, moved her out of her filth and toward the table. She fought, kicked, but after five days without food and little water, she was too weak to make a difference. He bathed her, each touch of the cloth making her want to vomit. Once in the demure nightgown, she lay back, defeated, on the table—his altar stained with blood—where he bound her to cold shackles mounted on the corners.

"It's time, Molly. Tell me or . . ." His evil smile took his words and buried them in the recesses of the room. He lifted his knife. High. Advanced. His eyes burned with the intensity of fire. He slid his fingers over her ear—gently, almost tenderly, then suddenly backed away.

Was he going to let her live another day? Hope fluttered in her chest.

He crossed the room. Lifted jar number four, the liquid sloshing as he returned to her. He blew the dust from the rusted lid. Fine particles lingered in the beam of light before dissipating in the stale air. He held the knife between his teeth, his eyes gleaming.

He started unscrewing the lid, slowly, each twist feeling like a nail in

Molly's coffin. He set the open jar on the floor, a pungent odor smelling like pickles floated up to her nose. Fear coursed through her body.

*Lauren. Remember Lauren.*

He slipped his hand into his pocket and two pearl earrings emerged. She fixed her gaze on the burn scars crawling over his hands, not on the earring. He inserted the first one into her left ear. The piercing stud ripped her skin, making her feel as if she were being nailed to a cross. To her death.

This was it, for sure. The end.

She held her breath. He placed the second earring and stood back, his eyes now vacant and his mind somewhere else. Somewhere his earring ritual had taken him.

His breathing grew rapid and shallow, his chest barely moving. Eyes glazed over, he raised the knife. His smile, teeth rotted and yellowing, was the last thing she saw as he bent closer.

"Tell me or not, my pet, it doesn't matter. The news coverage of my return will be legendary, and your death will bring Lauren to me. She won't miss your funeral."

The knife pricked her skin. Her heart seized and refused to beat. She ignored it. Ignored everything, her resolve still in place.

She'd die before letting this butcher near someone she loved.

And, as he'd promised . . . it would be today.


THERE. HE WAS OUT of commission, doubled over in severe pain.

*Perfect.* It was just what Agent Rebecca Lange wanted—her boss, Rolland Sulyard, the Assistant Special Agent in Charge of the FBI Portland's office, on his way to the hospital.

She spun and shot out her leg in a roundhouse kick, landing her foot solidly where his kidney would be located, sending the red heavy bag in a swirling rotation. She recovered, imagined his face on the worn bag, and fired a jab to his nose.

*Take that, Sulyard. No one shuts down my investigation.*

"You trying to kill that thing, Lange?" a beefy local police officer asked as he passed by.

She shot him a quick look and swiped with the back of her arm at sweat running down her face, but didn't bother to respond.

"You should give it a rest before you stroke out," he added, then laughed as he headed for the locker room.

Maybe it was time for her to hit the showers, too. No. Anger still boiled in her gut. Thirty minutes at the bag and she was still mad. Good and mad. At Sulyard. At herself.

He'd shut down the credit card identity theft investigation that she'd been heading up for the agency's Cyber Action Team. Months of hard work wasted. Just like that, in one fell swoop. She had yet to tell the team. She dreaded it. Especially telling her co-agents and friends Kaitlyn Murdock and Nina Brandt. Then there was the new intern, Taylor Andrews. She'd take it especially hard, and Becca's reputation with the newest team member would be tarnished before it even got off the ground.

Worse yet, victims were going without justice due to her failure. She should have worked harder. Smarter. Done better. If she didn't help those in need, who would?

She slammed a fist into the bag again. Another. Then another. *Bam, bam, bam.*

"Remind me never to make you mad." The male voice came from behind her.

Her brain stalled, and her hands stilled.

What was *he* doing here? He was the last person she wanted to see today. A perfect addition to a perfectly dismal day.

She took several deep breaths and let them out. He'd think she was just winded, but in fact, she needed a clear head to face Connor Warren, a detective for the Portland Police Bureau. She had this thing for him when she was in no position in her life to have a thing for any guy.

Another few cleansing breaths, then she pivoted and found his gaze pinned on her, as she expected. Her heart did a quick somersault, and she chastised herself for responding.

He must have noticed her discomfort as he smirked. "Do you mind dropping those gloves so we can talk?"

She looked down to discover her hands were still raised. She swatted at hair stuck to her face and lowered the gloves. "What're you doing here, Connor?"

He grinned, his smile lopsided and cute at the same time, turning her insides to mush. Seriously, how did he do that to her every time she saw him?

This mutual thing had started when they'd met two years ago on an investigation. It was there every time they laid eyes on each other, which was often. Too often for Becca's liking. His partner, Sam Murdock, married her friend and Cyber Action Team member Kait, so Becca ran in to Connor all the time.

He tipped his head at the bag. "Whoever you were trying to pummel, you succeeded."

As usual, he avoided her question and went off on his own tangent while he let his gaze take her in from head to toe.

Fine. Let him look. She would too. She ran her gaze over his six-foot-two body, lingering on his shirt molded to hard pecs and biceps.

His auburn hair was more red than brown and cut short. His jaw was square, and his eyes, when he wasn't smiling, held an intensity she understood all too well.

His grin widened. He got that she was into him. He'd have to be blind not to see it, but then, he probably had women taking a second and third look all the time. Shoot, she'd taken a whole lot more than a second look over the years, much to her annoyance. And it had to stop now.

"So, are you here to join the gym?" she asked, hoping the answer was a big fat no. She didn't want him here. She found her relaxation at the gym the way many women found it in a spa. The words *relaxation* and *Connor* had nothing in common.

He shook his head and lifted a folder clutched in his hand. "I have information on a case Sam said you were taking lead on."

"Oh?" She made sure to play down her interest to keep him from wanting to stay.

"He said you've been working a credit card fraud ring in the area."

*Right. The investigation that Sulyard just shut down.*

"I think I can help you with it," he said.

"Oh, yeah? How?"

He looked around, then lowered his voice. "I'm working a homicide where a man was murdered for his credit cards. At least, that's our theory right now. I tailed a suspect to an apartment in the northeast and watched the place for a few days. Struck out on finding anything that could give me probable cause to enter, but it looks like I stumbled on your theft ring's base of operation. I took some photos you might want to see."

Pulling off her gloves and tucking them under her arm, she stepped closer. She took the folder, making sure to avoid touching him. She started flipping through the photos of teenagers carrying shopping bags taken outside a rundown apartment complex. "Did these kids all go to the same apartment?"

He nodded. "We checked the lease, but as you might expect, the ID was bogus. The manager said the rent was paid in cash three months in advance, which for that neighborhood, is a great deal for the manager, so he didn't ask any questions. He did describe the guy who rented it. Five-ten. Dark hair. Late forties."

"Seriously? It could be just about anyone with that description."

Connor gestured at the folder. "You won't find him in the pictures. No one over the age of twenty ever showed up at the apartment."

"Not surprising. Credit card fraud crews are often recruited from runaways and homeless teens, and it's rare to find the mastermind behind the operation." Which was why Sulyard had shut down her investigation. It was going nowhere.

"Exactly how do they work this scam?" Connor asked.

She might not want to talk to him, but she was always happy to explain how this kind of fraud worked. "It starts with a ringleader who obtains stolen credit card information from the Internet. He then uses an embossing machine to make new cards, and recruits runaways to make fraudulent purchases at local retailers. These groups have been moving up and down the I-5 corridor and we've really been trying to bust one of them. If we catch the kids, we're hoping they'll flip on their ringleader. Did you get any of their license plates?"

"They took the bus. TriMet and street cams didn't help ID them either."

Becca went back to the photos to withdraw five pictures for Connor. "I can ID these five right now. If we combine your information with mine, I should have enough to get a search warrant."

"Exactly what I was hoping for. We can work together. If we give you the ID ring's evidence you're after, you can probably get us in there. Then, hopefully, I'll find something related to the homicide."

*Right,* they'd have to work together. Her heart dropped.

"It'll be a win/win." His eyes, bright with enthusiasm, locked on her, daring her to say no. She didn't flinch under his gaze, but she was just a moment away from turning tail and running. She didn't like what he could do to her insides. Didn't like it at all. And working with him on an investigation? What would happen then?

No, she didn't need that. She didn't need him.

"I have all my information in the car." He gestured outside, but kept those steely blue eyes locked on her. "We could head to your office to iron out details for the warrant."

She swallowed hard under his continued gaze. "How about you give me the files, and I let you know when the warrant has been approved?"

"Yeah, right." He rolled his eyes and widened his stance. "Either we collaborate on getting the warrant and serve it together, or you keep punching that bag, because your case is going nowhere."

She gaped at him. "You'd give up a lead on a homicide case, just like that?"

"Nah," he said with a half-smile that crooked up in the corner. "Just like I know you would never turn your back on a lead for your investigation. Which means you'll end up working with me. So, why fight it?"

He had her, right where he wanted her, and she felt herself caving. If they went straight to her office, she could get the information to Sulyard before he left for the day, and her case would be back on track.

"Okay, we'll do it," she agreed, hoping they might actually be able to handle a professional relationship. "But I need to take a quick shower."

"I wasn't planning to say anything, but since you brought it up, you *are* a mess." He let that gaze trail over her again, his eyes heating up. "Not that I mind a woman all sweaty from taking her frustration out on a bag. I find it kind of hot, actually."

Her heart gave a rebellious flutter. So much for the professional. One second, and it was gone. She shoved the folder into his chest and grabbed her gloves, thinking for a moment of wiping the look from his face with a well-placed punch.

She took a breath instead. "You can wait for me in the coffee shop across the street."

She wouldn't hang around for his rebuttal. Why bother? It would be a smart-aleck quip that she didn't need to hear. She headed for the locker room. She felt his eyes on her as she walked.

Fine. Let him look. She hoped he enjoyed what he was seeing. He needed to get it out of his system so they could collaborate on this investigation as professionals.

"Yeah, right," she muttered under her breath as she swung into the locker room. "Maybe you should listen to your own advice for once."

# Chapter Two

IN THE FBI'S WAR room, Connor swirled the last dregs of his coffee in the paper cup and didn't try to hide his study of Becca as she presented her warrant request to her supervisor, Assistant Special Agent in Charge Roland Sulyard. They'd been talking for fifteen minutes, and Connor thought she was making progress.

*Talking, shoot.* They'd been arguing in the hallway, but Becca didn't back down. She'd changed into a boring navy business suit with a tailored white blouse. Her eyes were wide, her stance firm, and she wore her usual fierce "defender of the downtrodden" expression. Some might think she was haughty. He knew she was simply passionate about her work.

He'd seen that expression often enough—showing her need to help those who couldn't help themselves. That was her motto. And she wasn't straying from it today.

Sulyard took a step closer to her. He was six-four, wore a black power suit, and his bald head gleamed in the light. His voice was low and controlled. "This is it, Lange. You fail to develop any solid evidence, and I won't hesitate to shut down the investigation like I did this morning."

So that was why Becca had been beating the bag in the gym. He could still see her—her body-hugging tank top plastered to curves she usually hid under one of her infernal suits, and faded blue shorts revealing legs as long as he'd imagined them to be. Man, she was all curves and silky skin. He tried to sound like he was kidding when he told her it was hot, but he was deadly serious. He did find it hot. Maybe not with other women, but everything Becca did got his blood boiling.

"Don't let me down," Sulyard said. After a long look, he turned and walked away.

Becca slipped back into the room, her eyes alive with their upcoming challenge. "We're a go. Judge Obrien is already on standby for a different warrant, so Sulyard will submit this one along with it."

Connor fixed what he hoped was a casual gaze on her. "Sulyard shut down your investigation, huh?"

She lifted her shoulders and stared at him. "We're back on track. As long as your lead isn't a wild goose chase. If it is . . ." The blue in her eyes darkened, her expression judging his merit.

He sat forward. "You doubt my intel?"

"No, but the crew could have made you and moved on."

"They didn't make me," he said, irritated that she thought him incompetent enough to let some pimply-faced teenager catch his surveillance.

"We still need to act fast. This group never stays in one place long, and could be on the move soon."

"Then let me map out the location for you, and we can form a plan." He grabbed a legal pad to start sketching the apartment complex, parking lots, and adjoining roads. She bent over him, her clean, fresh scent from the shower instantly grabbing his attention.

He didn't need to be thinking about her like this. Didn't need to keep flirting with her when she wasn't interested. She was into him, that was patently clear, but she didn't have time for a man in her life. She was too busy saving the world all on her own. And he was a fool for trying anything when he didn't really want to get involved with a woman again either.

He sat up and she took a quick step back. He slid the drawing over in front of the next chair, forcing her to move even farther away so he could concentrate.

He tapped the drawing while she took a seat. "Apartment's on the second floor here. Patio slider on the back here. We'll need someone to cover the rear exit."

She nodded. "You can do that while I take the front."

He gave her an as-if look. "I'll call in reinforcements, and we'll go in together."

She appraised him for a moment. "Who did you have in mind?"

"Sam."

"I'm good with Sam joining us." She sounded amenable, but suspicion was lodged in her eyes. "I've asked our intern to tag along."

"You're kidding, right? An intern?" He dropped the pencil on the table. "This is important, Becca. We don't want a green-behind-the-ears recruit screwing this up."

She eyed him. "Taylor may be fresh out of Quantico, but she's far from a green recruit. She's served on an FBI Evidence Recovery Team for years, and has seen more than most law enforcement professionals."

"So she's seen the aftermath of man's inhumanity to man. That still doesn't mean she isn't green as far as serving a warrant goes."

She planted her hands on her hips. "We may not make nearly as many arrests as you do, but we've been around the block a few times. We can both handle this."

"I was kidding." He wished they could just relax around each other. This tension between them, hanging just below the surface, ready to erupt at any time, sapped all of his energy.

She didn't return his smile. "You won't terrorize Taylor, then? Because we need her. With the rise in cyber intrusions, we've added a slot on our Cyber Action Team. After shadowing me for a few weeks, she'll take that job."

"Another geek in town. Just what we need." He laughed again, but he had to force it out this time.

She stared at him. "I need you to take this seriously."

Right. Serious. Her middle name.

He stood and looked into her eyes for a moment, something he'd much rather do than go serve a warrant, even if it *was* for one of his investigations. But she was right. He had a job to do, and despite her considering him too laid-back at times, he never shirked his responsibilities. He wouldn't start now.

RESTRAINT. REGINALD Zwicky needed to learn restraint. Restraint would have kept Molly alive until she gave up Lauren's address. He paced the basement, his mood as dark as the dank space. Even that earthy, metallic scent of blood couldn't erase his black mood.

He'd screwed up. Let his emotions get the best of him. How? He'd learned patience, or at least he thought he had. He'd practiced restraint all these years, honoring Mother's request to stop cleansing girls in the nineties with the taste of blood fresh in his mouth. He'd wanted to continue, but no, she'd seen the news report that he'd failed and a girl had gotten away. She'd beaten him until he'd told her about both Lauren and Molly escaping from him and admitted that Molly had attempted to seduce him. He'd fallen prey to it and they'd struggled. She'd caught him off guard, and managed to get away. Then Mother had nagged and nagged him to find them until his ears nearly bled with her harping. At least it was a change. Usually, her sharp fingernails would pierce the tender cartridge, dragging him across the room to his closet.

"Don't you see, Mother?" he said, her spirit still living with him though she had passed away six months ago. He pointed at Molly's virginal body in her gown. "I found her. For you. Cleansed her. She'll lead us to Lauren. Then you can truly rest."

He waited for his mother to answer, but the building was quiet, save for the rats running in the rafters above.

He kicked an empty oil can across the room, the sound ringing through the space.

What a despicable place. He couldn't even leave a body here overnight. Not with the rats. He'd had to construct a wire mesh cage to keep them from tearing apart the bodies. It was especially needed for Molly. The police had to see her peaceful repose to understand his mission.

He went to the stained porcelain sink, took the Lava soap his mother insisted he use, and scrubbed his hands. Waves of red swirled from his fingers and down the drain.

"Are they clean, Reginald?" Mother had always asked before inspection. If he'd failed to meet her expectations, she'd scoured his hands with the pumice soap, leaving his skin raw.

"You'll be proud of me, Mother. The police will be in awe of everything you have trained me to do."

He imagined them finding Molly and being impressed with his ability to cleanse. He wanted to do more. His body fairly vibrated with the need to continue his life's work. To rush right out and find another girl and offer her the same purification. But he couldn't. Not yet. He had to lie low until Lauren showed up for Molly's funeral. Then he'd follow her. Take her. Evaluate her. If she was still pure, he'd make her his for life. If not, he'd cleanse her. It all depended on how she'd lived these past sixteen years.

Until then, he'd have to forget the lingering taste of blood, forget that nothing could assuage the desire for more. He'd gone nearly sixteen years without killing. Years without ever laying a hand on another young girl. Years of listening to his mother's teachings. Enduring her discipline so he could achieve nirvana. She'd been his guide and spiritual leader until her sudden death from a heart attack six months ago.

Now he was a man, on his own. A disciple. Ready to save the girls.

"A man or a loser?" Billy's voice whispered through Reginald's mind.

"Be quiet," Reginald told his childhood friend.

Billy was everything an imaginary friend needed to be. He'd gotten Reginald through many terrifying incidents, but he'd turned into a nagging voice that never left Reginald's head for long.

"You're a loser." Billy's tone was now high and nasally, mixed with irritation and judgment. "A madman like the news media claimed in the nineties. Sick and depraved."

"No." Reginald clamped his hands over his ears. "I'm not. I'm their savior. The one who cleanses. I saved their souls. I gave them the peace they need."

"Then why hide it? Why not proclaim it to the world?"

"Humility, you fool. Didn't you listen to Mother all these years? We must be humble."

Billy started lecturing him, and Reginald tightened his hands over his ears until Billy went silent the way he always did when Reginald spoke unadulterated truths. But he'd be back. He always came back. Questioning. Pressuring. Trying to get Reginald to ignore his mother's teachings.

Except during the ritual. Then there was peace. Blessed peace. Like the girls must feel. A release to a higher place.

Like Molly. At rest. He lifted her jar. Admired the curve of her ears and the glow of the pearls. "Perfect, Mother. Just like you taught me."

He placed the jar on the shelf, then ran his fingers along the others. There. Excellent. Number four, filled and in place where it belonged, at last. No longer would Molly suffer in this world from the base physical longings she couldn't control. He was glad for the simple way to help her. A pair of earrings. The symbol of purity and chastity. Of humility and innocence as his mother had first told him, her switch following each word, after she caught him with one of the fast girls at school who would sleep with anyone. Even him, with the twisted trail of scars running over his body.

Mother had been furious.

"Purity, Reginald," she had snapped, dragging him by the ear and forcing him to the floor in the closet. "It's a virtue you must learn, must keep, until you find the equally pure woman you will marry. I know it's hard. Especially at fifteen with all those hormones rushing through your body. Let me help you learn control as my father taught me. Your father could never grasp the concept of control. It was the reason he had to leave us."

She ripped his shirt from his back, took a tighter hold on his ear, and cracked the belt across his naked skin. The pain bit into his body, racing along nerve endings, begging him to cry out. But he wouldn't. Didn't. Just as he hadn't during the fire. She would see it as his carnal nature calling out, and she'd keep going, crack after crack until it was extinguished.

Now he was the master and it had been worth it. Superb in every way. Untouchable, as long as he remained smart and in control. And he was smart. His control still needed perfecting, however. Molly had proved that.

"See. I told you, you're a loser," Billy said.

Reginald ignored him and stepped around the space, looking for anything he'd missed that could lead the police to his doorstep. At the shelves on the far side of the wall, he knelt on the ground to shine a flashlight into the dark recesses.

There. In the corner. A hair thingy Allie—his lovely wonderful girl number seven—had worn. Powder blue, the same color of the eyes that had stared up at him for so long. He carefully retrieved it and stuffed it into his pocket. He'd been careless. Now he'd have to go back to the clearing to add it to the bag of clothing he'd buried last week. He'd kept it all for a long time. Touched it. Smoothed it over his skin when the urge grew too strong. But when he'd found Molly, and then learned Lauren was alive, he knew he had to divest himself of all traces of the other girls. For Lauren. She'd be jealous to learn he'd moved on.

*Lauren.*

Why had she deceived him? Faked her death.

"And you were stupid enough to believe it all these years," Billy mocked.

"Everyone did."

"But you're supposed to be this big guru. You should have known. Instead, you had to find Molly, then dig up Lauren's coffin to look for her tiny ear bones to complete your collection." Billy laughed. "Man, that was a day. You finding the coffin empty. Never seen you quite so shocked."

"Wouldn't you be shocked to learn she'd faked her death?"

"Nah, I'd go with the flow."

"That's because you weren't called on to save the world like I was." He reached into his pocket and drew out the jeweler's box. "But now, I know her escape was meant to be. She's pure. She didn't want what Molly wanted. What the other girls wanted when they agreed to meet me. She only came to me to save Molly. She was pure. And if she still has that purity, she could be the one."

He gently cupped the box. Blue velvet with a midnight-black lining that accented his mother's pearls so nicely. They rested in slumber as she, too, rested. He ran a finger over the bright white lustrous orbs. Took one out. Stroked it along his cheek.

His mother's pearls. A gift from her father. The finest. Worth thousands. Not that he would sell them. They were for the woman he would marry.

Maybe Lauren, when he found her.

"She's alive, Mother!" he exclaimed. "Really and truly alive."

He wouldn't be alone after all. Lauren was the one. The only one.

# Chapter Three

THE RAID OVER, Becca jogged down the steps of the tired two-story apartment building located on a busy thoroughfare of cheap hotels and rundown retail stores to get the evidence bags from her car. They'd apprehended one young teen without ID who would only say his name was Danny, and Connor was hauling him over to the transport vehicle. The kid had been belligerent and uncooperative, tempting Becca to shake some sense into him. But she had a weakness for wayward kids, so she'd resisted her urge.

Becca continued on, catching sight of Taylor. She was almost comically stiff while standing guard at the raid. Becca remembered her rookie days—she would have been doing the same thing. She'd been so gung-ho, she'd likely have taken it up a notch from Taylor and would have still had her gun drawn.

Becca approached Taylor. "Thanks for standing duty down here. Sam will go along with the kid to County to make sure his fingerprints are run immediately. I want you to go with him. Call me the minute we know anything."

Taylor frowned. "I'd really like to stay and observe. Wouldn't it be possible for Sam to call us?"

*Odd.* "It's nothing you haven't done a thousand times before. Forensics will process the scene, and we'll catalog the evidence."

Taylor nipped her full lower lip. "Once I join the team, I won't likely get this close to a murder investigation again."

Becca could sympathize with Taylor, but she wouldn't let that sway her decision. "I need you to take the kid in, but then you're welcome to stop back by here."

Taylor smiled. "Okay, then. I'll be back as soon as I can."

"Let me grab some things from the back of the car first." Becca turned and caught Connor watching her.

Maybe watching Taylor? She was a beautiful girl. Thick dark hair, olive skin, deep brown eyes, and a curvy body. Becca could see him or any guy going for her. But it didn't bother Becca that *any* guy might be attracted to Taylor. Just Connor. The man she had this love/hate thing with. Okay, to be fair, she didn't hate anything about him. That was the problem.

"You two got a thing going on?" Taylor asked.

Becca snapped her mind back to the job at hand. "What? No. Nothing going on."

"Relax. So what if you two have a thing?"

"We don't have a thing."

"Okay, fine, not an actual thing. I get it. You're both keeping it on the down-low, but it's there. I'd have to be blind not to notice it. So hey, when I come back, I promise not to invade your territory."

Becca felt heat flush up her neck. "Come back if you want. Invade if you want. It's none of my business."

She spun and marched to her car, grabbed the evidence bags, and slammed the hatch harder than necessary before returning to the apartment that had walls lined with bookshelves filled with the suspected stolen merchandise. A metal folding table held three computers, a printer, and a magnetic card reader/writer for making bogus credit cards. A stack of cards and plastic blanks for making others sat on the table, too.

They'd located a gun of the same caliber as the one that killed Connor's victim, but they had no proof it was linked to the murder he was investigating. So, as the warrant holder, she'd take the gun, plus the stolen merchandise and credit card paraphernalia, into evidence. She started by bagging the gun and ammo clip for safety, then sat down behind the table and turned her attention to logging the credit cards.

"I guess all this stuff is what you were hoping to find," Connor said as he came back into the room.

"Yes."

He pointed a gloved finger at one of the computers. "It would be nice if we could take a look, but I know we have to wait for the techs."

She glanced at him. "Good to see you're up on computer seizure protocol."

"It's not hard to keep straight." He lifted his index finger. "Number one, don't touch them." His second finger went up. "And number two, wait for the experts to take them."

She smiled at his simplified version of the procedure. "Your department has trained you well."

"You can thank our Detective Yates for that. He played solitaire one night on a vic's computer while he was waiting for the ME to arrive." Connor chuckled. "I don't pretend to understand why we can't touch them, I just know we can't."

"The tech has to take an image of the hard drive to prove the state of the machine when we arrived, and that we haven't made any changes."

"Okay, an image," he said. "That tells me nothing."

"Think of it like finding blood on a crime scene," she said, starting a story she'd told many times to officers. "You've just arrived and see a pool of blood. But before you can get out your camera to document the scene, someone walks through the blood and leaves footprints. You still take a picture, but you know you'll have to explain to a jury why there's a footprint in the blood."

"Once you do that, they'll start questioning all of the forensics." He nodded. "I get it. And computers are the same?"

"Exactly. An image is like taking a snapshot of the hard drive. You start messing with a computer, and it leaves a trail, just like footprints in blood."

"Makes sense." He gestured at the shelves. "So here's the thing I still don't get. They buy the stuff, but short of selling it on the street or on eBay, how do they get their money?"

"They return it."

"But that would put a credit on the card, which doesn't help them at all."

"They don't use the card for that. They go to a different store to make the return without the receipt and get cash or a store gift card. If they get a card, they turn around and sell it to businesses that resell gift cards. I know it doesn't sound like big bucks, but the ringleader recruits a ton of associates and the numbers add up."

Connor's phone rang. He glanced at the screen.

"It's Sam," he said. "He couldn't possibly have fingerprint info yet. Maybe Danny gave up his full ID."

Connor answered the call, and she took the time to discreetly study him. He wore black pants with a black knit shirt that looked like it had been tailored to fit him. He suddenly squared his jaw, and his normal easygoing expression was replaced with an intensity that concerned her.

"You're sure?" He shoved a hand into his hair before starting to pace. "It's Van Gogh, for real?"

*Van Gogh.* Becca's heart dropped.

The abductor and killer of at least one fifteen-year-old girl in the mid-nineties, and likely two more. The girl had been in the system, like Becca and her foster sister Molly. Not only did he murder the girl, but he also cut off her ears and stored them in a jar, marked with the number one.

He'd taken Molly and Becca, too.

While she'd been held captive, Becca had noticed three jars sitting on the shelf, each holding ears, but only one body had ever been located. Becca had gotten away, but she suspected Van Gogh had killed Molly. There was no proof, though, so Becca had searched for Molly all of these years.

Becca pressed her fingers against the back of her own ear, felt the scar from the tip of the knife pricking her flesh. She saw Van Gogh hulking over her, his meaty fingers with twisting scars clamped around the large serrated knife. Evil eyes, usually hollow and vacant, alive with excitement. She could still feel his intensity, as if he were standing over her now.

"Could be a copycat," Connor said, completely oblivious to her reaction. "I mean, we haven't heard a thing about him in what, sixteen years?"

*Sixteen years, eight months, and fifteen days to be exact.*

Becca had continued to search for him, but he'd been silent. So why was he back now? Killing again. Maybe he'd learned of her name change and decided to come for her. Or had the body the police had just discovered been in the ground for years? Could it be Molly?

Panic raced to overtake Becca, but she gulped in air to fight it off.

Connor glanced at Becca, a quizzical look in his eyes. "Yeah, she's still here. I'll ask her."

Connor hung up, his probing detective's stare locking on her. She obviously hadn't done a good job of hiding her fear.

"You okay?" he asked. "You look a little pale."

"I'm good." She bit the inside of her mouth to keep from crying out.

"So, like I said, that was Sam." He stepped closer. "We caught another homicide. A big one that will trump this investigation for the time being. A teenage girl found in Forest Park. The crazy rain we've been having washed away the soil and a hiker found her in a shallow grave."

"Oh." She struggled to show little interest when what she really wanted was each and every detail about the killer who'd once kidnapped her.

"Here's the thing." Connor lowered his voice. "We think it's Van Gogh."

"Why?" she asked, dreading the answer.

"The girl's ears have been cut off."

At his official confirmation, Becca felt the color drain from her face and her knees go weak. She swallowed hard and tried to control the shaking of her hands, but they refused to cooperate so she shoved them under her legs.

"I heard you say it might be a copycat. Maybe you're right." She hoped, prayed he was correct, and her worst nightmare hadn't returned.

Connor arched a brow. "Sam says you studied this guy at Quantico."

"All the rookie agents do," she said, testing her voice for stability and deciding she was hiding her turmoil well enough to continue. "They dream of being the first law enforcement officer to crack the case. But they lose interest when they leave Quantico and find themselves up to their necks in their own workload."

"Not you, though, right? Sam says you stayed with the investigation and are the leading expert on Van Gogh." He gave a mock shudder. "Kind of creepy, if you ask me. Why would you want to spend your free time on such a guy?"

*Because I witnessed Van Gogh's depravity personally. And I left my best friend to die at his hands,* she thought. But she would never tell him or anyone else about that. "One of my foster sisters, Molly, disappeared in the nineties, and we suspect she was one of Van Gogh's victims."

"Oh, man, I'm sorry, Bex. No wonder you haven't let this go." He reached out to pat her shoulder, but she slid out of reach.

She didn't like him using her nickname. Her friends called her Bex, but Connor never had. That made this personal. *Him* personal. And it was more than she could handle right now, especially now that Van Gogh had resurfaced.

Hurt flashed in his eyes for a moment, then he seemed to do a mental shrug. "You haven't given up, right? You're still into the case?"

Into it? If he only knew how into it she was. But he wouldn't. At least, he wouldn't hear it from her, and he wouldn't find any mention of Rebecca Lange in the police files either. He could find details on a fifteen-year-old Lauren Nichols who'd been taken by Van Gogh and escaped. What he wouldn't find, however, was what had actually happened to that girl. When Van Gogh hadn't been caught after three months had passed, the police had faked her death and changed her name. The lead detective had promised to keep that out of the files.

"Becca?" Connor appraised her.

She had to answer, or he'd start to dig deeper. "I've never given up on solving that case, if that's what you're asking."

"So maybe you can give me some insight into the guy before I take off." He looked at his watch. "The quick version, if possible. Once this scene is secured, I need to get up to Forest Park ASAP."

"A quick insight into Van Gogh? Hardly. He's far too complicated for that."

"Come on, Becca. We could really use your help."

"Then I'll go with you to the crime scene." The words tumbled out before she took the time to think them through. If she had, she'd have likely chickened out, and run as far in the other direction as she could go.

It was something she was good at. After all, she'd done it once when she'd left Molly in the hands of that lunatic to save her own life.

# Chapter Four

CONNOR RUSHED after Becca and grabbed her arm before she reached the door. "What are you thinking? Running out of here like that. Van Gogh's victim isn't going anywhere, and their scene is secured, which is more than I can say for this one."

He expected her to be embarrassed by ignoring protocol, not to mention ignoring the case that a few minutes ago was top priority to her, but she seemed far too distracted to respond.

"Becca?" he asked. "Did you hear me? Van Gogh might be a career-making case, but I have a family counting on me to find the person who murdered their husband and father for his credit cards. I'm not leaving until we document the scene properly and your forensic team takes control."

"I got it." She sounded more relieved than disappointed, confusing him.

In his experience, she wasn't one to waffle like this, and he didn't know what to make of it.

She went to the table and seemed to collapse on a chair, then started sifting through the stack of credit cards, effectively dismissing him. Not that he intended to go anywhere. He continued to watch her, trying to read the thoughts she wasn't willing to share.

Was this about Van Gogh? Or was she just trying to keep him at arm's length, as she'd been doing from the moment they'd met? Met, shoot, she'd done it every time they'd run in to each other since then, including telling him outright to back off the day of Sam's wedding.

What a day that had been. As the best man, Connor had been thrown together with her all day. Her dress had been a seriously deep blue color that clung to every curve and was cut deep enough at the neck to fuel his imagination. It had been no hardship standing next to her. Or dancing with her. Until he hinted at dating. Then she'd gone into her I-don't-need-anyone mode and said she wanted to keep things professional. Made him mad. Good and mad. Which was stupid, considering he wasn't looking for a relationship either. No way was he giving another woman a chance to betray him the way his ex-fiancée Gillian had done.

He'd never gotten around to telling Becca that or asking what was wrong with having a little fun together. She was just too serious about life for her own good.

*And it's not your job to loosen her up. Forget about her and get this scene documented so you can move on to Van Gogh.*

He texted Sam to tell him Becca would be joining them, then grabbed his sketchpad and focused on drawing the layout of the small apartment. With Becca holding the search warrant, she or Taylor would perform the same task for the Bureau, but he wanted a clear record of the evidence for his case files as well.

He dug out his camera and started snapping pictures for documentation, keeping his eyes open for anything out of the ordinary. He glanced at Becca, and found her staring at a stack of credit cards, her mouth turned down in a frown. She didn't seem to be making progress on her work, nor was she willing to discuss the evidence. It was odd behavior from a woman who lived for her work. So what was her damage?

It had to be him. "Did I do something?"

Her head popped up. "What? Why would you ask that?"

"All I've been getting since I stopped you from taking off are one- and two-word answers."

"Sorry. You were right. We can't leave a crime scene unsecured. I'm just trying to focus so we can get done faster."

"Yeah, right." He squatted down to get her attention. "You look freaked out about something. If you're not mad at me for stopping you, then the only other thing it could be is what's going on between us."

"No it's—"

"We're going to be working together on this case," he interrupted before she could deny there was a problem. "Not to mention running in to each other all the time like we do at Sam and Kait's functions. I'm tired of walking on eggshells around you. Don't you think it's about time we clear the air and move on?"

She studied him for a few moments and seemed to come to some conclusion. "So we what? Just say a few magic words and this stupid attraction goes away?"

"Stupid?" he asked, surprised at how much the word hurt.

"You know what I mean."

"Yeah. It's unwanted, that's for sure." He forced out a smile. "I think just getting it out in the open will put an end to it. You know? Admit that if things were different, we might give it a go, but right now, it won't work for either of us."

A shadow crossed her face, her eyes darkening for a moment. "Maybe you're right. Putting it out there will take the mystery out of it and it'll burn out faster."

"That's what you want, right?" he asked, just to be sure. Or maybe to give her a chance to say no.

"It's what I want."

He grinned, hoping to lighten things up now that they'd made things official. "Then let's hope you don't fall prey to my charms and change your mind."

"I won't change my mind and it *will* burn out." She set her jaw, her expression daring him to argue.

He held up his hands. "Don't worry, Becca. You're coming through loud and clear. We can now get back to work and not have this hanging over us."

She gave a firm nod and went straight to her task. She seemed more focused, but he was more confused.

They'd cleared the air. Exactly what he wanted, right? Then why was his gut twisted in a big old knot?

BECCA OWED CONNOR her job. If he hadn't stopped her from bailing on the crime scene, she would have run out on the investigation she'd fought Sulyard so hard to continue. Then he would likely have disciplined her for making such a stupid move. Maybe even fired her. Sure, she had a good reason, but she couldn't tell him that.

Now that she was over the initial shock, she'd prioritize her tasks and work smart so she could get her job done, then go with Connor to the crime scene.

*Prioritizing.* Her specialty. Starting with setting goals for Taylor.

After discovering that Danny's fingerprints didn't produce a match in the system, she'd returned. That allowed Becca to take advantage of Taylor's skills in evidence collection. She could supervise the computer techs and Evidence Response Team, freeing Becca up to go to Van Gogh's crime scene without losing any time on the credit card fraud investigation.

Taylor should have all of this wrapped up by the time Becca got back to the office, and Becca could review the report and assign duties before moving on to Van Gogh. She'd have to work late and wouldn't get much sleep, but with Van Gogh on the hunt again, she wasn't likely to get much sleep anyway.

Taylor stepped away from their ERT tech, Henry Greco, and joined Becca. "Henry seems very capable."

"He's one of the best techs I've encountered."

"That's because you never worked with me." Taylor smiled, her gaze lighthearted and eager.

What Becca wouldn't give to feel that way. Just once. For a minute. An hour maybe. But Van Gogh had stolen that from her. Or had she simply lost it when she'd left Molly behind?

"Any idea how long you'll be?" Taylor asked.

Becca shook her head. "I should be back in the office by the time the techs finish imaging the computers. If not, start reviewing the electronic files right away."

Taylor nodded, her expression more serious. "Hey, thanks for trusting me with all of this."

Becca felt a smidgen of guilt. If Van Gogh hadn't resurfaced, she wouldn't be trusting Taylor with anything. But Van Gogh *was* out there, and that meant compromise.

"Call if you need me for anything," Becca said, then went to join Connor.

The apartment door shot open, and her friend Kait stepped in, her gaze immediately going to Becca. She rushed across the room, her regal posture making her look like she was gliding. Even her basic suit didn't detract from the image of royalty, Becca thought, smiling in spite of herself. Kait seemed a little off-putting at times, but Becca couldn't find a more caring friend.

"What are you doing here?" Becca's question came out laced with suspicion.

"Kait," Connor greeted warmly. "I thought Taylor was taking over for Becca."

"She is." Kait met Becca's gaze. "Sam told me Becca was going to the Van Gogh scene with you, and I'm here to stop her."

Becca wasn't surprised at the pronouncement. Kait was just looking out for Becca, but it irked her all the same. "They need my help, and I'm going."

"Help is one thing, but this? Sam says the scene is gruesome. Besides, after all these years without a sign of Van Gogh, what are the odds that it's actually him and not a copycat? You'll have been exposed to that atrocious scene for nothing."

"I'm not sure I agree with you, Kait," Connor said. "Van Gogh could have been killing all this time, just doing so under the police radar."

Kait fired an irritated look at Connor. "Did Becca tell you about her friend Molly? We think Van Gogh took her sixteen years ago."

"Becca mentioned her."

Kait's eyes widened. "And you're still good with involving her in this investigation and bringing back all of that pain?"

"Good with it?" He shook his head hard. "No. Willing to accept her help to bring in a depraved killer? Yes."

"Enough." Becca crossed her arms. "You two can argue about me all you want, but I'm the one who will decide. I think I can help stop Van Gogh, so I'm going to the scene. End of discussion."

"Okay." Kait frowned. "But I'm coming with you."

"Now wait a minute," Connor said. "Sam isn't going to allow that."

"I might be married to Sam, but he doesn't control my professional decisions."

"Fine. Make him mad. That's your choice. But I don't have to let you onto the crime scene. Having Becca there is one thing. It's going to be hard enough to explain her to our lieutenant, but you? You have no reason for being there."

Kait linked her arm with Becca's. "We're a package deal. You want Becca, you get me, too."

Becca stepped back. "I can't ask you to do that, Kait."

"You're not asking. I'm volunteering." Kait drilled Becca with a resolute look. Obviously, no matter how much Becca argued, her loyal friend would be right by her side. In fact, now that Becca thought about it, Nina would likely be standing right here too if she wasn't off work preparing for her wedding to Quinn Stone.

As much as Becca was irritated by Kait's determination to join her, she was thankful for her friends. Becca smiled at Kait. "Thanks for your support."

"Good. That's settled then." Kait turned her attention to Connor. "Becca doesn't need to hang out with you and Sam all day, so I'll drive her."

Connor arched a brow. "Not sure I agreed to this."

"Come on, Connor. You know you're no match for the two of us. You'll eventually give in. Why not just do it now so we can get out of here?"

He nodded reluctantly, his attention quickly going to the phone ringing in his pocket. He looked at it and frowned.

"Sam," Connor answered then listened intently. His frown deepened, and Becca assumed Sam was passing on bad news. She was afraid to ask, and yet, afraid not to hear it.

"I'm leaving now." Connor looked at his watch. "It'll take me about a half hour to get there." He hung up and looked at Kait. "You have directions?"

"That was Sam?" Becca asked.

Connor nodded but kept his gaze on Kait. "Directions? You have them?"

"Yes," she said.

"Then we should get going." Connor grabbed his bag and headed for the door without another word. She and Kait followed, but he picked up his pace, jogging down the steps as if Van Gogh himself were waiting for him at the crime scene.

By the time Becca and Kait reached the car, Connor's vehicle was long gone. Kait quickly merged into traffic, and Becca curled as close as she could into a fetal position without drawing Kait's attention. Connor's final comment to Sam kept echoing through her mind.

"It'll take me about a half hour to get there," he'd said, the phrase innocent enough.

One half hour, Becca thought. Thirty minutes. Eighteen hundred seconds until she had to summon up the courage to get out of this car and face her greatest nightmare.

# Chapter Five

ONCE SAM TOLD Connor about a second body, he hightailed it over to Forest Park, not caring if Kait kept up. He stopped to talk to the officer of record posted as a sentry at the path leading up to the crime scene.

"Add Agents Rebecca Lange and Kaitlyn Murdock to your list of approved visitors," Connor told him. "They should be here soon."

Connor waited for the officer to jot down the names, then he started up the path lined with big leaf maples and alders. Enormous ferns peeked through rusty leaves beaten down to the ground in the heavy rain.

Connor reached a bend and paused to shift his bag and catch his breath. This was one of the most difficult paths to traverse in a park that covered more than seven miles of the eastern slope of the Tualatin Mountains. The trail's difficulty meant it was used less often than easier trails—a perfect place for Van Gogh to dump a body without being seen. It also meant Van Gogh had to be in reasonably good shape to haul the girls up the steep path. Connor was struggling enough with his bag—he couldn't imagine carrying a hundred-plus-pound girl over his shoulder. With that kind of load, he would have to stop to rest, and he worked out daily.

He started off again, keeping his focus on the sides of the trail, looking for any hint of evidence that Criminalist Dane Harwell or Sam might have missed on the way up. Sam had briefly described the setting, mentioning that a lack of blood near the body indicated the girl hadn't been killed at the burial location. Connor stopped at a spot that had been recently trampled, and saw Dane's evidence marker number, A1, sitting next to a cigarette butt. If Van Gogh had climbed this path with a girl, he wasn't likely a smoker. Still, Connor snapped a quick picture for his records and continued on up.

Near the apex of the trail, a small clearing covered in ankle-high green grass opened to the left. Hills surrounded the area with tall pines and maples fighting for sunlight under gray skies. Rain had carved the thick grass into a deep gully running from the top of the hill to the bottom. Connor couldn't see the girl from his location, but the spot was cordoned off with crime-scene tape. Sam and Dane stood fifty yards to the east. Sam wore his usual jeans, boots, button-down shirt, and a PPB windbreaker. Dane's clothes were covered in a white Tyvek suit, and his head was bent over as he slowly moved around the edge of the clearing.

Connor started toward the body, his feet sinking into the waterlogged earth. The pungent, rotting decay of human flesh drifted on the breeze, and Connor swallowed hard. No matter how many murder scenes he'd witnessed in his career, it was never easy. He stepped under the fluttering yellow tape, and Sam greeted him from a distance with a grim shake of his head.

Connor took his first look at the girl. His lunch came rushing up, and he swallowed hard. He'd seen dead bodies in his five years as a homicide detective. Some murdered. Some dead from natural causes and car accidents. But today? The sight of the recently murdered young girl peeking from the shallow grave, clumps of clay soil hugging her body, brought him as close to hurling on scene as he'd ever come.

He'd make her as mid-teens, fitting Van Gogh's preference. She was dressed in a white gown that looked like satin with lace trim. A demure gown, like a young girl might wear to bed. Her arms were folded across her chest, her legs crossed, her mouth open in a scream, her ears missing. Sawed off.

Connor gagged again and went to join Sam and Dane who was still staring at the ground. A former patrol officer, Dane carried himself like a cop with confidence and an assessing eye. He was near six feet tall, with broad shoulders, and had a muscular build from his recent commitment to working out. Criminalists were sworn staff members at PPB, which meant Dane carried a gun just like any other officer, but it was hidden under his protective suit. He'd served seven years on the street, and that time had taught him to think like a criminal, a valuable skill for a criminalist.

As Connor drew closer, he saw something poking out of the ground. It looked like a stick. Maybe it had been used in the crime somehow, but Connor didn't immediately get the importance. Maybe it had to do with the second body Sam had mentioned on the phone.

"Not a pretty sight over there," Sam said in greeting.

Connor nodded his agreement. "So what's everyone looking at?"

"A foot, or more precisely, a toe." Dane squatted and used a fine brush to remove dirt from the item Connor had thought was a stick until it became clear that Dane had indeed located a bone.

"Looks like a metatarsal," Dane said. "Big toe. The phalanges either washed away or never surfaced." Dane stood. "I'm no expert, but the bone is small so, I'm guessing it belongs to another girl."

"I know this is kind of an obvious question, but did you check to see if the first girl has all of her toes?"

"You had to ask?" Sam mocked pulling a knife from his chest.

"Okay, fine. Just double-checking." Connor focused on the bone and moved his gaze across the grass to where he would expect her head to be located. "Ground's intact."

"Which means she's been here awhile." Sam ran a hand over the back of his neck.

"You're positive it's a human bone?" Connor asked.

"Positive, no. The ME can weigh in, but I think we'll need the OSP forensic anthropologist for a firm confirmation."

Connor had already expected they'd need resources from the Oregon State Police on this investigation. He just didn't expect that would include an anthropologist. They'd have to call their lieutenant to arrange it.

"I'll get her out here ASAP," Sam said, his eyes going to the trail.

A fiery redheaded woman wearing coveralls rolled up at her ankles crested the hill. It didn't take Connor long to recognize her as Marcie Jensen, the best medical examiner on the team. She was accompanied by Tim, her often acerbic tech. He was a string bean of a guy, who usually made the business of collecting bodies more difficult than it had to be. Still, he was competent, or Marcie would have fired him long ago.

"I'll go meet Marcie." Sam looked at Connor. "Dane will secure this area. It'd be great if you'd start mapping the scene."

Connor dug his sketchbook from his field bag as Sam stepped off in long strides. Connor traced each tree, each large boulder, the gully with the grave, and the path, while Marcie and Sam studied the body. Connor labeled everything in neat block letters, making sure it was legible. He then used his surveyor's wheel to plot the precise location of each item of evidence Sam and Dane had marked A2 through A17. And as he did so, he looked for additional evidence. Dane was doing the same thing, but Connor believed in being thorough. They could compare notes when Dane completed his drawing to be sure they hadn't missed anything.

Connor ended back at the second body, now identified by Dane's crime-scene tape.

Connor wondered who this poor girl might be. What had her dreams been? Whatever her aspirations, they'd been cut short by the lunatic Van Gogh. A thought suddenly hit him, and his heart sank.

"Hey, Dane," he called out. "Can you come here a minute?"

Dane strode over to him. "Whatcha need?"

"This bone. How long would it take to become skeletonized like this?"

"Depends. It could happen quickly if the body wasn't buried the whole time. A few weeks, I'd guess. Or if she'd been buried, six months or longer. Or we could be looking at a girl who's been here for years."

"Like sixteen years?"

"Sure."

Connor resisted letting his mouth fall open. This toe, this little bit of a human being, might be part of Molly's body. And today could be the day Becca found out her foster sister hadn't escaped Van Gogh's clutches after all.


HE WAS BACK, AND Becca couldn't breathe.

She forced herself to plant one foot in front of the other to make her way up the path. The air was thick with moisture, and large raindrops hit her in the face. She swiped a hand over her forehead to dislodge hair matted against her skin and paused to catch her breath.

"Tough climb." Kait panted next to Becca.

"Imagine carrying a body." Becca swigged her water and started up the path again.

Her mind went to the sight that she knew awaited them, and her skin crawled.

She'd had nightmares of this day. Dreamt about it over and over for sixteen years. Awoke sweating. Terrified. Unable to breathe. Much of the time, she'd been seeking Molly who'd run away, becoming a whispery shadow on the horizon, and Becca had never been able to catch up to her.

It was fitting, considering that Becca had run from Molly. Just as Van Gogh made the first cut into Becca's ear, Molly had offered herself instead. Distracted, he turned his attention to Molly without properly securing Becca. The chance to escape opened up, and Becca had taken it.

She'd run. Fast and far. Telling herself with each step that she was putting enough distance between them to be able to find help without risking capture. But she'd raced past help. Run hard. Down the road. Around corners . . . until she'd collapsed. Until she could run no more. Until she had no idea how to get back to the house where Van Gogh held Molly.

And Becca had never seen Molly again.

What kind of person left her foster sister to die at a lunatic's hands? A terrible person. One who thought only of herself.

They crested the hill. Becca's gaze went straight to the grave. Sam charged across the field and stepped in front of Kait. Becca slipped past him, not bothering to see if they followed. She didn't care. She'd left Molly alone, and she deserved to be alone, too.

Connor stood on the far side of the grave talking to the medical examiner. She didn't make eye contact with him, but could feel him carefully watching her. He was worried for her, and he wasn't bothering to hide it. She appreciated his concern, but she hadn't asked for it. Hadn't asked for anything from him. All she wanted was to be treated like a fellow colleague. This monster of a mess was the reason. She could never share her secret. Never tell anyone else she'd abandoned Molly. If she did, they'd run the other way. So even if she did feel more than a physical attraction for Connor—which she wasn't saying she did—she wasn't about to do anything about it.

And then there was the possibility that Van Gogh could find out she was alive and come after her again. Maybe hurt someone she cared about in the process. That was why she chose not to tell Kait or Nina. And no matter how big and tough Connor was, she wouldn't risk exposing him to Van Gogh, either.

She moved closer, catching the fetid smell as she looked at the grave. The girl, the poor, poor girl wore the same style of nightgown Van Gogh had dressed Becca in, right before putting the pearls in her ears. Before the knife came out and he paused to stare at her, a sick smile plastered on his face.

Was he here, watching now? Did he see her? Did he somehow know, after all this time, that she was Lauren? That she was alive?

She searched the area and honed in on the trees, looking for life, for the man who'd terrorized her and Molly for days. She saw nothing, but he could be there. Deeper in the woods, binoculars in hand. Enjoying her distress.

Her throat closed. She could barely breathe. *No*. He couldn't win. She forced her mind back to today and looked at the girl's face. The mouth and eyes were open. Terrified. The face morphed into Molly's face. This wasn't Molly. The body was too young to be Molly's. Besides, this girl hadn't been dead for sixteen years. But still, Molly would have felt the same terror.

A strangled cry escaped Becca's throat.

Connor grimaced and started for her, skirting Marcie with a deft foot. He gently took Becca's arm and turned her away from the horrific sight. She usually reacted to his touch, but she was so frozen in shock and fear, she barely felt his hand.

"I'm thankful for your help." He rested a hand on her shoulder and gave her a tender look that brought tears to her eyes. "But I wish you weren't here."

All she wanted to do was melt against his chest and let him hold her until the horrible memories of the night in the damp cellar disappeared, but she was here as an FBI agent and she needed to remember that. "I'm a law enforcement officer, just like you, Connor. I'm trained for this."

"Training and actually viewing a decomposed body are two different things. I oughta know. I deal with homicide victims all the time."

She wanted to heed his advice, but if she didn't check out the details, she couldn't help bring the monster Van Gogh to justice. "I'm good, Connor. Really I am."

She stepped around him. The foul odor caught on the wind.

*For Molly and the others,* Becca reminded herself and made her feet move forward.

Marcie looked up, smiled tightly, then focused on Connor. "Before you ask, my initial assessment is that the girl's been here for about a week. But there are so many factors when a body is buried that I can't be certain. We do have the presence of coffin flies, and putrefaction has started. Her face is swollen and her abdomen full of gasses so she's definitely—"

"That's enough, Marcie." Connor held up his hand. "We trust your skills and don't need the details of how you came to your conclusion."

She transferred her gaze to Becca. "Odd to see you here, Becca. You working a case that involves a murdered girl?"

"Becca's an expert on Van Gogh," Connor explained, grabbing Marcie's attention. "Any ID on the victim?"

"No, but then we didn't expect it, did we? Not if Van Gogh's behind this." Marcie shook her head. "Again, I'm not certain of her age yet, but this girl appears to fit his preference for fifteen-year-olds." Marcie fisted her hands and looked like she wanted to punch someone. "At least, if she's in the foster care system, we'll be able to narrow down the field a bit. There will be fewer missing girls to look for."

"Not necessarily," Becca said. "She may not have been reported as missing. Foster kids run away all the time. Some are reported. Some aren't."

Marcie's eyes widened. "How can that happen?"

"Most foster parents are on the up and up, but some are only in it for the money. If they don't report when a kid takes off, the checks keep coming, and it's one less mouth to feed."

Marcie grimaced. "That's disgusting."

"Unfortunately, it's reality. Still, it gives us a place to start." Connor frowned. "Do you have a cause of death?"

"I can't be sure until I do the autopsy, but I'd venture to say from the ligature mark around her neck that she was strangled."

*Strangled.* Van Gogh's MO.

Becca moved toward the body for a better look. As she stared down at the girl, Molly's face kept replacing Jane Doe's, and Becca had to back away.

"So is this a copycat or Van Gogh?" Connor asked, through clenched teeth.

That's what Becca was hoping to check. One detail had never been leaked to the press or to anyone outside the investigation, but Becca couldn't bring herself to raise the girl's knee-length gown to find out. And she couldn't tell the others without explaining how she knew about it. She could make up a story, she supposed, but she wouldn't. She was many things, but she wasn't a liar. Still, she couldn't keep this to herself. They needed to know if Van Gogh truly was back. *She* needed to know.

She opened her mouth to speak. Nothing came out. She swallowed hard and cleared her throat.

Connor stepped up to her and searched her face, kindness lingering in his eyes. "I knew you'd react this way once you saw the body." There was no accusation in his voice, no "I told you so," just sadness at their situation. "Just tell me what you know about the killer and take off. Okay?"

"I . . . it's . . ." She wanted to tell him everything about that night. Tell him her real name was Lauren. Even more, she wanted to confess her guilt. To admit aloud to saving her own neck and leaving Molly to be butchered by this madman. Her ears in his collection, preserved in mason jars.

Becca imagined Connor's reaction if he found out. Would he still ask for her help if he knew she'd nearly been victim number five? That she bore physical scars from her run-in with Van Gogh? And what if he learned she'd left Molly behind? What would he think of her then?

Bile rose up Becca's throat, and she swallowed hard.

"Becca?" Connor asked. "Is there anything you can tell us to help?"

She jerked her gaze to Marcie. "Check her stomach, Marcie. To the right of her navel."

"What am I looking for?" Marcie asked.

Becca wasn't going to tell them about the number. About Van Gogh's great joy as he carved a number into each girl's skin, branding them, claiming them as his. Not unless she absolutely had to. "Just look and describe what you see."

Marcie adjusted the victim's clothing. Becca's hand went to her own stomach. She'd had the number five removed, but the feel of it was burned into her soul. Seeing him etch the number four on Molly's stomach, a close second.

Marcie looked up. "That sick, depraved creep. He carved a number into her skin."

"This is no copycat." Becca managed to force the words up her parched throat.

"How do you know?" Connor asked.

"Van Gogh engraved a number on his victims' abdomens."

"A copycat could do the same thing."

She shook her head. "This information was never released to the public. No one else could know."

"Then how do you know about it?"

"I can't reveal my source at this time." She waited for him to push for the truth.

"And you're sure your source is reliable?"

She pressed her hand against her waist again. "Positive."

"So this is the work of Van Gogh, then." Connor sounded resigned to the horrific confirmation. "What's the number, Marcie?"

Marcie looked up, her face contorted with disgust. "Nine. This psychopath has killed nine defenseless girls."

Becca knew that wasn't true. Her body had been number five, so the max count could only be eight. And Becca still hoped that Molly was alive and the count was really seven. Still, even one girl losing her life this way was a horrific thought to ponder.

# Chapter Six

TAYLOR SHOULDN'T be doing this. She'd only been an agent here in Portland for like a minute before she'd realized she had her work cut out for her. If she wanted to make it, she was not only going to have to measure up, but she'd have to find a way to stand out against the talent and expertise on the Cyber Action Team. Three strong women. Strong agents. Yet real and personable. And hard to shine around. So today, Taylor was taking charge, even if it ended badly.

She tucked the folder under her arm and entered the Multnomah County Detention Center. Taylor had honestly been shocked that the county jail was located in the middle of downtown Portland. How many people who strolled down Third Street realized a maximum security facility sat behind the building's pristine architecture?

It took her only a few minutes to register and be escorted to a small square box of a room painted in a dingy gray, holding one table and two bench seats bolted to the floor. Her sweaty palms reflected her lack of personal experience in jailhouse interview rooms. She chose the seat facing the door and opened the folder to review Danny's statement, along with the photos Becca had received from Connor.

When Danny was escorted into the room, he dropped onto the bench with a sigh and eyed her. "So, what? They think they can send a pretty agent in here, and I'm going to talk? You may be cute, but I'm not saying a word."

It sure wasn't what Taylor had expected the kid to say. Of course, she'd never done an actual interview, either. Although she'd spent hours role-playing with her fellow classmates at Quantico, she had no real-world experience, so she shouldn't have any preconceived idea of what he might say. Still, he surprised her. She *did* know she couldn't let him think she was just another pretty face, or he'd walk all over her. That much she'd learned from shadowing Becca and watching Nina and Kait in action.

"It's my training and experience that you should really be watching out for," she replied, eyeing Danny until he squirmed.

*Good.* Now that she'd set the tone to her liking, she took out a micro-cassette recorder. She turned it on and recorded the date, time, location, and the names of the parties in the room. She set it on the table and sat back, doing her very best to look confident.

"So, Danny . . ." She paused and drew out the silence. "Tell me how you happened to be in an apartment for which you don't hold the lease. An apartment filled with stolen merchandise and credit cards."

He shrugged. "I was just hanging with my buddy who lives there."

"Okay, let's assume there was a buddy there before we arrived. He have a name?"

"Puh-lease." Danny snorted. "If I won't give up my name, why would I give his up?"

"Then we're talking about a guy. Thanks for narrowing it down." She allowed herself a satisfied smile.

"You already got that from the lease, so don't make it look like I've told you something new."

"See here's the thing, Danny." She leaned closer. "People lie on leases all the time. So we don't usually believe them until they've been confirmed. Which you just did."

"Big deal." He crossed his arms. "I didn't give up his name, though."

"If this friend is like you and has done nothing wrong, why not tell us his name?"

"You cops are all the same." He fired an angry look her way. "You won't believe a thing any of us say. I've seen it. Plenty of times on the streets."

She looked at his fingernails, saw the ground-in dirt in his skin and under his nails, the ragged nail edges, the rough, worn skin. "Are you living on the streets then, Danny?"

"Maybe," he said.

"I'm guessing you to be about sixteen, seventeen. Maybe you're a kid who didn't get along with your parents, so you took off. Only, living on the streets isn't all that easy. You could have been recruited by an ID theft ring. And maybe you even want to get out of it, but don't know how."

She studied him in silence for a moment, then added, "Since we found the gun in the room with you, you'll likely be charged with murder." She threw the last bit in, even though she didn't have a clue if the ballistics report matched.

He didn't speak, but his defensive posture had lessened.

"I can help you, Danny. This can end now. Give me your ringleader's name—the man who signed the lease—and I'll make sure the DA goes easy on you. If you're a first-time offender, there's a chance you'll be able to walk away from this." His expression softened more. "Go home. Start over again."

He tightened his arms and defiance returned to his eyes. "I'm not saying it again. No information."

She might be new to interviewing, but she could read people. The kid wanted to talk, and he wanted to get away from here. But he didn't want to go home. That was clear. She made a mental note to search for reported runaways, and since about a third of Portland street kids were, or had been, in the foster care system, she'd also check in with the Department of Human Services for missing kids. For now, she'd see if she could get a reaction from him on the other teens in the photos.

"Do you hang with any of these people?" She started flipping over Connor's surveillance pictures, one by one, watching his face for a reaction. When she came to a cute girl's picture, he visibly stiffened.

This girl meant something to him. She wasn't old enough to be the ringleader, but maybe she was a friend, or even a girlfriend. Either way, Taylor wasn't going to mention it and let him know she was on to the girl.

Taylor finished flashing the pictures without another reaction from Danny. She really had nothing else to ask the kid, and had basically struck out. She would get into trouble for this—that much was certain—but they'd go easier on her if she had something to show for her time. With her forensics background, her mind went to fingerprints and DNA.

They'd lifted no prints from the gun, but DNA was another matter. Odds were that a DNA test wouldn't be authorized for a fraud case, but she could unofficially get Danny's DNA and find a private lab to process it. She'd pay for it herself.

"I'm thirsty, how about you?" she asked casually. "Want a Coke?"

"I could drink something."

"Hang tight." She went to the door to talk to the deputy. She doubted they had facilities to supply the kid with a soda, but that wasn't going to stop her. She'd work her magic on the deputy, and the kid would have a Coke before she departed. Of that she was certain.

REGINALD HAD WORK to do. He'd have rather spent time daydreaming about Lauren than cleaning the old warehouse, but he couldn't risk getting caught. When he called the police with an anonymous tip on where to find Molly, they'd swarm the place, poking and prying into every crack and crevice with their CSI tools. He loved forensics television shows, and he'd seen how a single hair could lead the police to the killer. He wouldn't be that careless and give them anything to further their investigation.

He opened the back door of his van, snapped on a hairnet, and tightened the cuffs of his long-sleeved shirt before putting on gloves. Completely covered, he grabbed his shop vac and carried it to the basement that was starting to smell.

"Hello, Molly," he said, and paused to check the effectiveness of his rat screen. "Yes, good. I see they have left you alone." He spun and went back up the rickety stairs to retrieve bleach and rags.

Back in the basement, he used the shop vac to suck up Molly's waste, retching at the smell. He'd hoped to leave it as a special present for the police, but he'd questioned Molly in this very spot, and he had to make sure he removed every trace of his hair or skin cells. He moved the vacuum around the basement, concentrating on the cracks and crevices where evidence could hide.

Satisfied at his work, he got onto his knees and flooded the entire linoleum floor with bleach. Let the police spend their time trying to decide if any traces of blood they found was his. It would keep them from looking for any real evidence. He moved on to the sink, dousing it with bleach and scouring every bit of the drain and the corners with a toothbrush. His nose dripped from the caustic liquid. He wiped it with his sleeve to keep from leaving evidence, and then continued until every inch of the room had seen bleach.

Not satisfied, he went back to the floor and rinsed it with buckets of water, swishing it toward the floor drain with a rubber squeegee. He repeated the action with bleach again, then scoured the drain and turned on a large fan.

"Perfect." He was finished.

Now, he needed to go home and do the same thing, just in case the police learned his name and came calling. He took the empty crate and carefully packed his mason jars, then carried it and the supplies to his car before heading home.

On the drive, his thoughts went to his home basement—or his workshop, as he liked to think of it. He'd brought the first five girls there. Mother hadn't minded. She'd liked knowing he was getting on with his work, but when Molly and Lauren had gotten away . . . oh my . . . Mother had totally shut him down.

As a memento, he'd used each girl's blood to scrawl their name, along with the date of their cleansing, on the wall. Mother had ended that, too, when she'd made him paint over it.

Ah, the girls. Each special in their own right. They'd once made him feel powerful. Useful. But now, now he felt nothing but emptiness except on cleansing day. So what if Mother hadn't approved of him resuming his work before he'd found Molly and Lauren? Mother was dead and gone in physical form. He hadn't waited even a day before starting his cleansing again. Sure, she continued to speak to him but she could do nothing to interfere except scold him. No more ear-pulling or pinching. No more closet.

Now he was his own boss. The master of his destiny. And tomorrow, oh, tomorrow. . . . That would be his big day. The day of expectation.

He'd pull out the burner phone and voice scrambler he'd ordered on the Internet and dial 911. He'd tell them, quickly, but succinctly—no point in lingering—where to find Molly.

Oh, yes, he could see it already. See the police scramble out of their building, running for their cars. They'd race out to the river, break down the building door. Then they'd come out with admiration on their faces, impressed with Molly's sacrifice for purity's sake.

And then . . . then and only then . . . would his real search for Lauren begin.

# Chapter Seven

"THE NUMBER ISN'T NINE," Becca said matter-of-factly, though her expression remained horrified.

"Explain, please." Connor didn't want to make Becca rehash her knowledge of this madman, this creep who carved numbers into girls' bodies and took their ears, but that was the reason she was here.

"One girl . . . a young girl . . . fifteen . . . Lauren Nichols," Becca started haltingly. "She was abducted by Van Gogh in the nineties but got away."

"Tell me about her," Connor probed.

Becca's eyes went blank, all signs of earlier emotion gone. "She . . . Lauren . . . escaped. This happened before Van Gogh's first victim was found. She saw three jars with ears in them, labeled one through three. Lauren had the number five carved into her stomach, Molly number four." Becca paused, and a shudder claimed her body. "So that means there could only be eight murdered girls. And of course, I'm hoping Molly escaped, too. If she did, we'd only be looking for seven bodies out of nine girls abducted." Becca drew her shoulders into a straight line, and her expression filled with resolve.

Connor was impressed that she could hold it together, much less call up the determination he saw on her face. She was a tough woman. Stronger than most. After what had happened to Molly, seeing a foster girl treated with such disrespect today had to be tearing Becca up inside. Not that she wanted him or anyone else to see how badly it was affecting her, hence the squared shoulders and resolved look. But his training taught him to look deeper. That's when he noticed that the color hadn't returned to her face, making her large brown eyes stand out. She could be in shock.

And she'd definitely be, if he told her about the second body. But he wasn't going to do that without a positive ID, and that wasn't coming anytime soon.

She suddenly pivoted, her gaze going to the trail.

Connor turned to see his supervisor cresting the hill. Lieutenant Vance's gaze lit on Becca then traveled to Kait who was still standing with Sam near the trail. Vance came to a complete stop, his look bewildered.

*Dang.* Connor and Sam had obviously violated their lieutenant's first rule of investigation. If it was a big case, a hairy case, one that might bite any of them in the butt, Connor was to report every step, every move to Vance before taking action. Only neither he nor Sam had informed their lieutenant that Becca and Kait would be involved.

Had they asked, odds were good that Vance would have said no to Becca's help this early on in the investigation. Vance was unlikely to call in the feds before he had a grasp on the situation and determined the resources needed. It ensured that no details of the case were made public before Vance was ready.

Shoot, it was the last thing Connor wanted, too. At least, he didn't want any additional feds to come out here, which could easily happen on such a high-profile case, if the news hit the media. The FBI had no jurisdiction here, but if the press got wind of the murders, Vance would have to include them to make it look as though he was doing everything he could to catch Van Gogh, even if they didn't need the FBI's assistance.

Vance started across the space, and Connor turned to Becca. "Sam and I may have omitted telling our lieutenant that you and Kait were here. You should join Kait while I bring him up to speed."

She nodded and, without saying a word, walked over to Kait. Connor motioned for Sam to join him, then tipped his head at Vance. "Prepare yourself."

"I thought you told him," Sam growled, his smooth southern accent long gone.

"And I thought you did," Connor said, when what he really wanted to do was remind Sam that it had been *his* idea to include Becca. But Connor wouldn't. Mostly because he *should* have made the call for Sam.

Ever since Sam had married an FBI agent, he walked a fine line. He naturally wanted to support his wife. What guy wouldn't? Yet, locals and feds didn't always have the same motives, and there was often an underlying tension, putting Sam in a tight spot. Connor could have taken the heat for this and spared Sam. If Vance's stormy approach was any indication, they'd both get an earful.

Connor braced himself and watched the short and squat powerhouse of a guy mash the grass flat with his forceful steps as he strode across the field toward them.

"Heck of a place to bring your wife." Vance focused his intense study on Sam, standing there with arms crossed, waiting for Sam to provide a good reason for Kait and Becca's presence.

Connor had to admit to feeling relieved. Sam didn't seem inclined to give an explanation, likely because he didn't want to say anything about Kait that would make Vance mad.

"Kait's here as moral support for Agent Lange," Connor said, trying to take some of the heat off Sam. "Becca grew up in the foster system and—"

"Even better," Vance interrupted. "Bring her here to watch us dig up the missing foster girls."

"As I was going to say," Connor continued. "She's studied Van Gogh for the last six years, and she's the leading expert on him. She's already provided valuable information, proving that we're looking at the real Van Gogh and not a copycat." Connor brought Vance up to date.

Vance stared at Becca and Kait for a moment. "Do they know about the second body?"

Connor shook his head. "Not yet. Only Sam, Dane, and I know the details."

"We need to keep it that way."

"I wasn't going to tell anyone." Connor was offended that Vance felt the need to tell them how to do their job. Every good detective knew sharing details that suggested a serial killer had claimed multiple victims was foolish until they'd decided how much information to release to the public.

"Good, though if they're still here when the OSP anthropologist arrives, it will tip them off that we're looking at a skeletonized victim, too. I don't plan to let that happen." He spun and marched over to the women.

Sam and Connor traipsed after Vance.

"Kait," Vance said cordially, then turned his gaze on Becca. "And Agent Lange. Good to see both of you again." Vance was a master as schmoozing when he needed to be, but Connor knew the hammer was coming.

"We've come to a standstill in our investigation while we wait for additional resources. We appreciate your help thus far, but you're free to go now. I do ask that you not mention to anyone what you saw here today, or that we suspect Van Gogh has resurfaced."

"No," Becca said.

Vance's eyebrows shot up. "Excuse me?"

"I won't mention this to anyone, but you said I was free to go." Becca planted her hands on her hips. "And I choose to stay. So my answer is no."

Vance widened his stance. "Perhaps I wasn't clear. We appreciate your help, but now you need to leave."

"No," Becca said again.

If the situation hadn't been so serious, Connor would have laughed at the shocked look on Vance's face.

"Again," Becca said. "I choose to stay.'

Kait tugged on Becca's arm. "We've done our part, and we should go."

"Our part?" Becca's voice shot up, startling birds into flight. "If Van Gogh isn't behind bars then our part,"—she put air quotes around the words—"isn't completed."

Vance sighed. "I get that you're personally committed to finding Van Gogh, but it looks like it's clouding your judgment. I see that as an even better reason to ask you to take off."

Becca jutted out her jaw. "My judgment is just fine, thank you very much."

"Look." Vance took a step closer. "Since I haven't gotten a call from your supervisor, I'm sure he doesn't know you're here. If I tell him you're refusing to leave, he'll make you go. So why not take off on your own?"

Becca eyed Vance, obviously considering her options. Connor thought he'd realized the depth of her conviction regarding these girls, but it obviously ran deeper than he thought. She looked at him, begging him to help her. And he wanted to help, wanted to stand up for her, to do whatever it took to remove the look of panic on her face. But Connor knew his lieutenant, and Vance wasn't going budge. If Connor interceded on her behalf, it would only make things worse. He offered her an apologetic smile.

"Fine, I'm going." She met Vance's gaze with one that brooked no argument. "But I *will* work this investigation. No matter what you say, or my supervisor says, I'm not going away."

She stepped off, flashing a disappointed look at Connor as she passed.

"Look after her, Kait," Sam said. "Try to keep her out of trouble."

Kait frowned. "I'll try, but no one keeps Becca from doing anything she's set her mind on."

Connor almost mentioned that the same was true of Kait, but he sure didn't need Sam or Kait mad at him, too.

When they were out of earshot, Vance faced Connor. "She stays out of this unless I approve. Got it?"

Connor nodded.

"Fine. Now that we've settled that issue, let's get to work on formulating a plan." With a scowl on his face, Vance strode over to Dane.

Connor and Sam followed, and the three of them briefed Vance on the investigation.

"So you've done the basics, but we really don't have much to go on." Vance fixed his gaze in the distance. "What about Marcie? Did she give us anything?"

"Only that the girl's been here about a week and was likely strangled. But you know Marcie. She's not going to say much until she completes the autopsy."

Vance nodded and turned to Dane. "Get another set of pictures before Marcie takes the body. And once the anthropologist—a Dr. Williams—arrives, I want you glued to her side. Get a photo of everything—every piece of bone, clothing, etc. Clear, crisp pictures. Never has your work been as important to a case. You understand?"

"Yes, sir," Dane said, his words almost a salute.

Sam took a step closer. "I hate to bring this up when we've already got our plate full with two girls, but this is a large clearing. There could be additional bodies."

Connor had considered that, but he hadn't been willing to dwell on it.

"The thought crossed my mind." Vance let his gaze run over the area. "But I won't waste resources until Dr. Williams confirms we're dealing with another murdered teen."

"Odds are good we are," Dane said.

"Likely." Vance rubbed a hand over his face. "If so, I'll get cadaver dogs up here." Vance looked at Connor. "Until then, we need to get lights set up for Dr. Williams. This is going to be a long night."

*A very long night*, Connor thought as he headed down the trail with Dane to retrieve the items they'd need to light up the hillside of death.

BECCA STORMED DOWN the trail, her breathing quick and labored in the humid air. Her legs ached as she slammed her feet onto the clay soil packed into a hard slab. She took perverse pleasure in the pain. It helped numb her from what she'd seen, numb her from being tossed off the crime scene. Numb her from Sam and Connor's lack of support. Especially Connor's. That irked her more than anything. It didn't bother her that Sam had held back. He'd had to. He walked a fine line with Kait being an agent. Becca got that. But Connor? What did he have to lose, other than any hope of ever dating her?

"Right, like that will ever happen," she muttered.

"Hold up, Becca." Kait grabbed her arm. "I can't breathe in this humidity. What's the big rush, anyway?"

"I want to get back to the office before Sulyard leaves for the day. I plan to convince him to call Vance and find a place for me on the team."

"That's not a good idea." Kait came to a stop, halting Becca's movements. "If you were thinking instead of reacting, you'd realize that."

Becca shirked off Kait's hand. "I can help. They need to let me do what I can."

"Granted. And I know Sam and Connor will be working on that. But if you go rushing into the office all wild and crazy like this, Sulyard will see how off your game you are and bench you."

"He might not notice."

"Ha! He might not notice if I flew off the handle or Nina got all emotional, but you? The woman who is so organized and methodical that you keep an inventory of your paper clips? Trust me, he would notice."

Kait exaggerated, but Becca got the point. Still, what was she supposed to do? She'd left Molly in Van Gogh's hands and she *had* to atone for that.

"Let's just take a moment to breathe." Kait dropped onto a stump and took off her shoe to rub her foot. "What's going on with you? I've never seen you like this. Running off half-cocked."

As much as Becca wanted to blurt out her story, she couldn't. It wasn't as if she minded others knowing about her harrowing experience. If that was all there was to this, then she'd tell her story in a heartbeat. But telling people that she'd left Molly in the hands of a madman? No. After other agents heard that story, there was no way they would ever trust her to have their backs. Nor could she bear to see the disgust in her best friends' eyes. It was far easier to live a double life.

She shrugged.

"I get that you have this connection with foster kids, but you've worked other cases that were just as difficult and kept it together." Kait's face suddenly lit. "Wait, it's Connor isn't it? You have thing for him, and you're mad that he didn't stand up for you."

"He didn't stand up for either of us," Becca corrected.

Kait's mouth dropped open. "You didn't deny it." She smiled. "Am I right? You have a thing for him? I mean, how much more perfect could that be, right? Sam and me. You and Connor."

"It's not Connor." Becca's answer felt like a lie—they were attracted to each other, but that had nothing to do with her current mood.

Kait studied her intently, the fire in her eyes usually reserved for grilling a suspect. "It's the foster connection, then?"

Becca hadn't really been dwelling on that aspect of the situation, but it did make her mad that Van Gogh targeted foster girls because they were less likely to be reported missing. *That* was something she could discuss with Kait.

Becca found a nearby log to sit on, but since she didn't plan on being truly forthcoming, she looked at the path. "Foster kids have a connection. A strong one. Since they—we—are so alone in the world, we know how to look out for one another."

"I get it."

"Really?" Becca glanced at Kait. "I'm not sure you could ever understand what it means to be alone like these girls are."

"You're not alone, sweetie." Kait squeezed Becca's arm. "You have me and Nina. And Elise and Buck."

Becca moved back. "See, that's the thing you can't understand. Elise and Buck were the best foster parents I could ever ask for. I love them dearly, and we're still close . . . but it's not the same as having parents. There's nothing official tying me to another human being."

"You're talking about a piece of paper, like an adoption certificate?"

"Yes. Maybe." Becca sighed. "I guess what I'm saying is that I never felt like I had someone who would stay with me, no matter what I did or said. That I could really let my hair down and be myself without doing something to scare them off. That they were committed to me, for life. That I was cherished. Loved."

"You didn't get that from Elise and Buck?"

"Almost, but no. I turned eighteen, and their responsibility to me was done. They'll always be there for me if I need them, but at the time, I sensed an urgency to move on so they could make room for another child. They never came out and said that. At least, not in so many words, but it was there."

Kait opened her mouth to speak, but Becca held up a hand to stop her.

"I fully support their desire and encourage them to help as many kids as they can. They're such good foster parents, and I've always known that I'd have to share them. That meant I needed to step up and take care of myself, the way I did when I lived with my mom." Childhood memories came flashing back, and she shook her head. "It's so weird when I think about it. As a little kid, I took care of Mom and did things no kid should have to do. Then Elise and Buck freed me from that, and before I knew it, I'd graduated from high school, turned eighteen, and was basically on my own again."

Kait scooted closer. "I thought you and Elise had that whole mother/daughter thing going on."

"We do in a sense. I don't really know how to explain it. It's weird I guess, but we see each other so often mainly because I work with foster kids."

"So the girl—Jane Doe. How does this all relate to her?"

Becca didn't have to think about that. Not with memories of Molly overwhelming her today. "She was alone, Kait. All alone." Tears formed in Becca's eyes, and she swiped them away. "No one to call out to when she was abducted. No hope that a parent would move heaven and earth to find her. I can feel what she must have been feeling, and my heart aches for her."

Kait circled an arm around Becca's shoulder. "I may not be your parent, but if you ever disappeared, I'd never stop until I found you."

"I know. You proved how tenacious you are when you tracked down Rhodes after he killed Abby." Becca smiled and decided to move on. Kait had lost her twin sister, Abby, to a bullet from her brother-in-law, Fenton Rhodes's gun. But she hadn't lost her entire family, and couldn't possibly understand the hole in Becca's heart. The ache to belong. In some regards, she'd always hoped that falling in love and signing a till-death-do-us-part certificate could fill that hole, but after leaving Molly, Becca didn't deserve happiness.

Her phone rang, and she dug it from her pocket.

"Taylor," Becca answered enthusiastically, glad to give up the gut-wrenching topic.

"I thought you'd like to know that the hard drives have been imaged," Taylor responded. "I'll get started on reviewing them and let you know if I find anything."

"I'll be back in the office in less than an hour to help."

"Okay." Taylor sounded disappointed. "See you then."

Becca disconnected the phone and stood up. "That was Taylor. I have hard drives to review for my credit card fraud investigation so we should get going."

Kait got up and stretched. "Are you sure you want to go back to work after this? I caught what Taylor said, and it sounded like she was willing to handle things for you."

"I'm not going to shirk my responsibilities just because Van Gogh is back." Becca started down the trail.

Kait caught up. "I know you won't shirk your responsibilities, but maybe this is the time to step back for a moment and recover from today's shock."

"Like I said, I'm good."

Kait grabbed Becca's elbow. "You're not really going back to the office to talk to Sulyard, are you?"

"No, you convinced me not to," Becca said, her mind already on her next steps.

She had to keep things together. Keep her focus. Not make anyone question her judgment, as Kait was hinting at, or she'd lose the job she'd worked so hard to earn. She would work the credit card case this afternoon because that was what she was being paid to do. But once she got home tonight, she'd dig out her files on Van Gogh and find a bargaining chip she could use to force Vance to involve her in the investigation.

She squared her shoulders. "I *will* find a way to get on the investigation."

"And just how are you going to justify that? We're computer experts, sweetie. This case has nothing to do with technology."

"Everything in our world today has to do with computers. I'll find a connection."

"And Sulyard? How are you going to get around the personal connection you have to the case?"

"I'm not sure yet, but I'll find a way." She crossed her arms.

"Say you do get past Sulyard's objections. That still doesn't mean Vance will let you get involved."

"Why not? With his team's workload, he should be happy for the help."

"Help from an unbiased person, yes. From you? No."

Becca tightened her arms. "I will work this case, Kait. Once I set my mind on something, I don't back down. This won't be any different."

*Except it will tear my heart apart.* She kept that thought to herself. No one needed to know that. No one.


THE SUN SLIPPED BELOW the trees, leaving the clearing with an eerie red glow in the background. It was fitting for the gruesome scene, Connor supposed. They'd hauled the portable klieg lights up the path, and they now shone a bright white light on the area, perhaps eliminating a bit of the horror. Perhaps.

Dr. Williams had arrived hours ago and was working with Dane to unearth the second body. She'd revealed the pelvis, which she said confirmed they were looking at another teenage girl. So Vance called in Lucky, the cadaver dog, and his handler Glenna Dexter.

Glenna let Lucky off his leash, and he loped across the clearing. Suddenly, he stopped, put his nose to the ground and resembled a vacuum cleaner. His gait slowed a few times, pausing to sniff more intently, then he moved on.

He suddenly flipped on his back, then got up and followed a trail.

"He's got something," Glenna said.

"Then why's he still moving?" Connor asked. He'd never seen a cadaver dog at work, and to be honest, he was a bit skeptical about what the dog might find.

"The scent isn't always the strongest over the actual body."

Connor's skepticism flared. "That doesn't make sense."

"It does if you think about it," she said patiently, as if she'd explained the same thing to law enforcement officers a hundred times. "Scent can percolate down hills and gather in low spots. Animal burrows can make the scent more accessible, too. And scent can travel along vegetation roots, particularly tree roots. Where these roots surface, the scent is stronger."

Totally weird, if you asked him. "Then how do you know when you've hit on a body?"

"Lucky will tell us. Just give him time."

Lucky sniffed, sending puffs of air rising into the fog before he turned around several times. Connor thought this was the sign, but Glenna stayed put, watching, waiting. Lucky moved away, then came back to the low spot filled with a clump of plants that were different from the surrounding area. Lucky never looked at Glenna, just kept moving.

He suddenly stopped, turned in a circle again, then made a muffled sound. He sat and peered at Glenna. She pulled a stake from her bag. "We have the first one."

Connor was skeptical, but he'd seen Glenna's professionalism and was starting to believe in her and Lucky.

"I'll just mark the spot, then give Lucky a break. He'll move on in a minute." Glenna strolled toward Lucky, who continued to sit at attention.

Vance came up from behind him. "Anything?"

"Yeah, Glenna thinks Lucky hit on a body. She'll continue working across the clearing."

Vance gave a grim nod. "Guess Dr. Williams is gonna have her hands full."

Connor didn't respond. What could he say, with another potential body waiting for confirmation?

"Marcie called. Jane Doe One's prints were a bust in AFIS."

"So we won't get an ID the easy way, then," Connor said, wishing the FBI's fingerprint database had returned a match for the girl. "With our forensics basically nonexistent at this point, it's too bad Marcie didn't have anything else to offer."

Vance started pacing, a hand planted at the back of his neck, his fingers white with the pressure. He was thinking something through, and Connor wasn't about to rush his lieutenant into speaking. So he waited patiently, staring over the macabre crime scene as he did. Vance pulled his phone from his belt holder and Connor heard him talking with their captain, laying out the situation. But when Vance brought up Becca, Connor could hardly believe his ears.

Moments later, Vance shoved his phone back in the holder and faced Connor. He made strong eye contract, his hand still clamped on his neck. "The pressure to solve this case in a timely manner is already off the charts. It'll require resources we can ill afford to pull from other cases. Shoot, we're tapped out before we've even begun. We'll need additional resources." He dropped his hand. "No offense to the quality of Dane's forensics work, but it would be good to get an FBI evidence recovery team out here, too. I think we should bring Agent Lange in on this case."

Connor clamped his jaw to keep his mouth from falling open.

"As you said," Vance continued. "She's the expert, and we could use her help getting us up to speed on Van Gogh."

"She'd be a consultant, then?" Connor clarified.

"Yeah, something like that. The captain is running it up the flagpole, but I don't think we're ready for a full joint taskforce at this point. I'd like to keep her on through the investigation. She can prevent us from wasting time on leads that have been exhausted in the past. I'll set up a morning meeting with her supervisor to get the ball rolling."

"Sounds good." Connor's gaze moved back to Lucky. No more than ten yards from the first flag, he flipped on his back then moved into the circling behavior again.

Connor pointed at the dog. "Looks like another hit."

Vance mumbled a curse. "I'll get Sulyard on the phone right now."

"The sooner the better," Connor said and couldn't help wondering how many more flags would be stuck in the ground before the night was over.

# Chapter Eight

REGINALD COULD NO longer abide the smell of bleach, but at least the work in his home basement was done. Not that he really thought it was necessary. He'd been so careful with the latest girls that the odds of the police locating him were next to none. And, of course, he'd left no connection to Molly or the other delightful girls from the past year either. Still, his mother had taught him to be cautious.

"And you're still helping me, aren't you Mother?" he said, glad that though she'd passed on, she was still listening and helping him.

He'd struggled the day she'd died. But then he'd developed such a strong longing to cleanse additional girls, he was sure it was his mother directing him. She'd since told him otherwise, but without her here to physically hold him back, he'd begun his work in earnest. He remembered her disapproving smile and a vision of her appeared in front of him.

"Remember, Lauren," she said, a sour pucker to her lips.

"Lauren," he repeated. "You'd be so proud of me, Mother. I'm very close to having Lauren in the fold again."

"Don't be so certain the funeral will bring her out of the woodwork, Reginald," she cautioned. "You must keep investigating on your own to find her, in case she fails to make an appearance."

"Yes, yes of course. I thought of that, Mother. Really I did, but I've been too busy cleaning. I'm finished, though, and I'll get right to it." He blinked hard and she disappeared. For a moment, he wondered if she had actually been standing in front of him. But that was craziness talking and he was far from crazy.

He hurried up to his office and sat behind his computer to search out details about Molly's life. After all, she was his only lead to Lauren. Thank goodness he'd become a pro in IT, so he shouldn't have any trouble digging up information that wouldn't easily be found. Computers had always come easy to him. He'd started honing his skills after the fire. There wasn't much else for a boy whose face looked like a patchwork quilt of lumpy Playdough to do. He could still hear the kids when he'd gone back to school. Every day at recess, they'd call out in singsong voices, "Icky Zwicky. Icky Zwicky. Touch his face, if you dare, it will make you sicky."

His mother took pity on him after that and home-schooled him. She'd let him spend his free time immersed in computers, probably due to her feelings of guilt over the fire. Still, it had taught him skills to survive in this world without ever having to leave his house where people stared and pointed. As a bonus, he'd amassed a fortune, hacking and selling data right under the noses of local law enforcement.

He ran his fingers down a long, prominent scar on the side of his face. The touch reminded him of his mother, tenderly applying antibiotic cream on his burns. He smiled as thoughts of the most horrific and yet best time in his life came flooding back.

He was eleven and she'd locked him in a closet in their rundown apartment so she could go to the market and be assured he wouldn't get into mischief. It had been a common practice for her. He'd wanted to go with her to the store, but she told him that since his father had left them, it was one of the few times she could be alone. He understood. He liked time away from her, too. And the closet wasn't bad. Not with Billy there beside him.

But that day was different. An electrical fire had started in the attic. Advancing rapidly, it had slithered across the ceiling above. He'd panicked, but Billy had kept him calm. Under Billy's direction, Reginald had pulled down a shirt and tied it around his mouth, then covered his hands with his shoes for protection and huddled in the corner. His clothing—his favorite jeans and shirts on the shelves above—caught fire, falling on him like blazing raindrops. He'd batted the largest pieces away with the shoes, but the fire continued to rain down on him. His head would be a burning mass for brief moments, then he'd find relief after he'd brush the burning material away. But more continued to fall. The pain grew intense. He nearly passed out as smoke filled the space. He could feel his life slipping away. At least the pain would have stopped.

But then he heard the firefighter's voice. "Fire department. Call out."

Reginald had screamed, his throat dry and painful as if he'd swallowed a box of razor blades. The door suddenly wrenched open, and he was rushed to the hospital. His mother told the police he must have locked himself in the closet. With her standing over him, he confirmed it. They were skeptical and questioned him alone. But Mother had told him long ago that the authorities would take him away if he told them about her teaching and discipline. So he'd lied, and there was nothing the police could do.

After that, Mother had tended to him. Gently, sweetly singing while caring for his wounds as if he were a newborn babe. Until he'd healed. Then it all stopped, and they resumed the training. Now, here he was, a full-fledged disciple with years of work lying ahead of him. He'd better get going.

He snapped his chair forward and looked at Molly's credit report. He hoped to track back her movements and see where they might intersect with Lauren. Molly had recently moved back to Portland and had one other address in Maine, with a reported occupancy date of 2000.

"So you ran all the way to Maine," he said. "Didn't you know your flight was futile?"

"Why?" Billy asked. "She already knew you were a loser for letting her and Lauren get away. Why would she think you'd be able to find her in Maine?"

"I'm not a loser," he shouted at Billy. "She just underestimated my abilities."

"What abilities?" Billy asked.

"I tracked her down, didn't I?"

"Um, not really. You found a girl on social media who looked like she needed to be cleansed. Turned out she was Molly's daughter. I'd say that was more of a coincidence than any skill."

Reginald ignored Billy and opened a picture of Haley. She was a beautiful girl, just coming into her own. The spitting image of her mother as a teen. She was like Molly in other ways, too. Flashing her picture all over the Internet. Blatantly flirting with boys, with men. All men. Dirty men who would corrupt her. Reginald knew their motives, knew why they wanted to connect with her. He had other ideas, but first, he'd had to deal with Molly.

"It may have been coincidence that I found her, Billy, but what I did with the knowledge was pure genius," Reginald said and waited for Billy's comeback.

There was no response.

"You're quiet because you know I'm right," Reginald said. "Haley was the perfect bait. What a good mother Molly was. Promising to meet me instead so I'd leave her daughter alone."

Molly had been so blind. He had no intention of leaving Haley alone. Not with her indecent behavior. She needed him. But Molly hadn't understood that. Maybe she did now, in the afterlife.

Haley would, too, after Lauren was his, once again. Then he could cleanse Molly's pretty little Haley and any other girl who flaunted her body on the Internet.

BECCA SUCCEEDED IN quickly reviewing the hard drives, even with her mind wandering to Van Gogh every few minutes. The trick she'd learned as a kid came through for her again. It had worked when her mother was drunk in the next room, the latest man visiting. And it had worked in all of the various foster homes she'd been in, with too many kids and no solitude. She simply used the "five more" rule. Five more minutes of reading. Five more minutes of homework. Five more minutes of reviewing.

She could do five minutes. Easy-peezy. Then another five minutes and on and on until she'd completed her task.

Today had been no different. Only this time, it was the noise in her own mind she was tuning out.

"Anything?" Taylor asked from behind her.

Startled, Becca swiveled her chair to see Taylor leaning on the edge of the cubicle, a thick folder in her hands. She looked tired, and Becca glanced at the clock. Ten p.m.

"Where did the time go?" Becca asked. "Did you get dinner?"

"Yeah, don't you remember? I left to grab a sub, and I asked if you wanted something?"

"Honestly, no."

Taylor frowned.

"What's wrong?" Becca asked, almost dreading the answer.

"You. You're . . ." Taylor shrugged. "I don't know. Different today. Like something's bothering you. Is it that thing you went to do with Connor?"

The mere mention of Connor brought back her frustration over his lack of defense when Vance had thrown them off the scene. She'd love to sound off about it, but she wasn't going to discuss it with the new intern. Nor could she mention Van Gogh.

"I'm fine," she lied, something she made a point of never doing. "Now you, on the other hand, look exhausted." Becca forced out a smile. "How am I going to exploit your desire to do a good job tomorrow if you're too tired for me to do so?"

Taylor laughed, and she looked as young as she was, a wrinkle-free twenty-seven. Becca hadn't ever been that young and carefree, even as a child. She was only thirty-two, but she'd seen far too many bad things during those years. Van Gogh was the worst. He'd stolen so much from her. It was a good time to go home to review her files to help catch him before he took even more.

"C'mon." She stood. "Let's get out of here. Go grab your things while I pack up, and we can walk out together."

Taylor went to her cubicle, and Becca loaded her backpack then joined her co-worker. "Ready to go?"

Taylor looked up, that carefree look gone. She glanced down at a folder in her hand and chewed on her lip.

"Something wrong?" Becca asked, hoping it wasn't something that took a lot of brain cells to deal with. Hers were zapped.

Taylor's gaze darted between Becca and the folder as if she wanted to say something but didn't know how to start. This was obviously going to take some time. Becca set down her pack and leaned on the edge of the cubicle, waiting for Taylor to get to the point.

"I did something I shouldn't have today," she finally blurted out, her gaze fixed on the folder. She shook her head and looked up, made eye contact for a moment, then stared into the distance. "I don't usually do these things, you know?" She met Becca's gaze. "I follow the rules. Honest, I do. I know that's important at the Bureau, and I don't want to lose my job, it's just—"

"Hold up." Becca flashed up her hand. "Take a breath. It can't be all that bad. Just tell me what you did, and we'll go from there."

Taylor opened her mouth to speak, but words seemed to fail her. She took a deep breath, then blew it out. Took another one.

This had to be bad. A feeling of dread settled over Becca.

"I went to the jail to question Danny," Taylor said on a long sigh.

"What? That's all?" Becca shook her head. "You had me thinking you broke the law or something serious."

"All?" Taylor sounded incredulous. "I went to visit a prisoner in jail without the case agent's permission. What if I screwed something up? Screwed up the investigation?"

"Did you?"

"I don't know . . . I mean." She wrung her hands. "I don't think so."

Becca took a seat, trying to keep her frustration with the day from her tone. "Sounds to me like you're upset because you broke the rules more than anything else."

"I don't know." She looked down at her hands. "Maybe you're right. I never . . . I mean I try not to bend them. So breaking them . . ." She ended with a shrug.

"You're making no sense, Taylor. Or maybe I'm just too tired to see this, but why did you go there, then?"

She looked completely crestfallen. "I thought I could help."

That didn't sound like enough of a reason to go against her ingrained nature. "That was it? Your only reason. You wanted to help?"

"Yes, I wanted to help." Taylor squirmed like a kid caught by her mother in a lie. "But I also thought I might do something to prove my worth on the team."

"Worth? What in the world are you talking about?"

Becca noticed Taylor flinch, and she instantly regretted her biting tone. "Look, Taylor. I'm sorry for snapping. I'm tired, and I've had a trying day. Go ahead and explain it to me, and I won't be such a grouch." She forced out a smile. "I promise."

"It's probably not going to make sense, but you, Nina, and Kait are so well-respected. I've felt like such a novice since I got here, and I wanted to prove to the three of you that I belong."

"You don't need to prove anything." Becca tried not to sound like a scolding mother, but she knew a subtle reprimand lingered in her tone. "Here's the thing. You were chosen for the team for a reason. Vetted once, twice, shoot, maybe three times. That means your credentials speak for themselves and you have nothing to prove. Well, nothing other than showing us that you can make sound decisions and have our backs. Going off and doing something half-baked doesn't do that, and it won't endear you to us. We're a team. We work together on everything. We have no room for loners."

*Right, except for your little secret about Van Gogh.*

"Message received." Taylor suddenly shot to her feet, a mix of relief and contrition in her eyes.

Becca probably should do something more formal about this infraction, but Taylor had just demonstrated that she'd be far harder on herself than Becca could ever be. Besides, Becca respected agents who took the initiative. It looked like Taylor was going to be one of them. She just had to learn when and where to do it.

"If it helps, I *did* learn a few things in my interview. Nothing earth-shattering, but Danny did admit he was homeless." She opened the folder and selected a photo of a girl, then handed it to Becca. "He seems to have a connection to this girl. Romantic, I suspect."

Becca recognized it as one of the pictures Connor had given to her at the gym. "What did Danny tell you about her?"

"Nothing. It was his expression that tipped me off." Taylor closed the folder. "When I got back to the office, I got to thinking about all the foster kids who take off. So I spent the rest of the day searching the Department of Human Services database. It took a bit of digging, but I found files on a few girls who've disappeared. They're all about his age, but unfortunately, the pictures didn't match this girl."

*Missing foster girls. Van Gogh.*

Becca's pulse kicked up and she schooled her voice not to give away her anxiety. "Do you still have the info on the girls you found?"

"Sure, but their pictures don't match the ones we have." A look of frustration flashed over her face. "They could still have been recruited for the credit card ring, though, and Connor didn't get pics of them."

"Agreed. I'd like the information so I can follow up."

"I'll email it to you in the morning."

"Can you do it now?"

"Now?" Her gaze locked on Becca's. "It's that important to you?"

Becca nodded and kept her mouth shut before she inadvertently mentioned something about the Van Gogh investigation.

"Sure, okay." Taylor leaned over her computer and sent the email.

"One more thing I should mention. Since Danny's still not giving his name, I collected his DNA so we can run a search."

"Resourceful." Becca picked up her backpack. "But if Sulyard approves the DNA request, which I doubt he will, I'm betting Danny will give up his name long before the test gets through the lab's backlog."

"We could use a private lab to get it done sooner."

"Sulyard would never spring for such a high cost in a simple fraud investigation."

"I could pay for it myself or try a few of my contacts in the forensic world to see if I can come up with someone who can—"

"Hey, wait a minute," Becca interrupted. "I've got someone local who might be able to help. He's a weapons expert, but he shares leased office space with a lab. Maybe he could get them to run the test for free. I'll give him a call and get it to him if he agrees."

Taylor frowned. "I'd like to see this through myself. Would it be okay if I took it to him?"

"Sure. Fine," Becca said and started down the hall.

Taylor caught up, and they headed for the parking garage together. A cool wind blew through the space, but the air was waterlogged and the fall temperatures were unusually warm. That meant she'd find fog on the run she planned to take the minute she got home.

Once they reached her car, Taylor turned to Becca. "Thanks for not getting mad at me."

"Honestly," Becca said. "We've all done something like this in the past. But it didn't take long for us to wise up and realize teamwork is a better option. You're part of the team, Taylor, and we have your back. Now go home and get some sleep. If Jack agrees to help with the DNA, you're going to need it to deal with him."

Taylor cast Becca a quizzical look, but there was no way she'd be able to explain Jack Rains, so Becca went to her car. Taylor would just have to experience him for herself. Even with her fatigue, the thought of rookie Taylor coming eye to eye with world-weary Jack made Becca smile. He just might be the best lesson Taylor could get on why going rogue wasn't a good idea.

Becca stopped to pick up a turkey burger and salad on her way home and shoved them in her refrigerator. She dressed in moisture-wicking running clothes before heading back outside for a long run to clear her mind. By the time she returned home, she was drenched in sweat, but she didn't take the time to change. She could cool down while digging out boxes of Van Gogh records.

She'd accumulated twelve file boxes of information over the years. Reports, forms, sketches, and crime-scene photos. She'd neatly organized it all in labeled folders by date. The once-crisp folders were now worn from her semi-annual review of the information. She'd practically memorized it all, but that, in itself, could be a problem. She might skim or skip over something important. Hence the need for a clear mind.

She pulled out the main folders to create a murder board on the long wall above her sofa. First up was a sketch of Van Gogh created from her description in the nineties. Next to it, she added an age progression sketch that she commissioned every year on the anniversary of her abduction. Then she added Molly's picture, as well as the photo of the girl whose body was discovered in the nineties. She'd been buried two weeks longer than the girl found today so it had been a gruesome sight. Next to that, she put up blank white poster boards where she noted the main case leads that didn't pan out and the reasons why.

On her dining table, she set her copy of Detective Orman's case murder book. She'd had the chance to interview him several times before he passed away this past year. He'd not been happy to see her at first. He'd said she reminded him of the most important case of his career, the one he'd never solved. He'd continued to investigate, but he didn't like the thought of her getting involved. He feared she'd get close to Van Gogh, and he'd somehow figure out that she was alive. But that hadn't happened, and on her last visit to Orman, he gave in and handed over a copy of his murder book. Actually, it was a copy of a copy. The original had to remain in PPB's files. He shouldn't have taken copies of the files either, but when he retired and the case remained unsolved, he couldn't let it rest.

She got out colored pens, sticky notes in various sizes, and colored flags to mark report pages. She added two sizes of notepads, a stapler, and paper clips to the table.

Standing back, she assessed the room. Perfect. Just the way she organized her investigations at work. Her next step would be to post everything she knew about today's Jane Doe to the board.

She printed out a map of the park and surrounding area, then highlighted nearby residential areas. Multi-unit homes in yellow. Single family homes in orange. On the computer, she panned the map out far enough to include the site where the girl had been found in the nineties. She printed it and marked the addresses on both maps. She tacked them up and studied them.

On the surface, no correlation appeared for the two locations. They weren't even on the same side of town. The first burial site had been a vacant lot in an undeveloped area of town that now held an apartment complex.

So what did the two locations have in common? Had Van Gogh lived near the first site in the nineties and moved nearer the current burial site during that time? Or had he, in both cases, simply searched for an isolated location to dump the bodies?

She needed a more detailed map of the area surrounding today's discovery to draw any kind of working hypothesis. She headed back to her computer, and her phone rang on the table. The sound startled her and sent her heart rate soaring.

Was it Connor? Had they found another body?

She quickly grabbed her phone and eyed the screen. Elise, her foster mother.

Okay, good. Not another body. Likely a foster kid in trouble.

Becca sighed out a breath.

"Since when has a foster kid in trouble become something to take lightly," she mumbled as she decided if she would answer.

She wanted to help this kid, whoever it might be—she'd never said no to kids in trouble—but tonight was different. Tonight, she was dealing with Van Gogh, and she didn't have the emotional strength left to talk about another suffering child.

Before she could make a decision, the call went to voicemail. Fine. Decision made for her. She went back to work, printed out the new map and highlighted it, then hung it on her wall. Her phone rang again.

The same jolt of adrenaline shot through her, abating only when she spotted Elise's name again. Elise had been the one who had taken Becca in after her name change. She'd been told about Van Gogh and the danger that could follow Becca. Still, she'd said yes, and it was her tender care that had kept Becca sane. Becca couldn't continue to ignore Elise, no matter what was going on in her own life.

"Elise," Becca answered but kept her gaze on the map in hopes of finding the clue she was missing.

"I need you." Elise's voice was barely loud enough to hear. "I'm at the ER."

"Are you hurt? Sick?" *Please don't say you're dying. Please.*

"It's not me, it's Frankie."

*Frankie.* A sweet teen and one of Elise's current foster kids.

"She's dead, murdered, and it's all my fault." The words came out on a choked sob.

*Van Gogh.* Had he found out Becca had lived with Elise? Was he punishing Becca for running from him by going after one of Elise's girls?

"How?" Becca held her breath for the answer.

"That's why I need to see you. Please come. Hurry. Before it happens to another one of my precious kids."

The line went dead, and a grim certainty settled over Becca. Van Gogh had struck and once again, it was close to home.

# Chapter Nine

IT WAS ONLY TEN P.M. and Connor was dog-tired. Despite the time, he should be falling into bed instead of pulling up to Becca's apartment, but there was no point in turning in yet. All he'd see when he closed his eyes would be the faces of murdered girls. Jane Doe number one, her face nearly decimated by decay. Jane Doe number two, now a skeleton, her face totally missing. And the third and fourth girls located by the cadaver dogs? It was still too early to see their faces. Dr. Williams had to take her time unearthing the bodies so they didn't miss any possible leads. She couldn't even determine a time of death yet . . . and might not be able to. Ever. She'd just have to wait and see what she located.

Which meant Connor had to wait, too. At least until tomorrow. Maybe longer.

He wasn't good at waiting, and after spending time with Becca today, he wasn't good with being alone, either. He hated to admit it, but that was his real reason for coming here.

He parked his truck and looked up to see her lights filtering through blinds. He wasn't sure if that was a good or bad thing. Good because she was awake and he really wanted to talk to her. Bad because of the potential consequences of violating every kind of protocol by sharing information with her before Vance cleared her.

*Too dang bad.* Connor needed her help on the investigation, and if this was what he had to do to find closure for these girls, then he would.

He slammed his truck door and crossed the lot to the main stairway leading to her second floor apartment. He'd barely planted a foot on the first step when her door suddenly opened. She was wearing serviceable running shorts and an Under Armor T-shirt. Her outfit should have made her look like a tomboy, but the shirt hugged her curves and the shorts gave him a nice view of her long legs. She carried a small backpack, and her face glistened with sweat, as if she'd already been running.

"Going for a run?" he asked.

She dropped to the ground, her hand going to an ankle holster, before meeting his gaze. "You scared me."

"Sorry about that."

"For your information—though I'm not sure why you need to

know—I just came back from a run."

"Kind of dangerous to go running alone at this time of night, isn't it?"

"My neighborhood is safe." She patted her ankle. "And as you can see, I don't go out unprotected." She stood and jogged down the stairs, stopping a few risers above him

He looked up at her. This close, he could see how tightly the fabric clung to her curves, firing his imagination. His heart gave a kick, and he regretted coming here. He should have known, in his exhausted state, that she would get to him even more.

He'd crack a few jokes then get out of there. "Guess I'm destined to find you all hot and sweaty from now on."

She eyed him. "It's late, Connor, and I'm not doing this whole witty banter thing with you." She crossed her arms. "Either tell me why you're here or take off."

"Crabby much?"

"Goodnight, Connor." She moved to push past him.

He stepped in front of her. "I was hoping you'd give me a rundown on Van Gogh."

"It's late. Read the case files." She dug her keys from her pack and tried to maneuver around him.

"I plan to." He widened his stance to make a solid wall in front of her. "But I thought we could get going on the investigation faster if you gave me a quick summary of what transpired in the nineties."

Her eyes narrowed into tense little slits. "You're really something, you know that? Expecting me to help you after your boss tossed me off the crime scene."

"Oh, that? That was just Vance. He's kind of a control freak, the same as Sulyard is."

"I'd have to have been deaf and blind not to figure that out." She eyed him. "But what I'm talking about is the fact that not a word came out of your or Sam's mouth in our defense. Not a single word."

"Hey, wait . . . what? You're mad about that?"

She crossed her arms. "You're darn right I am."

"I'm sorry, Bex. Honest. But if I'd spoken up, it would have made things worse. Vance would have zoned in on you even more."

"Right."

"Think about it. If you questioned or contradicted Sulyard in front of PPB officers, what would he do?"

"Get mad and let me have it when we were alone." She relaxed her arms. "Okay, fine. I see your point."

"So you'll help me?"

She stared right through him. "In the morning. Right now, I have somewhere I have to be."

He gaped at her. "Now? Dressed like that?"

"I really have to go, Connor."

His failure to move elicited another sigh from her. "I have to get to the hospital."

"Are you all right?"

"I'm fine. It's my foster mother, Elise. She called. One of her kids, Frankie, was murdered tonight. She needs me *now*, so I didn't take the time to change."

"Murdered." He let her pronouncement settle in. "In the Portland city limits?"

Becca shrugged. "Elise lives in the city and the hospital's within the city limits, so likely."

He dug out his phone and thumbed through it. "I didn't get notification of a homicide."

"She just called from the hospital. Maybe the responding patrol officer hasn't requested a detective yet."

"Maybe," Connor said, his mind running through the possibilities. "You think this is related to Van Gogh?"

She shrugged again, but her eyes gave away her fear.

He wasn't leaving her alone when she was feeling this way. And if the murder was related to Van Gogh, he had to know as soon as possible. "I'll go to the hospital with you."

Becca shook her head. "Look, I appreciate your concern, but you've got enough on your plate right now. If this ends up being connected to Van Gogh, I'll give you a call."

"Not happening," he said firmly. "I'll come with you. If the murder occurred in my jurisdiction and it's not related to Van Gogh, then I'll take Elise's statement, and we'll go from there. Okay?"

"Fine," she said, but her tone told him otherwise. Apparently, spending any time with him was unpalatable.

He jingled his keys. "I'll drive."

Her chin jutted out. "I'll drive my own car, and we can meet up at the hospital."

Everything between them was always such a struggle. At the moment, he was tired of it, but if he was honest, he also liked the sparring. His brothers had all married easy-going women, but he found the challenge Becca presented interesting.

Just right now, he wished she'd give it up so they could get going. "I was hoping to talk to you about Van Gogh on the drive over."

"Fine," she grumbled.

He was starting to hate hearing that one word from her, but he'd take it as long as she didn't drive off alone into the night.

He gestured for her to precede him, and then followed her to his truck. He opened the door for her and stepped back. She gave him a look that told him she could get herself settled, so he took the hint and jogged around the front of the truck and got in.

Once on the road, he glanced at her. She'd taken a moist wipe from her backpack and was running it over her face and neck. Her eyes were narrowed in worry, it seemed, not in anger or frustration as they had been with him. She was probably thinking about her foster mother. He'd been so focused on Van Gogh and the way Becca made him feel, he'd completely forgotten that Becca had a connection to the murdered girl.

"Tell me about Elise," he said gently. "And Frankie."

Becca gnawed on her bottom lip. "I thought you wanted to talk about Van Gogh."

"I do, but it'd be good to get some background on your foster mother before I arrive."

Becca appeared lost in thought for a moment, but then a tremulous smile broke free. "Elise's a mom, through and through. You know, the one you'd always imagine you would have. The type who stayed home and was waiting for you each day after school with fresh-baked cookies. Who was there for every event in your life, cheering you on."

"Sounds like my stepmom. Except when all of us kids would fight, which was often. There were four boys in the family."

"You have three brothers?"

"Not only three brothers, but a sister, too. Poor Beth. She's the youngest, and she had it rough. We picked on her all the time." Happy family memories assaulted him for the first time in a long time, making him question all the reasons he'd left his past behind when he left home. "Of course, she had four brothers to defend her, too. And as we got older, we learned to appreciate her."

"You sound like you're close."

"Close?" Were they? All of the others were tight, but him? Not so much anymore. Not that they wouldn't want him to come around more often. "I suppose we're as close as we can be, with me living three hours away." He knew the words weren't true as soon as they came out of his mouth.

He could make more of an effort to visit—to want to visit—but the same smothering feeling he always got when he thought about his family came rushing back. His mother had walked out when he was fifteen, and as the oldest, he'd had to keep things running while their dad worked. He'd taken on all the responsibility while his siblings got to live their lives, and he had to admit, he grew to resent them. As soon as he'd been free to leave, he'd done so.

"Where do they live?" Becca asked, completely oblivious to the civil war going on in his gut.

"My dad and stepmom own a retreat center in central Oregon. Everyone in the family works there except me."

She swiveled to face him, fear gone from her eyes and sincere interest there instead. "Why did you leave?"

That was a loaded question. He wanted to tell her about his overwhelming childhood. About how his mother had bailed on them. But he didn't know Becca well enough to trust her with that information. The only other person who knew about his past was Sam, and the bro code kept him from telling anyone. Even Kait. Connor would give Becca the story he told people. It was true after all.

"When I was a kid, there was a rash of burglaries and vandalism in the area," he said, already feeling bad for not sharing the whole truth. "Our place was hit hard. I found the investigation fascinating and decided to be a detective right then and there. Since there wasn't much chance for that in the boonies, I moved here."

"Do you miss the country life?"

"Sometimes, but I really like what I do." Guilt had him focusing on the road when what he really wanted was to look at her. "Of course, my family doesn't understand why I'd rather hunt down lowlife murderers instead of being with them, but . . ." He shrugged. "I make it a point to get back there now and then. Especially to see my nieces and nephews."

"Sounds like there are a few of them," she said.

He detected longing in her tone. She was the last woman he took for wanting a house filled with kids. Maybe he didn't know her as well as he thought he did.

"What's the matter?" she said, her eyes lit with humor. "Can't remember how many there are?"

"There's eight. No, wait. Nine, now. My sister just had a girl." He smiled at the memory of his four-week-old niece. "Everyone has a minimum of two kids, except me."

"Hmm." She tapped her lips, her very kissable lips. "No wife. No kids. You live in the city. You really are the black sheep of the family aren't you?" She laughed. "Any prospects?" She acted like she was simply making small talk, but he heard the sincere question in her voice.

They'd spent far too much time talking about him. He wasn't about to discuss why he was still single and would remain so for the foreseeable future.

"Not at the moment," he replied, making sure she knew he was done talking.

He could feel her watching him, and he wanted to face her. To tell her something that would make her think he hadn't clammed up, but he wasn't going to reveal how his mother's infidelity and abandonment had affected his ability to trust. Or his hideously bad breakup that had sealed the deal. No way was he going there. Not ever.

# Chapter Ten

BECCA STEPPED INTO the ER entrance. The smell of disinfectant, mingled with an orange-tinged air freshener covering the stench of sickness and death, brought her feet to a stop. She hated hospitals. She'd hated them since her alcoholic mother had crashed their car, killing herself and nearly killing Becca. There were days in recovery when she'd wished she'd died, too. Even days after recovery. Like the day she'd arrived at her first foster home. The leering father, with his touchy-feely hands. She'd immediately asked for a transfer, but he'd made her life a nightmare until the paperwork went through.

The next home was better, but her new guardians had been only into fostering for the money and rarely gave her any attention. She was used to that. Her mother's drinking binges had given Becca plenty of time on her own, but surprisingly, she missed her mother. More likely, she missed having someone to take care of and tend to, so she didn't feel so utterly and completely alone.

So she'd sought a way to keep busy . . . by getting into trouble. She'd been kicked out of one foster home after another. And then she'd found Molly and they'd formed a bond of sisterhood. Van Gogh had ended all of that, and Becca had once again been alone.

Finally, she'd found Elise and it had all changed. Becca had known things were different the night she'd been arrested for underage drinking. She'd waited for Elise to toss her out, as every other foster mother had before that. But Elise had wrapped Becca in a hug and told her no matter what Becca did, she had a place in her home. Becca hadn't believed it, but Elise had proved it, day after day, year after year, even when Becca didn't deserve it.

Of course, if Elise had ever found out that Becca had left Molly behind, even Elise wouldn't have loved her. But Becca wouldn't dwell on that. She'd do as she'd always done, trying to make up for Molly's loss by helping others in whatever way she could.

She approached the ER front desk and forced a calmness into her voice that she didn't feel. She held out her FBI credentials to the woman manning the desk. "I'm looking for Elise Cobb. She'd be with a patient you admitted, a Francine Otto."

Despite the woman's smile, she looked harried and belligerent. "I'm sorry, but I can't give you any information."

"I'm her foster daughter. She's expecting me."

The woman arched an eyebrow. She clearly didn't believe Becca, likely figuring this was a ploy to gain access to Elise.

Connor stepped up to the desk. "Now, come on, Sandy. That's no way to treat my friend." His voice was filled with humor, his smile easy-going.

"Connor." Sandy returned his smile. "I didn't see you there. Let me check this out for you." She turned to her phone and dialed. Connor leaned against the desk, his ankles casually crossed, the smile still on his face.

Becca gritted her teeth. She hated it when law enforcement officers flirted to get their way. She'd never flirt, but she had to admit, it often succeeded. Especially for guys who looked like Connor. Or maybe she hated this because it *was* Connor, and that likely meant he was doing the same thing with her. Worse, she was falling for it.

Sandy hung up. "The nursing staff is going to tell Ms. Cobb you're here and arrange for a room where you can meet."

"How's your slacker of a husband doing?" Connor asked, humor still in his tone.

Sandy sighed. "He's still flat on his back."

"Tell him to quit faking and get back to work. Our records department needs him." Connor laughed, making the woman chuckle as well.

Becca often wished she could be so laid-back, but it had never been in her nature. Nina was a lot like Connor. Even Kait was more relaxed now that they'd arrested her sister's killer. But Becca? Nah, she just couldn't take the time. There were too many people needing her help.

A woman wearing a hospital wristband approached the desk, and Sandy sobered. "Go ahead and take a seat, Connor. I'll let you know when you can go back."

Becca crossed the room with Connor. A cold blast of air from the automatic door suddenly made Becca conscious of her attire. Or lack of it. She'd wanted to get to Elise as soon as possible, but still, she should have taken the time to change. If not because of the weather, or the lack of professionalism, but because Connor kept looking at her legs.

She leaned closer to him so no one could overhear. "Did you ID Jane Doe yet?"

He shook his head. "Fingerprints were a bust. Our team is searching every known database for missing girls in general, but so far, nothing."

"What about the crime scene? Find anything there?"

He hesitated, then looked away and took a breath.

Irritation that only he could seem to bring out in her fired hot. "It's that way, huh? You want me to share my stuff, but you hold yours close to the vest."

"No . . . I . . ." He rubbed a hand over his face etched with fatigue, and she felt a moment of regret for pressuring him when he had so much on his plate already. "I don't mind telling you because I know you'll keep it confidential, but I hate for you to have to hear this. Oh, shoot, I'll just come out and say it. Looks like we found three more bodies."

She gasped and felt that all-encompassing panic return. "So it's Van Gogh's private burial ground."

"Yes." Connor's one word held the weight of the horrible discovery.

"Three more," she said in disbelief and thought about her movements at the crime scene today. Had she crossed over these bodies? Trampled on them. "Where are the bodies located?"

He frowned and hesitated again. She appreciated his consideration but she had to know. "Where, Connor?"

"Near the back of the clearing." Reluctance slowed his words. "All three were neatly lined up and evenly spaced out, as if Van Gogh made an effort to carefully measure the spacing."

Becca sighed out a relieved breath. She hadn't moved any deeper into the clearing than Jane Doe, so she hadn't stepped on their graves. Wait, graves? She'd been so worried about her movements, it took her a moment to fully process the fact that three more girls had lost their lives. It was official. Van Gogh had killed three more. Three more!

Or were these bodies from the nineties? Molly's face came to mind. *No. No. No. Not Molly.*

"How long have these girls been buried?" She held her breath.

"We don't know yet."

"When will you know?" she asked, needing the answer but hating to hear it.

"Dr. Williams has to fully excavate the bodies. When I left, she was still working on the second girl and had a long way to go. She said it could take a few days, but suggested I stop by tomorrow for an update."

"So we could be looking at his latest victims or the girls from the nineties."

"Yes."

"That means if he really killed eight girls, we could find three more bodies up there."

"It's not likely. At least not in the clearing. The cadaver dog didn't light anywhere else. But we'll check the area with ground-penetrating radar to be sure. I've got a strong hunch we've found girls numbered six through nine. Since the girl in the nineties was found elsewhere, it seems unlikely we'd locate the other two up there."

Not find them? They had to. If they'd all been in the foster system, no one else was looking for them. Girls like her. Like Molly. Like Frankie.

*Frankie.* Becca had almost forgotten about Elise and Frankie. Becca looked at Sandy, hoping to get the green light to go in.

Sandy met Becca's gaze and mouthed, "Soon."

Becca nodded, but if Sandy didn't give them the all-clear in a few minutes, Becca would prod her along.

"Are you thinking Van Gogh is still targeting foster girls?" Becca asked.

"Nothing we've found says he isn't."

"Taylor searched databases today for the credit card investigations. She came up with the names of a few girls who have been reported missing from foster care. She gave the information to me, but I haven't had a chance to look at it. Maybe there's a link between those girls and the ones in the clearing."

"You tell Taylor about Van Gogh?"

His lack of faith in her discretion stung, but she wasn't going to let him know it. "No. Like I said, it was for the credit card ring."

"Right," Connor said. "Sam's coordinating the search for the girls. Could you forward that information to him?"

She nodded as a horrific thought flashed through her mind. "What if number nine isn't the end, Connor? What if Van Gogh has simply moved to another area to bury others?"

"It's not a stretch, I suppose. Especially with the first girl being found clear across town sixteen years ago." Connor blew out a long breath. "You know what? Let's not think about that. Not until we have a reason to go there. We already have five unidentified girls with no leads to speak of. Not to mention two others from the past. That's enough to turn my hair gray." He shook his head grimly. "I can't even begin to think about the possibility of others."

He was right. There was no use in speculating. They'd work the cold, hard facts. Make a plan and stick to it. Setting goals and careful planning had always worked for Becca, except in her quest to find Molly. And it would work now, moving them forward and keeping her focus on the situation, not on how it made her feel.

"Okay," she said with resolve. "About the anthropologist, this Dr. Williams you mentioned. If you think she needs help, the Bureau has plenty of qualified individuals. I can arrange to have on site by morning."

He shook his head. "If we reach out to the feds, someone is bound to talk. This case will hit the media, and we'll have that circus to deal with, too." He paused then added quickly, "No offense. It's just that the fewer people who know, the better."

She wasn't offended. But she was concerned about getting the best people on the job. Oregon State Police was a skilled and professional agency, but was it up to FBI standards? "Is Dr. Williams qualified for something like this?"

"She may not be a fed, but she's one of the top forensic anthropologists, and she's been called in to consult on cases worldwide. So, qualified?" He scoffed. "Yeah, she's up to the fed's standards."

"Wait, no. I didn't mean it like that. We can't be fighting about fed, local, or state at this point. We just need to get the best person on the job."

"We'll go with her for now, and I'll ask her if she needs or wants help tomorrow."

"Sounds like you've got this all worked out."

"I do know what I'm doing, you know. Even if I'm not a fed." He grinned.

"That's not what I meant."

"I know, but I can't miss a chance to try to put a smile on your face when we're dealing with something so dismal."

She tried to smile, but just couldn't manage it. Not with Van Gogh still out there killing and Elise inside waiting.

"This is taking too long. I'm gonna check with Sandy." Becca started to rise.

Connor shot out a hand to stop her. "Sandy's very capable. She'll tell us the minute you're cleared."

Connor was probably right, but Elise needed Becca. She eyed Sandy again, who was talking with another patient. Becca would wait until she finished with that person and then ask.

"So what else did you find?" she asked Connor.

He frowned. "That's all for now. We ran out of daylight, but the cadaver dog will start searching the entire trail and nearby areas tomorrow. Maybe expand their search through the park."

"There's no way you can cover that much ground, is there? The park is seven miles long."

"We can check out the two other difficult trails that have easy parking access and would be less used, like this one. Plus, we'll go over the two adjacent trails. And as I mentioned, we'll get going on the GPR."

"Our agency could probably help with that."

"Good. Vance will be all over not having to foot that bill. You can suggest it at our first status meeting tomorrow." He shifted in his chair.

"Meeting? What in the world are you talking about?"

"Vance has decided he'd like your help on the case after all. He called Sulyard. They're meeting first thing in the morning to discuss the terms of your service."

"Just like that." She crossed her arms. "You throw me off the scene, and then you want my help and assume I'll just go along with it?"

"Won't you?" He grinned, and it made her madder.

"Yes." She sighed. "But it would have been nice to have been asked."

"Then after Vance makes the arrangements, I'll make sure he asks you." Connor's grin widened.

She wanted to wipe the smile off his face, but she knew his jokes meant nothing. He was just Connor being Connor. A laid-back guy who seemed to know how to balance his job with life and not get bogged down in the ugliness. She could learn a thing or two from him. Shoot, probably more than two things.

"I'll look forward to his call then," she said.

"You should clear your schedule for the day. I'm not sure of the meeting time, but as I said, I'll be heading back to the scene to talk to Dr. Williams. You might want to come along for that."

"Thank you. I would." Her mind immediately went to possible ways to keep the identity theft investigation on track and work the Van Gogh case at the same time. She'd ask Sulyard to get someone else to fill in for her on the credit card case, but after she fought so hard to keep it going, she had no intention of completely withdrawing. Taylor would earn her keep, that was for sure.

"Okay, Connor," Sandy called out, drawing their attention.

They rose together and crossed the room.

Sandy gestured at a door. "The nursing staff will escort you."

When the door opened, Becca forgot all about her attire. About Connor. About the antiseptic smell of the hospital. Instead, she wrapped her mind around what she was about to see. Elise, the person who had singlehandedly turned Becca's life around, waiting for her in a sterile room. A girl she cared for, no longer alive.

"Right in here." The nurse opened the door to a small conference room.

A man wearing a clerical collar who Becca assumed to be the hospital chaplain sat next to Elise. She was dressed in a professional suit, not something she wore unless she had to go to court for one of her kids. It was rumpled, and her eyes were red and puffy. Becca expected her husband Buck to be here, but he was probably home with the other kids.

Elise shot to her feet and hurried over to Becca. "Thank goodness, you're here. If anyone can get to the bottom of this, it's you."

"What happened?" Becca asked.

"Frankie's appendix ruptured, and they gave her an antibiotic. Cefoxitin."

Becca shot a glance at Connor. His relieved expression matched her inner feelings that floated away when a tortured sob slipped from Elise. There was no relief when Elise was suffering so much.

She twisted her hands together. "Why didn't I know someone had stolen her identity? Why? I was supposed to protect her. Now she's gone." She started sobbing, and Becca put aside her questions about the stolen identity comment and drew her former foster mother into a hug.

Becca, who'd had so little human touch as a child, often felt awkward hugging others, but not Elise.

"Shh." Becca rubbed Elise's back until her sobbing slowed, and Becca led her to a chair.

Connor moved closer and leaned against the wall.

Becca sat next to Elise. "This is Detective Connor Warren with PPB."

Elise looked up at him. "Did the hospital call you?"

"Connor was with me when I left to come here."

Elise arched a curious brow for a moment then shook her head. "The hospital is probably dragging their feet until they can get their attorney to weigh in, since they had a part in this."

Becca's curiosity was piqued. "Tell me what happened, Elise."

"It's terrible. So terrible and senseless." She sniffled and grabbed a tissue. "Buck and I were in court for a hearing today. Frankie got violently sick at basketball practice after school and passed out from the pain. The substitute coach couldn't get hold of us, so she called 911. The hospital continued to try to contact us, but you know you can't have a phone turned on in court. We got the message as soon as we got out of court and we called. By that time, Frankie's appendix had burst. They gave her the Cefoxitin and took her to surgery." She shuddered and wrapped her arms around her waist. "Frankie's allergic to several antibiotics and Cefoxitin is one of them."

"She wears an alert bracelet, though, right?" Becca asked.

"Yes, but she takes it off for practice, and the sub didn't know about Frankie's allergy."

"What about emergency cards? Didn't the school have one for Frankie?"

"The sub couldn't find them by the time the ambulance arrived. She rode along with Frankie and called the school, but it was after hours and no one was working in the office."

"What I want to know," Connor said, "is if the hospital didn't know about her allergies, why on earth did they give her any antibiotics?"

"Standard procedure is to look at past records when no one can update the medical information. They claim she was seen here two weeks ago when she completed a patient information form. Her record indicated there were no known allergies." Elise shook her head hard. "She's never been treated here."

"Never?" Becca asked. "Then how does she have a record?"

"That's what I asked and demanded to see the paperwork. And it was there. Right in her file. It said Frankie was treated for bronchitis and it also showed no known allergies." Elise slumped lower, and Becca took her hands for support. "The hospital believes someone used Frankie's social security number and insurance information to impersonate Frankie and get free medical care. That person had no known allergies, so Cefoxitin wasn't added to Frankie's record."

Connor scowled. "That's taking identity theft to a whole new level."

"Theft of medical records and insurance information is on the rise," Becca said. "Nina recently worked a similar case where a woman's information was stolen from her doctor's office. Thankfully, she didn't die, but her entire identity has been compromised."

Elise reversed their hands and clutched Becca's with a death grip. "That's why I called you. I want this person found and prosecuted for murder. They will do that, right?"

"It depends," Connor answered for Becca. "If this information was obtained through computer hacking, the hacker is complicit in Frankie's death. If the person who used Frankie's ID wasn't the hacker, identity theft in Oregon is still a felony. A death as a result of committing a felony is considered murder, accidental or not, but it will be up to the DA to determine the actual charges once he sees the circumstances."

Elise nodded and stared at Becca. "I figured that the local cops would take on the case because of all the jurisdiction stuff you tell me about. But I'm worried about the safety of my other kids." Tears started flowing again, and she grabbed another tissue. "If the thieves got Frankie's information from our house somehow, then all the kids might have a problem, and it's all my fault."

"Don't start blaming yourself," Becca said. "There's a good likelihood that the security breach occurred at one of Frankie's doctor's offices or even at DHS where records for foster kids are held."

"You really think so?" Elise asked, a bit of hope in her tone.

"Absolutely. The healthcare industry and government are still reliant on aging computer systems that can be easily hacked. And believe it or not, medical records are worth more on the black market than stolen credit cards. That's why this type of theft is on the upswing."

"Why are these records worth more?" Connor asked.

"Credit cards get cancelled quickly. Health insurance companies aren't as quick to react or may never even know the records were stolen. A criminal can bilk an insurance company for a long time before the problem is caught."

"You know all about this. That's why I need you." Elise grabbed Becca's hand. "You've got to look into this for me, Becca. You just have to. Please."

Becca looked at Connor. "Since we're in your jurisdiction, I assume you'll be opening a case file."

He nodded. "I'll get it started, but with my caseload, it will likely be reassigned."

Becca turned back to Elise. "Can you excuse us a minute?"

"Sure." Elise grabbed a fresh tissue. "I'm not going anywhere."

Becca gestured for Connor to join her in the hallway. She looked up at him. Exhaustion hung in his eyes—not necessarily physical exhaustion, but the fatigue that came with working such mentally and emotionally draining cases.

"I know you're swamped. Just working Van Gogh would tax any detective. And you have other cases, too."

"But you want me to take this one?"

"Yes."

"Back at your place, it sounded more like you wanted me to stay far away from this."

"I did, but it was strictly for personal reasons. You know . . . this whole attraction thing. But Elise and her kids trump all of that." She rested a hand on his arm. "I wouldn't ask, but she's very important to me. I'll get my team working the ID theft if you could take the hospital investigation."

"I'll have to hand off tasks to others, but I can oversee the case if Vance allows it."

She squeezed his arm. "You're a good man, Connor Warren. I won't ever forget your help."

He grinned. "So you owe me, then?"

"Yeah, I owe you big-time."

His grin widened. "You know I'll collect, right?"

She laughed and shook her head.

"No, I mean it." He stepped closer to her, his scent filling the air. Her heart started beating harder.

*Step away, now.*

She should move, but she was mesmerized by the shade of blue in his eyes. By the unfettered interest she saw in them.

He raised a hand and softly brushed a thumb over her cheek. "I'll collect, Becca. But be aware, it may not have anything to do with the job."

# Chapter Eleven

"I'LL WALK YOU TO your door," Connor said in the parking lot of Becca's apartment.

"Thanks, but I can take care of myself."

"I get that, but I was hoping to talk you into a cup of coffee and a bit more information about Van Gogh."

Her eyes narrowed, and he could almost see the thoughts racing through her head. "I'll give you thirty minutes. Then I'm kicking you out."

He wanted to argue, but he'd take what he was offered and try to renegotiate later.

She slipped her key in the lock, took a single step inside, then backed out and hastily pulled the door with her, as if she had something to hide.

"You know," she said. "I'm more tired than I thought. Can we do the Van Gogh thing in the morning?"

"You said you wanted to accompany me to talk to Dr. Williams in the morning."

"I know, but . . ." She shrugged, but didn't look at him.

"You're not a very good liar, Becca." With a quick palm to the door, he shoved it out of her hand, revealing a living room filled with boxes and a murder board.

"Whoa," he said as he studied the space.

Poster boards with notes scribbled in various colors of marker were posted next to pictures and other documents. A laptop sat on a table next to open folders spilling out papers. File boxes stood in three rows, four high near the far wall.

"Van Gogh," he said. "This is all Van Gogh?"

She crossed her arms. "You didn't think I'd quit thinking about the case just because your lieutenant sent me packing, did you?"

He stepped past her, his focus going from item to item. "You keep this stuff out all the time?"

She stared at him. "I may be interested in Van Gogh, but I'm not some crazy obsessed person."

"No, wait. I don't think that. Honestly. You're normal. I think, I mean I don't know you *that* well, but . . ."

She eyed him for a moment, then laughed. "You should see the look on your face. Mr. I-have-a-response-for-everything is at a loss for words." Her smile widened. "Priceless."

He probably should feel embarrassed for wondering if she was a nut case, but instead, he grinned. "Hey, even if you do have a screw loose, I'd like to hear your take on the investigation."

"Then have a seat, and I'll make the coffee." She closed the door and motioned to a leather club chair.

"I'd rather look around."

"No," she said firmly. "It'll all make more sense if I explain it to you."

"Ok-a-a-y," he said.

"If you're not going to sit, then come help make the coffee."

"That I can do." He followed her to the kitchen, but he'd rather be digging through her information. Her reaction just now had been over the top. It seemed like she was hiding something from him. Or maybe he was being overly suspicious, and she was just trying to protect years' worth of case files.

In the kitchen, he spotted another stack of boxes in the corner where a table should be. "More files?"

She looked up from grinding coffee to shake her head. "I haven't fully unpacked."

"When did you move in?"

"Move in?" she said absently as she spooned coffee grounds into a filter. "I guess it's been about a year now."

"And you haven't unpacked?"

"Old habits die hard." She grabbed the carafe and took it to the sink to fill.

He joined her, inching closer. "What habits?"

She didn't seem to want to answer.

He nudged closer, eyeing her until she sighed.

"Fine." She planted her hands on the countertop. "Foster kids never fully settle in because they don't know when they'll have to move again. And I was one of those kids. After a while, it just gets easier to leave some of your stuff packed and dig it out if you need it."

He could see her as a kid. His tough, strong Becca, keeping things packed. Keeping a part of herself packed, too. People had let her down, over and over, obviously.

He slid his hand across the counter and covered hers. He waited for her to jerk away, but she didn't. "I'm sorry, sweetheart. That kind of life must have been hard."

She said nothing.

"How did you end up in foster care?" He pushed, but he suspected she'd clam up or redirect the conversation.

"My mom was an alcoholic," she said softly. "She crashed the car. Killed herself, nearly killed me."

"And your dad?"

"I never knew who he was. After Mom died, the police spent like half a second trying to figure out his identity, but my mother freely slept around, so it was an impossible task."

He took her hand and turned her to face him. "And I whined about my family today when I should just be thankful for them."

"Hey, it's no biggie."

As a cop, Connor knew the conditions of some foster homes. Given Becca's unwillingness to unpack, he suspected she'd run in to some of them and carried the damage with her.

He looked into her eyes. "I'm sorry you had to go through all of that. I really am."

She peered at him for a long moment, then freed her hand and turned to the coffeepot. "It was a long time ago and belongs in the past."

She was right. It did belong in the past. But as much as she claimed she was over it, it was clear that she wasn't. He was suddenly very glad that Vance had sent her away today. Otherwise, she'd have been there to see the cadaver dog light on death time after time. To see Dr. Williams carefully dig around the flags to prove that one more terrified girl had lost her life. To prove that the shocking number of seven, maybe eight, lives lost to Van Gogh was seeming more likely by the minute.

"Your time is ticking away." She raised her shoulders into a solid wall that seemed impenetrable. "You want to spend your half hour dissecting my past or talking about Van Gogh?"

"Both," he said, surprising himself.

She looked over her shoulder at him, studying him for a tense moment before a monster of a frown claimed her face. "I can't do both. You'll have to choose."

"Message received. Your past is off limits. I'll take Van Gogh."

She spun and headed for the family room. He traipsed behind her, his disappointment in her unwillingness to talk to him a physical ache. He'd let his guard down around her and let her get to him. Really get to him. And he had no idea what to do about it.

She gestured at the club chair. "Have a seat."

He did as asked, but couldn't help wondering why she felt such a need to control the situation. He dug out his small notepad, then shook his head. "With all of the information you've dug up, this little thing isn't going to cut it." He tapped the table that looked like an office supply store had thrown up on it. "Mind if I borrow one of these legal pads?"

"Go ahead." She took a deep breath and started. "I know we've covered part of this, but I'm going to start at the beginning of the timeline so I don't miss anything. On Valentine's Day in 1999, a fifteen-year-old girl, Lauren Nichols, was found huddled in the doorway of a storefront."

She shared the exact address, and though it would be in the case files he'd review tomorrow at the office, he jotted it down so he could look it up on the Internet as soon as he got home.

"She was dressed in a white gown like the one Jane Doe is wearing."

"Can I see the pictures of Lauren?"

Becca shook her head. "There aren't any in the case file."

"None?"

"None."

"Don't you find that odd?"

"Perhaps there are some in the official files, but I don't have access to them." She took another breath and continued. "Lauren told a story of a madman who'd abducted her and Molly and held them in a basement. He'd cut off the ears of three girls, had preserved them in canning jars that Lauren saw on the shelf, and he was trying to cut hers off, too." She paused and swallowed hard. "Then she said that he was holding my foster sister, Molly Underhill."

"And the detectives believed Lauren's story?"

"Mostly. She showed them the slice behind her ear where Van Gogh had started his cut before Molly interrupted him and the number engraved on her stomach. She also had contusions around her wrists consistent with being tied up and trying to escape."

"And your friend? This Molly? Did Lauren show the police where to find her?"

"Lauren was so terrified when she ran that she'd gotten turned around and couldn't lead the police back to the house." Becca jutted out her chin as if she felt a need to defend Lauren's action. "That put some question in the detective's mind, but a few days later, Van Gogh's first victim was found, minus her ears."

"Since you've worked this investigation over the years, do you have a current address for Lauren Nichols?"

Becca shook her head. "We have the old foster home address, but she didn't stay there after the abduction."

"And you've looked for her?"

Her eyes widened. "You have to ask?"

"No. I guess not. You wouldn't let a chance to talk to Van Gogh's only eyewitness pass you by." He made a note on the legal pad to try to locate Lauren.

Becca took a sketch down from the wall and handed it to him. "They did a rendering of Van Gogh in '99. It was on the news, but you may not have seen it." She retrieved another drawing. "I had another sketch done with his age progression. He'd look like this today."

"You had someone draw this just this afternoon?" Connor studied the sketch.

"No, I have one made every year on the anniversary of Molly's disappearance."

He wanted to say that was all kinds of crazy to be so obsessed with the case to commission an annual sketch, but he'd seen law enforcement officers consumed by cases that they were unable to solve, and they weren't crazy by any stretch of the imagination. They also didn't have personal connections to their cases, the way Becca did.

He studied the picture. "Burn scars?"

She nodded. "Lauren said his entire face and hands are covered with them. She thought he was in his mid-twenties at the time of abduction, and she said the scars looked old. Detective Orman jumped all over that. He had his team scour hospital records for anyone with severe facial burns, but found nothing. They even got the FBI involved in nearby states, but there were no leads."

Connor held up the sketch. "You would have thought that, with this extensive facial disfigurement, someone would have recognized him from the news, back when the first girl's body was found."

"I always thought it was odd."

"I suppose he could be a hermit, not getting out of the house except to stalk these young girls."

"He has to eat and do all the regular things people do."

"He could have his groceries delivered, though. Today, a person can get most everything he needs from the Internet. And he could work from home."

"Sure, that's likely today, but not so much in the nineties. People didn't work at home as much then."

"But it wasn't unheard of."

"True, but to never leave the house? I guess it's possible. It just seems like a stretch, unless he had someone living with him. But if that's true, why didn't they turn him in?"

"Maybe he lived with his parents. Parents rarely report their own children."

"Lauren said he often talked to his mother, like she was in the room with him. I initially thought that meant she was dead, but maybe he was still living with her."

Connor handed the sketches back to her. "Can I get a copy of the current drawing?"

She nodded. "So what else do you want to know about the investigation?"

"Prime leads that fizzled and why. Your opinion of the lead detective. Did he do his job well? Sloppy, thorough? What did he share with you that's not in his case file? That kind of thing."

"What makes you think I talked to him?"

"Really?" he asked, rolling his eyes. "You're a pro. You'd leave no stone unturned."

"Okay, fine, I did. It took me four years of pestering him before he agreed to see me. Then, out of the blue, he called and said he was ready to talk about the case. I later learned that was when he received his cancer diagnosis."

"He's dead?"

"You didn't know?"

"Vance just said he wasn't the same after that case. So when he retired, he didn't stay in touch with the guys and no one at the precinct could tell us anything about his current life. I was planning to try to locate him tomorrow."

"The closest you'll come is his daughter, Eva Waters."

"The TV reporter?"

Becca nodded. "Start by asking her questions, and you'll find your name as a headline on the six o'clock news."

"Did you ever talk to her?'

Becca relaxed against the wall. "We talked for a few minutes back when her dad was sick."

"So if you questioned her now, she wouldn't think much of it. She'd just think you were trying to run down Van Gogh."

"I suppose so."

"That's even more of a reason for my lieutenant to add you to the team."

Her body stiffened. She blinked a few times then looked at him. "Is that what you want to happen? Me on the case?"

*That's the big question of the day.* "Do I want you all wrapped up in a horrific serial killer case? No." He continued to look at her, her expression softening and morphing into something he couldn't read from across the room. Something he'd have to see up close to decipher.

He got up. Started for her.

*Don't do it.*

He ignored his brain's feeble warning and crossed the room. She drew in a shallow breath and held it, her eyes glittering with something he'd never seen there before. Keeping his eyes on her, he planted his hands on the wall on either side of her head. "Do I want to have your input on this case and see you on a regular basis? Yes."

"Don't go there, Connor," she chastised, then licked her lips.

It was nearly his undoing. "I get that we agreed to put aside our personal feelings, but Bex, I gotta tell you, instead of making it easier, I think it's making it harder for me. You know, the forbidden fruit thing."

"You'll just have to try harder then. I mean it, Connor. We need to focus. Now more than ever." She pressed on his chest, trying to push him back, but he refused to budge.

"Um-hm," he said, but for some reason, he couldn't take his eyes off her mouth as she talked.

"Don't look at me like that."

"Like what?"

"Like you're starving, and I'm the last morsel of food on this earth."

"I am starving, honey, and I'm starting to think you're about the only satisfying thing on the menu."

# Chapter Twelve

REGINALD DIDN'T LIKE the cold, and his clunker of a van didn't much like it either. It huffed and puffed up the final hill toward the trail entrance.

He patted the dash. "You can do it, Wilbur," he said, mocking the voice of Mr. Ed, the talking horse on television. His mother had watched that show nonstop, and he'd memorized nearly every word of it. Especially Ed's lines. Reginald had loved that horse. He was so funny.

As he crested the hill, Wilbur coughed, but Reginald couldn't be concerned with that. At the far side of the parking lot, the spot just below the trailhead, a Portland police officer stood guard. His car sat in the lot next to a crime-scene van and what looked like another official state van parked on the other side.

Reginald's heart rate kicked up as he kept the van chugging toward his secluded parking space, but when he reached the spot, his instincts screamed at him to keep driving.

"What do you make of this, Wilbur?" he asked. "Could they have found the girls? Not possible, right? I was so careful. And there was nothing in the news about it. Surely, they couldn't have found them without it making the news. Mother was all about humility, but even I know how much the world would clamor to meet me if they learned of my special skills. The news stations would be compelled to report it."

He turned down a side street, then another for good measure, and parked the van on a road filled with cars to blend in with. In many cities, a classic VW van like his would stand out, but not in Portland. There were plenty of the old VWs around the town where California hippies had migrated in the seventies.

He found his small flashlight and binoculars under the seat and headed toward the park. He had a special observation spot that he'd used to confirm the trail was abandoned on the nights he'd brought the girls up here. He'd never run in to anyone this late. Honestly, as much as it was exciting, it was equally annoying that he couldn't dispose of Allie's hair thingy, but he couldn't let it get to him. He still had to be careful.

He moved slowly through the dark, not a step out of place. He was used to the darkness. Used to hours and hours confined to his room and required to sit without any light so he didn't disturb Mother while she tuned in to *Mr. Ed* and other old re-runs of the shows she'd watched with her father when she was younger. More of her alone time, she'd claimed.

Not needing his flashlight, Reginald felt the ground through his Chuck Taylor high-tops as he moved into location and perched on a fallen log. He was close enough to see the cop, hear him if he spoke. Reginald planted his elbows on his knees and focused his binoculars to get a good look at the cop's face. The burly guy strode back and forth a few times, lumbering like it was a big deal to move. He suddenly shrugged and went back to his car where he sat with his door open.

As Reginald watched, the cold, damp air settled into his body, making him cranky. Minutes ticked by like a slug approaching Mother's favorite spring primroses. He heard a car before it turned into the lot. Another cop car. Maybe a shift change.

The first cop got up. Stretched and yawned. The other climbed out, two cups of coffee in his hands.

"Man, am I glad to see you," the first one said. "I've been jonesing for something to do."

"So, no action here, then?"

"Not much. The lady anthropologist is still in the clearing, but she's not saying a thing." He stepped closer, as if he feared being overheard. "But you gotta know there are more bodies up there besides the one the ME hauled off. They wouldn't have called in the anthropologist otherwise."

*No.* They'd found the girls. They were disturbing their peace after he'd worked so hard to drag them to their resting place, using a tarp he'd fashioned into a large canvas bag. Then he'd erased every track, every mark with a rake. He hadn't been sure he'd gotten them all, but then the rain had set in. The blessed heavy rain, washing the marks away. Maybe that's how they'd found the girls. The rain had been a real gully washer. It could have exposed one of them, he supposed.

He knew he should have dug deeper, the way he had for the first girls. Dug deep and chose burial sites around the city instead of laying them all to rest in the same location. His heart ached as he lowered his binoculars. One thing was certain. He wasn't going to hang around here. Allie's hair clip would just have to go into a dumpster.

"Reginald." He could hear Mother's scolding voice. "Haven't I told you? Every bit of the girls' possessions from before your cleanse must be buried, just like the girls are buried, or the cleansing won't work."

"That doesn't mean it has to be in the same place," he said under his breath as he got up to leave. He'd bury the clip somewhere in the boonies. Then what?

Did the fact that the cops had found the girls change anything? Maybe.

This was sure to make the news, and he'd suddenly be a hero for saving these girls.

"A hero?" Billy's voice broke the quiet. "More like a zero. The press is gonna crucify you like they did in the nineties."

"Be quiet, Billy," he whispered so they couldn't hear him. "They have no idea who I am so it shouldn't interfere in my plans." But he couldn't be too careful. He needed a clear head to think this through. He'd have to delay the call about Molly until he'd sorted this out.

"Just for a day," he promised himself. "Just until you're sure you've covered all the bases."

He'd waited a long time for Lauren. Mother had taught him patience. He could wait one more day.


IT WAS THREE A.M. when Becca finally closed the door behind Connor. What a night. She should have sent him on his way after thirty minutes as she'd threatened, but it felt good—oh, so good—to talk to someone about Van Gogh after working the investigation alone for so many years. She hadn't been able to stop. They'd thrown out thoughts and ideas and worked side-by-side through the possible leads. It was so much better than talking to herself.

True, she had to be on guard every moment, and it was hard to watch her words and not accidentally slip and say that she was Lauren, but she'd managed. At least, she hoped she had. Connor's lack of questions indicated as much.

Maybe he was too distracted with his crazy infatuation with her that he simply didn't notice. She touched her cheek, remembering the feel of his hand on her face as he'd said goodnight, and a smile found its way to her lips.

Maybe the real reason she hadn't sent him packing was because she'd simply liked his company. His teasing. His easy jokes, which lightened her usual no-nonsense, get-it-done-now behavior. She even liked the way her heart beat faster when he looked at her. When he touched her.

Honestly, she felt alive around him. Really alive, and her hope for a normal life came alive too. A hope she'd buried for years.

"Not good, Rebecca Ann Lange. Not good at all," she scolded herself. "You don't get to have that kind of life. And wishing for it will just make things worse for you."

Shaking her head, she went to the table to pack up her files.

Diligence. That's what she needed. A recommitment to being cautious around Connor. She'd always found staying busy to be the key to avoid these impossible emotional desires.

"That you have," she mumbled before a yawn caught her.

She could use some sleep, but if she wanted to free up time to help Elise, she needed to head into the office now to get organized so she could assign tasks to Taylor when she arrived.

Becca shoved the reports into a folder, then took a quick shower and dressed in one of her many suits. In less than an hour, she was parking in the FBI's secured garage. A car that Becca recognized as Nina's sat in the space nearest the door. Odd. Nina was on vacation and shouldn't be there. She was probably checking on one of her investigations. Agents never really turned off the job. Not even for vacations. At least Becca didn't, but Nina was more laid-back.

Becca entered the building and went straight to the bullpen housing agent cubicles. The room was pin-drop quiet. It was a perfect time to work. She could get so much more done without interruptions and distractions.

As she approached their workstations, she heard fingernails clicking on a keyboard.

Yeah, Nina was here. She was the only one on the team with long nails that sounded like birds pecking as she typed. Ones that were usually perfectly manicured and polished in bright colors, Becca might add. She didn't understand why anyone would waste time on a manicure. Snip and a quick file was all Becca needed. Then again, she couldn't imagine Nina with plain nails either. They were as much a part of her personality as were her brightly colored clothes and southern accent.

Not to mention her messiness. To a casual observer of her cubicle, it would appear as if she'd been in a fight for her life, lost, and had been abducted. She'd always been messy, but now that she was engaged to Quinn, she had even less time to organize herself at work.

Becca approached. "Thought you were on vacation."

Nina shot her head around, her hand going to her chest. She took a few deep breaths, her bright fuchsia blouse rising and falling.

"You like to have killed me," she drawled. She worked hard to curb her deep Alabama drawl at work, but it came out in times of stress.

"Sorry." Becca dropped into the chair at the end of the desk. "What happened to your vacation?"

"I'm about to lose my mind with all the wedding plans and couldn't sleep. I thought a few hours of mindless paperwork might tire me out."

"Are things not going well with the wedding plans?"

"Oh, no, no." She waved a hand. "But you know Quinn. He's got to have a say in everything." She wrinkled her nose. "I figured Mr. Tough Guy wouldn't want to participate, but he's weighing in on everything."

"A former SEAL . . . choosing colors and whatever else you need to decide on for a wedding? That's got to be quite a sight." Becca laughed, and it felt so good.

Nina smiled. "He's really into it. Not that he'd admit it. He says it's because his former team will be there, and he's trying to protect his cred by keeping things from being over-the-top girly." Nina leaned closer. "Between you and me, he really cares about the day. It makes a girl's heart melt." She sighed and a dreamy look claimed her face.

Nina's peaceful and contented expression accentuated the heavy weight of sadness in Becca's heart. It was an ache, a physical ache. She might not want marriage, but she wanted contentment. She'd longed for it, ever since her mother died. Sure, she had a difficult life with her mom, but it was *her* life, and she'd been fine with it. Until the accident and then Molly.

Rare tears welled up. She closed her eyes to stem the flow. She was just weepy because of what had happened with Frankie. Not to mention Van Gogh resurfacing.

"What is it, hon?" Nina asked. "What's wrong?"

"Nothing." Becca swiped at her cheeks with the back of her hand.

"Puh-lease." Nina rolled her eyes. "I may be all wrapped up in my own life right now, but I've never seen you cry. Ever. So, something big is going on with you, and we're going to sit right here until you tell me about it."

Becca had never met an agent who wasn't tenacious, and Nina was no exception. She would keep Becca there until she gave in. So she gave Nina the sanitized version of what was going on with Van Gogh, the story she told everyone else, and then told her about Frankie's death. "Guess it's just too much. Both things happening at the same time, I mean."

"Of course it is." Nina squeezed Becca's hand. "I'd be bawling like a baby over just one of them."

Becca laughed. "That's not hard to believe. You cry at sappy YouTube videos."

She swatted a hand at Becca. "I sure hope Sulyard agrees to let you work the Van Gogh case. I know how much it means to you to find closure on Molly's abduction."

"It does, and that's part of my problem. I desperately want to find Van Gogh *and* the person who hacked Frankie's medical record, but I only have so much time in a day. I feel like I'm really needed on the Van Gogh investigation right now and the fact is, someone else can track down Frankie's killer. But I don't want to hand off Frankie's case and disappoint Elise."

"So instead, you came to work in the middle of the night so you could do it all." Nina shook her head. "You can't keep doing that, hon. You'll burn out before you know it, and then, you won't be able to do either."

"I know."

"Besides, there's not really much you can do on Van Gogh at this point, right? At least until Sulyard tells you you're officially on the team."

She nodded. "Even Connor is pretty much on hold until they recover all of the bodies."

"So for now, why don't you work on Frankie's death? I'm sure Connor will let you know if something changes."

*Connor.* Right, the guy who was starting to worm his way into her life. Nina sat back and appraised her. "Is that part of the problem, too? Connor, I mean."

"So, is everything going according to plan for your big day?" Becca asked, desperate to change the subject.

Nina watched her carefully for a moment. "I'm right on schedule, thanks. Although today, I was thinking about a last-minute change in the bridesmaids' dresses. Would you mind giving me your opinion?"

"Me? I'm the last person you want to weigh in on this." Becca ran her hands down her suit. "You know that, right? Otherwise, you wouldn't have had to do a fashion intervention with my closet."

"You are pretty hopeless." Nina smiled, then frowned. "I really would like another opinion. Maybe I'll still be here when Kait or Taylor come in."

"I'd be happy to look at what you're considering. Just don't be surprised if I give you bad advice."

Thirty minutes later, Becca was still trying to understand the difference in the fabric trims Nina was suggesting, but she was hopeless.

Nina finally held up her hands in defeat. "You go do what you do best, and I'll wait for Kait."

"Sorry."

"No worries." Nina made a shooing motion with her hands.

"The Van Gogh thing. I need you to keep it between us for now."

Nina mocked zipping her lips, and Becca went to her cubicle and booted up her computer to get started on Frankie's investigation. In the next few hours, she learned that five credit cards had been opened in Frankie's name with a post office box as the address. Buck and Elise's credit seemed clear, but Becca printed the report to review with Elise. Further searching proved that Frankie wasn't the only one of Elise's foster kids whose identity had been stolen. Roxanne, Neal, and Steven had obviously been compromised, too.

Becca sent all of the reports to the printer then sat back to think. She could see that the kids' credit had been compromised, but what, if anything, did this mean in relation to the insurance information theft? And how was this thief getting access to that information? Was one of Elise's current foster kids involved? Or could one of Elise's prior foster kids have stolen the info?

"Guess your comment about us needing sleep just meant me," Taylor said from behind her.

Becca looked at the clock. Five a.m. She peered up at Taylor's good-humored expression.

Becca smiled. "And I see you listened, too."

Taylor chuckled. "I wanted to be here the minute you told me it was okay to take in Danny's DNA sample. Have you called your friend?"

"Jack? No. I'm not calling him this early in the morning. Not if we want him to agree to help."

"I take it he likes to sleep in."

Becca shook her head. "He has a morning exercise and meditation ritual, and he gets grumpy if he's disturbed."

Taylor nodded at the computer. "You working on our ID theft case?"

"No, but I could use your help." Becca gestured at her side chair and told Taylor about Frankie.

"Man, Becca." Taylor shook her head. "I'm sorry. Real sorry."

Nina came around the cubicle yawning. "I'm heading out, unless you need anything from me."

"Mind giving me your thoughts on something?" Becca asked.

"Oh, hon, you know I'm always up for giving my opinion." Nina laughed.

Becca shared the information she'd discovered on the Internet. "The kids see different doctors, so the odds of the info coming from them are highly improbable. I'm leaning toward ruling out a doctor's office hack."

"Makes sense." Nina's eyes narrowed in thought. "The home computer seems the most likely connection to me. And that means it's someone local with a connection to Elise or even someone in the family."

"It could just be someone trolling for unsecured networks in a neighborhood," Taylor said.

"With all of my harping about network security, I'd hope Elise's computer is secure, but I've never looked at it." Becca drew her notepad closer to jot a note. "I'll have an image taken of her computer and router and go from there."

"I don't suppose I could get in on this investigation," Taylor said, her eyes aglow with interest.

"With everything on my plate right now, I'd appreciate the help."

"Name it."

"Easy, tiger." Becca laughed. "I first need to run it by Sulyard when he comes in. If he's on board with us taking on this part of the investigation, you can get a warrant for the PO Box and credit card statements for the bogus accounts, and get a tech out to Elise's house to image her electronics."

Taylor lifted her coffee cup. "Then here's hoping Sulyard agrees."

Nina yawned.

"Get out of here, Nina, before you make me tired." Becca made a shooing motion with her hands.

Nina waved and set off down the hall.

"I'm really looking forward to meeting Quinn," Taylor said after Nina had taken off.

"He's just like you'd expect a former SEAL to be. But he has a softer side, too and a good heart."

"So he's the perfect man, then." Taylor laughed.

"I'm pretty sure no such animal exists." Becca couldn't stop the thought of Connor popping into her head. He wasn't perfect by any means, but he was the only man who'd ever made her question her life choices.

Maybe she could have more . . . if only she found the nerve to take it.

# Chapter Thirteen

TAYLOR CLUTCHED Danny's bagged soda can and stood by her car to wait for Jack's arrival. After hearing the things Becca had said about the guy, Taylor was beginning to wonder if she was there to meet some nut job. It didn't matter, of course. Nut job or saint, Taylor would talk to any person Becca directed her to meet, and Taylor would do it to the best of her ability.

A large black SUV pulled into the lot, and her pulse kicked up. She might just be delivering a can and waiting for results, but after going rogue and visiting Danny, she was a bit nervous about screwing up again.

The car slid into a parking spot on the far side of the lot. She resisted running over there and looking like the newbie she was. The door opened and long, jean-clad legs slid out. Hiking boots covered in a thick layer of clay hit the ground with a thud, and Jack soon stood tall next to his vehicle. She made him at well over six feet. He wore a black button-down shirt with the sleeves rolled to the elbow. His hair was black and cut short. With his back to her, she could see his broad shoulders narrowed to a trim waist.

He wasn't all that different than she expected a weapons expert to look, she supposed, though her initial reaction on seeing his build was that he'd likely be as good at firing weapons as he was at studying them. He reached into the vehicle and pulled out a rifle case that he slung over his shoulder. He slammed the door and finally turned to look at her.

His eyes were as dark as his hair, and when they landed on her, they cut through her like a knife. If she hadn't been leaning against the car, she'd have automatically taken a step back. This was a guy you didn't mess with. As he swaggered across the lot, he ran his gaze down her body, then back up to her face. Even from a distance, she could see she didn't measure up to the person he was expecting. He could probably tell she was a raw recruit.

She would have to work extra hard to hide her nervousness. She pushed off the car and widened her stance. She felt a bit foolish, but with his gaze still raking over her, she had to do something.

He stopped in front of her, his eyes locking on hers. She held his gaze and committed to not be the first person to look away.

"You gonna give me the soda can or not?" he asked, sounding put-out.

"You must be Jack Rains." She held out her hand. "I'm Special Agent Taylor Andrews."

He ignored her hand. "The can."

She offered it to him, and he took it casually. "Tell Becca I'll get the results to her in a few hours." He started to leave.

"Wait a minute." She grabbed his forearm and relieved him of the bag. He shrugged free and glared at her.

She got the message loud and clear. Hands off. As if she wanted to touch him in the first place. Okay, fine, she wouldn't mind it, but. . . . *Focus.*

"I'm going to wait with you for the results."

"Not going to happen."

She was starting to get mad at his he-man tactics. "Actually, it is, and nothing you can say is going to stop me."

He watched her carefully. "Fine. You can sit in the lobby. Take it or leave it."

She didn't want to compromise, but she had no choice. Not if she didn't want to disappoint Becca. "Then lead the way."

He started off, and she had to take long strides to keep up with him, which, at five-eight, was something she rarely had to do. But there was no way she'd let him ditch her. And she wouldn't be hanging out waiting for the results in the lobby. She didn't know how she would accomplish it, but she'd be sticking with Jack Rains no matter what he said.


CONNOR WENT TO THE lobby to meet Becca and bring her up to the status meeting. She was wearing another conservative navy-blue suit and her hair was pulled back with a clip. Dark circles ringed her eyes, but despite her fatigue, she was still haltingly beautiful.

She caught his gaze and offered a smile that he could see was forced when he'd expected her to be glad to see him. They had worked so well together in the wee hours of the morning. Both of them had been too tired to put up any pretense, and they made a good team, finishing each other's thoughts and sentences at times. He'd never had that with anyone but Sam. He'd certainly never had it with a woman, and Connor wanted more. But their interaction this morning? Nah. They were back to being strangers, and that was as comfortable as a bed of nails.

He shook his head. He had to quit waffling like this and make up his mind about what he wanted. Should he decide to trust Becca, and go for it, or put it behind him once and for all?

He stepped up to her. "You doing okay today? No bad dreams after yesterday?"

She curled her fingers into a fist. "For about the thousandth time. I. Am. Fine."

Right. He'd offended her desire not to need anyone.

"Hey." He held up a hand. "I didn't mean any disrespect."

"Wait, no. It's me. I'm sorry. I guess I'm just . . . I don't know . . . I'm crabby today or off my game or something." She sighed, and he heard a world of frustration in the depths.

He nodded, but he suspected there was more to her bad mood than she was letting on. Still, they didn't have time before the meeting to discuss it, so he led her to the elevator.

"Any updates on who stole Frankie's identity?" he asked, trying to ease the tension between them.

"I pulled credit reports for her and the kids last night. They each show several new accounts. Only, according to Elise, nobody has opened any new accounts."

"So, someone must have stolen their socials."

"It's looking like someone has hacked her home network and accessed her computer tax preparation program."

"Can you figure out who's behind it?"

"Maybe. Taylor's working on the logs for their home network, and she'll hopefully turn something up."

The elevator reached their floor and issued a sharp ding. When the doors parted, he escorted Becca to the conference room and introduced her to the PPB team.

"Welcome, Agent Lange." Vance shook her hand, his gaze apologetic. "I'd like you to start our meeting by bringing us up to speed on Van Gogh."

"Be happy to," she said, not even a hint in her voice of irritation at Vance for sending her packing yesterday.

She took a position at the head of the table and opened a folder from which she extracted Van Gogh's current sketch. She handed it to Sam who was sitting closest to her. She took a long breath and closed her eyes for a moment before recounting the same story she'd told Connor last night. But today, he had the luxury of watching her and seeing the nuances behind her words.

Her voice sounded robotic, her tone flat and devoid of any emotion. It seemed almost as if she didn't care about this girl's murder, which Connor knew was far from the truth. The only hint she gave of her uneasiness was the way she was worrying the paperclip in her hands, as Sam and the rest of the team, comprised of Lieutenant Vance, detectives Frank Yates, George Adams, and Olivia Lee, fired off the same basic questions Connor had asked last night. Becca stood strong as usual, but he got the feeling that she could drop at any moment.

"Van Gogh called himself Adam Smith when he chatted online with Molly, but the police exhausted all leads pertaining to that name," she said, then seemed to sag, as if she was grateful to have the story told.

"Has the Bee-ur-eau ever done a profile on the guy?" Yates asked in his usual snide tone. He was an Old Guy on the force, and many of the OGs didn't much like FBI agents or women in law enforcement in general, so Becca had two strikes in his book.

She nodded. "Do all of you hold the same opinion of profiling as Detective Yates, or would anyone else like the details?"

"Trust me." Olivia stared at Yates. "Very few of us at Central have the same opinion as Frank here. Especially not women. I, for one, would like to get more insight on Van Gogh."

Others chimed in, and Yates didn't even have the decency to look embarrassed. Connor didn't think he was a bad guy. He simply hadn't adapted well to change.

Becca tapped a finger on the sketch of Van Gogh that had made its way back to her. "We know from Lauren's description that Van Gogh is a white male. At the time of her attack, she thought him to be in his early twenties, which puts him in his early forties now. He's a detailed and organized man, rigid, and in control at all times. The placement of the graves at the crime scene confirms that he still has this need for symmetry. The ears in the jar that Lauren described were never recovered in the nineties, but she'd reported that they'd been pierced, with pearl studs in all three sets of ears. He had identical earrings waiting for Lauren and Molly. Lauren was wearing them when she was found."

Becca grabbed the table, as if to steady herself, clasping it hard before continuing. "It's believed he was abused as a child by a woman, most likely his mother."

"Let me guess," Yates said. "Mommy Dearest wore pearl earrings."

"Our profiler suspected, that yes, she wore pearls, but not necessarily earrings. They believed that the removed ears could hold another meaning for him."

"Like what?" George asked, seeming fascinated.

"He may be trying to silence the girls. Or another theory is that the white gown the girl was dressed in, coupled with the angelic pose, expressed virginity, and he was trying to keep her from hearing something."

"Was his first victim a virgin?" Olivia asked.

"No."

"Did this Lauren girl say anything about this being sexual?"

Becca shook her head hard. "He never made any sexual advances and rarely spoke to the girls. He did, however, talk to his mother quite often. It was as if she was in the room, though she never made an appearance."

"Did they ever ID the first girl they found?" Olivia asked.

Connor couldn't help but notice she also took a personal approach to this case rather than clinical. Likely a woman identifying with a woman in a way the men in the room couldn't do. Connor was glad to have her on their team.

"No," Becca said.

Sam's frown continued to deepen. "I assume the investigators visited local jewelers to see if anyone recognized Lauren's earrings or to ask if someone had purchased multiple sets of pearl earrings."

She nodded. "Nothing came of it."

"What about the jars?" Vance asked.

"Without having them in hand, it was hard to tell anything about them. Lauren's description put them at standard sixteen-ounce canning jars." Becca suddenly shivered and Connor wanted to rest his hand on hers, but this meeting wasn't the place to get personal. Besides, she'd pull her hand back anyway.

"The detectives suspected Van Gogh used formaldehyde as the preservative," she continued. "And they did get a little traction on that. It wasn't as readily available back then—no Internet orders at that time—which narrowed down the places he could have purchased it. They found a small chemical supply company in northeast Portland where a cashier remembered a man with a scarred face buying formaldehyde under a name and address that led to a dead end."

"I hate to ask," Sam said. "But since it's used as a preservative, and I'm guessing it doesn't go bad, did he buy in bulk?"

"Not really. Formaldehyde is sold by the liter. He bought three one-liter bottles, claiming he was a new science teacher and they were preserving frogs."

Vance grabbed a marker and went to the whiteboard. "Okay, so a liter is around thirty-four ounces, which means he bought enough at that time to fill six mason jars. With yesterday's Jane Doe being number nine, he'd have to have replenished his supply." Vance looked at Olivia. "Start with the original supply place to see if they're still in business, and ask if anyone has bought in quantity."

He turned to Becca. "Okay, Agent Lange. This is where I ask you, as the leading expert on Van Gogh, how would you proceed if you were taking lead on this case?"

"I'd start by trying to answer my own questions." She didn't take time to think through her answer, but Connor knew that was because she'd been thinking about this case for years. "How did Van Gogh get the girls up the trail without anyone seeing him? They weren't heavy, but most of us climbed that trail yesterday and know it's a bear. Can you imagine having a body over your shoulder? What does this crime scene have in common with the first burial? Why did he change locations? Should we be looking at nearby clearings?"

"Slow down," Vance said from the whiteboard where he was attempting to jot down all of Becca's questions.

She nodded, but started right back in. "Then there are the bodies. Are they all girls? All the same age? All foster kids? Do they have something in common besides foster care? Anything in common with the girl found in the nineties? She was strangled. Were these girls strangled, too?" Becca paused for a long moment. "And then the biggest question of all, why is this creep dressing young girls in white gowns, cutting off their ears to preserve them, and killing them?"

"I can tell you're not a detective." Yates sneered. "It's easy to ask all those questions, much harder to come up with concrete steps to answer them."

"You want steps?" she asked, sounding irritated for the first time. "Okay. Step one. Meet with the ME and anthropologist to see what they've learned. Is there a way to ID the skeletonized girls? Fingerprints, dental records, DNA, physical and race description, etc. If so, proceed with trying to ID them. In any event, search for missing girls in the area. Use all police records—city, county, neighboring cities, other states. FBI. Where there's a likely match, interview their parents. Maybe we can get forensic sketches made of the skeletonized bodies to compare to the missing girls' photos. Talk to street kids to see if any of the girls they know have gone missing. Then, of course, we'd want to follow up on any forensic evidence that has been collected and track down any leads from there. And, you've already mentioned the formaldehyde." She looked directly at Yates. "Is that enough of a start for you, Detective Yates?"

*Attagirl,* Connor thought and resisted giving Becca a fist pump for standing up to Yates. He did smile at her, though, and the corner of her mouth tipped up in satisfaction.

"Okay, let's get busy assigning all the items Agent Lange suggested." Vance was clearly impressed. "And maybe along the way, we'll catch ourselves a killer."

"I WON'T BE LEFT OUT here to wait." Taylor planted her hands on her hips and stared at Jack.

He quirked a tight smile. "Don't see as you have any choice in the matter."

"Why? What are you hiding in there?" She tipped her head at the closed door behind him.

"Not hiding a thing, but no one from the outside is allowed in the lab. I'm sure you can understand that." He said it in a way that insinuated she wasn't too bright.

"I get it. But that also means once you turn over the evidence, you won't be hanging out in the lab either."

He arched a brow, looking like a marauding pirate. "I'm giving a weapons seminar. Not something you'd be interested in sitting through. You'd likely fidget, squirm all over in boredom, and end up distracting me."

"I'd find your weapons seminar quite interesting."

"It's for seasoned shooters."

"I'm seasoned."

"At your age?" He rolled his eyes. "A princess like you? Give me a break."

She curled her fingers into a fist. "I'm older than I look, and I'm no princess."

He just kept staring at her, and she glanced around, looking for a solution. She caught sight of his handgun, a tricked-out Kimber 1911 Custom II. An idea formed.

"Tell you what." She tried to keep the excitement from her voice. "I'll prove my abilities. Give me your handgun. I'll field strip and reassemble it in whatever timeframe you give me. If I don't meet your goal, then I'll sit out here. If I do meet it, you let me sit in on the seminar."

"My timeframe, huh?"

She nodded. "As long as it's reasonable."

"You've got a deal." He stuck out his hand.

She grasped it, and as she connected, a jolt of something fired in her belly. Stunned, she forgot to move . . . or breathe.

"Hope your gun skills are better than your wimpy handshake." He turned and pressed his thumb on a biometric reader that scanned it and unlocked the door. "Wait here while I deliver the evidence. Then I'll come back for you."

"Ha! Like I trust you to come back."

"I always keep my word, Taylor." His steely gaze scared her as much as it thrilled her. "If I say I'll be back, I'll be back." He held out his hand. "I'll take the evidence to my friend so she can get started."

Taylor didn't know if she was being played, but for some reason, she believed him to be a man of his word. She gave him the can, then regretted it the moment it left her hands. He had to know he was good-looking. Maybe this whole unapproachable vibe was his way of garnering a woman's interest. At least, it was working on her. She couldn't resist a good challenge, and he certainly was that. He wore no ring, so she suspected he was single. Not that she was interested in a relationship while trying to establish herself in the new job, but she'd grudgingly admit she was interested in finding out what made the man tick.

She sat in a stiff chair and composed a text to Becca. *Waiting for the*

*DNA results. This Jack guy is something else.*

Becca replied quickly. *Cut him some slack. He's hard to get to know, but he's one of the most ethical and compassionate men I know.*

Taylor texted back. *Hard to get to know, right! Try impossible.*

The door swung open, and he filled the doorway.

"We'll have the results in a few hours." He gestured over his shoulder. "First door on your left."

She stepped past him, taking in everything in sight. The place was minimal in décor, but tight on security. Another biometric reader led to a windowless room. Jack opened the door, and she stepped into a conference room that resembled a bunker with more weapons mounted on the walls than she'd ever seen in one place. Rifles, automatics, semis. Pistols of every variety and make. Even a rocket launcher.

She let out a low whistle. "Now I see why you have all the security."

"Wouldn't do for someone to break in."

"But I don't get how you're connected to the lab."

"They require a similar level of security, so I lease a space with them. It's worked great for us both for the last few years."

"You're not actually associated with the lab, then?"

He shook his head. "Just on friendly terms with the owner. She's an old friend."

*Friendly terms,* Taylor thought. He was a fine-looking man, but unless he had charms that she didn't see, his association with the lab owner was likely professional. Taylor hated to admit it, but she liked thinking he might not be in a relationship.

"Okay, the test." He picked up a cleaning mat and spread it out on the table, then snapped his Kimber from his holster and ejected the magazine. He grabbed an empty magazine, inserted it, and laid the weapon on the padded mat.

"You have ninety seconds." He looked at her with amusement.

He expected her to fail. Of course he did. A Kimber wasn't as common as a Glock or Colt. And it was more difficult to disassemble. He probably expected her not to realize that the spring was under tension, figuring she'd make the novice mistake of letting it fly, but she wouldn't. She wasn't a novice by any means, and the Kimber 1911 was one of her dad's favorites.

She picked up the gun and pretended to look it over as if she didn't know what she was doing. It was a mean thing to do, but he was trying to play her and she intended to return the favor. She hadn't told Jack that her father owned a gun range, or that she'd been raised around a variety of weapons. Her dad had always wanted a son, but got her instead. If she'd wanted to spend any time with him, she had to learn to love guns, too. His

idea of fun was the field test he'd designed using his former military training. She'd taken his test so many times with a wide variety of guns, that she
could take apart and reassemble many of them with her eyes closed.

She hefted the gun in her hands, getting the feel of the amazing
weapon. "Ninety seconds, huh? You sure you don't want me to close my
eyes, too?"

He raised a brow. "I'm good with the conditions, but I admire your
spunk."

His compliment slid over her like a warm blanket, and she totally got
lost in eyes that had warmed to a cool gray.

"Ready," he asked, holding out his wrist to study his black diver's
watch.

She shifted the weapon into her left hand and banished thoughts of
anything but the gun from her brain.

"Start," he snapped out like a starting gun.

She ejected the magazine and pulled back the lever to make sure no
bullet remained in the chamber, then went on autopilot disassembling the
gun. She laid the seven pieces on the mat in military order as her dad had
drilled into her.

"There, field stripped and ready to reassemble," she said as she reversed her actions. Once reassembled, she inserted the empty magazine,
cycled the slide, and pulled the trigger.

"Time," she called out.

"Fifty-five seconds." Jack stood staring at her, admiration burning in
his eyes. "You've obviously had weapons training. I can tell you're not
military, but you laid down the pieces in military order. "

"My dad's a former Marine. He owns a gun range, and I was the boy he
always wanted. I entered shooting competitions almost as soon as I could
walk." She laughed.

"You might have mentioned that before we struck a deal." Humor
lightened his deep voice.

"And you might not have jumped to the conclusion that, because I'm a
woman, I don't have much knowledge of guns beyond Bureau-issued
weapons."

"Touché." His smile widened, proving how irresistibly handsome he
was. "You may look all soft and feminine, but I promise I won't
underestimate you again."

She hated that he admitted to letting her looks sway his judgment.
Even in today's world, she faced sexism on the job. But sexist or not, she
liked seeing the warmth in his eyes when he let his gaze glide down her body
and back up. Too bad she wasn't going to work with him for long. Life
could get mighty interesting.

# Chapter Fourteen

THIS HILL WAS EVEN harder the second day. Becca figured it was because she knew what awaited her at the top, or maybe because she hadn't gotten any sleep last night. Regardless, she tried not to show her fatigue as she trudged up the path alongside Connor, but her breathing had been labored for the last few minutes. Not Connor's, though. He strolled on as if he'd stepped out for a walk down the block. They both regularly worked out and were in great shape, and yet, she was the only one the hike left breathless.

"Hold up." She lowered the hood on her raincoat to get some fresh air on her sweaty head. "I need to catch my breath."

He stopped and turned, that usual adorable smile on his face. He wore only a PPB windbreaker, no hood, and his hair was damp from the constant drizzle.

"Can't keep up with such a fine specimen, huh?" He winked at her.

Despite their grim task, she smiled back and felt a bit of her burden lift. "I know when I'm beaten."

"Ha!" he said and laughed again. "I've never once heard you admit defeat."

He was right. She didn't accept defeat. Never had and probably never would again. Maybe she just wasn't cut out to enjoy the carefree life.

She turned her thoughts back to their task at hand—figuring out how a current-day Van Gogh had managed to trudge up the path, a dead girl over his shoulder.

She just couldn't see it. "I keep thinking about carrying another hundred pounds or so on my back. I don't think I could do it. Van Gogh wasn't in great physical shape in the nineties."

"So, do you think he killed the girls here?"

"No." She shook her head firmly.

"You seem certain."

"I believe he killed them in his basement lair like he did in the nineties. The table was set up like an altar and was saturated with blood. The floor, too. It was stained with it." The memories of the rusty-red table came flooding back, and she looked away before Connor saw her angst.

"Sounds like you've pored over these case files so much, you can imag-

99

ine yourself in this scene."

She didn't respond. After all, anything she said would be an outright lie, and she'd been careful not to lie when talking about herself as Lauren—at times answering questions with questions of her own to avoid it. "How about dragging the bodies or using a wheeled device of some sort? Like a wheeled garbage can. He could pull that up the hill and stop to rest along the way. If he was dressed like a city worker, anyone he ran in to would simply think he was just cleaning up trash."

"Maybe, but we found no signs of such a trek."

"True, but the rain could have washed everything away." She paused and thought about it more. "I can't see him coming up here in the daylight, either. Not with the scars on his face. People could freak out and report him."

"So he probably brought them up here at night. Unfortunately, that doesn't help us narrow down how he did it. Dane's combed every inch of this trail, but I'll get him to do it again." He studied her for a moment. "Ready to go, or should I send someone down here to help you up the trail?"

"You're so funny." She lifted her hood and stepped past him.

He came rushing up from behind and walked beside her when his longer strides could have easily taken him into the lead again. "I'll stay by your side in case you need help."

His crooked grin with a single dimple had always been her undoing, and it drew a smile from her. If he could get her to smile under such dire circumstances, she could see how he could lighten up her life on a day-to-day basis.

When they arrived at the clearing, Becca's breathing was strained, but not stressed. Still, she paused to take in the entire scene now that she was aware of exactly what she was looking at. A thin, uniformed officer stood sentry at the edge of the path, looking bored. Connor nodded at him, and he acknowledged it with a quick nod of his own.

She peered past the officer to where they'd found Jane Doe yesterday. Her body had been removed, but yellow crime scene tape cordoned off the area, fluttering in the breeze, and a white canopy stood overhead. At least today the wind didn't carry the nauseating scent of death, but Becca was wise enough to expect lingering smells from body fluids when they got closer.

From this distance, she couldn't tell if the other three cordoned-off graves were empty. They each had a large tent covering them. A woman, with short gray hair and wearing army-green rain gear hunkered over the first grave. Dane stood at her side, his camera out, and he was busily clicking away. Three younger workers were scattered at the other graves and appeared to be digging.

"C'mon," Connor said. "Let me introduce you to Dr. Williams."

He lifted the crime-scene tape, and they scooted under it. They passed the first grave with flies swarming around it.

Connor stopped outside the canopy. "Dr. Williams," he called out.

The woman looked up and shoved damp bangs from her forehead. Her face was thin, her features sharp, but she had a pleasant smile that made her seem very human, something that made what they were dealing with a little easier to take. "Detective. Good. I was just about to call you."

"I see you've made progress on all three bodies."

She got to her feet, clutching her lower back as she moved. "I'm getting too old to do this." She tipped her head at the other workers. "I'd let my grad students do all the work, but I don't trust anyone as much as I trust myself." She laughed and crossed over to them.

Connor made quick introductions, and Dr. Williams simply nodded her acknowledgement to Becca.

"So you've found something?" Connor asked.

"Yes, but before we start, I need to explain the identification system we have put in place so we all know which girl we're discussing. We've ordered the girls in number by the location of their grave. Jane Doe One is the girl Marcie has taken back to the morgue." She looked down at her feet. "This girl is Jane Doe Two, the next Three, and the final Four." She looked back up at them. "Are we clear?"

They nodded.

"Okay, then we'll start with Three." She clomped across the grass to the closest body. Her bright red rubber boots covered with thick clay soil made sucking noises on the moist soil. "Okay, kids, move out of the way for a minute."

Two women Becca guessed to be about her own age scrambled away from the body.

"Come in closer." Dr. Williams curled a finger. "The bones won't bite you."

Becca liked the woman's no-nonsense approach, but she didn't feel as if Dr. Williams thought of these bones as sweet teenage girls whose final hours must have been absolutely horrific. She moved to the left side and gestured for Becca and Connor to take the right. Becca looked into the shallow grave and saw exactly what she'd expected to see. A small skeleton, a stained white nightgown lifted up to the chest.

"Have either of you worked on a dig like this before?"

They both shook their heads.

"Then I'll be sure to explain my findings. First, let me say, the skeletons are intact and unless your killer is an expert at placing bones, the bodies were buried while still quite fresh. Additionally, I can tell you all three girls were around age fifteen and Caucasian."

It was what Becca had expected to hear, but still, her knees felt weak.

"No cause and time of death?" Connor asked.

"Ha!" she laughed. "Just like you detectives. Give me the cause of death and the postmortem interval and do it yesterday."

Connor's face morphed into a sheepish look, but he remained quiet.

"By the way, cause of death is officially Marcie's job," Dr. Williams said, referring to the medical examiner.

Connor looked surprised. "Then why isn't Marcie here with you?"

"She was, actually. But once we uncovered enough of the skeletons to determine there was no soft tissue left on the bones, she turned the girls over to me."

"How and when they died is critical to finding the killer," Becca said, more out of frustration than anything.

Dr. Williams appraised her. "I wish I could wave a magic wand and give you the information you need right now, but we'll get there. You'll just have to be patient."

Patient. Right. While Van Gogh ran around killing girls. Becca bit her tongue to keep from voicing her thoughts.

Dr. Williams squatted and peered at the body. Becca could see the heartache in the woman's eyes. She really did care about this girl, which somehow made this terrible death more bearable. "I assure you, I'll give this my all and provide you with as much information as I can, but it's going to take time to get these girls back to my lab and look at each and every bone for the kind of trauma that might give us a manner of death."

"You said they were all girls around fifteen," Becca stated.

"Yes. That's right. Let me explain my findings." She knelt by the pelvis. "I can say with certainty the wide girth here"—with gloved fingers, she pointed at the large pelvic opening—"suggests this is a female, and the lack of parturition pits tell me she has not borne a child." She scooted up to the skull and pointed at the forehead. "The more globular forehead, rather than a sloping forehead and brow ridge, further confirm this is a female." She gestured at the area where the nose would be located. "The narrow nasal root and bridge, and narrow face also tell me she's Caucasian."

She sat back on her haunches and looked up. "Now. The age. That's a bit more complicated. We classify bodies in three broad categories. Very young, teen, and adult. Bone growth places a body in one of these categories. There are primary and secondary areas of bone growth that continue until the secondary areas fuse to the primary area and all growth ceases."

"And that helps you how?" Connor asked, putting voice to the impatience burning in Becca's gut.

"Studies over the years have given us approximate ages at which the bones fuse. I won't bore you with the details, but suffice it to say, after examining a variety of bones, I put this girl around fifteen."

"Any way to tell how long she's been here?" Becca asked.

"Hopefully, but it's going to take a bit more time. I can give you a general idea, though." She stood and nodded to the side. "Let's head over to Jane Four, and I'll explain."

She took a few steps then glanced back at her students. "What are you waiting for? I want this girl out of here by nightfall."

When they reached Four, Dr. Williams faced them. "The soil around the body can tell us a lot about when and how each girl died. Bodies leak fatty acids into the ground as they decompose. The profiles of these acids vary over time, so analyzing them can show how long she's been dead and how long she's been buried."

Dr. Williams stopped to stare down on the girl for a moment, her expression one of sadness mixed with anger. She shook off whatever she was thinking and started again. "We also know a body buried two feet underground, as these girls were, will take about six months to skeletonize. However, a body will skeletonize faster if it is buried in acidic ground, and pine forest soils are highly acidic. This variable means my initial estimate could be off, but at a minimum, I'd say they've all been here for about six months. I can't be more exact than that until the soil is evaluated, but I can tell you one thing for sure—this girl has been here the longest."

"But not sixteen years," Becca said, trying to keep her tone level.

"No, definitely not that long."

Connor shared a smile with Becca and she let out a sigh of relief that Molly wasn't buried in one of these graves.

*Thank you, God!*

Dr. Williams knelt near the ribcage and looked up at them. "When bodies first decay, they are quite toxic to plant life in the area, but then they serve as excellent fertilizer and attract plant roots. Notice the roots from the nearby shrub have grown and intertwined in the rib cage of this girl. There's not a heavy mass of roots to suggest she's been here for a long time, but still, it's been long enough for the roots to grow a few feet."

"I didn't notice any roots near the other girls at all," Becca said.

"Exactly. That's why I believe Four has been buried the longest." She paused. "But let me caution you. This could simply be a moister patch of ground and the roots were looking for water."

Connor stepped closer and looked down at the grave. "Does your dig indicate that?"

"No."

"But you still can't say how long any of them have been buried?" Connor clarified.

"I'm sorry. I know it would help if you had a narrow window, but all I can say, at this point, is that I'd start looking for girls who have been reported missing about six months ago. But again, it could be less because of the acidic soil and I'll—"

"Know more when the soil is analyzed," Connor interrupted.

"Exactly."

"I've never dealt with anything like this and had no idea how complicated it could be." Connor suddenly smiled. "I'll admit to watching *Bones*, and I know the show isn't accurate, but . . ." He shrugged.

Dr. Williams sighed. "Real life is rarely like they portray on those shows."

"Then how do you determine the cause of death?" Becca asked.

"Manner," Dr. Williams corrected. "It's often in the bones. Bone trauma is a moment frozen in time. While the rest of the body decomposes, the bones remain, and we can search them for trauma that will provide clues, such as a gunshot wound, stabbing, etc."

"And positively identifying these girls?" Becca asked. "With no clue as to who they are, dental records won't be of help. And they obviously don't have fingerprints."

"I'm glad you asked." Dr. Williams smiled as she came to her feet. "First, I can give you each girl's approximate height, so you can compare them with the heights of other missing teens. If you find a match, we can move on to the next step. All of these girls' teeth are intact, so if dental records are available for the girls you locate, we could do a comparison and ID them that way. However, I have to caution you again. Three has severe dental decay. I doubt she's seen a dentist in quite some time."

"And if dental doesn't pan out?" Becca asked.

"We can most likely extract DNA from the bones or hair. If the girl is in CODIS, then we'll have an ID."

Becca was glad they had the option of searching the national DNA database, but the only way the girls would be in there was if they'd been convicted of a crime serious enough to warrant the cost of DNA processing, or if they were a victim of a crime involving DNA. "The odds of that are slim, though."

"True," Dr. Williams said. "We can also analyze their hair to determine the part of the country where they've most recently been living and that would allow you to better search for missing girls outside our immediate area."

"I've never heard of that," Becca said. "How does it work?"

"Basically, everything we eat or drink ends up in our tissues, and hair is no exception. It's like a linear tape recorder and acts as a timeline of where we went and when we were there. Recent developments allow us to narrow down regions of the country based on water. So, if one of these girls is from outside our immediate area, we can discover that through her hair. But another caution. This technology is new, not widely used, and it's pricey. I can call in a favor and try to get the test done for free. If not, cost will make it a last resort."

"Interesting stuff, Doc," Connor said enthusiastically.

She nodded. "And of course, we can test for drugs, hair dye, etc., in the hair as well. It won't give us an ID, but it will help us determine manner of death."

"And if none of this works?" Becca asked.

Dr. Williams looked at the girl again. "Facial reconstruction is a possibility. We could have a forensic artist recreate their face in clay, then make a sketch that we could publicize. If we have any calls, we can then use dental records to make a positive ID."

"All of that will take time."

"Yes. Weeks. Maybe months. But I do have some good news for you, too. We can easily ID Jane Two."

"How?" Becca asked, excitement starting to build.

"Let's head back over there, and I'll show you."

They stepped past the curious students and stopped by Two.

"Of these three, I venture to say she has been here the shortest amount of time. And"—Dr. Williams dropped to her knees—"she has something the others don't." She pointed at a shiny object.

"She had a knee replacement?" Becca's voice shot up.

"Yes, and before you ask," Dr. Williams continued. "It's very odd for a young girl to have an implant like this. But she has signs of inflammatory bone erosion, so I suspect she had juvenile rheumatoid arthritis. The important thing here, though, is that the medical device is registered. I've given Marcie the information so she can call and find out the girl's identity."

"Talk about burying the lead, Doc." Connor smiled.

His shifted his gaze to Becca, and she felt the same satisfaction that was displayed on his face, but she tamped it down. There was nothing good about how these poor girls died.

Still, they were going to find out who this girl was. That was a start. But there were still three other girls to identify and potentially three more from the nineties that they needed to locate before the investigation was over. And one of them could be Molly.

# Chapter Fifteen

WHAT A GOOD IDEA. A perfectly wonderful idea. What better way for Reginald to determine if he should call the police about Molly's body than to watch them at the trail. To snap pictures of them coming and going like little worker ants from the trailhead and see if he could learn anything about their investigation.

He heard voices in the distance. A woman's and a man's. The woman's voice danced around his brain, searching for recognition. He zoomed his camera in and waited to see the face that went with the melodic voice.

She stepped into view. His camera auto-focused and the image cleared. He fell back in shock. Could it be? Yes!

He sat up straight. Zoomed in closer. His heart fluttered. It *was* her. Lauren.

"Like it'd be that easy," Billy said. "This nonstop focus on finding her has you imagining it."

Had he imagined it? He blinked hard and stared. She stopped to talk to the police officer, and Reginald zoomed in tight on her nose. There, at the bridge. The tiniest of bumps where she'd fractured her nose as a kid.

Praise, be, it was her. Lauren!

He started snapping shots, his finger pressing as if his life depended on the speed. A shot every second maybe more. His mind raced. What was she doing here? Had the police brought her in to consult on the case?

He studied each and every inch of her. Tall. Muscular. Lovely long hair. Eyes, those whiskey-brown eyes he remembered so well. He wished she'd focus on his area so he could see them even better.

Oh, happy day. She was back. He found her. He really had.

"Mother, do you see? It's her. Lauren," he whispered.

"You fool," Billy said. "Getting so excited when it could just be a girl with a broken nose."

"No," he whispered. "I know her voice. Her movements. I know her!"

She turned, and his mouth dropped open. She wore a navy windbreaker with FBI in big bold yellow letters across the back. Was she an agent? Had his little Lauren gone into law enforcement? No. The guy she was with must have lent it to her. But wait, he had a PPB crest on his jacket.

"Thanks a lot, Agent Lange," the uniformed cop said as he shook her hand. "I appreciate it."

Agent Lange. Her name was Lange. She was an agent. He wanted to lurch from his hiding spot. Run to her, hold her, and question her all at the same time. But he couldn't give himself away. He couldn't even risk following her. Oh, but it was so hard not to.

He would go home. Let his fingers do the work for him. He'd search the Internet, scour it, actually. Do everything he had to do to prove that fine-looking woman strolling toward a black SUV was Lauren. *His* Lauren. If ever he needed his best hacking skills, this was the time.

*Hold on, Lauren. Hold on.* He blew a kiss in her direction. *I'm coming to rescue you.*


"I'M SO OUT OF MY element here," Connor said, as he swung his truck into the Medical Examiner's parking lot. "Usually we have a time and cause of death, as well as the vic's ID by now, so we can move forward. But it just seems like we're in limbo, waiting for bone analysis and soil tests to get started."

"We can only work the leads we find."

He swiveled to look at her. "You seem awfully complacent about this."

She arched a brow. "Trust me, no one wants Van Gogh found more than I do. But we have to accept that the science in this case is going to take some time. Maybe Marcie will be able to gives us Jane Doe Two's name and we can work on that lead."

He wanted to believe her, but there was an underlying tension that made him question if she really was dealing with this as well as she professed. "You're right. Hopefully Marcie will have something actionable for us."

They got out of his truck and didn't speak as they walked inside. Maybe Becca was thinking about the graves. He sure was. He'd seen death before—many times—but he'd never seen a body reduced to bones. Three young girls, their black eye sockets staring up at him and imploring him to find their killer.

He stifled a shudder and held the door for Becca. She stopped for a moment, then squeezed his hand.

"We're smarter than Van Gogh, and we'll catch him." She peered up at him, her eyes soft with sympathy and understanding.

Never had he wanted to draw a woman into his arms as much as he did at this moment, even more than at the crime scene yesterday. He wanted to forget about the time. Forget about the place, about the horror they'd witnessed, and pull her close. Right there on the main steps of the ME's office.

"Connor." Marcie's voice came from the lobby breaking the moment.

"And Becca." She looked from one to the other then got a big smile on her face. "Of course. Why didn't I see it before?"

"Excuse me," Connor said. "See what?"

"You two are perfect for each other. Straight-laced goal-setting Becca with fun-loving Connor. You two balance each other perfectly."

Connor's mouth dropped open, and Marcie's smile widened. She linked her arm in Becca's and started through the lobby. Connor vaguely heard them chatting, but he was too focused on the way Becca moved to listen. He'd always been interested in her, but right now, he had a heightened sense of the fluidity of her body. An athlete, she didn't waste a single movement. Her legs were toned and firm, the pumps with spiked heels making them look even more so.

"Would you like a cup of coffee, too, Connor?" Marcie asked as she glanced over her shoulder.

Connor pulled his gaze free and nodded. "Coffee would be good."

They swung through a breakroom, and Connor grabbed a cup then loaded it with sugar and cream. Becca took hers black. They both sipped as they walked.

Marcie was right—they *were* opposites. He knew people always said that opposites attracted, but back when he'd been a patrol officer, he'd seen those opposing qualities cause a *lot* of intense drama. Someone always got hurt. So he'd tried to date women with like-minded thoughts, ones who'd been comfortable and compatible. Women like Gillian.

*Is that what you want in life? Comfort? Or do you want the fire that a life with Becca could offer?*

Besides, being comfortable with Gillian had simply made it easier for her to cheat on him. Maybe she was bored. He didn't know. He'd never given her a chance to explain. Instead, he'd just broken off their engagement.

They entered Marcie's office, and Becca crossed those long, long legs. He ran his gaze from the shiny black pump dangling from her foot, up the toned calf to the hem of her skirt. Perfection. He glanced at her face. She continued to sip her coffee and was oblivious to his watchfulness. She was having no trouble focusing. Why couldn't he?

*Get your mind back in the game, man.*

He straddled a chair and put his gaze squarely on Marcie. "So you've completed Jane Doe's autopsy?"

Marcie nodded then scowled. "Since I know your first question will be cause of death, I'll start by telling you that she was strangled. The ligature marks indicate he used wire."

Connor saw Becca wince.

"Just like the girl from the nineties. Is the time of death still the same range you noted at the site?" Connor asked.

"I've narrowed it down, and I'd estimate three days. I'd like to give you a more exact date and time, but with the body having been buried, everything changes." She took a deep breath and blew it out. Marcie was usually unflappable, but Connor knew her well enough to know something about this girl's death had hit her hard.

"Have you found anything to provide an ID on that older case, yet?" Marcie asked them, changing the direction of the conversation.

Connor shook his head.

"Maybe I can help with both of them, then," Marcie said. "I'll request the records from her autopsy and compare them with this one to see if there are any additional similarities."

"How long will that take?" Becca asked.

"We didn't keep computer records sixteen years ago, so the files will have to be pulled from storage. I'll put Tim on it. If he's his usual acerbic self over there, they'll bump up the request just to get rid of him." She laughed, but it was forced.

Connor forced an equally unfelt smile. "We just came from the scene where Dr. Williams filled us in on the other girls. You'll continue to coordinate with her, right?"

"Yes. If I thought I could be helpful, I'd be right there digging alongside her." She reached for another folder. "The good news is that I was able to obtain an ID on the girl with the knee implant." She slid the folder to Connor.

He scanned down the report. "Allie Fields. Age fifteen. She lived on the east side near Westmoreland."

He pulled his crime-scene sketch from his notes and jotted Allie's name on the grave where they'd located her. The act seemed so final, as if he was sealing the poor girl's fate. But he hadn't. That was sealed the day she'd gone missing.


BECCA TOOK THE sidewalk to the Fields's pricey home and rang the doorbell, then stood back. As the lead on this investigation, Connor would handle the death notification. As far as Becca was concerned, that was a good thing. She was too involved in this case to do it. Besides, she had no experience in delivering such difficult news.

A regal woman with graying hair pulled back into a bun opened the door. "Can I help you?"

"Mrs. Fields?" Connor asked.

"Yes."

He took out his shield and displayed it.

"Oh . . . oh . . . oh no. This is about Allie, isn't it? Is she?"

"Her remains were located yesterday. I'm so sorry for your loss." Connor's words sounded harsh, but Becca knew the first thing an officer learned in making a death notification call was to let the person know right up front that their loved one had died, so they didn't hold out hope.

A strangled cry came from Mrs. Fields's mouth, and she wobbled. Becca gripped the woman's elbow and steadied her with an arm around her back.

"Can we come in and ask you a few questions?" Becca asked, mainly so she could help this poor woman sit down before she collapsed.

Allie's foster mother nodded half-heartedly, her eyes glazed with pain and anguish. She was already in a state of shock. Becca escorted her through an open foyer with expensive furnishings to a large family room with colorful designer touches. Becca felt as if she'd been teleported into one of Nina's decorator magazines.

Mrs. Fields sat on the edge of the gray sofa, her back straight, her manicured hands clasped in her lap. "Where are my manners? Can I get you anything to drink?"

Her reaction might have seemed odd to some people, but it made perfect sense to Becca. The woman was obviously close to a breakdown, but falling back into her comfort zone by offering refreshments kept her from losing it.

"No, thank you." Becca sat across from Mrs. Fields. "When was the last time you saw Allie?"

"Five months ago," she said, the tears coming faster now. "We had a fight. We'd discovered she'd been using drugs. For some time, actually. She had juvenile rheumatoid arthritis, and she said the drugs were the only thing that relieved her pain. I believed her, but my husband Fred didn't. He gave her an ultimatum. Check in to rehab or leave. I thought he was being too harsh, but that's Fred. He's a cut-and-dried no-nonsense kind of guy. He thought I let Allie get away with too much because of her health issues. So he put his foot down." She turned and looked at the foyer. "The last time I saw her, she was walking out that door. She never came back. Never will come back." Mrs. Fields broke down sobbing, and her gaze darted about the room.

Becca pulled out the tissue packet she'd thought to add to her pocket and handed it to her.

"I didn't tell Fred, but I tried to look for her." The woman fumbled with the packet and finally freed a tissue to dab at her eyes, smearing her mascara. "A couple of street kids in Portland recognized her, but I never found her." She looked back at Connor. "I suppose she overdosed."

"We're still looking into drug use," Connor said vaguely. "But I'm sorry to tell you, we believe she was murdered."

"Murdered?" She wrapped her arms around her waist and started rocking. "Oh, no. No. No. No. My poor, sweet baby." Her gaze flew to Connor's. "Did she suffer? Please tell me she didn't suffer. With her health issues, she already had so much pain and suffering in her life."

Becca knew Connor couldn't offer such an assurance, so she jumped in before he had to tell the distraught mother the truth. "How long was Allie gone before you reported her missing?"

"Gone?" She looked startled, as if she hadn't remembered Becca was in the room. "I wanted to call when she didn't come home that first night." A soft smile played on her face then evaporated. "I remember when she ran away as a child. She'd just come to live with us as our first foster child."

"Was she still in the foster system or did you adopt her?" Becca asked.

"Her mother wouldn't allow adoption, so we were never able to do so." She crossed her arms and jutted out her chin. "But we've had her since she was four, so she's more ours than hers. Now she's . . ." She wrenched her hands together and looked so lost.

"Do you have other foster children?" Connor asked.

She shook her head and relaxed her fingers. "After Allie was diagnosed with JRA, we knew she'd need special care, so we decided to direct all of our efforts to her."

"If you don't mind me asking," Connor said. "Why foster, when you could have adopted?"

"I was fostered as a child, and I wanted to give back."

Becca nodded. "I had the same experience."

An instant bond formed between them, and Becca could more readily identify with this woman. "So what happened when Allie ran away as a child?"

Mrs. Fields smile returned. "She got to the corner. She knew she wasn't allowed to cross the street, so she came home. When she left this time, I knew she'd go farther . . . but I really thought she'd come back that same night. Or stay at a friend's place. So I called around, but no one had seen her. Fred said to give it a few days. I waited two full days, then called the police and her caseworker. They kind of sided with Fred, saying she'd likely come home on her own. I thought she would, too. Especially for her medicine. Without it, she must have been in so much pain."

Becca could hardly stand to see the woman's grief. It reminded her of the days following Molly's abduction, and made her consider how she would have reacted if she'd heard this news about Molly back then. Shoot, then? Even though Becca suspected Molly had died, she knew she'd still fall apart if her suspicions were confirmed.

"You mentioned Allie's friends," Connor said. "Could we get their contact information from you?"

"Yes. Yes, of course. I'll get that for you." She rose slowly, regaining her regal posture when she reached her full height.

After she'd stepped from the room, Becca looked at Connor. His compassion, combined with strength in this situation, made her see him in a new light. He worked with death on a regular basis, and yet, he had an easygoing approach to life. It took an amazing person to be able to balance that.

"I don't know how you do this all the time." A shudder claimed her body.

"Hey." He took her hand. "First off, it's not often that I'm dealing with a kid like this, which trust me, is harder. Second, our murder rate here in Portland is much lower than a lot of cities, so I have it better than most homicide detectives."

"Still, I couldn't do it." She smiled at him. "I've gained new respect for you, Connor Warren. You're quite a guy."

He opened his mouth to respond, but Mrs. Fields returned. He jerked his hand away, his professional demeanor back in place.

"I wrote them down for you." She handed a piece of paper to Connor, but didn't sit, indicating the visit was over.

"Would you mind if we took a look at Allie's room?" Connor asked.

"Her room?" Mrs. Fields's forehead furrowed. "What could you possibly want to see in there?"

"I know it seems like an invasion of your privacy, but we hope to find something to lead us to the person who killed Allie," Becca said softly.

"Oh, right. Yes. I want this person caught." She gestured at a hallway off the family room. "Her room's down the hall. Third door on the right. I'll just call Fred and then join you."

Becca followed Connor down the hallway, dreading what she might see. It was another first for Becca and something she didn't want to repeat. But she feared she'd have to do a lot of things she didn't like before they arrested Van Gogh and put him behind bars.

# Chapter Sixteen

BECCA MEANDERED down the sidewalk to the tree-filled park across the street from Elise's house where homeless teens were known to hang out. She was hoping to find a few of the street kids who were willing to talk about Allie, or the credit card fraud.

A sharp wind picked up and cut through her jacket. She huddled into the coat's downy warmth. She'd be a whole lot warmer if Connor was by her side, but he'd headed back to the station with a smile on his face. He was picking up a new portable fingerprint scanner that had arrived this afternoon. He was also meeting with Sam and Lieutenant Vance to update them on today's events. She hadn't been invited.

Maybe that was for the best. She was getting used to having Connor around, and she honestly missed him. It would be good for her to be away from him for a while.

Her phone buzzed and she looked at the screen to see Taylor's name.

"What's up, Taylor?" Becca answered.

"I just left Elise's house. It looks like her foster daughter, Roxanne, is inadvertently responsible for the hack. She gave their network password to a homeless girl named Willow and with all the network logins listed on the logs, it's clear she passed it on to others."

"Why on earth would Roxanne do that?" Becca asked.

"Willow and Roxanne used to be in a foster home together, but Willow took off. Now she hangs out in the park across the street. Roxanne felt bad for Willow and wanted her to have access to free Wi-Fi." Taylor paused. "I also reviewed the hospital security footage for the day of Frankie's supposed visit for bronchitis. It was Willow who impersonated Frankie."

Becca pondered the information. "I guess if she was the one to hack Elise's network, that makes sense."

"That's not all," Taylor continued. "She's also the girl Danny recognized when I visited him in jail. So it's looking like the credit card investigation is related to Frankie's death."

Though there was no concrete proof at this point, Becca had to agree. "I'm already at the park by Elise's house following up on another lead. If you'll text Willow's picture to me, I'll look for her, too."

"You got it. Oh, and I also got Danny's DNA report and ran it through CODIS. Unfortunately, it didn't turn up any results."

Becca sighed. "We're back to square one, then."

"On the DNA, yes." Taylor paused and Becca's curiosity grew. "But I got to thinking about other ways to ID Danny. I remembered that Oregon DMV has a facial recognition program."

Oregon had started taking digital photos for drivers' licenses in 2008, so when a driver applied for a new license, the computer ran a biometric comparison in their database to be sure the person was indeed who they claimed to be.

"Connor ran Danny's mug shot through the DMV database the day we arrested him," Becca replied. "It was a bust."

"Yeah, I know. But I followed up with the DMV and they said the mug shot and their photos weren't on similar platforms, causing the computer to reject that picture. I arranged to have a DMV camera taken over to the jail and took a new picture of Danny that fit their mapping. It worked, and we now know he's Danny Gains, aged seventeen, and a foster kid who ran away six months ago."

"Another foster kid," Becca said, pondering the implication. "Does he have any priors?"

"Squeaky clean."

Becca looked down the street at all the other homeless teens and wished she could do something to help all of them, or even to help Danny. But her first responsibility was to solve the crime.

"Can you head on over to the jail and let him know we have his identity? Tell him since he has no priors, we'll try to help him out on the theft charges if he gives up the ringleader."

"I'm on it." The excitement in Taylor's voice reminded Becca of her early days as a rookie, but she was far too cynical now to get excited over a simple lead like this one.

Unless, of course, it was related to Van Gogh. *That* she'd be all over.

Becca said goodbye and the text arrived with Willow's picture. Becca glanced at it before she pulled up her hood against the cold wind and tried to act casual as she searched around for Willow. She didn't find her, but spotted three girls and a guy sitting on sleeping bags down the street. She cautiously approached them. Their radar was up by the time she got there, but at least they didn't bolt.

"Hey." She kept her tone casual as she held out the picture of Willow. "I'm looking for this girl."

They glanced at each other, and it didn't take a trained agent to see they were planning on lying to her.

"What do you want with her?" the guy asked.

Becca could try to hide the fact that she was an agent, but if these kids had been on the street for any length of time, they'd know she was in law enforcement. Her jeans and hoodie only allowed her to get close enough for them to lie to her. That's also why she showed Willow's picture instead of giving them her name. If they knew she'd already learned Willow's ID, they'd realize the girl was in trouble.

Becca pulled out her shield and displayed it.

"She's involved in a case I'm working." She changed the photo to Allie Field's picture. "I'm also interested in information on this girl, too. Do you know either of them?"

The shorter girl rolled her eyes. "Like we're going to get them arrested."

Becca squatted to make herself less intimidating and decided to focus on Willow first by holding up her picture again. "See, here's the thing. We've got her boyfriend Danny in lockup. We caught him with merchandise and stolen credit cards. But he's determined to keep quiet and do time for his boss. Not a smart move. He may be under eighteen, but he could be tried as an adult and go away for a long time. If I can talk to his girlfriend, she could convince him to do the right thing and cut his sentence."

They looked at each other and finally the boy shrugged. "She doesn't hang down here anymore. Not since she hooked up with Danny."

"So where does she hang?"

"Their guy rented an apartment for them."

"Their guy?" Becca asked.

"The dude they work for." He rattled off a location and apartment number in the suburbs. "Sweet place."

"Hey, thanks." Becca held up Allie's picture. "What about my other girl, here? Do you know anything about her or any girls who've gone missing? Fifteen years old or so?"

The trio shared a look again.

The long, lanky girl sat up, her eyes filled with anger. "Don't know that girl, but there was this one, Karen something or other. She got all caught up with a dude who hung near the Lloyd Center. I never saw her again. Her mean old foster mother would never look for her, so I tried to find her."

Becca's heart skipped a beat at the mention of another missing foster kid. "And did you?"

"Nah. No one knew where she was. I figured he dumped her and she moved on. You know? To fresh territory."

"Nah," the guy said. "She'd come back here first."

She shot a fiery look at the boy. "Maybe she was embarrassed that she trusted a creep like him."

"Shoot, ain't nothin' none of us haven't had happen," the short girl said.

"Ain't that the truth," lanky girl added.

Becca held out Allie's picture again. "So you don't know this girl?"

They all shook their heads.

Becca dug out her business card and gave them each one. "If you find yourself in any situation you can't handle, call me first, okay? I've been where you are and can help."

The lanky girl flicked the card onto the sleeping bag. "You, living on the street? No way."

"Way." Becca stood. "Between foster homes. And before I realized that a creepy old foster father crossing boundaries was way better than trying to make it on my own out here."

She could see her comment resonated with the youngest girl. "Like I said. Call me. I'll help."

She headed down the street to talk to other teens. As she walked, she offered a prayer for these kids that they'd wise up and come in from the cold before they ended up like Allie—a murder victim left to rot like garbage at the landfill.

# Chapter Seventeen

REBECCA. HER NAME was Rebecca. Rebecca Lange.

Reginald's research showed that people close to her called her Becca. He would, too, because despite so many years passing since he'd seen her, they were closer than anyone else. Of that, he was sure.

With his favorite waltz playing in the background, he traced the outline of her face on his computer screen. She didn't have a Facebook page. Most law enforcement officers didn't. But there were plenty of teenagers who were glad to post pictures of her. Foster kids who'd been mistreated and she'd been their saving angel. He'd always known she was an angel. His angel. But apparently, she was an angel to others now, as well.

The pictures were amazing. She was as beautiful as he'd always imagined she'd be. He sent another picture to the printer, tore the teenager in the photo from the page, then tacked her image on his bulletin board. He ran his fingers over her face, kissing the lips that he remembered so well.

When would they be reunited again?

"How can you be so sure she's your Lauren?" Billy interrupted. "Still going with the bump on the nose? If so, you're the idiot I've always known you to be."

"It's Lauren. I know," Reginald argued.

"Prove it. Have her DNA tested."

"DNA." Reginald let the thought roll around in his brain. "I do still have her shirt from when we were together. It has her blood on it." He shot a look at the ceiling. "I'm sorry, Mother. I know I was supposed to get rid of everything, but Lauren was different. She hadn't been cleansed, so it didn't matter."

Mother didn't speak, and he feared she'd take away his disciple status. But when a few moments passed in silence, he knew she wasn't going to stop him.

"So," he said. "I need to collect a current sample from Lauren. I can easily get that from her apartment." The monitor dimmed, and he caught sight of his face on the screen. He ran his fingers over the lumpy skin. "I'll have to find a way to hide my face."

"Easy, you fool," Billy said. "Tomorrow's Halloween. Wear a mask. Not that you need one. That face of yours is enough to scare everyone."

He ignored the snub. "Halloween, perfect. And my lock-picking skills will come in handy. Lauren will never guess I've broken into her apartment."

*A lab.* He would need a lab to process the samples. One where he could get lightning-fast results.

He searched the Internet. He'd stick with his plan to reveal Molly's body in the morning, but if all went well in his search, he'd have the results he needed to prove Lauren's new identity by the following day. Then, it was just a matter of figuring out how to take her without anyone noticing she was gone.

He located a small local lab online and called. They were happy to take the sample and rush the results. Of course they were, for an extra fee.

Now all he needed to do was figure out how to grab Becca and bring her back here. With her being in law enforcement, it would be more difficult than it had been with most of his girls. They wanted to believe his lies. Becca wouldn't. A surprise smash and grab like he saw on TV shows with Mother should work. So how and where did he nab her?

He grabbed a pen and jotted down his choices.

1. In her home at night.
2. On the street.
3. In her car.

The first would be the best as far as not being seen, but he'd have to break into the apartment without waking her. As an agent, she probably slept with a gun by her bed.

"Okay, so that's not a good idea."

And grabbing her on the street was too public. Too much risk of being seen.

So that left her car. A carjacking, of sorts. It would have to happen at night in a deserted area. That was something he'd have to control. But how would he get her to stop where he wanted?

"Really, Reginald," his mother said. "You participated in that online car-hacking seminar. Can't you do your computer magic on her car?"

"Yes, of course, Mother. Good idea. I can do that. A little bit of research, some coding, and I can modify her onboard computer. Easy. And I can get a cell phone signal blocker. That way, when her car dies, she won't be able to call for help." He rubbed his hands together, then logged on to his computer. "Yes, Mother, as usual you have a plan. A very good plan."

CONNOR HAD BEEN trying to get through to Becca for an hour, but his calls kept going to voicemail. He didn't like not being able to reach her. Not one bit. He'd just have to keep trying her after he picked up a pizza at his favorite hole-in-the-wall joint. He found a parking spot just down the street, and his phone rang just as he started to get out. Becca's ID popped up. He quickly accepted the call.

"Where are you?" he snapped before she could say anything.

She didn't answer.

"Sorry," he said, taking a deep breath to blow out the anxiety that had been building for the last two hours. "I guess that came out kind of demanding."

"Kind of?"

"I tried calling you." He got out of his car and headed down the street.

"I saw the five missed calls."

"I was worried," he said, and didn't wait for her respond. "Why couldn't you answer your phone?"

"I've been talking to street kids, hoping they knew Allie, but I came up empty-handed. I did get a lead on an apartment that the credit card ring-leader leases for his crew." She gave him the Portland suburban address. "It's possible Allie was caught up with that business, too, so I'm staking the place out."

Something in her voice made her sound lonely. Maybe she needed a stakeout partner or maybe he just wanted to see her.

"Did you have any dinner?" he asked, ignoring the little voice in his head warning him to stay away.

"No."

"I'm just picking up a pizza. I could bring it by and hang out with you," he offered casually. Part of him hoped she'd say yes, the other part no. He knew good and well sitting in a confined space with her for any amount of time was a bad idea.

"Okay," she said less than enthusiastically.

Surprisingly, her attitude stung. "I could drop off the food and take off, if you'd like."

"No, it'd be good to have a second set of eyes on the place."

*Okay, fine.* She wanted him there. But she wanted the cop, not the man. It was the story of his life with her. He glanced at his watch. "I'll be there in thirty minutes or so."

"Connor," she said.

"Yeah," he answered, hoping she would tell him she was looking forward to seeing him.

"Could you bring me a bottle of water? I don't need the extra calories from soda."

"Sure." He hung up.

She was something. A tough nut to crack. But it just made him want to crack it all the more.

When he stepped inside the hole-in-the-wall pizzeria, his mouth watered at the tangy aroma filling the air. His usual order of sausage, mushrooms, and extra cheese pizza was piping hot and ready. After grabbing a bottle of water for Becca and a can of Coke for himself, he arrived at the apartment in less than the thirty minutes he'd quoted her. He made sure his jacket covered his gun and checked to see if anyone was watching before he slipped into her car.

"That smells so good." She smiled at him. "I haven't eaten since breakfast."

"Why didn't you say something this afternoon?"

"Honestly?"

"Of course."

"I figured it wasn't a good idea to sit down to a meal together. It might lead somewhere neither of us wants to go."

He opened the box and offered her a slice. "And this is different how?'

"I haven't eaten since breakfast." She grinned at him, and he had to laugh.

"Let me clarify, just so I get it right in the future," he said, her smile disappearing on the word future. "You won't share a meal with me unless you're starving, so I shouldn't bother to ask."

"Exactly." She chomped a bite of her pizza and groaned. "Is this as good as I think it is or am I just starving?"

"It's that good." He took a bite and chewed. "I discovered the best little pizza joint after a late-night stakeout with Sam. The place is kind of a dump, and I was leery at first, but they were the only place open. One bite, and I haven't bought pizza anywhere else since."

She gulped her water as if she'd just crossed a desert. "How long have you and Sam been partners?"

"Five long years." He laughed. "Don't tell him this, but he's the perfect partner. I've learned a lot from him. Plus, he gives me space."

"Like he's doing with the Van Gogh investigation, you mean?"

Connor nodded. "He may have been first on scene, but I wanted to take lead so he backed off."

"Why?" She peered at him. "Why'd you want to take lead?'

"Honestly?" he asked, mimicking her earlier question.

She nodded, but he could see she was wary.

"I wanted to keep an eye on you." She opened her mouth to speak, but he held up his hand. "Not in a personal 'let's go out' kind of way, but . . ." He shrugged when the words wouldn't come to him.

She simply sat staring at him, pizza in one hand, water in the other. Not moving. Not speaking.

Finally, he couldn't take the silence anymore. He'd start over. "Something about you makes me want to protect you, okay? I know it's an old-fashioned idea. And I know it's not necessary. You're in law enforcement and you can easily protect yourself. I get that. It's just . . ." He shrugged again. "It's not something I can really explain. I hope I'm not offending you."

She continued to silently stare at him. He'd expected worse.

"I don't mind," she finally said. "Since we're being so honest and all, I kind of like it. Not the 'he-man protecting the little woman' thing. It's just . . . I've never really had anyone else looking out for me. I mean, I've got people like Becca and Nina, and to some extent Elise and Buck, but otherwise . . ." It was her turn to shrug.

*Interesting.* "I thought that was the way you liked it."

"Yeah, it is . . . it was. I'm not sure anymore." She turned her attention to her pizza, and he did the same.

They ate in companionable silence, and he didn't push. He was thrilled they'd already gone this far. Shoot, they'd actually had a real breakthrough. She'd confided. Not as much as he'd like, but as much as she'd felt comfortable sharing. He'd like to hear more, but no biggie. His job gave him the ability to read people well, and he didn't think she was purposefully keeping something from him.

*Right, you didn't think Gillian was, either. Not until her little bombshell of infidelity fell into your lap.*

Becca was different. She wasn't hiding anything. She just wasn't big on sharing.

She finished her slice, dabbed a napkin over her mouth, then turned to him. "Did you and Sam make any progress on the list of missing foster girls I gave you?"

Okay, so they were back to business. "We ruled out two of the girls based on height. Sam's talking to one of the girls' foster parents right now. He thinks she's a match for Jane Doe Four. You should also know, she's been arrested for credit card fraud in the past."

"So she could be one of the kids in my investigation." Becca shook her head. "It's so hard to wrap my mind around the fact that she could also be one of Van Gogh's victims."

"Both investigations involve foster kids, so it's not too farfetched, I suppose."

Becca peered at him, her eyes creased in sadness. "Those poor parents. They opened their home and took in this girl. Now she's been murdered." She paused and looked like she was trying to gain control of her emotions. "I hate it, you know. But on the bright side, it's about time we catch a break on this case."

REGINALD'S HEART BEAT a mile a minute as he tapped 911 on the prepaid cell phone and waited for the operator to answer. He'd gotten a good night's sleep, and he could think of no better way to start the day, other than actually sitting across the small breakfast table from Lauren.

"911. What's your emergency?" The operator's pleasant voice came over the phone and the reality of his task hit him full on.

He was suddenly glad Mother had talked him into calling 911 instead of the detectives. It was safer, she'd said. Less intimidating. He held the voice scrambler over the phone.

"I want to report the location of another girl just like the ones they found in the park," he said, almost giggling at how he was enticing the police to act. "You know . . . the ones that were buried."

"You want to report a buried girl?" She sounded confused.

Of course. She was just an operator and wouldn't be in the loop about the girls, yet.

"Yes." He loved the sound of his altered voice reverberating through the room. "Call PPB detectives or better yet, Agent Rebecca Lange with the FBI. They'll want the information."

"Your name?"

"Ah yes. My name. Van Gogh, of course. Vincent van Gogh. And you'll need my address." He spoke slowly and carefully as he gave her the address for the fabrication plant. He made her repeat it back to him so he was sure she hadn't made a mistake in entering it into her computer. "I look forward to seeing the detectives and Agent Lange." He disconnected.

Imagining the detective and Becca sitting at their desks, then getting this call, he dropped the phone into the dumpster in a dirty alley on the east side.

He'd waited sixteen years for this moment. . . . Now the big reveal was only moments away.

# Chapter Eighteen

IT WAS A NEW DAY, a new chance to catch Van Gogh. But Connor didn't like what he was hearing from Sam, who was seated across the small table in the PPB conference room. Dental records provided by the foster parents Sam had interviewed positively identified Jane Doe Four, as they suspected. Phoebe Quade had been a runaway. Her foster parents had said she'd been just plain trouble, so they hadn't bothered looking for her, figuring she'd take off again.

Becca had expressed her concern over this family suffering, but when he called to tell her about Phoebe's treatment, he knew Becca would be furious. Shoot, he was furious. No kid deserved this.

"They threw her away," Connor mumbled, his mind filled with disgust.

"It was hard to hear them say it." Sam eyes narrowed. "At least they reported her missing."

"I guess they think that absolves them of the responsibility they promised to fulfill."

Shaking his head, Connor went to the murder board and jotted Phoebe's name on his crime-scene drawing. It gave him something to do, shifting their focus to actionable items rather than dwelling on something they couldn't control. "So we've identified two of the four girls. Other than the fact that they'd run away from home, what do we have that can connect them?"

"So far, all I have is that they were both in the system," Sam said. "Van Gogh has made it clear that he's still targeting foster girls."

"So how does he find them?"

"Maybe he has a connection to DHS, a caseworker or another affiliated position."

"That seems logical." Connor jotted the question on their board.

"I'll take a look at caseworkers," Sam said. "Maybe there's someone still working in the foster care department who was there in the nineties. I'll also talk to the girls' caseworkers to see if there's any connection."

"I'll follow up with Dr. Williams. And Marcie requested the records from Jane Doe One's murder, so I'll check in to see how she's doing with that." Connor noted both items on the board. "I'm going to interview

Detective Orman's daughter, too." He added that note and turned to find one of their clerks poking her head into the room.

"I've got a 911 operator on line eight who wants to talk to the detective working with Agent Lange." The woman sounded very harried for so early in the morning. "One of you want to take that call?"

Connor shared a confused look with Sam.

"I could take a message," she offered.

Connor waved her off. "I got it."

After a quick smile of thanks, she departed.

Connor crossed to the phone, closing the door on his way.

"I'll put her on speaker." He punched the button and answered.

The operator identified herself, but it wasn't necessary. Connor recognized her voice from his time as a patrol officer. "I just received a very odd call. It was a guy who claims he has information about another girl like the ones buried in the park."

Connor snapped his chair forward. "Is he still on the phone?"

"No. He hung up. But before he did, he said to call PPB detectives or Agent Rebecca Lange. Since he was talking about bodies, I called homicide." She sighed. "I think he was using one of those voice scrambler things. Or he just has a really weird voice. I figured it was a prank call, but I wanted to follow up anyway."

"Exactly what did he say?" Sam asked.

"Not a whole lot. He told me about the body, gave his address, and said he was looking forward to seeing you. Oh, and he said his name was Vincent van Gogh, which has to be a prank right?"

"Hold on a sec." Connor grabbed a pen and paper. "Give me the address."

She fired it off and he jotted it down. Sam snatched the page, then started typing the address into his laptop.

"I'll need you to email a recording of his call ASAP." Connor opened the Internet on his own computer.

"So this is for real?" she asked.

"Likely a prank as you said, but we have to check it out." No way was Connor going to tell her about the bodies and have this case explode in the media. "I want two units dispatched to secure the address he reported, and I'll need the officers' cell numbers so I can coordinate."

While waiting for her to dispatch the officers, Connor plugged the address into his map program on the computer. The operator soon came back on the line and gave him the officers' phone numbers before disconnecting.

Connor zoomed in on the map. "Industrial area. Northeast. Near the airport."

"I've got the tax records," Sam said from behind his computer. "Property's owned by the city. It looks like it was a metal fabrication plant. The company went bankrupt, and the city took over when the company failed to pay the property taxes."

Connor switched to street view to get a good look at the place. "There are far too many exits in the building for you and me to cover. We'll need SWAT."

Sam looked up. "What about Becca? Want to include her in this?"

Connor didn't even need to think about it. No way he'd put Becca near a reported Van Gogh sighting. He shook his head.

Sam arched a brow. "Is that a personal response or professional one?"

Connor thought about it. "Both I guess. I don't want her to get hurt and it could just be a prank. So why get her out there for nothing? Besides, she wouldn't be much help in a raid. If we do find another body, we can bring her in then."

Sam watched him for a few moments, then shrugged. "Your call. But prepare yourself. She's bound to be mad."

Connor imagined her reaction, and he knew he'd be in for a tongue-lashing. But he'd deal with that when and if the time came.

"I'll update Vance and get the approval for an assist from SWAT." Connor snatched up the address and jogged to his lieutenant's office.

It didn't take him long to receive SWAT approval and within the hour, the entire team was standing in full tactical gear in front of the warehouse, waiting for Connor's direction.

He ran his gaze over the long building nearly the length of a football field. The main door was secured with a padlock, but that wouldn't have stopped anyone from entering the building through broken windows and rotting wood.

Connor checked with Sam. He nodded his readiness, and Connor gave the signal to proceed.

The SWAT commander directed the front team to the door. They stacked in a line and the commander cut the lock. Unlike TV shows where detectives run in first, Connor and Sam brought up the rear. SWAT wore tactical vests, helmets, and other protections where Sam's and Connor's vests were lighter weight. It would have been foolish for them to go in first and take a potential rifle round to the gut.

Once the door was open, the men moved in like a swarm of bees, fanning out in the large space. Several stepped to a door on the left, and others went straight in, their footsteps sounding like an army and ringing to the high rafters. Connor and Sam followed the second team, then held position behind a large machine.

Connor soon heard, "Clear," called from all directions, indicating that the peripheral rooms were safe. One man was stationed at the entrance and the rest of the team moved forward, reaching the end of the building without locating a person or a body. Or even a place where a body could be buried.

Only one door remained, and it boasted a shiny new padlock.

"Bust it open," the commander ordered.

An officer quickly took care of the lock and jerked the door wide. "Basement."

The strong caustic odor of bleach drifted up. Connor got a bad feeling in his gut. Bleach was often used to clean up blood and cover a trail. He wanted to get down there and check it out, but heading into the unknown, unprotected, was dangerous. It was a task best left to SWAT.

The officer snapped on the light and stepped through the door. He lowered his shield and slowly descended.

"We have a body," he called out.

He disappeared into the basement, but soon charged back up the steps gagging and drawing in deep breaths. "It's a female in a white gown laid out on a table. She's obviously been there for a few days. Otherwise, we're clear."

Connor glanced at Sam, his expression grim and angry.

The team leader raised his visor, his eyes filled with questions he didn't ask and probably didn't want to know the answer to. "You're clear to go in."

Connor made his way down the stairs, his gun drawn and at the ready. These guys might have pronounced it safe, but Connor wasn't taking any chances. He heard Sam's footsteps close behind.

At the bottom of the stairs, the unmistakable stench of death mixed with bleach greeted him in the airless hole in the ground. He covered his mouth and nose, then looked around. The room was cold and stuffy, the ceilings low, and the walls made of stone. With no windows and only a single light bulb hanging overhead, the room closed in on Connor.

The space looked much like an old-fashioned root cellar, he supposed. Shelves lined one wall with old metal castings discarded on them. Shackles were bolted to the far wall, low to the floor. A long, rough-hewn table sat in the middle of the floor and held the body covered with a fine wire mesh cage. The body, as the officer had said, was female. Her ears had been removed and she was wearing a similar white gown to the girls in the park. But she definitely wasn't a fifteen-year-old girl.

She'd been sealed in a large plastic bag that looked like it once covered a mattress, which thankfully kept the bugs away. Unfortunately, he suspected it would have also kept the body warm and hastened decomp.

"An adult female." Sam came to stand next to Connor.

Together they approached the body. The smell intensified. Connor gagged and forced himself to ignore the disgusting odor. He straightened the plastic to get a better look at the woman's face.

"The fact that she's in the bag might make it hard to determine her time of death." Sam snapped on gloves. "At least it's cold down here. Hopefully, that will counterbalance the effect of the plastic."

Connor moved down to her hands. "We should still be able to get a print. Let's take some pictures and cut this bag open to better see what we're dealing with."

"Right." The word stretched out in Sam's Texan drawl. "Cut the bag. That's exactly what I want to do."

"It can't be helped. I'll get my camera *and* the fingerprint scanner." Connor knew Sam would have something to say about his recent purchase so he gave Sam a pointed look and waited for it.

"Okay, fine," Sam said reluctantly. "I'm glad you bought the scanner. Now go."

Connor didn't need further encouragement to leave this horrific stench behind. He took the stairs two at a time. Upstairs, he gulped in deep breaths, then when he hit the crisp fall breeze blowing outside the building, he took a few minutes to focus on pulling in even more. Never had fresh air smelled so good.

SWAT was packing up, but the patrol officers would remain on site as long as Connor and Sam directed them to. Connor stopped to instruct them to set up a perimeter, and for one of them to serve as officer of record at the entrance. Connor also phoned Dane, asking him to assign someone else to help Dr. Williams at the clearing and to get over here ASAP.

Connor dug behind his seat and located the tote bag holding his essentials, including his camera and the print scanner. He returned to the basement and handed a sketchbook to Sam. "Dane's on his way."

"I called in to request Marcie, too," Sam said, flipping open his sketchbook. "She's in a meeting, but she'll be free in about an hour. I'd like to move forward, but she's worth waiting for."

"Agreed." Connor snapped a photo of the plastic-encased woman while Sam started measuring and drawing on his sketchpad.

When Connor finished taking photos, he looked at Sam. "You ready to help me take her prints?"

"As ready as I'll ever be." Sam snapped his Leatherman tool from his belt and sliced down the middle of the bag. The smell ballooned out like the fallout from a nuclear bomb, sending them both back to the entrance.

When Connor adjusted to the odor, he returned to the body. Her face had been badly beaten and he cringed when he spotted cigarette burns on her arms, missing fingers, and the nails pulled out of others.

"You think the girls went through this kind of abuse, too?" Sam asked.

"There was no mention of torture or abuse in the old case files."

"So maybe, since she's an adult, Van Gogh's motive was different."

Connor looked at her face again. "He still took her ears and dressed her in a gown."

"Let's get the prints. If we get a match, maybe her ID will shed some light on this scenario."

Connor took out the electronic device that looked like a smart phone. He turned it on and pressed the victim's index finger, then her thumb on the screen and saved it. He had to connect to the computer in his car to see if there was a match in AFIS. "I'll upload this to my computer and be right back."

"I could use some fresh air," Sam said, sounding uncharacteristically morose. "I'll come with you."

They wasted no time exiting the building. Connor was glad to see the officers had cordoned off the area, with one standing duty at the door as he'd directed.

The officer lifted the logbook to show he was doing his job. "How's it going down there?"

"Let's just say it's a good day *not* to be a detective," Connor said in passing.

He stepped to his car, sent the prints, and tried for a moment to forget the woman in the basement. He liked his job, really he did. But ever since catching this Van Gogh case, he was questioning so many things.

Things like . . . if the job was still the only thing worth living for, as it had been for him the last two years. At the moment, he'd give it all up for what his siblings had. A wife, a family, and life in a small community where everyone cared for one another. A place where people weren't viciously beaten and murdered.

The computer dinged, and both Connor and Sam turned their attention to the screen.

"A match," Sam said excitedly from where he leaned on the door-frame.

Connor opened the file and stared at the name. It had been added to AFIS after a fingerprint check for teacher clearance. Molly Park, maiden name Underhill.

"Man, oh man." He shook his head. "It can't be. Poor Becca."

Sam shot a look at Connor. "You think this is her friend Molly?"

"The age is right. Let me check to see if the maiden name matches the name Becca gave me." He swiveled to dig through his bag where he kept his notes on the investigation. He flipped pages until he found the right one. "Name and birth date match."

Sam let out a low whistle. "So Molly *did* get away from Van Gogh back in the nineties."

The sick irony left Connor with a hollow feeling in the pit of his stomach. "Only to have him catch her—and kill her—sixteen years later."

# Chapter Nineteen

SOMETHING BAD had happened.

Nothing visible or apparent, but Becca could feel it, the heebie-jeebies making her twitchy. Because she'd basically had to fend for herself since she was a child, she'd developed a sixth sense—a kind of warning system. It wasn't accurate all the time, but more times than not, it was spot-on. She'd learned to pay attention to it.

Today, she just didn't know what *it* was, but she was going to find out. She pushed away from her desk to check on her friends. Before she could, Taylor rounded the corner and stepped up to Becca's cubicle.

*Here it comes.* Becca braced herself for Taylor to open the folder she was carrying and hand over the bad news.

"Here's Danny's DNA results for your files." Taylor planted her free hand on her hip. "Jack was just like you said he'd be, but he came through for us, which I suppose is all that matters."

Becca eyed her protégée and didn't like what she saw. "A word of warning. Jack may seem like the mysterious guy you want to dig deep and unravel, but many women have gone before you and failed. More importantly, they got hurt in the process."

Taylor gave an offhand shrug. "I've run in to his wounded hero type at my dad's gun range. Trust me. I know better than to try to save him."

"So you say." Becca laughed. "But your interest in Jack is written all over your face. I'm guessing you're not much of a poker player."

Taylor bit her lip, then scowled. "I've been working on my game face since I got this job. Guess I'll have to try harder."

"Especially if your emotions are of the romantic type," Becca warned. "Let those fly around here, and Sulyard will bench you before you know what happened."

Taylor handed the folder and another sheet of paper to Becca. "This's the rental agreement for that address on Frankie's credit report. You're gonna be surprised."

Becca scanned the document, and her mouth dropped open.

"Exactly," Taylor said. "I never expected the bogus address on the credit report would match the apartment where we found Danny."

Becca looked up at Taylor. "Maybe this goes deeper than we expected, and it's not just about Willow stealing Frankie's ID."

"Makes locating Willow even more important."

"I agree," Becca said, as she pondered their next move. "How would you like to stake out the apartment where we think these teens are living?"

"Are you kidding?" Her voice brimmed with excitement. "Of course, I'll do it. My first solo stakeout."

Becca didn't have the heart to tell her she'd likely spend several long, boring hours sitting in a car where she might or might not even catch a glimpse of Willow. "Just make sure to call me if Willow shows." Becca paused for effect. "Whatever you do, don't approach her."

"Got it." Taylor turned to go.

Becca got up and looked over the cubicles. "Have you seen Kait?"

Taylor shook her head. "I just came back from lunch."

"Guess I'll go find her."

Taylor left, walking toward her own cubicle at the end of the row. Becca searched the bullpen but found nothing odd—just agents, heads down, focused on their cases as usual. The routine hum of computers, the copier, and the sound of low voices on the phone were also all normal. Nothing was out of order at all.

So what was making her so jumpy? Could this feeling of dread have something to do with her personal life? Someone she cared about?

That list was short. Only four strong and it wouldn't take much time to check up on Elise, Buck, Nina, and Kait. Taylor was also working her way into the fold. *So is Connor*, the thought came unbidden. *But I'm so not going there now.*

She started her search at Nina's cubicle, just in case her friend had popped in to the office, but it was empty. Becca fired off a text and got a quick reply that all was well. She moved on to Kait's cubicle. She wasn't in hers, either.

Kait always checked in if she planned to step out of the building so Becca knew she was still at the office. As Becca went in search of Kait, she texted Elise. Becca took the long hallway to the breakroom and found Kait standing outside. Her posture was perfect and her back was to Becca as she talked on the phone. Her hair was pinned in her typical bun, not a strand out of place. Becca loved Kait, but the woman spent way too much time making sure everything was neat and tidy. Give Becca a shower and a hair clip, and she was out the door.

Becca's phone chimed with an all's well text from Elise. So that left Kait, who turned and met Becca's gaze. Her face was dark with anguish. Bingo. Becca's intuition was right on the mark.

Her heart starting to pound, Becca stepped up to her friend. "What is it? What's wrong?"

"Let's go back to your cubicle and talk." Kait tried to take Becca's arm.

She sidestepped Kait and planted her feet. "Now. Here. Just tell me. I can take it."

Kait sighed and stood silently.

"C'mon, Kait. Spill."

"It's Molly," she finally said.

*Molly.* Becca's heart sank. She knew deep in her soul, in that spot where anguish over leaving her best friend lived, that they'd finally found Molly. But Becca had to hear the words. "What about Molly?"

"They found her," Kait said reluctantly. "It was Van Gogh."

The words registered, and Becca's legs refused to hold her up. She grabbed the wall, her breath stolen from the pain. Kait slipped a hand under her arm and walked her back to her cubicle to settle her in her chair.

Becca dropped hard, her mind racing with the news. Her friend had died. It was something Becca had expected for years, but the pain that radiated through her body? That ache was far more excruciating than anything in Becca's wildest imagination, and her chest constricted with the loss.

Kait squatted next to Becca. "I'm so sorry, sweetie. I know how much Molly meant to you."

Becca searched for a response, but what could she say? Molly. Dear, sweet Molly. She was gone for good.

A fresh ache pierced Becca's heart. "Are you positive it's her?"

Kait nodded. "Connor ran her fingerprints."

"Fingerprints?" A burst of hope raced through Becca's veins. They were wrong. They had to be. It wasn't Molly. "If he'd killed her sixteen years ago, her body would have decomposed long ago. There'd be no chance of taking her prints."

"No, you don't understand. She was just killed a few days ago."

"Wait, what?" Becca's gaze flew to Kait. "She's been alive all this time?"

"Yes."

Molly hadn't died back then. She'd been alive for sixteen years, and Becca wasn't responsible for her friend's death after all. A flash of relief flooded Becca's body. Yes. Good. Molly had had more time on this earth. She'd lived, maybe loved and had a good life. But now, now she'd been murdered.

*Oh, Molly. How I loved you.*

Pain swept in again, leaving a physical ache in Becca's gut.

"Talk to me, Bex," Kait said.

Becca couldn't form any words.

"I'm sorry that you couldn't reconnect with her," Kait continued. "Sam said she had a family and two kids. She'd lived in Clackamas. Her husband reported her missing six days ago."

Molly in suburbia. Becca couldn't imagine it.

*She's dead. Molly's dead.*

Becca's gut roiled. Her heart splitting, she started to rise. "I need to see her."

Kait shot to her feet and pressed down on Becca's shoulder. "That's not a good idea, sweetie."

"It doesn't matter if it's a good idea or not. I'm going." Becca shook off Kait's hand, reached for her backpack and pulled out her keys. "Where is she?"

Kait eyed her and didn't speak.

It didn't matter. Becca had to see Molly. "Tell me, or I'll call Connor."

Kait crossed her arms. "Then you're going to have to do that, because there's no way I'm telling you where to find her."

Becca couldn't be angry at Kait for interfering. Becca would have probably done the same thing if Kait had been in this situation. But Becca also wasn't going to let it deter her. She dug out her phone and dialed Connor.

"It's Becca." She buried her pain, something she was good at, and tried to sound in control. "Where's the scene?"

A long hiss of air filtered through the phone, followed by silence.

"The address, Connor," Becca insisted.

"It's not a good idea to come here, Bex." His tone brooked no argument, and it wasn't hard to imagine the stubborn set of his shoulders as he spoke.

"Will everyone quit telling me what's good for me?" She sighed, trying not to lose her temper. That would get her nowhere with Connor. "Just give me the address. Please."

"On one condition."

"What?"

"Promise me you won't come alone. Bring Kait or Nina."

"I will."

"No, Becca. Promise."

"I promise, already."

He gave her an address located in the industrial area in northeast Portland, an area Becca wouldn't expect suburban Molly or the street-smart Molly she remembered to frequent. She'd always been so savvy, except when it had come to Van Gogh that first time. Still, she would have known that part of town could be bad news. Maybe she worked over there. There was so much Becca wanted to know.

She looked at Kait. "Connor made me promise not to come alone. Either come with me, or I'm sure Taylor will."

Kait grabbed Becca's keys from her hands.

"Hey." Becca tried to snatch them back.

Kait's lightning-fast reflexes kept them out of reach. She put her hand behind her back. "You're in no condition to drive. I'll take you."

Becca sighed out her relief. Kait wasn't going to continue to argue. Becca's legs trembled and she hoped they would hold. She took several deep breaths, shouldered her backpack, and marched toward the parking garage, her steps frantic.

They settled into Becca's car, and she fell silent as Kait maneuvered into the midday traffic. Memories of Molly came rushing back and questions followed. Would Becca ever learn what had happened to Molly so long ago? Where she'd been all these years? What she'd been doing?

*Oh, Molly. Sweet, sweet Molly. I'm sorry. So sorry.*

Tears pressed hard against Becca's eyes, begging for release. To stem them, she filled her mind with her intention to hunt Van Gogh down and bring him to justice. She'd get him. Oh yeah, she'd get him. Hunt him down until she found him and he begged for mercy. There was no question now.

By the time they pulled up to the low-slung building, she had her head on straight and was ready to work this scene. She ran her gaze over the long building, rotting on one side and covered with bright red and yellow gang graffiti. The metal roof was rusty and curled at the corners. Their car bumped over potholes and crumbling asphalt in the parking lot. Why would a suburban housewife like Molly frequent a place like this?

"Who found her?" Becca asked as she noted three police cruisers and one unmarked vehicle parked near the building.

"Van Gogh called 911 and reported it."

*Van Gogh called?* "He wanted us to find her," Becca said, her mind rushing over the reasons he could have for telling them about Molly.

"He mentioned you and Connor by name on the call."

"Me?" She shot Kait a confused look. "How does he know anything about me?"

Kait shrugged. "He must have somehow figured out you and Connor were working the investigation."

Was that it? Had he only mentioned her name because she was the agent on the case? Or had he figured out she was Lauren, and he wanted her to see what he'd done to Molly? Wanted her to know what he'd do to her if he caught up with her again?

Fear raced through her veins and she scanned the lot, peering into the shadows, the bushes, searching for Van Gogh. He could have staged this whole thing to bring her out in the open to kill her. No, he was smarter than that. He wouldn't try anything in front of so many police officers. He likely learned she was working the case just as Kait had said. That was all.

But how? How could he possibly know?

Kait parked next to Connor's car, and Becca was out the door before her friend turned off the engine, bolting for the officer of record standing at the door. He was tall, wide, and powerful. His narrow-eyed gaze was meant to intimidate. He might look imposing to some people, but nothing was going to stop Becca.

She stepped up to him and flashed her ID. "Detective Warren is expecting me."

He crossed his arms. "He didn't tell me that, and I'm not letting you in until he does."

"But they're expecting us," Becca argued.

He widened his stance. "Sorry. Orders are orders."

Kait joined them and displayed her ID. "You might recognize my last name. Murdock. As in Sam Murdock's wife."

"Oh, hey, Ms. Murdock." He smiled broadly. "Give me a minute to let them know you're here." He bent his head toward his shoulder mic, announcing their arrival.

Becca was a bit irritated at having to wait, but the officer was to be commended for protecting the scene so well. His diligence would help prevent contamination of evidence, and that meant a faster arrest of Van Gogh.

He lifted his head. "Sam's on his way up to get you."

"Up?" Becca asked. "There's a basement here?"

He nodded grimly. "Unfortunately, yes."

Becca assumed that was where they'd found Molly's body. Becca could almost imagine the room. It would be like a dungeon. No windows. Maybe airless. Dank and musty. And Molly. Dear, sweet Molly, who'd do anything for anyone in need, had been left behind like trash.

A shudder ran over Becca, and she crossed her arms to keep warm, though the sun was beaming down on them. Smiling on them, belying Molly's death. Becca's loss.

She heard footsteps on a wooden floor and soon Sam was striding toward them. He wore his usual blue jeans with big belt buckle and cowboy boots. Becca could easily visualize him sitting astride a horse. Maybe wearing a Stetson on his head. Not coming to tell her about Molly's death.

"I'm sorry for your loss, Becca." He gave her arm a squeeze. His clothing carried the lingering scent of death and decay.

Becca jerked back, the knowledge of what she was about to see becoming very real. She'd breathed in the smell of death the other day, but it hadn't been the final scent of someone she knew and cared about.

Sam watched her carefully, his lips a flat line. "Are you sure I can't talk you out of this?"

Becca shook her head. "I have to do it."

He turned to Kait. "I wish you'd think twice and stay here. I can accompany Becca. Between Connor and me, we'll look out for her."

Kait flashed a beaming smile at her husband. "I know you'd do a fine job, but Becca needs *me* with her." She rested a hand on his shoulder. "It'll be okay."

"Then let's go." He led the way inside the fabrication plant.

Giant lathes stood like headstones, marking the grave of the former company. Metal shavings littered an old pine floor that had rotted in places. The few windows that weren't broken were sprayed with so much graffiti, the interior was dark and ominous even in the daylight.

"Watch your step." Sam pulled out a flashlight and gingerly stepped over cracked floorboards leading to the crumbling end of the building. At a doorway that had once been boarded up, he turned and looked at Kait. "I wish you'd reconsider."

She fired him a terse look. "I'm going."

"What is it with you two?" He sounded angry now. "The scene is gruesome and neither of you will be the same afterward."

"He's right, Kait," Becca said. "You stay up here. I'm fine."

Kait frowned and made a shooing motion. "Go ahead, I'm right behind you."

Becca led the way down worn wooden steps. As she neared the bottom, the caustic scent of bleach mixed with a heavy musty odor and the unmistakable smell of a decaying body assaulted her.

Becca ignored it and turned the corner. The odor slammed up against her face and almost forced her lunch up and onto the cracked flooring. She put her wrist up to her nose, breathing in the scent of fabric softener that clung to her cuff, but it didn't help, and she gagged. She looked back at Kait. She wasn't faring any better.

Sam stepped in front of Kait. "Now are you ready to stay put?"

Kait shook her head and put her arm around Becca. Together, they stepped forward. Becca saw Connor standing near the far wall, his back to her. His broad shoulders were stiff, his feet planted wide, as if he was forcing himself to remain in the basement. He was talking to Dane and another criminalist she didn't recognize. She moved on, settling her gaze lower. She spotted a table. It was the same table that she'd lain on with her hands bound. Today, there was a large plastic bag draped over it. Her gaze traveled higher, and she gasped.

On her back, Molly was wearing one of the white nightgowns. Her hands were folded over her chest. Her face was beaten and swollen. Becca took a step forward. When she thought she might collapse, she felt Kait's hand under her elbow. Together, they approached the table. Connor turned.

"Aw, honey, why'd you come?" he said as he stepped closer. He stuffed his notebook and pen in his pocket and took her hand. "I'm so sorry. I know she was like a sister to you."

Becca dropped his hand, and, as if in a trance, she moved alone toward Molly. Her long-lost friend's hair was matted against a face covered with purple and yellow bruises. The yellow ones were more difficult for Becca to see. They meant that Molly had been here and suffered for some time before Van Gogh had finally killed her.

Becca turned back to Connor. "Gloves," she demanded and held out her hand.

She knew he shouldn't let her touch Molly, but he withdrew large latex gloves from his pocket. She snapped them on, for a moment transfixed with the excess size. Then she took a deep breath and went to Molly.

"I'm sorry, Molly," she whispered, moving the hair from her friend's battered face. Becca let her gaze roam the body. She saw cigarette burns on Molly's arms and palms, noticed that her fingers were broken and the nails ripped out. Two fingers had been severed and were missing. "I wish I could have been here to stop this. To keep this evil person from hurting you again."

She heard Kait crying behind her, and Sam comforting her. Then Kait came and placed a hand on Becca's shoulder, urging her to leave.

Becca looked up at her friend. "Can I be alone with Molly? Please?"

"Everybody out," Connor shouted and the staff obeyed, making a hasty exit while casting pity-filled gazes at Becca on the way out.

"You guys, too," she said to her friends.

Sam shook his head. "I'm sorry, Becca, but one of us has to stay for evidentiary reasons."

"You two go," Connor said. When Sam and Kait moved toward the stairs, he turned to Becca. "I'll wait over in the corner. Tell me when you're finished."

Becca wanted to argue, but Connor was just doing his job. They couldn't leave her alone with the body. The body. Ha! When had Becca started calling her friend the body?

Becca believed in God. Molly had been the one to teach her about Him. About living a life with purpose, making a difference. And that's what Becca had spent her life trying to do, even as she tortured herself for leaving Molly behind.

Becca took her friend's beaten and battered hand to offer a prayer. When she finished, she stood quietly by Molly as time ticked past. Becca dug deep for the resolve that she'd used to get through life thus far. She'd been around and had seen things no kid should have to see. Lived a life that no kid should have to live. But then came Molly. Her friend. The girl who proved that there were good and decent people in the world.

Tears clouded Becca's vision, but she couldn't stop the direction her thoughts were going. Molly had been right. There were good people in the world. Becca had been blessed to know several of them, but now . . . now there was one less.

And Van Gogh was going to pay.

# Chapter Twenty

CONNOR HATED EVERY moment of watching Becca's agony, but she needed this time to find closure on a lifetime of torment regarding Molly. The moment Becca released her friend's hand and stepped back, he crossed over to her. Her shoulders were pulled back, that fiery look of determination in her wounded brown eyes.

"I'll walk you to the car," he offered.

"I'm staying with Molly until the ME collects her."

"Molly's gone, honey. She won't know if you're here or not. And Marcie will take good care of her."

"I don't care. I'm staying." The tears he'd expected earlier slid down her cheeks, and she blinked rapidly. "Kait said Molly had a family. Have they been notified?"

"Not yet. I'll stop by to see her husband after we finish with the scene, and I clean up."

"I want to go with you."

"I hate to sound like a broken record, but that's not the best idea."

"For who?" She eyed him. "It will be better coming from me. I knew Molly. Loved her. They'll want to hear that."

"But having you there could affect the husband's willingness to speak freely." *Not to mention distract me.*

"Then I'll step out of the room, if necessary."

"I'm not going to win on this, am I?"

"No," she said sadly. "If you don't let me go with you, I'll head over there and tell him myself."

"Then we'll go together."

"Okay to come in?" Marcie poked her head around the corner. Even in the dark, dank basement, her red hair shone brightly.

"Please," Becca said, and Connor was thankful that Marcie had caught the case. She'd treat Molly with the utmost dignity.

Marcie entered wearing a Tyvek suit rolled up at the ankles due to her petite stature. Her feet were covered in booties, her hands with gloves, and she carried her field kit. She stopped next to Becca and squeezed her arm. "Kait told me the victim was your foster sister."

Becca nodded, and Connor could see she was still working hard to control her tears. He hoped she wouldn't fight them for long. She needed to let go and release some of her pain.

Marcie stepped over to the body and stared down at her as Connor and Becca took the other side. Becca took Molly's hand in hers, as if protecting her from Marcie. Connor wanted to do the same thing—take Becca's hand and lead her out of this mess to protect her from additional pain.

Marcie gritted her teeth and peered at Becca. "I'll do everything within my power to make sure the creep who did this is caught."

Becca nodded. "She's obviously been tortured, but can you see a cause of death?"

Marcie shook her head, her corkscrew curls vibrating, but she didn't speak. It was unlike her. Connor figured Marcie was likely holding her tongue because Becca was in the room.

"How about time of death?" Becca prodded.

Marcie looked at Molly. "I would only be speculating, and it wouldn't hold up. The best thing I can do to advance the investigation is to get Molly to the morgue."

"You can't even hazard a guess?" Becca asked.

"I know you want answers, Becca, but it's going to take time. Please be patient with me while I do this the right way," Marcie said firmly. "I'll let my assistant know that we're ready to load up the bo—Molly." She started for the stairway.

"Marcie," Becca called after her.

Marcie turned. "Yes."

"Thank you for being here for Molly."

Marcie waved a hand. "No thanks necessary. I'm glad to do whatever I can to help."

Becca turned her attention back to Molly. There was nothing Connor could do for Becca so he stood to the side as they waited for Marcie to return with her assistant. Today, Sandra accompanied Marcie, walking into the room with her gaze fixed on the floor. Sandra rarely made eye contact and seemed to live in the same world as the corpses she helped deliver.

Becca helped Marcie and Sandra move Molly's body into a black body bag. Connor expected Becca to move away when the odor released from moving the body filled the room, but she stood strong. Marcie started closing the zipper on bag.

Becca blew a kiss to Molly and tucked her friend's hand into the bag, then stepped back. When the bag was fully zipped, her tears flowed freely. Connor's intention to allow her some space shattered at the sight of her grief. He circled his arm around her shaking shoulders and escorted her out of the room.

On the upper level where the air was clearer, he took her in his arms and held her while she sobbed. Marcie and Sandra trudged up the steps and loaded Molly onto a gurney that creaked over the rough wood floors. Connor continued to hold Becca until her crying subsided. Law enforcement officers were a tough breed, usually managing to keep it together, in even the most difficult situations. They grieved, railed, and fell apart in private.

Becca would be embarrassed in the morning for breaking down, but at least he'd kept her out of view of other officers.

When she stilled, he leaned back and resisted swiping away a tear. "Let's find Kait and have her take you home for a shower. I'll do the same thing when I'm done here, then pick you up to go see the husband. Okay, honey?"

She nodded, her lower lip trembling. She pressed her fingers over his shirt where her tears had darkened the fabric. "I've made a mess of your shirt."

"No worries," he said. "It's there whenever you need it."

She smiled up at him. A tremulous smile that tugged at his heart. He backed away before he did something stupid like kiss her. That was the last thing she needed right now. The last thing he needed, too.

"You good to go?" He gestured at the door.

She dabbed her eyes with the cuff of her shirt. "I'll bet I look a mess."

"Kind of raccoonish," he admitted.

She rubbed under her eyes and looked at him, the red rims evidence of her sorrow.

"Better." He forced out a smile.

She started for the door and with each step, her shoulders came up higher, and her trembling eased.

Outside, he breathed in the clean air, but he knew the stench of death still clung to his body. They met Kait and Sam by the car. Kait eyed Connor, not missing the wet patch on his chest.

"I'm so sorry, sweetie." Kait put an arm around Becca. "Let's get you home."

"Can you stay with Becca until I pick her up later?" Connor asked. "We have to notify Molly's husband."

Becca narrowed her gaze. "I don't need a babysitter. Or even a friend right now. I just want to be alone to process my thoughts."

"I'm still driving you home," Kait said.

"And I'm here if you need me," Connor added.

When she frowned, he shook his head slowly.

Becca was so strong. So independent. She didn't really need anyone in her life. Even with this horrible shock, she wanted to be alone. Maybe she really did want to spend her life alone. No husband. No family.

As Connor watched her and Kait drive away, the thought made him sadder than he'd been in a long time.

REGINALD ZOOMED IN the scope on his long-range sniper rifle to focus on Becca's face. She was stronger than he'd imagined. He'd suspected she would fall apart at seeing Molly's body, but then, he'd always wondered if Becca understood his purpose and that's why she let Molly go first. To make sure her friend experienced the joy of his cleansing.

She took a step closer to that big, burly cop from the other night. Reginald didn't like the man. He seemed far too involved with Becca. Reginald would have to watch that. Watch to see if she was sleeping with the guy.

"She'll be no use to you if she is," his mother said. "You must test her to be sure of her purity."

He put the rifle down to think. "Hopefully, she'll leave her backpack at home when I go in to get her DNA sample. I'll add a GPS tracker to it so I can tell where she is at all times. It would be better if I could track her via video or voice, but I just don't have those capabilities right now. At least not at a long distance. But . . . I could record her conversations and listen to them later."

"That would help," his mother said.

"Yes," he said absently, getting lost in his thoughts.

Maybe she'd provide positive proof that she was Lauren and the DNA he'd try to obtain tonight would just be icing on the cake.

THE SCALDING WATER pounded against Becca's shoulders, but she couldn't get rid of the smell of death. Molly's smell. She'd soaped her body several times, washed her hair at least four times. Nothing worked. She knew it was likely just her imagination, which couldn't let go of the gruesome crime scene. She should have listened to Kait, Connor, and Sam and stayed away. But if she had to do it all over again, she'd still spend time with Molly before Marcie performed the autopsy.

Besides, Becca had needed to see it. How else was she going to truly believe another person she loved had been taken from her?

She twisted the knob and toweled dry so forcefully that her skin burned. With the towel still wrapped around her body, she went to her closet and stood there, staring, trying to figure out what to wear. What did a person wear when she had to tell someone their loved one had been brutally murdered?

Did she wear a suit to make them realize it was a professional call from the get-go? Or did she dress casually, in her jeans and a T-shirt, so as to not give any warning until the words were out? She just didn't know. She'd never had to do it until she and Connor visited Allie's mother. It was bound to be even harder when the news pertained to someone she cared about. And she'd loved Molly. Fiercely.

In the end, Becca chose a compromise—khaki pants, a button-down blue shirt, and semi-casual shoes. She dressed quickly and towel-dried her hair before pulling it back in a ponytail.

"You can do this," she said to herself in the mirror, while slathering on face lotion. "You've survived worse things than doing a death notification."

*Like losing Molly*, Becca's mind screamed. Tears fought for release and she closed her eyes, forcing her thoughts to her single priority in life, now that Molly had been found. She had to find her killer. Find Van Gogh. Keeping busy was the way to deal with loss. No time to think. No time to feel. She'd done it before. She'd do it again.

Hoping Kait had somehow decided to take off, Becca stepped into the living room. Kait sat on the couch. She'd taken a quick shower in the spare bathroom and changed from her suit into jeans and a comfy top that Sam had dropped by. It looked like Kait intended to sit with Becca all night, but Becca wouldn't allow that, of course.

Kait stood, her eyes creased. "Feeling better?"

Becca wasn't about to start this conversation with Kait or she'd never leave.

"I'm good." Becca picked up her phone to see if Connor had called or texted. Nothing. "Does Sam have any idea when Connor will get here?"

"He's on his way now." She rested a hand on Becca's shoulder. "Why don't you sit down, and I'll make you a cup of tea?"

"I'm not sick, Kait, so don't treat me like I am." Becca took a deep breath. "In fact, you should just go home. Like I said before, I'd like to be alone."

"Dear, mistaken Becca." Kait drew her into a hug. "You're heading right back to becoming the woman I knew when we first met."

Becca didn't return the hug. If she did, she'd start crying like a baby. And she also wouldn't say anything to encourage Kait to stay.

Kait pulled back. "You wouldn't let anyone get close then, and you're back behind that same wall, now."

"Nothing's changed." Becca sat down and pretended to check email on her phone.

"Right," Kait said. "You've just lost the woman you loved most in this world, and you're acting like it's just another day. If that doesn't mean you're hiding how you feel, I don't know what does."

"Give it a rest." Becca fired a warning look at Kait.

Kait's expression fell. Becca had hurt her. It was the last thing Becca had wanted to do. Kait, along with Nina, had been good friends for the last few years, and Becca didn't want to ruin that now.

Becca softened her voice. "Please, let it go, Kait. For me."

"Okay, as long as you don't shut me out." Kait perched on the edge of a chair. "You can't keep this bottled up. You're holding on to enough other stuff already. There's no room."

Becca opened her mouth to argue, but the doorbell rang. She raced for the door.

"Don't think this conversation is over," Kait called after her.

Becca took a moment to compose herself, then opened the door. Connor stood waiting. He'd changed into dark jeans, a long-sleeved shirt, and a blue jacket that brought out the dark color in his eyes. His hair was still wet, attesting to the fact that, after his shower, he'd raced right over there.

"Ready?" he asked.

Thankful he didn't ask how she was doing, she nodded. "Just let me grab my things." She turned and held the door for him to step inside.

"Kait," he greeted. "Sam's gone home to shower and will be over soon to pick you up."

Good, Sam was taking Kait home.

"Keep an eye on her," Kait said as if Becca wasn't in the room. "She's pretending to be okay with this, but I know she's not."

Connor eyed her, his gaze compassionate as he searched. Somehow, his intense study was different from Kait's, and Becca actually didn't mind it. Which was a problem, in itself. She was letting him get too close. *She* was getting too close. Hadn't Molly's death just showed her the pain that came with opening herself to love?

"We should get going." She stepped out the door and didn't stop until a group of costumed children charged across her path on the sidewalk.

"I forgot it was Halloween," she said to Connor.

"No problem. I've taken care of it for you." He opened the back door of his car and lifted out a garment bag. "Costumes for both of us."

She shot him a surprised looked. "You can't seriously think I would, a) ever dress up to go out on Halloween, and b) do it right after seeing Molly."

"Not for fun, no. But I thought we could keep an eye on the gang at the credit card apartment afterward. Maybe we'll get lucky and grab Willow."

"I know I said I wanted to go back there, but not tonight, Connor."

"I get that you're hurting and it cuts me to the core, but tonight is perfect. First, it'll take your mind off Molly. Second, we're dealing with teenagers, and they'll be partying. Their guard will be down. We can hang out on their street and no one will be suspicious. We won't get another chance like this again."

"I suppose you're right." She mulled it over for a second, her curiosity growing over what the bag contained. "What kind of costumes did you get?"

"Ah, see, that's where you're going to have to trust me. You'll have to agree to come with me first."

"That's not fair." Trusting was the hardest thing for her to do. With his astute detective skills, he'd have to have picked up on that by now. Maybe this was a test. An easy one, really. How bad could it be?

"Okay, fine," she agreed, albeit reluctantly. "We'll do it. But not to have fun. It's all business."

"It always is with you," he said sadly. "It always is."

He reached for the passenger door to open it for her. She didn't know if he did it out of pity, or if he was just an old-school kind of guy. Either way, she could open her own door, which she did and plopped onto the seat.

His work car was immaculate, but the cup holder held two lidded foam cups.

"I got you some tea." He pointed at the cup closest to her. "Sam said you liked chai."

"Thanks," she mumbled, hating this feeling that everyone wanted to do something for her. She didn't need help. She had things under control.

He merged the car onto the road, and she lifted the cup. "Would you mind stopping with all the pity? Everyone has been treating me like fragile china today. It honestly makes me uncomfortable. So just be yourself. Please. Even if that's more annoying."

"I'm happy to oblige." He grinned. "One annoying detective at your service."

# Chapter Twenty-One

THE MASK ITCHED. Reginald resisted lifting the chin and scratching until he was safely inside Lauren's apartment. He glanced down the deserted hallway, and then worked the lockpicks in Lauren's door. He'd mastered this skill at his mother's insistence. She'd said he never knew what kind of situation he'd need to overcome to take his girls.

The lock clicked, and he took one last look down the hallway before stepping inside and closing the door. He appreciated the cover that the costume provided, but he didn't need it inside, so he ripped off the infernal ninja hood. The irony of the night made him mad. Halloween was the only night of the year he could go out in public and not worry that someone would run in revulsion from his scars. They'd stare at him as usual, but then compliment him on his mask, maybe ask him where he got it. It drove him crazy, but at least he could spend the day out of the house. But tonight, he couldn't risk being recognized by a cop on patrol, or getting picked up by security cameras that were everywhere these days, so he'd worn the costume he'd bought online when he was younger.

He clicked on his flashlight and fell back against the door in surprise. The room was filled with information about him. A current drawing. Police files. Pictures of the girls. He was at first repulsed, but then he got it. This was perfect. Lauren had been looking for him, too. He hadn't counted on that. She must have realized she shouldn't have run and wanted to be with him as much as he wanted her.

"Yes!" He shot his fist up. "I knew we had a connection. She felt it, too."

"Really?" Billy said. "How can you be so dense sometimes? You haven't even proved Rebecca Lange *is* Lauren. All this proves is that an FBI agent is trying to catch you."

Reginald ignored Billy's insult. Reginald preferred to think he'd been right the first time. His gut confirmed it, so he wouldn't bother thinking about that until the DNA results came back.

He flexed his fingers in the latex gloves. The temperatures had fallen throughout the day, becoming much more like fall in Portland, and the cold weather always tightened the scar tissue and made his hands ache. The tight latex caused them to throb even more. Maybe he'd sell the house and move to Florida with Lauren. If he let her live.

He went to her bathroom and studied her hairbrush with a magnifying glass. He collected not only the minimum five strands of hair with roots for the DNA test but took as many as he could find. He pocketed the sample and went back to the living room where he'd seen her backpack and laptop.

He carefully unloaded the canvas pack. He stroked the side of his face with her gloves, inhaling her scent. He remembered that smell. Becca was Lauren. There was no question in his mind.

"Or are you just wanting it to be so?" his mother asked.

"No, Mother. I'm sure. This is Lauren."

"We'll see."

He rarely got mad at Mother, but she was pushing it.

He used his pocketknife to make a small slice in the interior lining of her backpack in the bottom corner where she'd never notice. He slipped in his mini GPS tracker and looked at the pack. The device was obvious if he stared at it, but then, how often did she unload everything from the pack and stare at the bottom? Never, he hoped.

He reloaded the pack and wished he had time to study every item, but he couldn't take the chance of getting caught. He moved on to her laptop that was sitting on the table surrounded by files containing information about him.

"Oh, Lauren, you are so detailed," he whispered. "You really do want to be with me, don't you?"

It took several tries to discover her password, but on a lark, he entered the word "Molly" along with the date he'd taken her and Lauren in several configurations. Bingo. He was in. He opened a Word document and took note of the most recent file names so he could reopen them and not leave a trail of his work.

Now. The note—a suicide note. When she disappeared with him, he hoped her fellow law enforcement buddies would see her suicide note and stop looking for her. He typed . . .

*If you're reading this, I am dead. I'm sorry, but after seeing Molly, I can't go on any longer. I've tried, but life holds no meaning without her. Please don't waste your time searching for me. I've always been fascinated by drowning and think this is the best way to go. Forgive me if I've hurt you. I don't mean to.*

*Love, Becca*

Yes. Perfect. He saved the document in an obscure part of her hard drive so she wouldn't find it, but when she disappeared, the cops would discover it in a computer search.

He closed the document and reopened the most recent documents in order, leaving everything as he'd found it. Then he logged out and watched until the screen went back to sleep before closing the lid and stowing it again.

He smiled. He was almost there. Almost with Lauren. He put on the mask again, not even caring now that it was hot and itchy. With a quick check of the hallway, he was on his way toward the street without notice.

At the end of the hall, he turned to look at her door one last time.

*See you soon, my love. Very soon.*

"A PRINCESS, REALLY?" Becca tugged at the low-cut neckline and shoved the garment bag holding her clothes at Connor. "You see me as a princess?"

"Not in the traditional sense, no." He latched on to her gaze. "I just think you've gotten some rough breaks and someone needs to see you as their princess. You deserve to be spoiled for a night."

Her expression instantly softened, and Connor knew he was lost. Totally and completely lost and under her spell. He touched her cheek.

"Will you be my princess for the night?" he asked, inserting humor in his voice to lighten the mood.

Mixed emotions flashed through her eyes. "On one condition."

"Name it," he said, and waited for her demands.

"If we arrest Willow, you'll book her. Because I'm definitely not going to go into the station dressed like this." She took a step back and planted her hands on her hips.

Her reply wasn't at all what he expected. Couple that with the consternation on her face and her hands lodged on hips that the dress accentuated, and he couldn't contain his laughter.

She socked him in the chest, then grinned, too. "Of course, you might not want to go in dressed like that, either."

"What's wrong with my knight costume?" He took a step back and bowed. "I made sure to get one with pants instead of tights, and I am armed, after all." He clapped his hand on the hilt of his plastic sword. "Just think of me as a medieval police officer."

She rolled her eyes and shifted the bodice of her costume. "You just picked this stupid costume for the cleavage."

"Hey, now," he complained. "I chose the most modest outfit I could find. I could have gotten you a naughty nurse or Cat Woman costume, instead. Or even worse." He gave her an evil grin.

She laughed. "You were right. As much as I hate that this is happening on the same day we found Molly, I needed a laugh. And I know she would approve of me trying to solve this thing instead of wallowing in my grief."

Connor shoved the garment bag in the police issue sedan and held out his arm. "Then come, my princess. Let us alight onto the streets and make merry."

She slipped her gun and shield into the small drawstring purse that came with the costume. "You'd better hope I don't need this to back you up. It's gonna be a real pain to get my gun out."

"Me, need backup, with this at my side?" He tapped his sword again. "Never."

She laughed, and put her hand on his arm. They'd parked near a convenience store to change in the bathrooms, and the apartment was several blocks away. As they walked, contentment settled over him for the first time in years. It felt as if something that had been worrying him was finally resolved, but he didn't know what it was. Strolling down the street like this, arm in arm, Becca's lighthearted laughter of a moment ago still ringing in his ears, he could imagine the fun they'd have on a date. On many dates.

"I think Finn took the news about Molly as well as could be expected, don't you?" Becca said.

She quickly burst his bubble of contentment, bringing up the memory of telling Molly's husband about her death. "I think, considering that she'd been missing for nearly a week, he expected to hear something like this. At least, I would have."

"But you're a cop. You always expect the worst."

He opened his mouth to refute her comment, but she was right. Anyone in law enforcement for any amount of time came to expect bad things and was pleasantly surprised when things went the other way.

"I wish Finn could have given us something to help find Van Gogh," Becca continued. "People don't just up and vanish. There has to be something the detective handling the missing person case missed."

Connor didn't like that she automatically suspected that someone in his department had screwed up, but grieving people often had to place blame, and he'd give her a pass tonight. "I'll meet with him in the morning to pick up his files."

She looked up at him. "Don't forget to ask for the computer they took into evidence."

"I'll get it to you as soon as I can."

They turned the corner, and he spotted a raucous party on the porch of the house next to the apartment building.

"You up for a party?" he asked.

She smiled again. "Thought you'd never ask."

They approached the walkway, and Becca came to a stop. "There. On the right side. Do you think that's Willow?"

Connor focused ahead. "Maybe. But that would be too easy, wouldn't it?"

"Yes. At least, based on how this investigation has gone so far."

Connor surveyed the scene. Ten people stood on the porch, a dozen or more in the yard. They were rowdy. Drunk. Which translated to unruly and hard to reason with. Things could get ugly fast.

"We need to get her off the porch and away from the crowd," he said. "Let's work our way up to her. Casually. Maybe grab a beer from the keg on the way past. I'll hit on her. Get her to step off the porch with me. You come up from behind. Cuff her." He turned his back to the crowd, lifted his shirt, and jerked his cuffs from the belt. "You got room for these in your girly bag?"

She scowled at him and snatched them out of his hand. "I promise you will pay for this costume."

"I already did. It wasn't cheap."

She rolled her eyes.

"Okay." He stretched, as if he was headed into a boxing ring. "Time to get my game on with Willow."

"Fine." Becca stared up at him. "But you don't have to sound so happy about it."


BECCA WAS NO LONGER having fun. Watching Connor flirt wasn't all it was cracked up to be. It was even harder because he was really good at it, and Willow had fallen for his lines. She was dressed as Snow White, and with her short, dark hair, she looked the part.

He suddenly swooped her off her feet and started across the porch. "Make way—a fair maiden in distress needs to be rescued."

She giggled and wrapped her arms around his neck. The crowd parted, and the men whistled and cheered him on.

*Like he needs encouragement.*

He appeared to be enjoying every minute of this charade—the way Willow kept touching him, whispering in his ear. Becca hated it, hated each and every minute of being forced to watch him flirt with someone else. Even if it was for a case.

He put Willow down on the ground, but her arms remained around his neck. He peered over her head, looking at Becca and urging her to hurry up. She reached into her bag for the handcuffs as she eased up behind Willow. Not that she needed to be so careful. Willow was far too wrapped up in Conner to notice.

Connor took both of Willow's hands from around his neck and spun her around, clasping her wrists together. Becca snapped on the cuffs.

Connor turned her to face him. "Sorry, fun time is over, Willow." Connor held out his shield. "I'm Detective Warren and this is FBI Agent Rebecca Lange."

"This is about the credit cards isn't it? Danny finally cracked and told you about me."

"You're gonna wish it was just about the credit cards." Becca's anger over losing Frankie came through in her voice. "You're under arrest for identity theft *and* the murder of Frankie Otto."

"Frankie? You mean Roxanne's little sister? I didn't kill her." Her eyes were wide with fear.

Becca stepped closer. "But you did impersonate her at the hospital, at which time you created a record under her name stating she had no allergies. FYI, Frankie was deathly allergic to Cefoxitin. The doctors checked her records before dispensing the drug, but because you claimed she had no allergies, Cefoxitin was administered. She died."

"Oh, no . . . really . . . no. I didn't mean . . . I just was so sick. I couldn't afford—oh no."

Connor looked at Becca. "You want me to call a uniform to take her in?"

Becca shook her head.

"But the costume," he reminded her.

Becca's desire to see Willow behind bars overrode her need to look professional. "I've changed my mind. Let's get her booked."


BECCA LOOKED UP at Connor as they stood outside her apartment door. "Do you think Willow was on the up and up? That she didn't hack Elise's computer and didn't give the network password to anyone else, much less the credit card kingpin?"

"What she said made sense, that her boss didn't need one little home computer when he had connections to data that we couldn't begin to fathom."

"But that's what confused me. First, we have a number of logins on the network so she had to give it to other people and I think she's lying to us about that. Second, this guy is into running local credit card scams, but Willow made it sound more like he was into Internet hacking for insurance data. Considering that's such a lucrative business, why would he be running these local scams, too? Maybe she's lying about that, too."

"Maybe he simply buys data from a hacker," Connor suggested.

"Okay, say he gets the insurance information that way. It still doesn't explain opening credit cards in the foster kids' names." Becca shook her head. "It makes no sense that he'd be engaged in both of these areas."

"You'll figure it out, I know you will."

Becca looked up a Connor, her heart heavy. "Yeah, eventually. But if it takes too long, we could have another report of a hospital visit gone very wrong."

"Sleep on it. Maybe it'll make more sense in the morning."

She nodded. He lifted a hand as if he was planning to touch her, but she backed up and opened her door. "Goodnight, Connor."

"Becca," he said, then fell silent and shook his head. "Sleep tight."

The last thing she was going to do was sleep. She didn't even take off the infernal costume before booting up her laptop. She grabbed a glass of water and sat down to check her email. An alert popped up on the screen, catching her by surprise. The message box noted three failed login attempts during the time she'd been out with Connor.

Someone had been here. In her apartment. On her computer. They could still be there.

Fear raced down her spine. She jerked her gun from the little purse and put her back to the wall as she pondered her next step. She'd grabbed a glass of water from the kitchen after saying goodnight to Connor at the door, so she knew the kitchen was clear. The living room was obviously clear, as well. That only left the bedrooms and bathrooms

She eased down the hallway, one foot at a time. Swinging the guest bathroom door open, she searched the space. Nothing had been disturbed. Back in the hallway, she slowly approached the bedroom and glanced quickly inside. Then she looked again. Clear, too.

She hurried to her bathroom, then her bedroom, taking a longer look. She checked the walk-in closet, then got down on her knees to check under the bed. Dust bunnies, but no intruder.

At the front door, she found no sign of a break-in. Maybe there was a slight nick on the deadbolt. It could be from lock-picking tools, or maybe it had been there all along. She'd never looked at the lock that closely. No one else had a key to her apartment except the property manager.

She dialed the after-hours number for the manager.

"Yeah." His sleepy voice came on the line.

"Did you let someone into my apartment tonight?" she demanded, then cautioned herself not to sound so accusatory.

"No."

"You're sure?"

"Look, lady, I've been home with the wife all night. If you don't believe me, ask her."

"No, I believe you." *I just don't like what that means.* She apologized for disturbing him and hung up.

So, now what? Did she call the police? If she did, what could they do?

Write a report. Take prints. Tell her to be careful. Fingerprints, yes. She definitely needed prints, and she didn't have the necessary equipment to lift them. She could call a tech guy from her office, but it would probably be good to have a police report on file in case this had nothing to do with Van Gogh.

*Right, not Van Gogh. You're nuts if you think that. He knows who you are, and he's coming after you, like he came after Molly.*

So, the cops. Should she call them? If she did, she could cause all kinds of problems for Vance. He still hadn't released the info about Van Gogh to the rank and file. One look at this room, and the officer would know what was going on. And she couldn't put all of this away without disturbing the crime scene.

There was only one thing to do. Call Connor.

As she dialed his number, she wished that making this call bothered her half as much as it would have when they'd first partnered on this investigation. Now she was glad he was there for her.

"Warren," he answered, sounding distracted.

"I need your help."

"Becca." His voice was suddenly alert. "What's wrong?"

"Someone tried to log in to my computer while I was out. When I booted it up, I got the warning screen."

"At your apartment?"

"Yes, I cleared the place," she continued, letting him know she was okay. "But I thought it would be a good idea to check for prints on my keyboard. I didn't want to bother you, but if a patrol officer came in here with all the Van Gogh information on display . . ."

"He'd put two and two together, and the word would get out." He sounded like he was moving around in his car. "You're sure you thoroughly cleared the space? Closets. Under the bed, the—"

"I know what I'm doing, Connor."

"I know, I just . . . I'm on my way. Keep the door locked and your weapon handy."

"I will. See you—"

"No! Don't hang up. I'm only a few miles away, and I want you to stay on the line with me until I get there."

"Isn't that overkill?"

"No, geez, Becca. We're hunting a psychopath here. Don't let your guard down. Ever. Not even as long as it takes me to drive a few miles."

# Chapter Twenty-Two

"THANK GOODNESS you're okay." Connor dropped his bag to the floor and grabbed Becca up in a hug. She held her body stiff for a moment, but then she melted into his arms. Her head came down on his chest, and he inhaled her unique vanilla scent, reminding him of coming home after school to fresh-baked cookies. "You scared the crap out of me."

She leaned back to look up at him. "But I told you I cleared the place, and I wasn't in any danger. Then you talked to me all the way here, so you knew I was fine."

*Cleared?* He needed to double-check. He set her away and drew his weapon. "You stay here. I'm just gonna have a look around."

"It's not necessary, Connor."

"Yes it is," he snapped a little too forcefully, his mind back to the threat. He didn't care if Becca pronounced it safe and was glaring at him as he made his way through the apartment. The thought that someone—maybe even Van Gogh—had been there, in her home, touching her things, made Connor's skin crawl in a way he'd never experienced before.

It was time he admitted that he'd let Becca get to him. Fully and completely. When she'd called, he forgot all about the women who'd betrayed him in the past. He knew Becca wasn't anything like Gillian or his mother. He could trust Becca.

He finished his inspection, including looking for any cameras that the intruder might have planted, and returned to the living room where he found Becca going through her file boxes.

"Anything missing?"

"Not that I can tell, but then there's so much stuff here, I might not notice until I need it."

"There's no sign he's disturbed anything else. I checked for any cameras he might have placed, just in case."

She shot him a surprised look. "I didn't even think of that. Thank you."

He watched her for a long time. Despite residual concern, he had to smile.

"What?" she asked.

"I thought you hated the costume."

She groaned. "I was going to change."

"I don't know, I might never change out of mine," he laughed. "It worked wonders on Willow."

"Ah, but Willow is all of sixteen and has no taste." She gave him a pointed look. "Can we get started with the prints?"

"Why? You have somewhere else to go in that dress?"

She rolled her eyes.

"Okay, fine. Enough teasing. We can print the place, but I have to be honest with you. If your intruder got in here undetected, it's likely he wore gloves." Connor grabbed his bag from by the door and reached for his fingerprint kit.

Becca eyed him. "You don't think this was Van Gogh, do you?"

He shrugged.

"It has to be him. I . . ."

"You what?"

She suddenly looked away. "Maybe you're right. Maybe I'm just being paranoid. It could be related to the credit card investigation instead."

"It's certainly not a routine break-in. Not with your TV and computer still sitting here." Connor started to open his kit, then paused to reassess. "You know what? This is too important to screw up. If it *was* Van Gogh, and he left any prints, we might be lucky enough to get a match in AFIS." Connor dug out his phone. "I'll call Dane."

"I'll put on a pot of coffee." She went to the kitchen, and Connor made the call.

"Dude, do you know what time it is?" Dane grumbled. "I've gotten like two hours sleep in the last three days, and I'm not on call."

"Sorry, man. But when you're the best at what you do, you're in demand."

"Sucking up isn't going to make me any happier," Dane complained.

"But at least, it might make you listen to my request."

Dane sighed out a long breath. "I'm listening."

"Someone broke into Becca's apartment tonight and tried to log on to her computer. There's a possibility it could be Van Gogh. If so, we might have his prints on her keyboard."

"Why didn't you say so in the first place?" Dane said.

Connor had no rebuttal, so he gave Dane the address and disconnected.

The smell of fresh coffee and a sweet, sugary aroma drew him toward the kitchen. The coffee was dripping into the pot, the oven on. Becca stood with her hands on the counter, her head bowed, her shoulders shaking. He hated to see her cry, but he knew she needed to find release from all of the stress. But that didn't mean she had to cry alone.

"Honey." He gently turned her toward him.

She sniffed. "I'm not usually like this."

"No need to apologize. So much has happened to you. Let it out and you'll feel better."

He was tempted to draw her into his arms, but held back, thinking his touch might be unwelcome. But when she looked up at him, her eyes glistening with tears, he gathered her close.

She settled back against his chest, into the spot that felt natural and right to him. He stroked her back while she cried, soaking his shirt again. He loved the fact that she didn't feel the need to keep him at arm's length any longer. When her sobbing slowed and turned to hiccups, she drew back and looked up at him. Tears clung to the hollows under her eyes.

He gently brushed them away. She seemed so fragile. His strong, stubborn Becca, fragile and needing him. That got his blood boiling, and he must have transmitted the change in his emotions because her eyes suddenly sparked with mirrored heat.

He unclipped her hair, letting it fall over his hands. He dropped the clip to the counter and slid his fingers in to cup the back of her head. "Becca, I . . ."

"I know," she whispered. "I know."

He lowered his head, questioning her with his eyes. She didn't discourage him, so he went for the kiss. His lips met hers softly at first to keep from scaring her, but she was the one who deepened the kiss and clung to him like a lifeboat. He lost all control and returned the kiss with a passion he'd never before felt, but wanted to continue to feel. Now. For today. For tomorrow. For as long as she'd have him. She might have closed off her emotions, but he'd take whatever she was ready to give.


BECCA VAGUELY HEARD the doorbell ringing. Connor was kissing her. Kissing her! His lips were so soft. Full, warm. Just like she'd thought kissing him would feel. She didn't want it to end, but it had to.

It was wonderful to kiss him, to be cared for by him, but that was all. A relationship wasn't possible. Not until she told him she was Lauren and she'd left Molly behind.

The bell buzzed again. She still couldn't break contact. Not yet. Just another moment. Then she would put up that wall again. *Yes, just a moment.*

Their visitor pounded on the door.

Connor suddenly lifted his head, his eyes glazed with longing. He took a deep breath and let it out on a shudder. "That'll be Dane. One look at you, and he's going to know what was going on in here." Connor ran a thumb over her lips, then down to her chin. "Sorry for the whisker burn."

"I didn't even know it was there." She touched her own face, her fingers locking with his. "Maybe I should go freshen up while you let Dane in."

He set her away, then grabbed her hand and jerked her back against his chest. Kissed her soundly again. "This isn't a one-time thing, you know."

"I know," she said. "But I'm not ready for more than this."

"Then we take it slow, okay?"

She nodded, willing to agree to anything at this point.

The knocking grew more urgent.

"Coming," Connor shouted, then released her.

She stood there, touching her lips, feeling bereft at his departure and relieved at the same time. She'd let her emotions go with Connor several times now. She'd never done that before, at least, not since Van Gogh. She needed a moment alone before seeing Dane. She fled in the other direction.

"To be continued," Connor called after her. "That you can count on."

She heard him laugh, then open the door and greet Dane.

"You call me out here in the middle of the night, then you leave me standing out . . . wait . . ." His gaze moved over Connor's shoulder to Becca. "Oh, I see. You two."

She glanced back.

"You two what?" Connor challenged in a tone that warned Dane to tread lightly.

"Nothing," Dane said. "Where's the computer?"

Connor caught her watching him and winked.

She hurried to the bathroom and caught her reflection in the mirror. Her face was flushed and her eyes glowed with something she'd never seen in them before—happiness. True happiness. The last few moments with Connor had brought her to life. Sure, there was a physical attraction, but this was more. She loved his integrity. His compassion. The way he could balance his easy-going nature with the demands of his job. This was a balance that worked for her. Besides, she liked being with him. Liked him, plain and simple, and wanted to spend time with him.

*It can't go anywhere. Not until you're completely honest with him.*

Her eyes lost their gleam and the fear that had lived with her for years returned. She might be in law enforcement, might put on a tough-guy act, but deep down, she was still that scared girl that Van Gogh had tried to mutilate. She was still Lauren, and would continue to be Lauren until she got some closure. More therapy? Maybe. Better yet, she had to find Van Gogh and make him pay for his crimes. She had to know he couldn't hurt her or anyone else, anymore. That's what she needed to focus on right now. Not Connor's kisses. Not the joy of having him around. She had to focus on Van Gogh and only Van Gogh.

Resolved, she splashed her face with cold water and patted it dry. Perfect. The tough agent had returned.

She thought about changing out of this confounded princess dress, but then Dane might think she wasn't taking this break-in seriously enough. So she kept the outfit on and joined the pair hunkered over her computer. Dane was concentrating so hard, he didn't even look up. But Connor did. His lips turned up in a suggestive smile.

She didn't return it. Wouldn't return it.

"Anything, Dane?" she asked.

"Got a few latents from the door and chair, but they could be yours." Dane finally looked up and grinned. "Nice dress."

"Halloween," she said, and let it go at that. "When you're done with the computer, I can pull up my prints on AFIS, and we can see if we have a match."

He nodded and went back to work.

Her kitchen timer beeped. "I forgot. I put one of Nina's famous cakes in the oven. Did you want some? Or some coffee?"

"You know it," Dane said. "Coffee, black. Cake, big." He chuckled.

"I'll help you get it," Connor offered.

"If you like." She knew she was acting really uptight, but she couldn't think of any other way to discourage him.

It didn't work. He traipsed behind her into the kitchen. The minute they were out of Dane's sight, he spun her around. "If this is a show you're putting on for Dane, you can knock it off. He's figured it out already."

"It's not a show," she replied. "I . . . we . . . shouldn't have kissed. Not now. Not when our focus needs to be on Van Gogh. We have to stop him. Getting involved with each other won't help with that."

"Becca," he said.

She held up her hand. "No. Van Gogh first. That's the only way I can deal with what's going on between us." She turned to the coffee pot and poured three cups, then pulled out the gooey cake. "Do you take anything in your coffee?"

"No."

It was only one word, but she heard disappointment, judgment, and anger mixed in the single syllable. She wanted to turn to him and take back her words, but this was the way it had to be.

She plated the cake. "If you'll grab a cup for you and Dane, that would be great."

"You sure it's not too personal for me to do that?" Connor's sarcasm stung.

"Connor."

"I know. That wasn't professional. Well, too bad." He took the cups and filled them, sloshing black coffee on the white countertop. She wiped it up and gave him plenty of time to get into the other room before following with her own coffee and the cake.

"Perfect timing. I'm done." Dane looked up and smiled. "We'll get your computer cleaned off after I have some of that cake. We can still check AFIS, but I think it may be a waste of time unless Van Gogh is a slight person."

"Explain, please," Becca said.

"There's a reasonable difference in the ridge density of prints from a male and from a woman, or a slight male, that I can see from casual field observation. If Van Gogh was able to get the girls up the trail, he's not likely a small guy, so the prints I lifted are most likely yours."

She nodded her understanding. "You guys go ahead and eat. I'll take care of the cleaning."

He patted the laptop. "Your baby, huh?"

"Exactly."

Dane tried to make small talk with Connor, but he continued to shut him down.

"Man," Dane said. "What happened in that kitchen anyway? It's like a freezer in here."

"Priorities changed," Becca said, and the room fell silent. She felt Connor watching her, but she stuck to her work and soon had her computer clean and ready to log in to AFIS. She brought up her own prints in the database.

Dane set down his cup, then carried a stack of white cards holding the fingerprints he'd lifted. He studied each card and frowned. "They're all yours."

"You're sure?" Connor asked.

"Positive," Dane said. "He must have worn gloves."

"So now we need to know what he was looking for. Maybe it wasn't even Van Gogh."

"If he modified any computer files, I'll be able to track his steps easily. If not, it'll take a bit more work." Becca started the search program running on her computer to look for modified files by date.

"I'm gonna take off." Dane started packing up his equipment. "Mind if I grab another piece of cake to go?"

"Help yourself." She continued to watch the search program as it ran through her files.

"Let me know what you find," she heard Dane say a few minutes later as he stepped out the door.

Connor remained standing behind her, looking over her shoulder and forcing her to work hard to keep her attention on the computer. The change log appeared.

"What in the world?" She sat back in surprise. "Weird. He added a Word document. Hid it in a folder I'd never look at. No one would, unless they were doing a forensic search."

"Can we open it?"

"Let me scan it first to make sure it's safe." She ran a virus and malware scan on the document.

"Okay." She double-clicked the icon. The document opened. She quickly read the message. She gasped and shot a look at Connor.

"It's a suicide note," she said in panic. "A suicide note."

"I can't see this being related to your credit card investigation." Connor started pacing. "I suppose it *could* be related to another one of your investigations." He stopped and stared at her. "Did you recently make anyone mad?"

She felt the weight of his question. "I send bad guys to jail, so of course I did. But not lately. And my password was related to Molly. Who else would have figured it out?"

"Then it has to be Van Gogh. But why you? Why take Molly as an adult? Why the change in his MO?"

Becca opened her mouth to tell him about her first abduction, to say she suspected Van Gogh was filling his empty jars and completing his collection, but the words wouldn't come out.

"Well, I'm not letting him get to you." Connor pulled her to her feet. "C'mon. We're going to pack you a bag, and you're staying at my place until this is over."

*Oh really?* She stared at him, Mr. Neanderthal at his finest. His nostrils flared and his eyes grew dark and penetrating. She didn't like this side of him. Not one bit. But she did like the thought of staying with him. Liked it too much, which was why she couldn't let it happen. "I'm sure Sam and Kait will let me bunk at their place."

"No."

"Excuse me?"

"I said no. This isn't negotiable, Becca. You will be under my protection until this is resolved. You got that?"

"Don't let this costume fool you, Connor. I'm not some damsel in distress."

"No, you're a very capable agent, but you also happen to be someone I care about." He folded his muscled arms across his chest and eyed her. "Don't test me on this. You won't win."

She knew when to give in. "Okay, but it'll be strictly professional."

He held up his hands. "Don't worry, I got the message loud and clear—keep my big mitts off."

"Then I'll pack a few things and be out in a minute." She headed down the hall, realizing she'd just lost a battle that she honestly hadn't wanted to engage in.

Frustrated, she thought about simply tossing some outfits into a bag, but her sense of order wouldn't let her. After changing out of the dress, she carefully folded several days' worth of clothes and put a few suits for work into a garment bag before gathering her cosmetics and returning to the family room.

"That was quick," Connor said, sounding surprised.

"This is only the first wave."

He eyed her. "You don't travel light, I guess."

"You got that right." She hung the garment bag on a doorframe. "I need to take all of my Van Gogh files, too."

"What?"

"He could come back here at any time and destroy things. Plus, you never know when we might need something. It'll be good to have the files handy." She tipped her head at her clothing. "Why don't you take that out while I file all of the items posted on the wall?"

He opened his mouth as if to argue, then turned and picked up her stuff. While he went to the car, she made quick work of gathering the loose items into a folder and packing up her pens and Post-it Notes.

They soon had everything loaded in his car and made the short drive in silence to his apartment. She'd expected a masculine place filled with black leather furniture, a big TV, and little décor. Instead, she was surprised to see a tastefully, yet sparsely decorated apartment.

She picked up a picture of his family. Seeing the smiling faces on the big happy group, jealousy bit into her. This was her dream staring back at her in a picture. A dream that might be hers if she and Connor could get over their issues.

And once Van Gogh was in prison.

"Nice apartment," she said to keep things light.

"It's comfortable." He dropped three file boxes on the floor. "It's my sister's doing, though. She thought I'd have better luck finding a wife if my place didn't scream 'confirmed bachelor'."

"Guess she was wrong, then," she joked, but it fell flat.

He frowned. "I'll go get the other files. Keep the door locked."

She twisted the deadbolt behind him and stared at the boxes. What should their next step be, other than for her to watch her back? Maybe get a good night's sleep so she was alert in case Van Gogh came for her? Could she even get a good night's sleep with Connor just down the hall? That was the question of the hour.

He made a few more trips, then twisted the deadbolt behind him, dou-ble-checking it before stacking all of the boxes in the corner while she stood like a dolt and watched him.

He ran a finger over the label on the top box that read "Detective Orman's Files." "You mentioned Orman's daughter. I'd like to talk to her tomorrow to see if she had any files you didn't have access to."

*Files.* Orman would have only had the personal ones that she hadn't seen. They could contain pictures of her as Lauren. Could include the details of how she became Rebecca Lange. It might be a good idea to tell Connor about her past right now. She wanted to. But tonight? It wouldn't change anything. And they'd both been through the emotional wringer. It could wait until the morning.

She looked up to find him carefully watching her. "I'll give Eva Waters a call first thing in the morning and set something up," she said.

He picked up her tote and garment bags. "It's late. We should get some sleep. You can take my room. I'll take the couch."

She looked at his sofa. There was no way he would fit on the apartment-sized piece of furniture comfortably. "I'm fine here."

"No," he said firmly. "I want you to get a good night's sleep."

"I don't—"

"Another non-negotiable point." He headed down the hallway, and she had no choice but to follow him.

He hung the garment bag in the closet and dropped her other bag on the bed that was neatly made. He crossed to an oak dresser and pulled out a set of sheets. "Mind helping me change the bedding?"

"I don't need—"

"Yes, you do." He ripped the striped comforter and cream-colored blanket from the bed. "My stepmother raised me right. She'd shoot me on sight if she heard I didn't give you clean bedding."

They worked in silence and soon, fresh white sheets waited for her. The crazy events of the day hit her hard, and she was suddenly overwhelmed. Tears pricked her eyes again. She was going to have to get a handle on this.

Connor grabbed some things from his closet and went to the door. "I'll be in the living room if you need anything."

"I still feel bad about kicking you out of your room."

"Don't." He stepped into the hallway.

"Connor," she called out suddenly, not wanting to be alone.

He stood waiting, his gaze intense and questioning.

"Thank you. For this, for your help, for everything," she said. "I'm sorry for earlier. I know I change like the weather. Hot, then cold. I wish things between us could be different, but they can't right now. Still, I want you to know how much I appreciate your care and concern. I've never felt so cherished before."

"Not even with your foster parents?"

"Yes, and no. I mean, I knew they were there for me, but I also knew it was only temporary. With you, it feels . . . it feels . . . different somehow."

He watched her for a few moments, then lifted his hand and reached toward her face, before letting it fall. "You should go to bed before I forget why I shouldn't kiss you again."

"I wish things . . ."

"Just go to bed, Becca. Now!" He slung his clothes over his shoulder and spun. His footsteps pounded on the wooden floor as he strode quickly away.

She wasn't hurt by his frustration. She was just put-out. The difference—the *big* difference—was that he was better at keeping his emotions under control. It was something she apparently still needed to learn before she got seriously hurt.

# Chapter Twenty-Three

THE NEXT MORNING, Connor sat across from Becca at his small dining table. She was wearing an old college sweatshirt and those stretchy yoga pants that women liked these days. Her face was scrubbed clean, her hair messed up. They'd both gotten up early and had been on the phone or checking email for a good hour now.

She was focused on her phone and wasn't paying him any attention, and yet, he was glad she was here. Liked it, actually. It felt right, normal even. He wouldn't mind doing it on a regular basis. Of course, if that were the case, he might be holding her free hand, or pressing his knee against hers. Just so he knew she was here for *him*, not for what he could do for her, as he was beginning to think.

"I got a text from Eva Waters," she said without looking up from her phone. "She'll see us at nine."

He glanced at his watch. "We've got an hour. You want to shower first or should I go?"

Her head popped up, and she actually blushed.

"I'll go first, then." He left the room before he could ask what she'd been thinking that had given her the red-hot face. He showered, shaved, and was ready in fifteen minutes. He made sure to hang up his towel and wash any lingering whiskers from the sink, then put out clean towels for her. When he got back to the living room, he found her digging through files.

"You looking for something in particular?" he asked.

"Just checking to see if there's anything missing, but so far it's all here."

He jerked a thumb at the hallway. "I put out towels for you. Let me know if you need anything else."

She nodded and took off down the hall. If her desire not to be in the same room with him didn't hurt so much, it'd be comical.

His phone rang. The caller ID confirmed it was Dr. Williams.

"Please tell me you've got something for me," he said by way of greeting.

"Hello to you, too," Dr. Williams replied.

"Sorry. This investigation is going nowhere fast, and I could use some good news. Has the DNA come back?"

"Not yet, but I did call in a favor with one of my associates to perform the hair analysis for free and rush the results."

"And?"

"And it was unremarkable except for Jane Doe One. She's recently been living in California, so you might want to expand your search to that state." She cleared her throat. "You'll also be interested to know that all three girls had broken hyoid bones."

"Meaning they were likely strangled."

"Yes." She didn't need to add that strangling was Van Gogh's preferred method of killing. It was a given. "I also had them check the hair for drugs. Three's showed meth, which would explain her dental issues. Two was positive for oxy and One and Four were clean."

"So we have a teenage meth user, a girl from California and, as we suspected from our talk with Two's mother, a girl addicted to pain meds."

"Exactly." She sighed. "That's all I have for now, but I'll keep you updated."

Connor thanked her and paced the room, pondering the news. Becca returned, her hair wet and in a ponytail, wearing a hint of mascara and eye shadow. She wore a plain business suit with a tailored white blouse, as usual.

"Dr. Williams called." Connor relayed the news.

Becca nibbled on her lip for a moment, obviously lost in thought. "If One is from California, she could fit the profile of a girl brought up the I-5 corridor for sex trafficking."

"I was thinking the same thing."

"I'll check with our agent on the Innocence Lost Task Force to see if she knows anything about missing girls."

"It's a shot in the dark, but worth the call."

Becca dialed the agent while he cleaned up from breakfast.

Becca talked for several minutes then hung up. "Blair knows of two girls who have disappeared recently. She has fingerprints on file, but no DNA, which is a bust for us. She does have some pictures, though. If Dr. Williams can arrange the forensic drawings, we might find something there. Blair's emailing the info to me."

"You'll need to loop Sam in on this. He'll add the girls to his current list." Happy they were managing to be professional, Connor looked at his watch. "We should get going."

They walked to the car in silence. Connor's mind was racing with unanswered questions, and he was frustrated at the lack of progress they were making. Becca seemed lost in thought, too. She could be pondering the same thing, or she could be wondering if Van Gogh was hiding in the bushes waiting to pounce. Connor wasn't worried about that. He could handle Van Gogh if he attacked. The only way the guy would get to Becca on his watch would be if Van Gogh shot Connor dead first.

Connor parked down the street from Eva Waters's townhouse community in a pricey area of Portland. He looked at Becca. "Remember. No mention of Van Gogh's new victims. You're just continuing with your past research."

"And how do I explain you?"

"I could be a boyfriend who's humoring you by helping." He grinned, but after the way they'd ended things last night, he knew it had to look forced.

"I doubt Eva will buy that."

"It worked with Willow. Why not now?"

"You mean besides the facts that everyone was drunk at the party, Willow's sixteen, and Eva's a sharp reporter?"

"I get your point, but I won't need to fake a thing. Not with this chemistry thing going on between us. We've both been fighting it for days. We might as well get some mileage out of it."

"I guess it's worth a try." She sighed.

He shot her a look. "Don't look so upset. There are worse things in the world than having me for a boyfriend."

"Right, like Van Gogh."

"So you're putting me in the same class as Van Gogh, huh? I didn't realize being with me was that close to slumming it." Surprised to find himself frustrated by such an innocuous statement, he jerked open his door and got out.

Becca met him on the sidewalk. "I wasn't comparing you to Van Gogh."

"I know." He shut her down with his tone and knocked on Eva's door. He kept his gaze trained straight ahead until Eva answered.

She was dressed in a business suit, and her blond, chin-length hair was sprayed into place. She had a reputation for being tenacious when on the air, so he knew they'd have their work cut out for them to keep from leaking any information that might put up her radar.

"Hello, Ms. Waters," Becca said. "Good to see you again. I'm so sorry about your father passing."

Eva turned her focus to Connor, and he wasn't surprised by her failure to acknowledge Becca's condolences. "And you are?"

He introduced himself without mentioning that he was a homicide detective. He slung his arm around Becca's shoulders. He felt her stiffen, but he continued. "Just tagging along to help Becca out." He gave an obnoxious wink. "Not much I wouldn't do to keep her happy."

Eva stepped back. "We should get to this. I don't have much time."

They moved into a living room that connected to an open kitchen. The décor was sleek and modern, fitting the image she portrayed on TV. He led Becca to the sofa where she'd remain within reach in case he needed to further feign their relationship.

"Take it easy," he whispered. "You're going to give this away."

He felt her shoulders relax.

Eva perched on the edge of a club chair. "So, in your message, you mentioned something about wanting to see my father's old files."

Becca nodded. "When I met with him last, he said he'd put a number of files in storage. Unfortunately, he never got around to sharing them with me."

"That surprises me." Eva crossed long legs. "He knew he was dying for quite some time, and he had everything so organized, I didn't really have to take care of anything. If he'd wanted you to see the files . . ." She shrugged.

"Maybe at that point it just wasn't that important to him," Connor suggested.

"Or," Becca said, "he may not have thought the files contained anything that could help with my investigation."

Eva raised a perfectly plucked brow that was penciled in to appear darker. "Why are you so interested in Van Gogh, anyway? The guy quit killing a long time ago, and we haven't heard a peep from him, since." The question sounded innocent enough, but Connor heard a deeper interest.

Becca must have picked up on it too, as she took a moment before answering. "Van Gogh abducted my foster sister. For years, I haven't known what happened to Molly, and I still want to find closure."

She was being careful. Not lying, but not outright saying that Molly had been found, either. Or that Becca had gone from looking for her friend to seeking revenge for her murder.

Eva watched Becca carefully. "And you think these files might help?"

Becca shrugged, and Connor liked how well she was downplaying this.

"I suppose it wouldn't hurt to tell you what I know." Eva pressed her hands on her knees, the blood-red color of her nail polish standing out next to her gray slacks. "I think Dad might have had a storage unit somewhere. If he did, he didn't want anyone to know about it. I found a padlock key hidden in the false bottom of a wooden box, but there isn't a paper trail for a lease or payments so I just can't be sure."

Becca sat forward, and Connor squeezed her hand, wordlessly telling her to relax.

"Why suspect a storage unit, then?" Becca asked. "The padlock could be for any number of things."

"True, but there were no work files in his apartment, which was odd for Dad. I know the Van Gogh case haunted him, and he never let it go. I'd often stop by and catch him reviewing old paperwork. So, let's just say the reporter in me has to wonder where those case files went."

"Maybe he disposed of them," Connor said.

Eva shook her head. "He wouldn't do that. If there was even the slimmest opportunity to bring Van Gogh to justice, he'd take it. I can't imagine him leaving this earth without giving the files to someone." She seemed to get emotional and looked up at the ceiling. "He passed sooner than we expected, so maybe he never got a chance to do it. All I know is, he wouldn't destroy them."

"What about an old partner?"

She frowned. "There was bad blood of some sort between them, and they hadn't spoken in years. Dad did go to say goodbye, but he still wouldn't have handed over his files." She fixed her gaze on Becca. "I honestly thought he'd have given them to you. But since you're here, asking about them, I guess that didn't happen. That further cements my theory that he stashed them somewhere."

"You're a reporter, Eva." Connor tried to sound in awe of her profession when he wasn't very keen on the media in any format. "Surely, you tried to track down this suspected storage unit."

"I've done a bit of research, but came up empty-handed."

"Would you be willing to give us the key and let us take over the search?" Becca asked.

Eva raised her chin and looked down her nose at Becca. "I highly doubt that you will get any further than I did."

"Did your father have a computer?" Becca didn't seem at all flustered by Eva's condescending look.

"Yes, a laptop. But if you're thinking you can search it and find information about the unit, I've already done so, to no avail."

"Ah, yes." Becca smiled. "But I have access to the best computer techs in the world. They can recover deleted information from the hard drive. That, you cannot do."

Eva appeared to weigh the comment. "Okay, fine. I'll give you the key under one condition."

"Name it." Becca's eagerness made Eva narrow her gaze.

"Whoa." Connor grabbed Becca's hand and laughed. "Back off, honey." He winked at Eva. "My little pit bull."

Eva looked disgusted at his infatuation with Becca. He was laying it on thick. Maybe too thick.

"So, your condition?" he asked.

"If the unit contains information that leads to Van Gogh's arrest, I want the exclusive on the story."

"We can do that," Becca promised, but Connor wasn't so sure they could make such a promise.

"Give me your word, Agent Lange, and the key is yours."

"You have my word." Becca held out her hand. "If we arrest him based on your lead, I'll give you an exclusive story on Van Gogh, if and when we find him."

Eva stared at Becca for a long moment then shook. "I'll get the key."

After she left the room, Connor faced Becca. "You can't promise that."

"I didn't say I'd give her an exclusive on Van Gogh's arrest, I just said I'd give her an exclusive story on Van Gogh. I'll do my best to honor the first, but conditions might mean she'll have to settle for the second."

"Well, if this does lead to the guy's arrest, you'd better do your best to give Eva what she wants. Something tells me you don't want to make an enemy of her."

Becca nodded, but still, she took the key and reiterated her promise before they headed back to the FBI office. There, they gave Orman's laptop to an analyst named Jae. Becca had raved about Jae all the way across town, but when Connor got a look at the woman, he wasn't so sure she could pull this off. She was short, her dark hair in pigtails and bangs, and on her stubby little fingernails, she wore the most horrid shade of green Connor had ever seen. She looked and sounded more like one of the homeless teens they'd been talking to.

"Go away, Becca," Jae said after taking the computer and clutching it to her chest. "The last thing I need is an audience."

Becca didn't verbally respond, but just stepped into the hallway. Connor followed.

"Is she always that rude?" he asked.

"Rude." Becca seemed to ponder the question as they walked toward her cubicle. "More like single-minded without any social skills. We cut her a lot of slack because she's so good at her job. Or maybe because she reminds us of how we used to be."

"You were like that?" He jerked his head at the door.

She laughed. "Yes, until I got to Elise's house. That's where I learned basic social skills."

"But the nail polish," he said. "You didn't wear anything that outrageous, did you?"

"Why, Connor Warren." She looked up at him. "Were you a goodie-two-shoes growing up?"

He was taken aback by her question and stopped walking to stare at her.

"You were." She came to a stop.

"Is that a problem?"

"Not at all. But I thought a guy with your looks would probably get into *some* trouble along the way."

"With my looks?" he clarified.

"You know. Good-looking. The kind of guy girls fall all over. Maybe the football quarterback."

"So you think I'm good-looking, do you?" He grinned as some sort of satisfaction settled in his heart.

"I didn't think I'd managed to hide that from you."

"You didn't. But I just wanted to hear you say it." He chuckled.

She socked him. If they hadn't been in the hallway of the very formal and uptight FBI building, he'd have kissed her. Thankfully, they were surrounded by FBI agents, because kissing her again would be a big mistake.

Her phone buzzed. She dug it out. "It's a text from Jae asking us to come back. Maybe she's found something."

"Could she really have located a lead that fast?"

"Jae's done this for a long time and knows exactly what to look for, so yeah, she could." Becca pivoted and marched back down the hall.

Connor had to hurry to keep up with her.

Jae sat in a chair, her back to the computer, her fingers bent. She spotted them and lifted a hand to blow on her fingertips. "Who's the best analyst in the building?"

"You are." Becca laughed.

"You know it." Jae swiveled back to the computer. "Is this invoice for a storage rental unit what you were hoping to find?"

Connor looked at the screen and recognized the address for the storage facility not far away. "There's no unit number."

Jae looked up at him. "Now come on, detective. Don't tell me you need me to go over there for you and get that information out of the attendant. Just say the word and I will, but . . ."

Connor laughed. Maybe under other circumstances, he'd take offense to her attitude. But after all the dead ends they'd run in to on this investigation, it was good to finally have a lead. This time, he'd cut the wonder kid some slack.

# Chapter Twenty-Four

IT WAS TIME TO TAKE Lauren. Reginald couldn't wait on the DNA report. His gut told him Rebecca Lange was indeed Lauren, and he couldn't take the chance that the annoying detective who followed her like a shadow would discover his location. First, he'd have to prepare for an extended time away from his house so that he could follow her. Then he'd find the perfect opportunity to announce his presence.

He went to his bedroom, parted his clothes in the closet, and released the hidden door. He grabbed the flashlight mounted just inside and snapped it on, revealing his secret five-by-five space. His gaze immediately went to his father's picture.

"Hello, Father." He touched the gold frame. "We haven't spoken in a while. Mother has been monopolizing my time."

His father never talked to him as Mother did, but the frustration on his father's face reminded him that his father had been hurt that Mother had kept them apart. Of course, she didn't know about this space. It was a kind of shrine to his dad, who'd passed from cirrhosis of the liver five years ago. Reginald had constructed the room on one of his mother's hospital stays for the heart condition that had ultimately taken her life.

He stepped up to the wall of rifles. "I think I'll use the StG 44, Father. You always wanted to own one of these. Too bad I only found this one recently, or we could have fired it together. It's as exceptional as you thought."

He reached for the rifle, and memories of the times he'd spent with his father collecting and shooting guns played like a video in his mind. The time at the range. The hunting trips. Swap meets. Gun shows. Father and son together, the way it should be. Then Reginald had turned ten and it had all ended. Father had started sleeping around. There had been woman after woman . . . until Mother had caught him. She caught everything.

"Not this room," he said proudly.

To build the room, he'd bumped into the attic space where Mother never went. She'd said she wasn't afraid to go in there, but for some reason, the attic terrified her and it was the only chink Reginald had ever seen in her armor. Whatever her reason, it perfectly fit his plans and he loved having a secret from her.

"Poor Father. You should have been more careful like I was. Then she wouldn't have thrown you out and told you never to come back."

Reginald hadn't seen this man who'd brought laughter and light to his life since that day. That was also when Mother had decided to start training him. He'd had to become serious, she'd said, or he would end up like Father. Alone and lost.

Reginald didn't want that. He wanted a wife and family. A woman who could look beyond the scars and see him.

*Lauren.* He so hoped she would be that woman.

He stuffed the rifle into a case, along with extra ammo. "The Glock, too, I think." He lifted the gun from the peg. "And the knife you gave me, Father. It's a must. I've used it for all the girls, and it would be fitting to do so for Lauren if it turns out she's not the one for me."

He finished packing his bag, then looked at his father. "You'd be proud of me, Father. I've done everything Mother has told me to do, just like you said before you left. Obey her in everything, and I couldn't go wrong. Remember, that's what you said before that last hug. The one that I didn't want to end. You wanted to come back, but I know Mother wouldn't allow it. I couldn't follow in your footsteps. She had important work for me."

He took one last look at his father and closed the door. He carried the bags to the foyer, then went to his office, where he located his other projects—the computer to stop Lauren's car and the cell signal blocking device. He loaded them into a backpack, then added his laptop and iPad and put the bag by the door, too.

He straightened and looked around. There was nothing in the living room worth taking. He went to his room and packed clothing and toiletries, then stopped by the closet for several bars of Lava soap and the last nightgown on the shelf. He'd have to buy additional nightgowns—he had to continue his work. But he could do that later.

Right now, he could only think about Lauren. His sweet, sweet Lauren.

THE STORAGE FACILITY loomed large ahead, big and foreboding. But it wasn't the size of the building that worried Becca—it was what the unit contained. If they actually found Orman's files, Becca's secret would likely be exposed.

So, should she tell Connor now or wait?

Orman had been very cautious with her information, not even trusting his partner, which was the reason they'd fallen out. She suspected he'd never put anything in writing either. If she confessed her past now, and Orman hadn't included her in the files, she'd be telling Connor for no reason.

*No reason, huh? You're falling for the guy. If you tell him, it will likely push him away. Just what you want, right?*

She'd thought that at first, but was that what she really wanted? If so, she couldn't let him walk into the storage unit without telling him.

She glanced at him. He was oblivious to her inner turmoil, as he parked by the office, and they got out. Her nerves on edge, thoughts of exposing her past tumbled around in her mind.

He glanced at her. "You're awfully pensive."

She couldn't tell him the truth so she said nothing at all.

They crossed a crumbling parking lot to the older building, his gaze fixed on her, questions alive in his eyes. He held the lobby door for her, but she ignored the questions and passed him to march up to the attendant's desk.

She displayed her shield and hoped the man would honor her request without demanding a warrant. "I'm looking for the unit number rented by John Orman."

The older gentleman who looked bored with his job eyed her for a moment. "No can do without a warrant."

She laid the key on the counter. "I have a key for the unit. I'm not asking you to open it for me. Just point us in the right direction, and you won't have violated any confidentiality agreement."

He looked at Connor then back at Becca. "S'pose it wouldn't hurt." He moved over to an ancient computer and tapped a few keys. "Second floor, number 21."

Becca smiled at him. "Thank you."

"Just don't tell anyone you talked to me."

Becca took off before he had a change of heart and kicked them out of the building.

As they rode the elevator, she glanced at Connor who looked lost in his own thoughts. If she was going to tell him about Lauren, she'd have to do it before they opened the lock on the unit. She imagined what his reaction would be when he found out just how much she'd been keeping from him. She saw narrowed, angry eyes. Then she thought about how he'd look if he found out the truth from Orman's records instead of from her. Narrowed, angry eyes, too, but also disappointment and something she didn't want to think about.

She was better off breaking the news to him.

The door slid open and they walked down the hallway. She put the key in the lock, turned it, and the padlock dropped open.

"Yes!" Connor pumped his fist.

She'd finally found the best lead ever in her search for Van Gogh and should be as excited as Connor. But all she could think about was that she would ruin his mood by telling him.

Maybe the locker was empty. She lifted the door to see file boxes neatly stacked in piles going all the way to the back of the space.

"Jackpot," Connor said with enthusiasm as he started past her.

It was time.

Her heart sank, but she moved forward to prevent his access. He took a step back and studied her intently.

"There's something I need to tell you before we start digging into these records." The moment the words flew from her mouth, she wished she could take them back.

"You're kidding me, right?" His eyes flashed wide. "We just spent thirty minutes in the car without a word and now you want to talk?"

"Yes."

"What is it?" he asked impatiently, his attention on the boxes not on her.

"It's about Lauren."

He didn't bother to look at her. "What about her?"

"I'm Lauren."

His mouth fell open as he stared at her. "You're what?'

"I'm Lauren. The girl Van Gogh took in '99."

His eyes narrowed as she'd imagined they would. "If this is some kind of a joke, Becca . . ."

"It's no joke." She lifted her shirt to reveal the scar by her navel. "I'm number five. I had the number removed, but there's a scar."

He stared at her navel, understanding slowly dawning in his eyes.

She dropped her shirt, moved her hair back and flipped over the top of her ear. "He started to cut my ear off. Here's the scar from that, too."

"Oh, man, you're not making this up. You're really Lauren." He shoved his hands in his hair and turned, as if planning to leave. He took a few steps then came back. "You're Lauren."

Her heart racing, she nodded and took a deep breath before launching into an explanation. "After I escaped from Van Gogh, he came after me again. Detective Orman had stationed a patrol officer at my house, and he chased Van Gogh off. Unfortunately, he got away, but Orman knew he'd be back. So, Orman faked my death, changed my name, and found me a new foster home. All of it was done under the radar." She dragged in a breath and held it as she watched him, waiting for his reaction.

"You're Lauren," he said again, clearly in shock. "It must have been horrible. Yet you seem to have gotten over it."

"Got over it?" She shook her head. "How do you get over a man carving a number into your stomach? Slicing at your ear? Leaving your sister behind to be butchered by him?"

Connor's eyes reflected the horror of what she'd once gone through.

She hadn't been able to talk to anyone but Orman about this, and he'd been kind to her. But he'd also kept his professional distance so she didn't lose it every time she visited him. But it was different now, here, with Connor. He shifted on his feet and looked at her as if he totally got her pain.

"I'm so sorry, honey." He came close, peered into her eyes, and shook his head. "So sorry." He drew her into his arms. "What a horrible thing to experience."

It wasn't the reaction she expected. . . . Where was his anger? His outrage. She deserved his anger, could handle his anger. But this kindness, compassion? No. She wasn't prepared for that.

His strong arms tightened around her and, for the first time in her life, she felt safe and secure. She'd fallen for him despite her best efforts not to. His response told her he cared, maybe as deeply as she did. But that wouldn't last. Couldn't last. He would soon realize why she was only telling him now, and then the anger would come.

She pushed back. His expression was still filled with horror and questions.

"Why tell me now?" he asked, a hint of suspicion lingering in his tone.

And there it was. She stepped out of his arms and jerked a thumb toward the locker. "I thought Orman might have noted something in his files."

"And you didn't want me to find out that way?"

She nodded.

"Thank you for that." His gaze bored into her as he watched for countless moments. "Would you have told me if we hadn't found this locker?"

She wanted to lie. To tell him she'd have trusted him with her secret, but she shook her head and told the truth. "I doubt it."

"I didn't think so." The questions and horror on his face warred with pain, and the pain won out. "I totally understand that you would want to keep this to yourself, but I have to admit, I'm disappointed. I thought we had something developing between us."

"I know. Me, too. But I had to tell you the truth." She wrung her hands. "Maybe in time I'd have told you. But just not yet."

"Fair enough," he said, but the hurt lingered as he gave her hands a quick squeeze. "I'm really sorry this happened to you, Bex. Really sorry."

Tears pricked her eyes.

"We should get to the files," she said quickly before she started crying.

Part of her wished he would push her to open up, but he gave a clipped nod and stepped deeper inside the unit. She followed him. He turned on the light. Boxes stood neatly stacked along one wall, the other held a murder board much like the one Becca had created in her apartment. This board contained greater detail than hers did and was arranged in chronological order.

Connor started at the beginning of the timeline, while Becca moved to the far end just before Orman's death. She forced herself to concentrate on details, starting from the point at which she'd last talked to Orman. He'd jotted down a few notes after that date. The very last one read, *Molly time capsule-24b.*

A time capsule? What in the world was that? And the number 24b, did it refer to a log page in a diary or file box?

She'd start with a worn three-ring binder sitting on top of the nearest stack. She flipped open to the first page. An index listed each box by number along with notes explaining the contents inside.

She flipped to 24b and read a note dated the week before Orman died. *Molly's foster parents' remodeled home. Found a time capsule hidden in the attic wall. Believe photos are retouched pictures of Van Gogh.*

Becca suspected Molly had a secret hiding place—most foster kids did. She could have put a picture in there and wouldn't have come back to claim it, in case Van Gogh was watching the house.

Becca quickly scanned the containers in search of the right box. There it was, near the back wall. She jerked three boxes onto the floor and pulled out number 24, wasting no time tearing into it.

"You have something?" Connor asked as he joined her.

She relayed the story while lifting out the blue folder labeled with a big B. Pressing it open on the file boxes, she withdrew three photographs that were printed from a computer on aged paper. She forced herself to look at the pictures.

One caught and grabbed her attention.

*Van Gogh.* Just as she'd seen him, but without the scars.

"He retouched it," she whispered as the sight of him after all these years stole her breath.

Her knees gave out and she dropped the pictures to grab the box for support. They fluttered away and sank to the cold concrete floor.

Connor retrieved the photos, staring at them for the amount of time it took for Becca to catch her breath and gain control of her emotions.

"How would Molly have gotten a picture of Van Gogh?" he asked.

"Likely from him," Becca said, still not believing it herself.

"How?" Connor sounded as shocked as she was.

"Molly met him on the Internet. It was all my fault." Becca's voice fell off and she took another deep breath before continuing, "Back in those days, the Internet wasn't a big deal. Most people didn't have it, but our foster dad did. He worked in IT and encouraged my interest in computers.

I loved going online and finding new things. That's how I discovered chat rooms where Molly and I hung out all the time. She started chatting with this guy who said he was our age and they flirted. I thought it was harmless, but it was Van Gogh. Of course, we didn't know that at the time. When I wasn't around, she must have exchanged pictures with him."

Connor's eyes narrowed. "But you were friends. Why hide it from you?"

Memories of a ferocious argument with Molly flooded Becca's mind. "He asked Molly out and I told her it wasn't safe to meet him. She told me she wouldn't go, and said she'd stopped talking to him. But she didn't." Becca stared at the photos in Connor's hand. "I didn't know she had a picture of Van Gogh. And I had no idea her hiding place was in the house."

"You make it sound as if having a hiding place like this is normal."

"It is. Foster kids steal from each other for all kinds of reasons. Parents take stuff too. So we all had secret hiding places, usually away from our current home. We never knew when we might be moved and wanted to have access."

"But Molly never told you where she hid things?"

Becca shook her head. "As much as we trusted each other, even we didn't share our hiding spots."

Connor stared at the photo. "I can see the resemblance to your drawings, minus the scars."

All she could do was nod.

"This is good, then. We can scan the picture and run it through the DMV facial recognition database."

"But we might run in to the same problem we had with Danny's picture."

"I'm sure Jae or one of the other geeks at your office will make it work." Connor smiled. "With luck, we'll finally get Van Gogh's name and address."

She nodded again, but couldn't move. Connor was right. They had a lead, the best lead they'd come up with so far. Odds were good that Van Gogh's picture would be in the database.

She should be celebrating, but she couldn't get over seeing Van Gogh's face again, even in a photograph. Right. A mere picture.

What was going to happen when they found him? When she had to look into the depth of his hollow eyes? See him? Smell him?

Would her heart stop? Would she stay strong to give Molly the revenge she deserved?

Becca had no idea. Only time would tell.

CONNOR STOOD NEXT to Becca as they peered over Jae's shoulder. She used top-of-the-line scanning software that he knew his office didn't possess. Soon, Van Gogh's face filled her monitor.

Becca gasped and grabbed the back of Jae's chair. Connor wanted to steady her, but she'd been giving a "hands-off" vibe since they got back from the storage unit and he wanted to respect the way she wanted to handle this situation.

Besides, Connor could barely wrap his mind around the fact that they were looking at an honest-to-goodness picture of Van Gogh instead of drawing. They'd made a huge discovery and yet, it was shadowed for both of them by Becca's secret.

"He's not *that* freaky looking," Jae said and looked up at Becca. "Maybe the eyes are kinda vacant, but other than that, he's not that bad."

"These photos have been retouched. He has significant facial scarring," Connor told Jae so Becca didn't have to explain her shock and reveal her secret. "We've seen sketches and know what he really looks like."

"Gotcha," Jae said. "Okay, shooting off the image to our contact at DMV." She clicked "send" on her email.

Once Connor had told his lieutenant about the photos, Vance had wasted no time in getting permission from the DMV supervisor for one of their tech people to run Van Gogh's photo through their facial recognition program.

"How long until we know anything?" Connor asked.

"Our DMV contact's standing by for my email. He promised to do the search then get right back to me." Her computer soon dinged, and she jabbed one of her ragged fingernails at the screen. "See, he's acknowledged receipt of my email. Now we just wait."

Connor stood there, hearing the "Final Jeopardy" music ticking down in his head. He couldn't stand still, so he started pacing, something he never did. He was normally far more calm during an investigation, but this thing with Becca had him all tied up in knots.

He looked at her. She'd moved to a table and sat rigidly in a chair, her shoulders in an uncharacteristic slump. He doubted she even remembered he was in the room, when he was aware of her every breath. She'd hurt him when she'd admitted that she wouldn't have told him her secret. In his head, he understood her reasons. She deserved her privacy. And she hadn't let it impede their investigation in any way. But . . . man, he wished she'd wanted to tell him.

"We got several matches," Jae announced.

Connor tore across the room, but Becca beat him to the computer.

"Relax," Jae said. "I'll project them on the screen so you both can see them clearly." She tapped a few keys, then sat back as the projector came to life and lit up a large wall screen. "If what you said about the scars is true, the last one's our guy."

Five photos appeared on the screen, and Connor ran his gaze over them, zeroing in on number five.

"It's him," Becca said in voice low. "It's number five. Reginald Zwicky."

"Yeah, he matches the sketches all right," Connor added, but right now, he was more concerned about Becca. She looked like she might drop again. Not that he blamed her. Zwicky's scars, added to that empty look Jae had mentioned earlier and left him looking totally creepy.

"What a dweeby name," Jae said. "He doesn't sound like a serial killer to me. I have to admit, though, he looks like one. That long hair and intense stare." Jae tapped her forehead. "Looks like he's not all there, if you know what I mean."

"What can you tell us about him from the DMV record?" Connor asked to keep them on task.

"He drives a '64 Volkswagen van. Blue. Lives in the Eastmoreland neighborhood."

"Pricey," Connor said.

"This record is seven years old, so the address might have changed. Let me check."

"Can you also run him for priors?" Connor asked.

Jae responded by typing Zwicky's name and date of birth into the computer. "He's clean. No arrests. Not even any tickets. The address is the same, of course. And he's up to date on his car insurance."

Becca shook her head. "How does a serial killer have the wherewithal to remember to do normal stuff like that? I mean, he strangles a girl, then goes online to pay his car insurance? Crazy. Just crazy."

"Zwicky's lived at the current address since he applied for his learner's permit in the nineties," Jae noted. "Let me check property records to see if he owns the house." Her fingers flew over the keys. "Looks like he inherited the house from a Rowena Zwicky about six months ago."

"His mother, I presume," Connor said.

Becca shivered. "He talked to his mother all the time. It was really creepy."

Jae shot a questioning look at Becca. "Is there something you're not telling me?"

"If Zwicky is our guy," Connor said, to draw Jae's attention, "it looks like the date of his mother's death might have set off his recent killing spree."

Becca nodded. "Go ahead, Jae, and email me the details we'll need for a warrant. Then work your magic in the cyber world to find any leads on

Zwicky, his mother, and the address while we plan his takedown."

Jae nodded and went back to her computer.

Becca faced Connor. Her expression was once again all business. "Let's get those warrants going."

She headed for the door, and Connor trailed after her down a maze of hallways leading back to her work station. She dropped into her chair. "I'll gather the data you're going to need to request the warrant."

"So you're giving me the arrest, huh?" He tried to joke, but it came out flat.

"It's your case. I'm just consulting."

She responded in such a defeated tone, his heart creased with her pain. "I'll update Sam while you do that. Just so you know, I have to tell him."

She looked up at him, her eyes haunted, and her expression broken.

*Aw, crap.*

With one look, she got beneath the resolve he'd set only moments ago. "Sam has to know how we came upon this information. Otherwise, he won't be able to procure the resources we need to apprehend Zwicky and search his house." Connor hated seeing the disappointment in her eyes. "Sam will keep the source to himself."

She shook her head. "No he won't. He can't. Your lieutenant will need to know. And Sam will tell Kait, and then she'll tell Nina."

"Sam keeps professional things from Kait all the time. Your story will go no farther than Vance."

"You know what? It doesn't matter. Tell whoever you think needs to know." She turned back to her computer, effectively shutting him down.

The urge to help her work through these emotions was strong, but she obviously didn't want him around. So he went down the hallway to a break-room he'd spotted earlier. He dialed Sam, keeping his eye on the door to prevent anyone from overhearing him.

"Hey, man, glad you called," Sam said. "One of the names on that list from Willow, a Karen Erickson, looks like a promising lead. She was fostered like the others, and her height is close to that of Jane Doe One. I'll be talking to her foster parents in an hour or so."

"Good."

"Good? That all you got to say, man?"

Connor should be excited about identifying another girl, but his mind was focused on Becca and Zwicky at the moment. "I'm kind of busy with a lead of my own."

Connor provided the details for Zwicky and explained what had happened to Becca.

"Oh, man . . . dude . . . that's rough," Sam said. "She sure hid it well."

"She's gathering all the electronic information we'll need for the warrants," Connor said, trying to keep the conversation on track so Sam didn't figure out how deeply Becca's pain was hitting him. "And I'll request them as soon as she's done. I was hoping you'd coordinate an arrest plan with SWAT. With any luck, we'll finally have Van Gogh behind bars before the day is over."

# Chapter Twenty-Five

BECCA HAD BEEN tempted to race right over to Zwicky's house. But if they wanted to successfully arrest him, it would require planning and strategy, so it was two hours later before they pulled up to his house. She stared at the cute craftsman painted white with blue trim. She had been blindfolded when Van Gogh had taken her captive and when she'd taken off that night. The last thing she'd thought to do was stand and look at the house. The place looked inviting and safe, much like similar houses lining the street. Safe. Right. If Van Gogh lurked inside, it was anything but safe.

She swallowed hard and fought off her memories of the time in his basement. She started shaking and couldn't stop.

"Aw, honey, don't." Connor rested a warm hand on her icy one. "This is too difficult for you. Maybe you should wait in the car."

"There's no way I'm hiding like a scared little girl." She jerked her hand free and shoved the door open, glad for the chilly breeze rustling through the trees and cooling her face.

She had to see Van Gogh—Zwicky—or whatever his name was, arrested. Personally. She had to be standing right there beside him and slap the cuffs on his wrists. She stood by Connor's car and waited for the SWAT team to file out while a trio of officers scurried toward the back door. One of the officers glanced into the garage window and shook his head. So, there was no van in the garage and it wasn't on the street. Maybe Van Gogh wasn't home.

*No.* She refused to believe it. He had to be there. This had to end. Here. Now. It just had to.

The SWAT team marched up to the front door painted a bright red. The team was dressed for battle in their drab green gear with helmets and tactical vests, their shields up, rifles drawn, and sidearms strapped to their legs.

She and Connor wore vests, but they couldn't withstand the same caliber of gun as SWAT, so they hung back. Connor kept looking at her, checking on her. She appreciated his concern, but wouldn't give in to it.

The team leader pounded on the door and announced their presence. They waited for a few beats longer, then the leader made a louder announcement. A few more beats later, he signaled for the team to use the battering ram to break open the door. They entered cautiously, spreading out and scattering like well-organized ants.

Becca took off for the back of the house, where, if they were in the right place, she'd find the door to the cellar. Connor caught up to her and grabbed her elbow. "Slow down and be careful. You've survived too much to let him plug you with a bullet."

"Are you kidding? He's not brave enough to shoot me. He has to torture and maim under the cover of darkness." She shrugged off Connor's hand and found the basement door right where she thought it would be, near a landing with another door leading to the backyard. She made her way down the steps. Despite her urge to charge ahead, she heeded Connor's warning and moved cautiously. She crossed through a family room that she'd run through sixteen years ago.

"This is it." Terror washed over her, but she kept her cool. "I recognize the room and the basement layout. Even the furniture. We're in the right house." She gestured at a closed door. "He held us in the utility room behind that door."

She was suddenly aware of the smell of bleach.

"You smell that?" she asked.

"Unfortunately, I do."

Her heart racing, she ripped the door open and peered around the corner. Then, checking the other direction, she stepped in.

"Clear." She felt faint as the familiar room sent memories flashing through her mind.

The table. The knife. Molly in shackles on the floor.

She forced herself to make a complete circle and take in every inch of the room. "The table's gone and he's put down new flooring. The walls have been painted, too. Otherwise, it's the same."

Connor stood at the doorway, surveying the space. "It's clean. Too clean for a utility room."

"You think he killed the other girls here or at the fabrication plant?"

"Hard to tell. He's used bleach at both locations. He could just have a fascination with bleach. But I didn't smell it upstairs, so I'm thinking he was trying to hide blood evidence down here, too. If there's any blood still left, Dane will find it."

Blood. Her blood. Other girls' blood. He needed to pay. "Dane's good, but I'd like to call in our Evidence Recovery Team, too. Dane knows Henry Greco, and he's our best, so I'll ask for him."

"I'm good with that. But I need to check with my lieutenant first."

"No," she said defiantly. "I don't care what he says. I've toed the team line on everything so far. I'm not doing it here." She set her shoulders in a straight line and eyed him, expecting him to be angry.

He smiled. "I'm glad to see the old Becca Lange resurfacing. For a while there, I was afraid she was gone."

She'd been thinking the same thing. "Then you're good with Henry?"

"Call him, and I'll arrange for Dane. But not until we find out if Zwicky is hiding out like a little sissy in a closet upstairs."

"Agreed," she said and started for the stairway.

On the main level, the team leader informed them no one was home.

"We need to get uniforms and agents canvassing the neighbors and make sure we have someone watching for the return of Zwicky's van," Becca said.

"I'll get the uniforms on it." Connor stepped away.

Becca dug out her phone. She first arranged for Henry, then Taylor, who could not only help out on the neighborhood canvass, but learn a lot in the process. Or maybe Becca just wanted someone here from her own team for emotional support. It was support she'd like from Connor, but she wasn't ready for that yet. At least he didn't seem to be angry that she'd kept her true identity from him.

That earned him additional brownie points, but she couldn't even think about him as anything other than a detective until this was over. She also couldn't keep her secret any longer. She'd tell Taylor the truth when she arrived. As soon as they finished processing this scene, Becca would also phone Kait and Nina and tell them, too.

Connor walked in the door as she was stowing her phone. "We're set. Dane's on his way and so is my lieutenant."

"Ditto for Henry and Taylor," Becca said. "I'd like to do a walk-through of the rest of the house."

"I'll go with you," he offered.

She nodded and glanced around the living room decorated in a muted beige. The house had a normal exterior and a normal interior, too. The creep fit into the neighborhood just fine, the way many sociopaths did. It made them hard to apprehend.

She approached a long hallway with three bedrooms and two bathrooms. The first room held a desk and four computers as well as a laptop, an Apple desktop, and two Windows machines, both generic cases indicating Zwicky had built them himself. She glanced at a bulletin board, suddenly realizing it held her picture. She didn't say anything, but when Connor caught sight of it, he growled something that she couldn't make out.

Then Becca's gaze lighted on the picture next to hers. "It's Molly's daughter, Haley. Oh, no . . . please no. He's going after her."

"No, he's not," Connor snapped out and grabbed his phone. "I'll have a team at her house in a few minutes."

He paced a few steps then demanded to have a patrol car go to Molly's address and explained his reasons. "Call me back the minute we confirm Haley is okay."

Becca didn't have Finn's number or she would have called him herself. Though she was anxious, there was nothing to do but wait until she heard back from the officer who was on his way to their house.

Becca turned her focus to the desk and studied schematics for an automobile computer system. "Looks like he's a software engineer working in the auto industry."

"Odd that Jae didn't find any employer in her search," Connor said.

"Computers make sense, though," Becca replied as she moved on to the next room. "He met Molly online at a time when few people were into computers."

She stepped into a larger, tidier bedroom that was sparsely decorated. It smelled like arthritis cream mixed with garlic.

Becca's stomach wrenched. The odor had clung to Van Gogh's clothing, and the memories she'd been battling came racing back. Panic followed. A small cry of distress escaped her lips. She clamped a hand over her mouth and took a step toward the door.

Connor came to stand next to her. "What is it?"

"The smell. It's how he smelled. His clothes. His body. He reeked of it." She forced her shoulders back and continued to the closet where she found women's clothing.

"His mother's room," Connor said.

The bedroom creeped Becca out. "He's holding on to her things."

"You said he talked to her a lot."

She nodded. "He always mentioned something about cleansing, saying he was trying to cleanse us. It never made any sense." She frowned.

"What?"

"Molly kept pushing him on it. Asking question after question. It made him mad. I figured he would take her life first just to shut her up."

"But he came for you instead."

She nodded.

"You never said how he managed to abduct both of you at the same time."

"He didn't. Not really anyway." She looked up at the ceiling for a moment. "Molly told me she wasn't chatting online with him anymore, but I knew she was and was planning to meet him. When she snuck out of the house, I followed her to make sure she was safe."

That night came back in great clarity. The darkness. Van Gogh's creepy face peering at her through the fog. The terror in Molly's eyes.

Her mouth and throat dry, she swallowed hard before she could continue. "They met in the parking lot of an old abandoned theater. By the time I caught up to her, he had her wrists in handcuffs and a knife to her throat. I lunged anyway. He threatened to kill Molly if I didn't come with them."

Connor watched her for a moment, evaluating and weighing her story, she supposed. "So he hadn't planned to take you, then?"

"No."

"Which is probably why he wanted to get rid of you first."

"Maybe."

"So how did you get away?"

Becca shivered and crossed her arms. "He had me on the table. Here, in the basement. The very table we found Molly resting on. He'd somehow failed to close my cuff tightly and left the key on a nearby shelf. He started to cut my ear, and Molly called out to him. She told him she'd sleep with him if he let me go. She—"

"But he didn't try to assault either of you sexually before that," Connor interrupted.

Becca shook her head. "He never even mentioned sex. But when Molly brought it up, he came to life for the first time. He went to her, and that's when I discovered my cuff was loose. I wiggled it until I freed my hand and could grab the key. I started for him, planning to attack him, but Molly shook her head and motioned for me to go. I figured she was worried that if I tried to attack him, he might overpower me again. So I went for help."

The memories assaulted Becca. She had to stop again and take a deep breath. In and out. In and out.

Connor rested a hand on her shoulder. "I'm sorry you had to go through that, honey."

The warmth of his hand and his soft voice, touched her to her soul, and she wanted to give in to her emotions, but that would get them nowhere.

She pressed her hand over his. "The rest you know and I'm tired of rehashing the past. I need to *do* something."

She squeezed his hand then stepped to the door. Connor padded behind her. She entered the next bedroom. Van Gogh's room. Organized and utilitarian like his mother's. The same smell lingered, but it wasn't as heavy.

Connor's phone rang and he answered.

"Okay, I want someone sitting on the house twenty-four-seven until we locate the suspect." He shoved his phone back into his pocket. "Haley's at home and she's fine. So is her brother Todd, in case you wanted to know, though it would be odd for Van Gogh to go after the kid."

"Thank you for arranging a protective detail for them."

"When we get done here, I'll talk to Vance and make sure we have the best officers assigned to their watch."

Becca nodded her thanks and scanned the space before going to the closet. The hangers, filled with threadbare shirts and jeans, were spaced evenly apart as if he'd taken a ruler to them. So far, Van Gogh was presenting as obsessive and orderly, just like his profile had predicted. Except for the large gap that appeared in the middle of the hangers. *Odd.*

She felt Connor come to stand behind her.

"Something's off about these." He reached over her shoulder and separated the clothes even more.

The overhead light shone on the back wall, revealing a secret door.

"A safe room." Becca jerked out her gun.

"Stand back, and we'll see." Connor drew his weapon.

She wasn't going to give him first crack at arresting Van Gogh. She pressed the door. The spring lock gave way, and it opened into a small space. No light. No movement.

"Cover me." She dug out her phone to shine a light in the space, running the beam over the walls. No Van Gogh, but guns. Walls filled with them. Organized by category. Handguns. Rifles. Automatics. Semis. There was one whole wall devoted to knives.

She stepped into the small space and saw an old photograph of a man framed and hung on the wall. He looked like Van Gogh, minus the scars. His father?

Connor joined her and stared at the walls, a deep scowl on his face. "Check out the empty slots."

She saw three bare spots. A handgun, assault rifle, and knife were missing.

"He's loaded for bear," Connor said.

*Loaded for bear.* And with her picture on his bulletin board, it was looking more and more like she was his intended prey.


DINNERTIME HAD LONG passed, and Connor's growling stomach made him cranky. Processing the scene and canvassing neighbors had taken hours. It wasn't unusual and Connor normally didn't mind it. Of course, normally he didn't have Becca's secret to stew over while she was busy working right under his nose. Like now, when she stepped past him as if he were invisible as she went to talk to the tech who was removing Zwicky's computers. Her failure to make eye contact made Connor even crankier.

The FBI forensic tech, Henry Greco, came barreling into the bedroom and rushed up to Becca. "You won't believe what we found in the basement. You've got to see it."

She started across the room and glanced at Connor. "You coming?"

*Fine.* So she did know he was there, after all. He fell into step behind her, and they made their way downstairs.

Maybe this was their break. Dane and Henry had worked hard, but so far, they hadn't found a stinkin' thing. No blood. No clothing. No jars, ears, or spare nightgowns. Sure, they'd found pictures of Becca in the bedroom, and Becca had recognized the basement, but what they needed was concrete evidence that this was Van Gogh's house.

They stepped into the utility room. The lights were out, and Dane stood near a long wall with a spray bottle in one hand and his blue light in the other.

"Close the door," he said.

Connor complied, already knowing from Dane's tools and the darkness of the room that they were about to see blood residue.

"We found blood. Quite by accident and quite a lot of it." Henry nodded at Dane. "We'll spray luminol over a large area of the wall behind Dane. Keep your eyes open. The image will fade fast." Henry picked up a spray bottle and his own light.

"Ready?" he asked Dane.

Dane grinned. "Oh yeah."

Together they quickly sprayed the entire wall, then clicked on their lights.

Connor's mouth dropped open, and Becca gasped.

She took a step closer to the wall. "This is it! The proof we need to nail this guy."

"Amazing, right," Henry said.

"'Amazing' isn't a word I'd use." Connor let his gaze run over the wall where someone had written five names and dates in blood, then had painted over them.

Connor shook his head. "I didn't know you could detect blood so strongly through paint."

"I'm guessing Van Gogh thought the same thing, but we've got him," Dane said.

"Oh, yeah," Henry slapped a high five with Dane.

"Now all we need to do is find him," Connor said. "Can you spray the wall again so I can write down the names and dates?"

"I can do you one better." Dane grabbed his camera and displayed the digital screen for Connor. "I've got it on film."

Connor got out his notebook and pen and jotted down the names. He wasn't surprised to see Molly and Lauren in the number four and five slots without a date next to their names.

He turned to Becca. "He may have written each girl's name in her own blood. If he did, we can use it to match evidence Orman collected from the body in the nineties."

"And we can run DNA on the others to see if there's a match in CODIS," Henry said.

"Get a good sample of each name and date," Becca instructed.

"Great job, by the way," Connor added.

Dane preened. "Just doing our jobs."

"Now that we've got absolute proof that we're in the right place, I want a new grid search of this place from top to bottom," Connor told Dane. "We can't miss a thing."

Dane nodded and flipped on the light switch.

Connor followed Becca up the stairs where Taylor waited for them.

"You look beat," she said to Becca.

"It's been a trying day." Becca rubbed her forehead and filled Taylor in on what they'd found in the basement. Then she told her about being Lauren.

To Taylor's credit, she didn't gape at Becca or even gasp. She simply gave a crisp nod. "Maybe we should take off and grab something to eat."

Becca shook her head. "I'll hang here to see if Van Gogh shows up."

"He's not gonna show up with all the commotion going on out front," Connor said. "We might as well leave this to Dane and Henry."

Becca's gaze darted around the room. "Maybe I'll talk to the neighbors again."

"It's too late to be knocking on doors," Connor said. But in reality, it was just a waste of time—they'd already questioned everyone at length.

"Come over to my place," Taylor suggested. "We could grab a pizza on the way and then check to see if there's any link between the girls' names on the wall and the current victims. It might lead us to an alternate location where we can find Zwicky."

Becca pondered it for a moment then nodded. "Sounds perfect."

Connor didn't like the plan. Letting Becca out of his sight bothered him big time, but he couldn't stop her. "You'll be careful?"

She rolled her eyes. "We're both capable agents, Connor."

"Okay, fine. I guess I'll see you later then."

"You'll call me if you hear anything from Dane?"

Connor nodded.

"If I don't talk to you tonight, I'll give you a call in the morning." Becca reached for her backpack sitting in the corner.

"Wait, what? You're spending the night with Taylor?"

"She is." Taylor stepped up next to Becca and dared him to argue.

"What about clothes?"

"We're about the same size," Taylor said.

"Goodnight, Connor." Becca headed for the door.

Connor watched her go. He couldn't help thinking it was a mistake to let her leave without him. A big mistake.


SO THEY'D FOUND HIS home. How, he didn't know. He thought he'd been so careful.

"I'm sorry, Mother," Reginald whispered from his hiding spot down the street as he watched the police officers surrounding his house.

Mother didn't reply.

"I know you're angry, Mother, but I have a perfect plan to take Lauren. Nothing they can do will stop it."

"It had better not," Mother's harsh voice came from above. "We've lost our home because of her."

"The hacking has paid off handsomely, and I can buy us another house. A grand one. And we can continue to live in style."

"We?" Mother asked.

"Yes, we," he cried out. "Please say you'll always be with me."

"I don't know."

Reginald's gut cramped at her words. He'd simply wanted to be loved. To have someone who would be there for him through thick and thin. Mother had done so, but with reservation and conditions. Always conditions.

Maybe he was better off without her. Maybe Lauren could be his forever love. The person who stuck by him no matter what, who wouldn't abandon him when the going got tough.

"Will you do that for me, Lauren?" he asked as he hurried toward his rental car. "Will you?"

# Chapter Twenty-Six

BECCA WAS WEARY. Bone weary. But not even exhaustion could make her forget seeing her name written on the wall in Zwicky's basement. It felt odd calling him Zwicky, but in all honesty, the name was so less intimidating than Van Gogh. If she thought of him as Zwicky, she could believe they would actually catch him. Van Gogh, not as much.

"Do you have preference on pizza?" Taylor asked from the driver's seat.

"Connor told me about a great pizza place near him. I'd like to pick up my car from his apartment building, so we can grab one on the way to your place."

"Your car?" Taylor glanced at Becca. "I can drive you anywhere you need to go."

"I know, and you were a real sport to jump in when you did, but I have this thing about being able to take off if I need to."

Taylor eyed Becca with curiosity.

"It's a foster kid thing. I need to be in control and have a plan at all times. Without my car, I can't do what I want, when I want. It makes me edgy and I'm already on edge. I don't need more stress."

"So punch Connor's address into my GPS," Taylor said. "We'll drop your car at my place, and then go grab the pizza."

Becca added the address and they were soon heading in the right direction. She wasn't hungry, and she was tempted to tell Taylor to skip the pizza, but Becca knew she should eat, and she suspected Taylor wouldn't eat if she didn't. Becca used a phone app to order a large pizza, then sat back for the rest of the drive.

Once outside Connor's apartment, Becca settled into her car and was on the road to Taylor's place. Taylor followed close behind, and while waiting for her to park her car, Becca enjoyed the solitude and the chance to think.

She'd confessed her secret twice today, and the sky hadn't fallen. People hadn't harshly judged her for leaving Molly. She did see pity in their expressions, but it wasn't the kind of pity that would linger or make them treat her differently. She was still Becca to them.

Taylor opened the passenger-side door, and the smell of rain in the distance filtered into the car. Becca took a deep breath of the freshly scented air. Despite Zwicky being in the wind, she actually felt more optimistic than she had in years. Maybe it was the fact that her secret was finally out in the open, lifting a heavy weight from her shoulders.

Taylor buckled her belt, and they exchanged small talk while Becca drove them to the pizza place. She and Taylor stepped inside, and the spicy smell sent Becca's stomach rumbling. Suddenly eager to eat, Becca paid for the pizza and gave the worker a generous tip.

"Thanks." He got a big goofy smile on his face. "You made my night."

"Glad to," she responded and felt almost giddy as she returned to her car.

Taylor rested the pizza on her knees, and Becca quickly pointed the car toward Taylor's apartment.

"Good thing you live close by or I'd be tempted to dig into that pizza before we got there," Becca said.

"If you do, I'll join you."

"I'll just drive faster." Becca laughed and turned the corner.

She tried to speed up, but her car suddenly slowed. She pressed harder on the gas pedal with no result. The engine was running, but the gas pedal didn't seem to work. They were coming to a stop.

"I thought you were hungry." Taylor shifted to look at Becca. "Why are you stopping?"

"I'm not." Becca stomped on the gas pedal. "The car won't speed up, but the engine is revving. It's like the brakes are taking over."

"This is the worst time for car trouble," Taylor said.

Becca's car finally came to a complete stop, and she got out to look for the problem. She strolled around the car, but couldn't see anything wrong. She could lift the hood, but why bother? She knew nothing about engines. Resigned to having to call her road service, she turned back to her door.

A car pulled up behind them. Perfect. Maybe the driver knew something about cars and could help.

She waited by her door to see what the driver planned to do. Her hand settled on her sidearm just in case.

A man leaned out the window and yelled, "Car troubles?"

No. Oh no. Becca's heart dropped to her stomach. That voice. That horrible, graveled, mean voice. The one that had terrorized her for days.

*Van Gogh.*

He was here. He'd returned. For her? Likely.

She reached for her door handle. The locks suddenly clicked into place. Becca pounded on the window, her terrified gaze going to Taylor. "Unlock the door. Hurry. It's Van Gogh."

Taylor tried rocking the button back and forth, but the locks didn't respond. "They won't open."

Panicked, Becca glanced behind her.

Van Gogh had gotten out of his vehicle and moved closer, his scarred face gleaming in the streetlights. He held an assault rifle aimed at her heart. "Now, Lauren, there's no need to pretend you don't want to come with me."

The use of her former name sickened Becca on the spot.

"When I visited your apartment, I saw all the work you've done to find me. I'm flattered." His voice was low and oddly tinged with sexual innuendo.

How could he believe that she'd been looking for him so they could be together? Easy, he was insane. And he'd come for her. To claim her after all of these years.

She frantically pulled on the door handle, her heart racing.

He stepped closer, and above his heavy whiskers, she could make out individual ragged scars running across his face. Over his hands. It was as if she could feel him above her, as he'd been years ago, looking down, his eyes glittering with intensity. The cold knife slicing her skin.

"No, please. Let me be," she begged, the way she'd done at fifteen. She'd been a mere girl then. Now she was a grown woman, an agent. She gave herself a mental shake. She had to stop this. She wasn't going to let him have this effect on her.

*You're stronger now. Not a victim.*

She drew her gun and planted her feet. He might kill her, but at least she could get a shot off first and protect Taylor.

"Come along now, Lauren." He stopped and ran his eyes over her. "You are my Lauren, are you not?" His eyes caressed her, and she felt dirty. He took a few more steps toward her. "My sweet, sweet Lauren."

So he had some doubts as to her name. She'd play that up and maybe he'd leave her behind. "I'm sorry, but you've obviously mistaken me for someone else. I don't know any Lauren."

"We'll just have to see about that, won't we?" He arched a brow and inched closer.

She gestured with her gun to stop him. "I'm not going with you."

"Now don't say that, my sweet." He smiled, a sickly narrowing of his lips that made her gut churn. "I'll be forced to kill you and take Taylor instead. You know what that would mean for her, right?"

Becca glanced at Taylor, then back at Van Gogh. She'd tried to think of him as Zwicky, but seeing his face, hearing his voice, she could only think of the serial killer. Not a man residing in the cute house, living in the past when his mother was alive. Not when his eyes, locked on hers, were filled with venom and evil. She couldn't go with him. She just couldn't.

"Put your gun on the ground. Nice and easy. And if you're carrying a second one as so many law enforcement officers do, add that one, too. And then your phone." He waited for a moment, then shrugged. "Okay, have it your way. Taylor will join us." He started toward the car.

"No wait. Leave Taylor alone." Becca gently laid her gun on the ground. "I only have one."

Becca started backing away from the car and prayed for Taylor's safety.

"No, Becca, don't," Taylor screamed and drew her own weapon, but held her fire.

Becca knew Taylor wouldn't shoot as long as Van Gogh had his rifle sighted on Becca.

"Okay, now this way. Quickly." Excitement tingled in Van Gogh's words.

Becca went along with him, hoping that by now Taylor had called 911 and a patrol car would be screaming down the street in mere moments.

Memories of her last time as his captive assaulted Becca. The knife. The jars and ears. The terror for herself and Molly.

Fear pierced Becca's heart and she dragged her feet.

He pushed her ahead and directed her to the passenger seat of the small sedan. She tried to elbow him, but he shoved her inside. He dug into his pocket and pulled out bright yellow zip ties. He held them out to her. "Tie your ankles together. Nice and tight."

She didn't immediately comply.

He arched an eyebrow, crinkling the scars running across his forehead. "I can still get a clean shot off at Taylor from this distance."

Becca took the ties and bent down. "You won't get away with this."

He laughed, the sound other-worldly and ominous. She pulled the ties tight and sat back up.

"Now hold your hands out."

He would threaten Taylor again so Becca did as she was told, and he zip-tied her wrists together.

He bent to check the ties on her ankles, his gaze never leaving her face. He came back up, his fingers going to her hair, stroking it and letting it run through his fingers. "I've missed you, Lauren."

She gagged and thought to spit at him, but she feared he would take it out on Taylor.

"Don't worry," he said. "It won't be long and we can be together."

He slammed the door and strode around the front of the car, his gun still trained on her.

Right. Like she had any hope of getting away.

He didn't seem to hurry, which was a good thing for her. The longer he took, the sooner Taylor's call to 911 would bring police officers to the rescue.

He slid into the idling car and set his rifle between his knees. He took another tie and affixed her hands to the door handle.

She was truly his prisoner now and her stomach revolted. She swallowed hard against a dry throat.

He wound a scarf that smelled of his mother around her head, silencing her voice, and she was no longer free to call out.

"I'm sorry, my sweet," he said as he shifted into gear. "But as I'm driving you might yell for help, and I can't risk it."

Her stomach retched again. Not from the cloth, but from his use of "my sweet." She wasn't his sweet anything.

Humming, he drove off slowly and waved at Taylor as they passed. She held up her phone, frantically miming that it didn't work.

"Oh, yes," he said. "I forgot to mention that I've also blocked cell signals in the area."

Paralyzing fear climbed up Becca's back and nearly swamped her. Taylor might not be able to call out or move the car, but someone was bound to happen upon her and help. Becca knew Taylor would have gotten the license plate number to this vehicle. But the car wasn't registered in Zwicky's name, so it could be a rental, and she wasn't sure having the plate number would help locate her.

Still, she knew someone would come for her. Connor would come. At least that's what she had to believe or she might lose it completely.

Whistling, Van Gogh made several turns, and they drove for miles before he parked in a darkened alley behind another small sedan. Becca made note of each turn, each street, and this time, she would lead the police, lead Connor, right to Van Gogh if—no, *when*—she got away.

Van Gogh grabbed his rifle and stepped out. He went to the other vehicle and opened the trunk.

*No, please God, no. Don't let him change cars. They'll never find me.*

He put his rifle in the front seat then came back to the car and opened her door. She tumbled halfway out. He pulled out his knife, the same one that had carved the number five in her tender flesh, the same one that had sliced into the skin above her ear. The big, gleaming, horrifying knife.

She shrank back, but she was unsteady and couldn't move.

He sliced through the tie holding her to the door. Then he scooped her up with one arm, the other holding the knife to her throat.

She didn't care if he had a knife. She started to fight him.

"Now, Lauren," he said patiently. "There's no one watching anymore. No need to pretend you don't want to be with me."

If she hadn't been gagged, she'd have screamed her hatred for him, but all she could do was try to wiggle free. She bucked hard and lurched from his arms. Despite her tied ankles, she managed to remain standing. She started to hop, her balance precarious. He took her down in a swift tackle.

"I'd hate to mar that beautiful neck, so please don't fight me." He pressed the knife to her skin.

She was instantly taken back sixteen years. To his basement. The cold damp air. Her body chilled to the bone from lying naked for days. Wondering about his plans. Worrying. Terrified.

He bent closer. His smell, garlic mixed with the same old-lady scent in his mother's room that had lingered in Becca's nostrils long after she'd gotten away from him, now sent bile rising up her throat. She was numb with fear.

He got her to her feet and gently settled her on soft mats in a trunk with luggage piled high in the back.

"I'm sorry, my sweet, but I can't arrive at the hotel with you drawing attention to us." He reached into a cooler and took out a bottle with just a few sips of water in it.

"Yell and the knife comes back out." He removed her gag and held the bottle up to her lips. "Now drink it all."

She knew it was filled with drugs to knock her out, and she pinched her lips closed. "The knife, Lauren. Remember the knife."

She opened her mouth, and he dumped the water in quickly, forcing her to swallow hard.

He tossed the bottle into the trunk and sat on the bumper. "We'll just wait for that to take effect." He hummed a song she remembered him humming last time. A dance tune, she thought.

He reached for the hem of her shirt, and she tried to move back, but she slammed into suitcases and couldn't move. He lifted her shirt and *ts*ked. "You didn't like the number, my sweet? I could have given you a different one if you'd but asked."

She wouldn't comment as her response would only make him mad, and she'd seen what he'd done to Molly when he'd gotten mad.

"No matter. We can replace it." He gently pulled down her shirt.

She felt the first effects of the drug start to take hold. Since it acted so quickly, she suspected he'd roofied her. She knew she would soon feel very drunk, and it would last for up to eight hours or so. Eight hours when she'd have no idea what he was doing with her body.

She started floating, feeling as though she was rising up and out of the trunk. Eight hours like this. She started to cry. Despite being careful, despite Connor's protection, her worst nightmare had just come true.

# Chapter Twenty-Seven

TAYLOR HAD TO GET to a phone. Now! Hoping to escape via the trunk, she tossed the pizza on the driver's seat, turned on the overhead light, and dove into the back seat. She clawed at the back cushion. It didn't budge.

"No," she cried out. "It has to have trunk access."

She jerked harder. It still didn't budge.

She moved to the other cushion. Pulled. It gave a little. She ran her hands over the top. Yes, a release. She pressed it and jerked. The trunk opened wide before her.

*Good.*

She wiggled inside and felt around for the release. She scraped fingers against rough metal, but finally found the lever and jerked it open. The trunk lid popped. Fresh air rushed in. She scrambled out and drew her weapon. Just because Van Gogh had driven off, that didn't mean he hadn't left a trap. She spotted a laptop sitting on the ground where he'd parked. Likely the computer controlling the car brakes and locks. A small device sat on top.

She ran to the computer. Using her sleeve to keep from smudging any prints, she picked up the small handheld device. It was a signal jammer, as she'd suspected. She quickly turned it off. Looked at her phone.

Yes! She had a signal.

She dialed 911. "This is FBI agent Taylor Andrews, and I need to report an abduction." She provided details, including Zwicky's license plate number. "This is related to an ongoing homicide investigation. As soon as you're done dispatching patrol units, I need to be connected to Detective Connor Warren."

"Hold on."

Taylor knew 911 operators had to remain calm, but this one didn't seem to be getting the seriousness of this situation.

"This is a matter of life and death."

"I understand."

Taylor wanted to scream at her, but she bit her lip instead and paced as she waited.

"The operator said something about an abduction," Connor's deep voice came barreling through the phone. "You'd better tell me Becca is with you, and she's all right."

Taylor explained what had happened, each word fighting the last to get out.

"Give me the address." Fear mixed with anger darkened his tone.

She provided it. "I'm heading back to the car now."

"I'm on my way," he said. "And you'd better hope she's been found by then or so help me, Taylor . . ." He hung up.

She didn't need him to complete the sentence. She'd screwed up. She couldn't have stopped Van Gogh, but there were other things she could have done.

"Like not let Becca get her car or stop for pizza," she mumbled as she headed back to the car.

When she reached the vehicle, she inserted the key into the driver's door and tried to unlock it. The locks wouldn't budge. Van Gogh had to have modified the vehicle's computer. If Taylor got a good look at it, maybe she could find a way to locate Van Gogh. First, she needed to secure the computer sitting on the street. She dug through Becca's go bag for gloves and retrieved the computer. The urge to search the machine was strong, nearly overpowering her common sense.

*No. Hold off.*

This was a crime scene now and like any crime scene where a computer was an integral part, the machine had to be imaged first. She tucked the computer into a safe location in the trunk then called her office and requested a computer tech on scene ASAP.

She heard sirens winding closer, but she wouldn't stand around and wait. She had to act. She drew out a flashlight and climbed back into the trunk.

Bruises would cover her body in the morning, but that was nothing compared to what Becca's would look like after Van Gogh finished with her. Tears bit at the back of Taylor's eyes, but she wouldn't let them flow. If she wanted to help her fellow agent, she had to keep it together. She had computer skills and hopefully, by looking at Van Gogh's handiwork, she'd be able to give Connor a lead by the time he arrived.

She didn't know a lot about cars, but she suspected the computer would be accessed through the dash. She wrapped her body around the center console and shone the light under the dash. She found wires roughly secured, obviously not part of the factory install. She trailed them to a small gadget that was connected to another blinking device. She maneuvered her cell into position and snapped a few pictures.

Swirling lights suddenly twisted above her. Then a flashlight was shone into the window. She gave the officer a thumbs-up.

"Agent Andrews." The police officer's voice came from the trunk area. "You all right in there?"

"Fine. I'll be right out."

"Want me to break a window and make it easier?"

"No. We don't want to contaminate the scene."

"Mind my asking what you were doing under the dash?"

"Proving that Agent Lange's car has been hacked."

"Hacked like you hear on the news about big company computers?"

"Exactly," Taylor replied as she maneuvered around until she was upright and could think without blood pounding in her head. She looked out the window and caught sight of a traffic camera angled at the scene.

*Perfect.*

She could access the camera feed on her iPad and hopefully find the lead they so desperately needed right now.


CONNOR ROARED ACROSS town, his lights and siren running. He'd never been so afraid in his life. Van Gogh had her. Becca, his Becca, and it was all his fault. Not Taylor's, though he'd snapped at her on the phone. No, he was the one to blame. The only one. He knew better than to let Becca go with Taylor. But he'd let Becca's unwillingness to let him help her override his common sense.

By the time he got to Becca's car, two uniforms were there, cordoning off the area with crime-scene tape. Taylor sat in the front seat of a patrol car looking at her iPad.

Had she found a lead? He approached, and she looked up.

"Oh, good." She climbed out, her gaze wary.

"Before you say anything," he said, "let me apologize for going off on you when you called. You're not to blame, and I had no right to let you have it."

"I could have done things differently. Maybe if I had, Becca would still be here."

"It started when I let her leave the house with you."

"Look," she said, "why don't we shelve all this blame until after we get her back? Then I'll arm-wrestle you for it." She offered him a tight smile and her hand.

"Deal." He shook her hand, and at that moment, he knew she'd fit in fine with the rest of Becca's team.

Taylor pointed down the road. "There's a traffic cam on the corner, and I've just pulled up the feed." She held out her iPad and started the video.

He watched as Becca's car came careening around the corner then suddenly slowed, as if she'd slammed on her brakes.

"This is where Van Gogh used his hack to apply her brakes."

Her car came to a complete stop, and another sedan pulled in well back from her. She got out and walked around her car. The man in the vehicle behind leaned out and said something. She looked at him. Then, she suddenly spun and grabbed for the driver's door. She jerked the handle, but it didn't budge. Then she started pounding on the window.

"This is the point where she told me it was Van Gogh. He'd taken over the locks right after she got out." Taylor shook her head. "I was too busy trying to figure out what was going on that I didn't even notice until she tried to get back in and couldn't." Her voice shook with emotion.

Van Gogh stepped out, lifted a rifle, and Connor's heart refused to beat. Connor could sense the desperation in her body language. She must have felt him coming. She backed away. Her hand went for her gun, and she took a strong shooting stance. She looked into the car, then slowly set her weapon on the ground. She'd given up. Likely to protect Taylor.

That was Becca. The person who was out to save the world, even if it meant sacrificing herself.

Van Gogh took her to the car. Connor couldn't make out what he was doing, but he was likely handcuffing or securing her somehow. He drove off. But before he did, he paused near her car for a moment.

"I signaled to Becca that my phone wouldn't work, and he waved to me. All calm and casual, like he was going on a date. I'll admit, I panicked for a minute or two, but then I crawled out through the trunk and turned off the signal jammer."

"So he blocked your signal?"

She nodded. "I found it and a computer sitting on the curb where he'd parked. I suspect it's controlling her car's locks and brakes. I've got a tech on the way to take an image of the hard drive so I can look at the data. Maybe there'll be something else that can lead us to him."

"This is just crazy." Connor shook his head. "Who knew you could hack a car?"

"Cars are controlled by computers now, so they're just as vulnerable as any computer would be. Different cars are susceptible to different hacks, depending on their computer systems." She frowned. "Zwicky has proved his computer skills, and there's no telling what else he's planning to do."

The officer's radio squawked, and a report of finding the car about ten miles away bolstered Connor's spirit. Then the word "abandoned" was added, and he plummeted back into despair.

"I'm heading over there," he said to Taylor. "Want to ride along?"

"I have that tech on the way, and Henry will be here soon to process the scene. Besides, I need to make sure the car is handled properly."

"It's just a car."

"A car that Van Gogh tampered with. It will be evidence when we find Becca and bring her back home. Once we've imaged the laptop's drive, I'll spend some time analyzing it and maybe we'll find a lead on where he took her."

"Call me if you find anything."

"You do the same."

Connor took off, hoping he'd have something positive to report very soon.


BECCA FELT AS IF an elephant sat on her head, and she couldn't focus her eyes. She blinked hard. Blinked again. Everything was still fuzzy, but she heard water running in the background. Like a bathtub. She lifted her head to look around. She was in a small bedroom. A hotel room? She was lying in a bed, her arms still bound together and strapped to the bed posts. Her muscles ached from the strain. It was just like the basement, only the bed was softer than the table had been. Her ears were fine. Her stomach fine. He hadn't hurt her. Yet.

*Thank you. Thank you. Thank you.*

"Hello, my sweet," he said, coming into the room. "I hope you had a nice rest. Now it's time to bathe you and put on your gown. Then we can talk."

*Right, talk. As if.*

"Talk about what?" she asked. Her mouth felt as if it were filled with cotton.

"Why, what you've been doing all these years."

"What does that matter?"

He looked at her, that deadness in his eyes lightening. "It's everything, Lauren. I need to know if you're still pure, or if you've let a man defile you."

"Why?" she asked and dreaded the answer.

"Because my sweet, I want you with me. But if you're not pure, you'll need to be cleansed."

"Cleansed. Explain that to me."

He opened his mouth to speak, then closed it and looked up at the ceiling. "I know, Mother," he finally said. "I get it. No one is to know about the cleansing but us, or they'll all clamor for it."

"Why foster girls?" she asked quickly before he clammed up completely.

He looked down on her, his eyes vacant and dark again. "You don't know?"

She shook her head.

"I thought you understood. All of you. Forgotten like trash. So desperate for love. Thinking that what men offer is love." He stroked her cheek with his index finger, and she forced herself not to react when she wanted to turn and bite his finger.

He withdrew his hand and curled the finger into his fist. "It's not, you know. They don't love you. They just want to have sex with you and then you're impure. Then you—" He shot a quick look at the ceiling. "Yes, Mother, I know. Don't say any more."

"But how did you find the girls?" Becca asked, not only to know the answer, but also hoping to put off whatever plans he had in store for her.

"I'm a whiz with the computer. Once I learned how much those poor girls needed me, it wasn't hard to hack into DHS's database."

Hack DHS? They hadn't been able to find record of his employment, but the information in his office said he was a computer expert, so hacking made sense and it explained why he never had to leave home.

Becca needed more information, to learn how much he'd compromised DHS computers. She had to question him without letting him know what she was doing. "So you found the names in the foster child registry?"

"Yes, and then I researched the girls on social media." He shook his head. "What's with young girls today? All of them parading around half-naked and flaunting themselves in pictures. Selfies. The devil's tool, I tell you. If this continues, I'm going to be very busy."

"Don't you have to work?"

He chuckled. "My stroll through DHS's databases was very productive. Not only did I find the girls, I also discovered insurance information for all the children in the foster system. Did you know that insurance information is the next big thing in the identity theft world, even more than credit cards?" He tapped his chin. "I suppose you would know that, now wouldn't you?"

"So what do you do with this information?" she asked, now genuinely interested in his answer.

"Sell it, of course. We have a very generous local buyer who snaps up the data like it's cocaine." He laughed. "Of course, I only give him a little at a time to whet his appetite. Soon though, he'll be so addicted that I'll be able to raise my prices."

"A local man, huh?" she asked casually when in reality, she was beginning to connect the dots. "What's his name?"

He arched a brow, anger filling his eyes. "You're playing agent with me, and I will not have that. My secrets are mine alone. Not for the FBI to know about."

He let his gaze linger on her, as if he were seeing her, but not seeing *her*. The insanity shining through his eyes sent terror to her heart.

"We need to get moving. Your bath is getting cold." He withdrew his knife, and she held her breath, but he went for her hands to cut them free. She tried to flail out and catch him across the head, but the lengthy strain on her biceps kept her from moving them. She searched the area for something to use a weapon and spotted a pen. She could jab it into his neck, but she'd have to be in the perfect position to surreptitiously take it and ram it into his body.

He helped her to her feet that were still constrained by cable ties. The urge to run nearly overpowered her, but she kept her head and snagged the pen from the table, resting it in her palm out of view. She held her breath, waiting for him to catch her. He didn't notice.

*Thank you, God.*

He urged her forward, tenderly holding her elbow. What a contradiction! A gentle killer.

They slowly crossed the room with worn carpeting, stained bedding, and chipped walls. Of course, it was a seedy hotel. He couldn't take her bound and gagged to a five-star establishment.

He paused to pick up a white gown trimmed with lace, much like the gown she'd worn in the nineties. Her mouth went dry. Her legs felt as if they couldn't hold her up, and she wobbled like a struck bowling pin. He slowed and encouraged her with soothing comments that made her want to vomit.

In the bathroom, he lowered her onto the toilet seat. She made sure the pen remained concealed. She couldn't use it at the moment, but she'd find a way.

He drew his knife from a sheath at his belt. "I'm going to free you so you can bathe alone. Mother says that's the best thing, in case you're still pure. But I'll be right outside the door with my gun, so please don't try anything. Mother says I'm to shoot you if you do."

Mother, Mother, Mother. She was tired of hearing about Mother. He sliced through her leg restraints. She raised her hands and started to maneuver the pen into position. He suddenly sat back and looked up. She dropped her hands to her lap before he saw the pen.

"I'm sorry about the restraints. Mother thinks you will run, but I say you want to be with me. You do, don't you?"

"Yes," she managed to say despite her raw throat. She'd say anything to keep him off guard.

"I knew it." He stood and bent over her.

One swift slice through the cable tie and her hands were free. He stepped back and out of reach. "Take your time and use the soap I've left for you. You'll remember it. Everything needs to be perfect."

She remembered the soap all right. The rough pumice had been like sandpaper on her skin. She didn't want to use it, but the last time he'd sniffed her body to be sure she had. When she didn't smell like the bar, he'd scrubbed her arms and legs himself, tearing her skin. She wouldn't put herself through that again. All she had to do was lather it up in her hands and pat it on her skin.

He stepped out the door, and she sat for a moment pondering her next move.

"I don't hear you moving around, my sweet," he said. "Do you need help?"

"No." She got up. "The water's a bit chilly. I'll just add a little more."

She turned on the tap and looked around the space. When she finished bathing, she could stand behind the door and strike with her pen. It might work. Might not. She needed a fallback plan. She had a pen and the paper encasing an extra toilet paper roll. She doubted he would kill her here. He was likely just using the room for her to bathe because they'd raided his home. In the event that they did depart, she could leave a message. She unwrapped the paper and wrote,

*I'm FBI agent Rebecca Lange. I've been abducted. Call Detective Connor Warren at the PPB.*

She started to fold it then stopped to add the license plate number of his current car. She went to the toilet paper roll on the holder and unrolled several layers. She tucked the note inside and rolled it back up. He'd never look there. Hopefully, someone else would.

She turned the water off and undressed, then climbed into the tub that she suspected was dirtier than she was. But she had no choice. She'd have to wash her hair or he'd bring her back in here and shove her head under the water himself.

She finished her faux bathing, dried, and put on the gown, which felt like death sliding over and claiming her body. She shivered and stared at her reflection in the mirror. She was pale, her eyes unfocused, dark circles lingering beneath them. She looked like death already.

"No," she whispered. "Stop this. You aren't going to let him win."

She firmed her resolve, grabbed the pen, and stepped behind the door.

"I'm ready," she called out sweetly and waited for the chance to impale the man who'd haunted her dreams—and her life—for years.


AS TAYLOR WAITED for the image to be completed of Van Gogh's hard drive, she played the video surveillance tape over and over, hoping to find anything that might help. She was sitting in the tech's SUV while he imaged Van Gogh's machine on site so she didn't waste any time in transport.

She replayed the video, zooming in on Van Gogh. Then closer this time, focusing on the rifle. An AK-47?

She paused the video and checked the markings. Not an AK-47. A Sturmgewehr 44.

*That's it! The gun.*

She'd seen his gun collection at his house and had recognized quite a few of the weapons as sought-after older guns.

Her dad had looked for a StG 44 for years. It had been developed in World War II and was considered to be the first modern assault rifle. A collector's item, it wasn't commonly sold in gun shops. They might find Zwicky by tracing the gun purchase. And she knew just the person to help her find it.

She stepped out of the car and dialed. The phone made it to the fifth ring before he answered.

"You better have a good reason for calling me at this time of day," Jack grumbled.

"I need your help." She told him about Becca's abduction.

"Tell me what I can do," he said.

"Van Gogh has a gun collection almost as impressive as yours. He was carrying a StG 44."

"So he knows a thing or two about guns."

"I was hoping you might put out feelers in the gun community to see if you can track the purchase or locate his favorite place to shoot. Maybe it'll give us an idea of where he's gone to ground."

Silence filled the phone.

"Jack?" she asked.

"I can do what you ask, but you have to know, if I get involved, it's not going to be by the book like you law enforcement people expect." He paused. "Tell me now if that's not okay or that you're not prepared to deal with the consequences."

"I'm prepared," she said, remembering Becca's tortured look as Van Gogh drove off. "Do whatever it takes, Jack. Whatever it takes."

# Chapter Twenty-Eight

THE SUN PEEKED OVER the horizon and flooded the FBI breakroom with a warmth Connor didn't feel. Mount Hood stood in the distance, reminding him of the mountain they were climbing to find Becca.

She'd been gone for eight hours now. Eight long hours, while he'd spent the time beating himself up over leaving her alone. He'd failed her, this woman he'd come to care for more than any woman in his life. She proved to him that women could be trusted. She'd simply had a horrific experience in her past that she couldn't share . . . with anyone. She hadn't cheated on him. Hadn't bailed on him like his mother had. He'd run from that situation as soon as he was old enough to go, leaving his family behind. Now he realized he'd been wrong . . . and that he'd wasted too many years.

He wasn't going to do the same thing with Becca. Life was too precious, too short not to go after his dreams. And that meant finding Becca.

He tossed his coffee cup in the trash and went back to Taylor's cubicle. He wished he could say the coffee had refreshed him as Taylor had suggested it would, but it just left him feeling wired and jittery.

"Anything?" he asked Taylor, hoping she'd found even a hint of a lead on the computer Van Gogh left behind.

"I'm sorry, but no." She sighed and sat back. "Looks like Zwicky only used this computer to control the car."

"No email, web surfing? Nothing?"

"No." She looked up at him. "He's a computer professional, Connor. He knew what he was doing and carefully planned his moves not to leave a trail."

"Okay, so what about the computer itself? Can we trace the serial number, maybe find out where he bought it?"

"We can try, but he'd have to have registered it for it to lead back to him. Even then, it'll just give us his address, which we already know."

Connor clamped a hand on the back of his neck to keep from punching something. "Maybe he has a second address."

"Could be. I'll tell our analysts to add this to their list." She got up and trudged wearily down the hall.

He felt bad for her fatigue. He'd been pushing her hard. She was a rookie, and he should probably cut her some slack, but he couldn't. Not until Becca was found. They all had to give one hundred and ten percent. He moved down the row to Kait's cubicle. She and Nina had come in to personally review traffic cam footage in search of Van Gogh's second vehicle.

"Tell me you have something, Kait," he said.

She spun and looked up at him. "Nothing we can act on."

"Meaning?"

"Meaning, there's no camera near the alley where he ditched the car. We picked up a sedan a few miles away. The driver's a white male who fits Van Gogh's build. We ran the plates and they came back as a rental, so it could be him." She tapped a map program on her screen. "This is the last sighting of the vehicle." She clenched and released her hands. "I should get back to it."

Connor nodded and backed away to let her work.

Taylor came rushing up to him. "I may have something. Remember I told you Becca had me take Danny's DNA to a private lab where her friend has a weapons consultancy business?"

Connor nodded.

"When I reviewed the video footage at the abduction site," Taylor continued. "I recognized the model of Van Gogh's gun. It looks like an AK-47, but if you look closer, you can see it's a Sturmgewehr 44. A fairly rare weapon."

"And?" Connor asked, wishing she'd get to the point.

"I called Jack—the weapons expert—and asked him to try to track the gun. He discovered one was sold at a local gun show. The show was held at a nearby motel and was only open by invitation. Zwicky was on that list."

"Okay, and that helps how?"

"We can go to the hotel and ask around. With his face, he'd be easily recognized. Maybe someone knows where he hangs out."

Connor tried to tamp down his disappointment over the less than solid lead. "It's better than nothing, I suppose."

Taylor's excitement evaporated.

"Sorry," Connor said. "You found a lead, which is more than I've done. I shouldn't have discounted it. Where's this hotel located?"

She rattled off an address.

"That's close to the car we're tracking," Kait called out, drawing Connor and Taylor over to her cubicle. She brought the address up on her map. "He's about five miles away on our last sighting. But if he stays on the same road, he could be headed there."

Connor looked at Taylor, making sure to transmit the enthusiasm he now felt about her lead. "Let's you and I get over there and throw the jerk a nice welcoming party."

"Thanks for inviting me." She grinned. "I've always been fond of parties."

Connor gave Kait his cell phone number so she could keep him updated on the vehicle's movements, then took off for his car parked in the visitor lot out front. It didn't take long to get to the motel. He parked a block away to keep from spooking Van Gogh.

"Ready?" he asked Taylor.

"Absolutely." She tugged on the baseball cap she'd put on to keep Van Gogh from recognizing her and added a pair of mirrored sunglasses.

Connor looked around warily as they hoofed it to the office. He searched for the sedan Kait was tracking, but didn't see it anywhere. He went straight to the lobby that hadn't changed since the eighties. It was worn and as tired-looking as the clerk who seemed bored to death. The man looked up, his expression wary.

Connor slapped Zwicky's picture down along with his shield and eyed the clerk to let him know he wasn't fooling around. "You ever see this guy?"

"Yeah, a few times."

"When was the last time?"

"When he checked in last night."

"He's here?"

The guy shrugged. "Not sure if he's actually here right now, but yeah . . . he's registered in room 141."

Connor was surprised that the clerk gave him the room number without any hassle, but he didn't question it. "You got a map of the rooms?"

Without a comment, he set a map on the counter and pointed at the third to the last room on the side facing the road.

Connor nodded his thanks, then bolted outside to get eyes on the unit. The drapes were pulled. The door closed. The parking space in front empty. Connor's anger flared that Becca might be held behind those curtains in this seedy, rundown motel.

Taylor joined him. "I can't tell if he's here or not."

"Only way to find out is to get inside." Connor jerked his phone from the clip, dialed Sam, and gave him the lowdown.

"I'll get a SWAT team dispatched," Sam replied. "You want me to come out there, too?"

"Honestly, I think it's better to have you back at the office managing things. Unless, of course, you're jonesing to take this creep down."

"He's all yours, man."

"There's a grocery store a block south of here. I'll meet SWAT there to coordinate the assault."

"Roger that," Sam said, and they disconnected.

Connor turned to Taylor. "I need you to stay here and keep an eye on the room. If you see any movement, even a swish of a curtain, you call me."

Her gaze already fixed on the unit, she nodded and held up her phone.

"Also, I need you to email all of the license plates in the lot to Jae and have her run them. Got it?"

"Got it," she replied without looking at him.

Connor took off running and made the short drive to the grocery store.

Early-morning shoppers were already milling around, so he parked in an out-of-the-way spot to keep from drawing attention. He retrieved his vest from the trunk, grabbed his rifle, and then checked the ammo, before putting extra clips in his pouches.

Armed and ready, he tapped his foot until SWAT arrived. Together, they formed a strategy and charged the hotel room.

Connor didn't care if he was risking his life. He was the first one through the door. He hurried past the empty bed with the stained bedspread. Past the scarred dresser to the bathroom, his heart beating so hard he thought it might erupt from his chest. He held his breath. Pushed the door open. It was empty.

He was at once relieved and disappointed at the same time. Relieved not to find Becca's body. Disappointed she wasn't there at all.

"Clear," he called out then returned to the team. "Fan out. Go door to door. Search every room. Every car."

He set his rifle on the dresser and dialed Taylor to update her and warn her to remain in place, and keep an eye out for a fleeing car. Then he phoned Dane to process this room. Next, he started checking the area as he pulled out latex gloves from his pocket. He found a few zip ties that had been cut. One dangled from the headboard, telling him Van Gogh had tied her up here. He searched for blood. Found none.

"Thank God," he mumbled and moved on to the table with water rings marring the surface. A water bottle sat half empty. He lifted it to his nose and smelled it. Nothing odd. On the dresser, he found a large white box with tissue paper inside. It was the size and shape for a gift of clothing. Had he brought something along to dress Becca in? Maybe a nightgown?

Connor forced away the thought of what happened to females when they wore the nightgown and went back to the bathroom with cracked tiles and moldy grout. The tub was wet, the shower curtain dry, and one towel damp. So someone had bathed. A bar of strong-smelling soap sat on the edge of the tub. Hopefully, Dane could ID this as the same brand of soap found in the sink in Zwicky's basement.

Connor turned to leave when the toilet paper roll caught his attention.

The roll seemed bulkier in one spot. He pulled on the tissue and a slip of paper fell out. Just a fragment of the paper used to wrap a roll of tissue that likely got caught in the roll at the factory.

His hope plummeted, but he picked it up anyway.

He unfolded it and saw handwriting on the back.

*I'm FBI agent Rebecca Lange. I've been abducted. Call Detective Connor Warren at the PPB.* It was followed with a license plate number.

He dropped the paper on the counter and ran for his car where he entered the license plate into his computer. The record came up. It was a rental, but not the vehicle Kait had been tracking.

He dialed Sam and updated him. "Need an APB out on the car. We also need to check ALPR to see if the car's been picked up anywhere in the city."

PPB had sixteen cars that were equipped with Automatic License Plate Recognition cameras. The cars patrolled the streets of Portland, scanning plates to find stolen vehicles. In a rare emergency like this one, detectives could check the ALPR database to see if the camera had captured the plate number. If it had, they'd also receive the time and location the vehicle had been spotted.

"I'll wait here for Dane to arrive. Then Taylor and I'll go from there. You keep me up to date on the plate scan."

For the first time, Connor had real hope that they might find Becca. He just prayed they weren't already too late.


REGINALD CARRIED BECCA to the altar. He gently laid her on the wood where the last few girls had found their peace. He stared at her. Her freshly washed hair flowed over her shoulders, caressing the lace of her gown. Her face was pale and her eyes were restful from the last roofie he'd given to her. She was so beautiful, he could hardly keep from stroking her face, but Mother wouldn't approve.

Especially since Becca had tried that stupid stunt with a pen. Trying to stab him. Mother didn't like that at all. Now he needed to hurry up and find out if Becca was chaste before Mother got angrier. It was something he could only determine by questioning her. It might get ugly, like with Molly, but he was doing it for Becca's own good.

He cut the twist ties and shackled her hands above her head, her gown drawing up and revealing trim ankles leading to smooth calves. He had to touch her, just once.

He stroked his hand over her narrow foot. Over the ankle. Up her calf. Soft, delicate skin.

He waited for his mother to speak. She didn't. He slid his hand up to

Becca's knee. He felt his mother's fingers pinching the top of his ear and jerking him away, her sharp fingernails biting in. Branding him. The pain racing along his nerve endings.

Ears. He hated ears. Hated the way she'd used his to control him. Even as an adult, she'd dragged him around by the ear. That's why he'd chosen pearl earrings instead of a necklace to cleanse the girls. He'd enjoyed removing their ears as souvenirs of his hard work, but he actually kept them as a reminder of what his mother might do if he failed her.

Like now. Touching Becca. He jerked his hand away. Then he grabbed the last bag of zip ties, sliced it open, and fastened them around her ankles.

His phone vibrated in his pocket. He looked at the indicator. He had a new email from Genetics Inc. Perfect. Lauren's DNA. He clicked it open and scanned the message. One word stood out. Match. The two samples matched. His dear sweet Lauren lay in front of him.

"You see that, Mother? It is Lauren. It's her." He touched the side of Lauren's face.

"But is she pure, my son?" Mother asked. "Is she the woman you need her to be?"

Becca stirred, moving slowly as if rising from a sweet dream. Her eyes fluttered open, her look confused, a small smile playing on her face.

He stepped back, in awe, basking in her smile. He'd never seen her smile.

Her eyes closed again. She was at peace.

*Oh, please let her be chaste. Let her be the woman I have searched so long for.*

She stirred again. Their eyes met. Hers changed. Tightened. The joy vanished.

"Hello, Lauren."

"How many times do I have to tell you, that's not my name?"

"Ah, but my DNA test says otherwise." He held out his phone for her to read.

She jerked her arms. Her feet. She looked around, fear darkening her eyes. "Where are we?"

"Oh, this place." He waved a hand over the room. "It's an old gun shop. My father once ran it and Mother held on to the place for a nest egg. But she died before she could sell it. Now it's mine."

"What happens next?"

"Next?" he asked. "Next, we have that talk. Then Mother and I decide your destiny."

# Chapter Twenty-Nine

CONNOR SAT BESIDE Taylor in the FBI war room that had been set up as an emergency command center. The day had passed without a lead on Becca, the knot in his gut tightening more and more with each moment that passed. Had Van Gogh taken her life?

Jae poked her head in the room, her laptop in her arms. "You know those pictures that were found in the time capsule?"

"Yes," Taylor said.

"Something about them kept bugging me, so I enhanced them."

Taylor stepped closer. "Okay."

"Let me show you." Jae attached her computer to the projector and an image of Zwicky came onto the screen.

"What are we looking for?" Connor's gut churned as he studied the giant-sized face smiling at him.

"His eyes," Jae said. "There's a reflection in them."

Jae hopped up and went to the screen. "See right here. A building."

"Okay, so we have a building. Big deal," Connor said. "If this is important, cut to the chase."

"Geez. Way to ruin my big build-up that's going to save the day." Jae crossed her arms and scowled at Connor.

"C'mon, Jae," Taylor said. "Just spill."

She went back to her computer and zoomed in, then broke that section from the photo with an editing program and enlarged the reflection even more.

"Ace in the Hole Gun Shop," Taylor read. "And this is related to our case, how?"

"The shop was owned by Zwicky's parents. From what my research says, Dad and Mom split in 1987. Dad took over and it went out of business in the early nineties, but he never sold the building. So guess who it belongs to now?"

"Reginald Zwicky," Taylor said.

"Exactly." Jae clicked on another file. "Here're the blueprints on file at the city. It has a basement like Zwicky seems to prefer, and, wait for it . . ." She grinned. "It's only a few miles from the motel."

Connor grabbed Jae in a hug and swung her around. She actually looked embarrassed, but he didn't care. She might have just saved Becca's life.

He put her down. "Print a good set of recon maps of the area."

She sat behind the computer, her face still red, and pulled up aerial maps and street views for the front of the building and the rear. Paper started spitting from the printer in the corner, and she went to get it.

"Thanks, Jae, you're amazing." He took the pages from her, quickly reviewed the printouts and maps, and then shoved them at Taylor. "Let's go."

"Me?" she asked. "Don't you want to call SWAT?"

He shook his head. "I won't risk a standoff situation. If he's got Becca in a basement, there's no way she can win if a SWAT team forces their way in." Connor raced for the door.

Taylor charged after him. "So it's just you and me?"

"Yes. We'll go in low and hard and take Van Gogh down before he knows what hit him." He kept moving. "You have a vest and rifle?"

"In my car."

"Then we'll stop to get it."

At the elevator, she waved the pages at him. "I'm like all over this, you know that, right? But are you sure I'm the right person for this job?"

"Do you know how to handle a gun better than most people who work here?"

"You know I do." She grinned. "I was born to shoot."

He smiled back. "Do you feel bad about Becca being taken on your watch?"

"You know that, too."

"Then what more motivation could there be to free her?"

Taylor raised her eyes in thought as if she believed he was really looking for an answer.

"Love," she said as they got on the elevator. "I'd have to say love trumps it. At least Nina and Kait would say that about Becca."

*Yeah.* Taylor was totally right. Love did trump it. Add a healthy measure of guilt over her being taken, and that just about explained how he was feeling.

He discussed the blueprints and maps with Taylor on the drive to the shop, which didn't take them long at this time of night. To confirm the pictures were correct, he did a slow drive-by of the building located in a strip of old stores.

The storefront was covered in paper, the exterior paint chipped and flaking. The black letters that made up the Ace in the Hold sign had faded to gray and the A hung at an angle, looking as if a strong wind would rip it free.

Satisfied they were at the right place, he parked near the back of the building where the blueprints showed the basement entrance. They climbed out.

"Door's gonna be locked," Taylor said.

He produced a set of lock-picking tools. "That's not going to stop me."

"I can't believe you just pulled those out of your bag."

The tools were illegal if the owner's intention was to use them to commit a crime. Sure, breaking into the gun shop was technically a crime, but saving a woman's life trumped that.

"You mention it to anyone, and I'll deny it," he joked as he put on his vest and checked his rifle and ammo, hoping that they'd have better luck than the last time he'd worn the gear, to raid the hotel.

The lock was old and no match for Connor. He soon had it open. A nearly negligible light shone on the stairs, and he heard music playing. It sounded like classic ballroom music.

He glanced at Taylor, and she shrugged. At least it proved someone was here. He gestured that he would go first, and she was to follow.

He eased into the store, walking on the balls of his feet to keep from giving them away. He might be big, but staying out past curfew in high school and slipping into a house filled with family members had taught him how to be quiet.

He made his way down the stairs. Thankfully, the wall went all the way to the floor and the music masked any creaking of the old wooden steps. They reached the bottom, and he signaled to his right, then, with his gun outstretched, he took the corner. It opened to a hallway, dark and shadowy. At the end, light shone from a cracked open door, creeping out like it was trying to brighten the darkness around them. He silently made his way over old split vinyl tiles. Taylor crept behind him.

At the doorway, he heard Van Gogh's voice for the first time. "Tell me now, Lauren, or Mother will make me get the information from you. Like I had to do with Molly."

"I don't know what you want me to tell you," Becca replied, sounding calm and in control.

Yes! She was alive. Connor's heart soared. He remembered the horrific injuries on Molly's body and his heart took a dive.

"I've said everything there is to say," Becca added.

Connor loved hearing the spunk in her voice, even after all these hours in the hands of a killer.

"Then Mother says the number five goes back on your stomach, and you will be cleansed like the others."

"Do what you have to do." Becca sounded resigned but strong.

"You may be interested to know," Van Gogh said, "that Molly's daughter, Haley, is next on my list. She flaunts herself on Facebook. A real little tease. In fact, I found Molly through Haley. A happy coincidence for both of them."

"I'm sure my team will catch you long before you get anywhere near Haley."

"That's doubtful," he said, sounding preoccupied.

Connor figured Van Gogh's focus would be on Becca right now, so he risked easing the door open farther to take a quick look at the room.

It was a small root cellar, with a dirt floor and wooden shelves, with jars lined up, ears in each.

Connor stifled a curse. He'd known the jars existed, that Becca wouldn't lie about them, but seeing them sitting there all shiny and bright on the shelf brought his dinner up his throat. He searched them carefully, holding his breath as he looked for number five. He could only pray they'd arrived in time.


VAN GOGH HOVERED over Becca, but she wasn't afraid. She'd had enough of being afraid to last a lifetime. She'd wasted years of being terrified to face up to what she'd done in leaving Molly behind. Running. Shutting others out. And where had that gotten her? On Van Gogh's table of death, not having really lived at all.

At first, she'd struggled to get free. Strained, until her wrists were raw from the metal handcuffs he'd snapped on, all to no avail. He wasn't going to forget to lock her shackles again as he had when he'd abducted her last time. So she was trapped, unable to free herself. If no one came for her, she'd put on a brave face to the very end. But if help came?

Oh, if help came, she'd embrace life, find a way to get beyond her past, to live a life filled with laughter and love. *If.*

"You can still change your mind, you know. All you need to do is tell me." Van Gogh grabbed a rag from the table and polished the knife until it gleamed. "Mother says it's not too late."

"No, I'm good."

He looked at her quizzically. "You've changed over the years."

"You haven't. Still a big mama's boy." She couldn't get at him with a weapon, so she'd wound him with words. And they hit the mark.

He flinched. "That wasn't necessary, Lauren. Mother and I simply have your best interest at heart here."

She scoffed.

He moved closer, lifted the knife.

She saw movement at the doorway. Twisted her head to see Connor standing there with a rifle, Taylor behind him. She nearly shouted with joy.

He lifted his finger to his lips to silence her. She blinked a few times to acknowledge it, her mind racing as she tried to come up with a way to help him. When he started moving forward, she realized she could do something—she could distract Van Gogh so Connor could sneak up on him.

"Reginald." Her voice was so syrupy sweet that she almost gagged. "I'll tell you what you want to know, but I want to whisper it in your ear so your mother doesn't hear."

His head popped up. "Mother hears everything."

"I still want you closer when I tell you."

He moved up the table, his knife still in his hand.

"Closer," she said, trying not to vomit or spit in his face. "I know you have a thing for ears, and I want to whisper into yours."

A light sparked in his eyes, and he inched closer. His breath, a mixture of garlic and foul air, fell on her face. "Mother always hurt my ears. She didn't mean to, but when I was bad and needed discipline, she dragged me by them. I deserved it."

"I'm not going to hurt your ear." Becca swallowed hard. She sensed Connor nearing her.

Now was the time. She rested her head on the table. "Look into my eyes first, Reginald."

He lifted his head a fraction. She smiled, and with all the force she could muster, she head-butted him. He bumped backward. She heard feet pounding closer.

Connor's arm shot around Van Gogh's neck, the other karate-chopped his arm.

The knife clattered to the floor.

Van Gogh's hands came up to pry off Connor's arm. He gasped. His mouth opened and closed, making him look like a fish out of water.

"Secure the knife, Taylor," Connor called out then looked at Becca. "Are you okay, honey?"

"I'm fine." She should warn Connor to loosen his hold, but she simply watched Van Gogh struggle, his face turning red, his hands clawing at Connor's arm. Frantic. Terrified. It felt good to see him as the victim for once. To see him fight off pain and fear of death.

His eyes bugged out, and his mouth flopped open. He looked like he might pass out.

"He can't breathe, Connor," she finally said.

"So?"

"Let him go. We can have the pleasure of knowing he's behind bars for the rest of his life."

"He doesn't deserve to live," Connor growled out.

"It's not up to us to decide that."

Connor's gaze waffled.

"Please, Connor. For me. Let him go."

Despite the barely restrained fury on his face, he released his hold enough for Van Gogh to drag in air and start coughing. Connor spun him against the wall and quickly cuffed him.

Becca wasn't happy to see Van Gogh released from his pain, but it was the right thing to do. She closed her eyes and took a few breaths of her own. She offered a prayer of thanks for her safety, then, feeling like she could face the million questions that would be coming in a debrief and interview, she opened her eyes.

Taylor was just finishing a call to request backup. Van Gogh's breathing had calmed, though Connor still had him up against the wall, his hand planted on his back, holding him in place. Connor's body was rigid and nearly vibrated with anger.

Taylor came up beside him and took hold of Van Gogh's cuffs. "You tend to Becca. I've got him."

Connor watched Taylor for a moment, then he suddenly spun to face Becca. His eyes were a volcano of anger ready to erupt as he ran his gaze from her head to her toes and back up again. His focus rested on her face and his expression softened as the moments ticked by, slower than a malware-infected computer. He shook his head, as if shaking off his anger, and dug out his handcuff keys before coming over to her.

He rested a hand on her cheek and stared into her eyes, his concern masking the anger that had consumed him a moment ago. "You're sure you're okay?"

She kept her focus trained on him. The caring he was exhibiting was beyond anything she'd ever experienced. Love? Was this what pure and complete love looked like? If so, she wanted more of it.

"Honey," he said, breaking the trance. "Did he hurt you?"

She shook her head and smiled. "But if you don't mind, my arms are kind of getting tired of this position." She laughed.

He didn't crack even a fraction of a smile, but tenderly unlocked her handcuffs. She started to move one and the strain had her moaning in pain. He cursed under his breath and took her hands, moving her arm slowly until it lay by her side, then followed suit with her other arm. He started for her ankles but she grasped the back of his shirt and drew him back.

"Those can wait." She twined her arms around his neck, the pain in her muscles nearly stealing her breath, but she didn't care.

She gazed into eyes that were riveted on hers. Then he lowered his mouth and kissed her. The kiss became urgent, frenzied, as if he thought he might never see her again. She returned the emotion, ounce for ounce. Her arms ached and complained, but she didn't care. She was alive and safe and kissing the man who seemed to love her, a man she loved too. If that meant a little discomfort for a few minutes, then so be it.

"Um, guys," Taylor said. "Backup's here. I don't think you want them to find you this way."

Connor lifted his head a fraction, his eyes now filled with desire.

"Go put Van Gogh in a squad car," he said gruffly to Taylor who'd done nothing wrong other than to get in the way of his kissing Becca.

She started for the door, jerking Van Gogh roughly.

"Don't worry, Mother," Van Gogh said as he stopped to look at the ceiling. "I'll get out of this and my work will continue. You can count on it."

"Ha!" Becca shouted. "The only thing you're going to be doing is sitting in a five by eight for the rest of your miserable life. If you're lucky, that is. You know what happens to child killers in prison, don't you?"

Van Gogh blanched, and Becca felt free at last.

Taylor prodded Van Gogh to get him moving again.

"Hey, Taylor," Connor yelled. "Thanks for the help. You're gonna be a real asset to the cyber team."

Becca looked over Connor's shoulder. "Yes, thanks, Taylor."

Taylor stopped and grinned. "I guess this means he's off-limits after all."

"You know it," Becca said, and grinned at her teammate.

Connor's eyes narrowed. "What's this all about?"

Becca smiled reassuringly up at him. "It's a long story. With Van Gogh headed to jail, we'll have plenty of time to talk about it."


CONNOR WANTED nothing more than to be alone with Becca, so he waited while his lieutenant gave them both an attaboy for arresting the terrifying serial killer. He waited while Dane arrived and started processing the scene. And he waited while the medics checked Becca's vitals. But he was done waiting now.

He liked to cut to the chase, and the chase here was that he had no reason not to be with Becca. And if she had any concerns, he would do everything in his power to change her mind. Tonight.

He crossed the street and stared down the medic. "I'm taking Becca home."

He didn't give the medic or Becca a chance to argue, but gently lifted her by the elbow and escorted her through the chaos on the street.

Eva Waters stepped out from the crowd, her microphone dangling from her fingers. "Thanks for the exclusive. I honestly thought you were blowing smoke with your promise, but I'm glad to see you came through for me."

Becca gave a weak nod and continued walking. Connor settled her in the passenger seat of his car and held her hand for a moment, looking into her eyes, trying to transmit how important she'd become to him.

She smiled. Softly. Sweetly, as if this was all new to her. He could totally understand. He'd never experienced this depth of caring for a person outside his immediate family. They were both experienced law enforcement officers, but when it came to relationships, they were rookies.

He squeezed her hand and closed the door, then saluted Sam before running around the front and climbing in. "I hope you don't mind, but I'm taking you to my house."

"Kait has asked me to stay with them, and that's what I want to do."

An ache, the same one that had plagued him when he couldn't find her, tightened his gut.

She rested a hand on his arm. "Don't be upset. I need time to think. After Van Gogh took me, I came to some realizations. One of them is that I can't continue to live my life cut off from the world. I need to let others in."

"Does that include me?" he asked quietly.

She slid her hand down his arm and twined her fingers in his. "I hope so. At least," she said softly, "if you want it to."

He pulled his hand free and tipped up her chin. "Of course I do."

"But you said you weren't interested in a relationship."

"Despite what I said, you changed that. So come home with me, and we can talk about it." He cupped the back of her head then slid his fingers into her hair. He grinned and winked. "Or figure it out another way."

She took his hand down and kissed the palm. "That is why I have to stay at Kait's place. I want to figure out if I'm ready for a relationship, or if I need time to work through my junk. To do that, I need space."

"Does that mean I won't see you?" He heard the panic in his own voice.

"I'll be at your office first thing in the morning to be grilled by your lieutenant. And then there's all the paperwork we'll need to close out. Plus, I'd like to come with you to do the death notification calls for all the girls whose names we found on the wall."

"You don't need to do that, honey."

"Yes, I do," she said with sincerity. "If you want me to resolve the things that have kept me away from you, then yes, I do."

# Chapter Thirty

BECCA STEPPED BACK from Molly's grave and watched her friend's coffin being lowered into the ground. Seven days had passed since Van Gogh had been arrested, and Becca was starting to put her past where it belonged—in the past. But that wouldn't include Molly or her family.

The coffin disappeared from sight, and Becca's knees felt week. Connor supported her elbow and held her close.

*Goodbye, Molly. I wish I could have known you as an adult. But I know your kids now, and I'll always be there for them. I promise.*

Becca felt good about her promise. She could do this. It wasn't a promise made out of guilt, but out of love for her friend.

She dabbed her eyes and turned to Molly's husband, Finn. "It was a lovely service."

He nodded woodenly.

Haley, her eyes red-rimmed, stood next to him and stared at Becca. She put her arm around the teenager. "You know you can call me anytime. Day or night. I'm here for you."

She sobbed and nodded. Becca hugged her close and vowed to be sure this young lady had a better life than Becca and Molly had endured.

Becca pushed back and ruffled Todd's hair. "That goes for you, too, squirt," she said to the ten-year-old.

He took a step back and clung to his father. Becca was thankful they both had Finn, who seemed to be a strong man and parent.

"I'll call you later this week," Becca promised and stepped away.

She and Connor crossed the grass toward his car. Becca fought the tears, but she wouldn't keep them at bay forever as she'd done in the past. She'd gone to her first appointment with a shrink, and had high hopes that if she faced her emotions head-on, she'd eventually be free from residual nightmares. Doing the parental notification visits, like the final one she'd conducted with Connor that morning, had helped, too.

The sun shone down on them. It was a beautiful autumn day, and, despite the funeral, her optimism continued to flow. She stopped and looked up at him. "The funeral, the visits to the families . . . all of it has helped me to work out my issues."

He leaned against his car, the sunlight highlighting the red in his hair.

"You mean the guilt."

She nodded. "It's always easier to help others with their problems than to see them in yourself. That's what the parents have done for me. They only wanted the best for these teens. The same as I wanted for Molly. Maybe they made a mistake along the way, but they have nothing to feel guilty about. It's not like they'd neglected these girls."

"How can you be so certain? Especially after what you experienced in some of the foster homes you stayed in."

"When you're neglected as a child like I was, you can spot the signs."

He lifted a brow. "You've never really told me about your parents."

"Neither have you."

"Then let me fix that. Tonight. After dinner, we'll talk." He took her hands.

She felt the warmth spread through her body. He hadn't so much as hinted at touching her since the night they arrested Van Gogh, but she could see that he wanted to. She wanted his touch, too, but she'd needed the space, and he'd respected that. Another plus for him in her book.

"I agree," she said. "It's time we talk."

His brow creased. "Now you have me worried."

"You have nothing to worry about." She freed her hands and pressed a finger into his forehead to relax the muscles.

He smiled, the cute little one that deepened his dimple and made her want to kiss him. The atmosphere changed, and the air heated up between them. If they hadn't been standing at the cemetery, she suspected he would have kissed her.

Her phone vibrated in her pocket, and she grabbed it. "It's Taylor. I should answer."

"We've got him." Taylor's voice was filled with urgency.

"Got who?" Becca asked as she climbed into the car.

"Xiaowen Shen. The mastermind behind the credit card fraud."

"Perfect. Is he corroborating Willow's story?" Willow claimed that the ringleader had bought lists of foster kids' identity and insurance information from hackers. He employed Willow to create bills for a bogus clinic to defraud insurance companies, resulting in millions of dollars of Medicaid and private insurance fraud. Willow had recognized Frankie's name on the list and decided to use it.

"He's not saying a word, but we recovered a printout of insurance information at his house, confirming Willow's statement. Several of the others kids he had running the credit card scam and billing the insurance companies are rolling over on him, too."

"I'll bet he wishes he never graduated from credit card fraud to insurance fraud."

"He's going away for a long time."

"Unfortunately, Willow might be, too. Too bad there's no way we can help her."

"She made the choice to use the insurance info, and Frankie died. You can't change that."

"I know, but she's just a kid," Becca said, remembering how wild she'd been at that age and knowing something like this could have happened to her. "I just hate not being able to do something for these kids."

"Don't forget Danny. You're helping him."

"One bright spot in this otherwise messed-up investigation. Keep me updated on Shen. Especially if you confirm that he was the local who was buying information from Van Gogh." Becca disconnected and relayed the latest development to Connor then fell silent. She thought about Danny and how Elise had agreed to foster him. She'd have quite an impact on his life.

He'd known only abandonment from the day his mother gave him up for adoption at the age of two. She'd tried so hard to keep him, but he had a heart issue, and she couldn't get him the care he needed. She'd wanted him to have a better life, but he never got it. His heart issue put off prospective parents, so he remained in foster care, moving from home to home. He'd finally had enough of the system and took off. Not unusual. It was a sad thing, as far as Becca was concerned, and something she was still committed to help fix.

She told Connor about Shen, then they made the rest of the drive in silence, both of them pensive. But the silence was comfortable, something she'd never had with another person.

He pulled into the parking area at her office and squeezed her hand. "I'll pick you up at five."

"I'll be ready."

His fingers twined in hers, and she could tell he wanted to say more, but was waiting for the evening. He gave her hand one last squeeze and then she got out of the car, basking in the sunshine before she stepped into the security booth. The clean, crisp air blew softly against her face. Since Van Gogh's arrest, everything seemed so much clearer and crisper. She was grateful for her life, and planning to do whatever she could to make it count.

No more with the guilt and recriminations. She now recognized that the misplaced guilt she'd felt all these years was just a reason to stop living. A reason to keep herself from getting hurt again. She didn't need that anymore. She was free, free to come out of the shadows of fear. The shadows of guilt. It was time to live for the present.

"ARE YOU SURE YOU want to do this?" Connor asked Becca from the driver's seat.

The sun was dropping toward the horizon, a burning fireball hanging behind tall pine trees and large outbuildings. But the evening was still unusually warm and a fresh breeze drifted through his open window.

"Of course." Becca smiled, a carefree, wonderfully relaxed smile that made him hopeful for their conversation.

"Don't say I didn't warn you." He nodded at his parents' house. "It's going to be crazy in there. A room overflowing with people, all of them like me."

"Exactly like you?" she asked, her tone lighthearted. "Then I can't wait."

She'd been relaxed all afternoon at work, and now she was downright flirtatious.

He could get on board with that kind of attitude very easily. He leaned close, cupped the back of her head, and kissed her. The world exploded around him, and all he could think of was deepening the kiss.

"Ew, Uncle Connor." Fists pounded against his window. "Come out of there."

He lifted his head at the sound of his seven-year-old nephew.

"Go hide, Zach, and I'll be out to find you at the count of ten," Connor yelled, though he didn't take his eyes off Becca.

"Me, too, Unca Connor."

"You too, Emma," he said to Zach's three-year-old sister.

"Sorry for the interruption, but that's life around here." He took in a deep breath and blew it out, then trailed a finger down her face and sat back to clear his head. "Time to go in. The craziness will start as soon as I open the door. Consider yourself warned."

"Absolutely." She smiled, her expression easy. How far she'd come in such a short time. He knew she was still having nightmares and anxiety plagued her at times, but she was seeing a counselor and that should help over time.

Her opened his door and started counting loudly. Becca came around to join him and slipped her hand in his.

"Eight, nine, ten," he said even louder. "Ready or not, here I come."

A little girl's giggle came from bushes abutting the porch.

Becca chuckled. "She's destined for a covert law enforcement career for sure."

He grinned at Becca then cupped his hands around his mouth. "I'm sure Zach and Emma are way too big to fit behind the shrubs."

"No I'm not, Unca Connor," Emma said.

Becca laughed joyously, and Connor stood watching the sun set behind her back. He'd hated this place ever since his mother had walked out. Now he could see it from new eyes. From Becca's eyes.

Her laugher stilled. "You look awfully serious for a game of hide and seek."

He stared over her head at the bus stop and memories came flooding back. "It's my mother. She didn't neglect me, the way your mother did you. Instead, she walked out when I was fifteen. Put us all on the bus for school one morning like usual, and then took off. She told Dad that she couldn't handle the responsibility anymore. She had to be free. We never heard from her again."

"I'm so sorry," Becca said, but she didn't get all sappy like the women in his family would, trying to hug him and make it all better. She just stood tall and strong next to him, holding his hand and waiting for him to continue if he wanted to.

"As the oldest kid, a lot of responsibility fell on me. I wasn't allowed to be a kid anymore. I resented it when my brothers and sisters got to have fun, but I had to keep things running while my dad worked. It got to the point that I hated being here. That's why I left as soon as I could. And I hated coming back here. Until you."

"Me?"

"The people inside? The ones who are cutting up and having a good time? I'll walk in that door and they'll welcome me like nothing's wrong. I essentially turned my back on them, but they'll still be there for me. You didn't have the luxury of turning your back on your family. You had no one to run from. I can now see how dumb it was to take off, and I aim to rectify it."

"So if this thing between us keeps going, we'll both be getting a family, then."

"Yeah, I guess so."

His nephew stepped out from behind a wishing well. "Uncle Connor. Come on. You're not playing right."

"I'm done with all of that," he said to Becca. "These games with the kids? They're the only ones I'm going to play anymore." He squeezed her hand and took off to chase his nephew.

Zach screeched so loudly, it brought his mother to the door.

"Connor Warren, why didn't you tell us you were here?" she lectured, standing on the porch with her hands on her hips. "We would have come to greet you."

"I figured the longer it took for Becca to meet all of you, the more likely it is that she'll keep going out with me." He looked at Becca and winked.

His sister came charging down the steps and linked arms with Becca.

"Come on, Becca. You've had a long ride with this big dope and it's time you met the smart ones in the family."

Becca laughed hard and Connor strode over to her. He looked at his sister Beth. "We'll be in in a few minutes."

Beth winked at him, as if she'd read his mind and jogged up the steps.

Connor turned to Becca and circled her in his arms. "You seem happy."

"I am," she said battling with a wayward strand of hair the wind had pulled from her clip.

"I can think of no one who deserves to be happy more than you," he said and pressed the hair behind her ear, then slid his fingers into her hair to cup the back of her head. "And I promise to spend every day making sure you're treated like a princess."

She grinned up at him. "Even if you have to wear the knight costume again to make it happen?"

He winked at her and leaned in for the kiss that marked the beginning of a whole new happiness in his life, too. "Even then."

*The End*

# Acknowledgements:

Additional thanks to:

My super agent Chip MacGregor, whose book-publishing knowledge knows no bounds. Without you, this series wouldn't have become a reality, and your ongoing support in bringing my books to market and steering my writing career is priceless.

The very generous Ron Norris, who gives of his time and knowledge in police and military procedures, weaponry details, and information technology. As a retired police officer with the LaVerne Police Department and a Certified Information Security Professional, your experience and knowledge is invaluable. You go above and beyond, and I can't thank you enough! Any errors in or liberties taken with the technical details Ron so patiently explained to me are all my doing.

And last but not least, to the Portland FBI agents and staff for sharing your knowledge and expertise at the Citizen's Academy. I am forever grateful for the opportunity to learn more about what you do and how you do it. I am in awe of your skills, dedication, and willingness to put others before yourselves.